PRAISE FOR
THE VELVET HOURS

"Alyson Richman's writing sings in her evocative new novel set in Paris at the dawn of World War II. *The Velvet Hours* is a beautiful and compelling portrait of two women facing their unknown past and an unimaginable future as their world begins to crumble. Heartfelt and romantic."   —Kristin Hannah, #1 *New York Times* Bestselling author
of *The Nightingale*

"Alyson Richman deftly weaves fact and fiction to create an enthralling tale of love and sacrifice in *The Velvet Hours*. Richman slips flawlessly between time periods, her sense of place in depicting Paris in the 1880s and 1940s spot on. The reader navigates the streets of the City of Light alongside Solange and Marthe, two carefully crafted and worthy heroines. The author does a superb job of creating a Paris apartment full of exquisite treasures and a priceless painting, a world of light and shadow, beauty and darkness. Ultimately, this is a carefully wrought story of love, of what the heart chooses to give up, and what it chooses to keep. Highly recommended to readers who enjoyed Kristin Hannah's *The Nightingale*."   —Karen White, *New York Times* bestselling author

"A book as full of treasures as the Paris apartment that inspired it. . . . A masterful mix of the glamour of the Belle Epoque and the shadows of impending war as the stories of two generations twist and twine together in delightful, heart-wrenching, and sometimes unexpected ways."   —Lauren Willig, *New York Times* bestselling author

continued . . .

Books by Alyson Richman

The Mask Carver's Son

The Rhythm of Memory

The Last Van Gogh

The Lost Wife

The Garden of Letters

The Velvet Hours

THE

Velvet Hours

Alyson Richman

BERKLEY
New York

BERKLEY
An imprint of Penguin Random House LLC
375 Hudson Street, New York, New York 10014

Copyright © 2016 by Alyson Richman
"Readers Guide" copyright © 2016 by Penguin Random House LLC

Library of Congress Cataloging-in-Publication Data

Names: Richman, Alyson, author.
Title: The velvet hours / Alyson Richman.
Description: Berkley trade paperback edition. | New York : Berkley Books, 2016.
Identifiers: LCCN 2016001384 (print) | LCCN 2016005067 (ebook) | ISBN
9780425266267 (softcover) | ISBN 9781101615805 ()
Subjects: LCSH: World War, 1939–1945—France—Paris—Fiction. |
Grandmothers—Fiction. | Storytelling—Fiction. | BISAC: FICTION /
Literary. | FICTION / Historical. | FICTION / Jewish. | GSAFD:
Biographical fiction. | Historical fiction.
Classification: LCC PS3568.I3447 V45 2016 (print) | LCC PS3568.I3447 (ebook)
| DDC 813/.54—dc23
LC record available at http://lccn.loc.gov/2016001384

Berkley trade paperback edition, September 2016

Printed in the United States of America
1   3   5   7   9   10   8   6   4   2

Cover art: Woman © Plainpicture / Glasshouse / Peter Ogilvie;
Eiffel Tower © Jeannette Rische / EyeEm / Getty Images
Cover design by Sarah Oberrender
Book design by Kelly Lipovich

In memory of my elegant grandmother,
Hortense Elaine Kleiman
(1917–2016)

and

For Charlotte, my beautiful girl.

We write to taste life twice, in the moment and in retrospection.

ANAÏS NIN

Solange

June 1940
Paris

Outside, I could hear the sound of airplanes, and their rumble filled me with unease. The only thing worse would be the wail of a bomb siren. I bit my lip and hurried to grab my bag.

I moved through the rooms of my grandmother's apartment one last time. My finger trailed over the edges of her furniture, my eyes absorbing the image of her beloved porcelains, her carved ornaments, and, lastly, the magnificent portrait of her over the mantel. The only possession of my grandmother's that I would take with me was hidden underneath the collar of my blouse, and feeling it against my skin gave me courage.

I learned so many things from my grandmother in the few short years I had recently come to know her. She taught me that when making a change in your life, never be sentimental and always be swift. So I took my final glances of all her precious things and reached into my satchel for the key.

As I pulled the heavy door behind me, I thrust the key in the lock. My grandmother's apartment and her belongings were left as she requested. The place was now sealed like a tomb.

My new life began the moment I closed the door of that apartment, as I locked my grandmother's secrets and personal treasures deep within.

It would become yet another buried story in our family of re-inventors and name changers, alchemists, and connoisseurs of beauty and love.

My father, a pharmacist, had grown up unaware of his true mother's existence until he himself was eighteen, when the soft-spoken woman who had raised him presented him a letter written in my grandmother's hand.

"I made a promise once," the woman whom he had always believed to be his mother informed him. "And now I must tell you the truth."

The letter was on heavy, bonded paper, with a small gold butterfly embossed on the top. The return address read *2, Square La Bruyère*. The handwriting was flawless. A black fountain pen had rolled over the page in fluid peaks and arabesques.

My dear son, the letter began. *By the time you read this, you will have turned eighteen. It's hard to believe that I had you so many years ago, when I was but a child myself. But it's important you know I exist. Do not fear, I will not demand you call me "mother." Madame Franeau is the woman who will always deserve that title, and I make no apologies that I am hardly a shining example of maternal grace. But should you be curious, I am here, always available to meet you.*

Her signature was large and marked with flourish. The name was wholly unfamiliar to him. *Marthe de Florian*.

He folded the paper, straightened his back, and made an effort to disguise his disbelief. It was almost impossible to comprehend that the woman who sat before him was not actually related to him. They both had small brown eyes, thin mouths, and dark hair. They had delicate digestions, and preferred their books and hobbies to the chore of making conversation. They found comfort in small animals, dogs, cats, and birds. And the fact that he chose to study pharmaceuticals seemed natural to all who knew him as a young boy. For he had always loved chemistry—the glass beakers, the mixing, and the science of making things that had the capacity to heal.

Madame Franeau tried to adopt a face of stoicism as she put forth this unexpected revelation to him. Her eyes were wet and glassy as she watched him read the paper, but never once did her tears fall.

"I couldn't have children of my own," she finally began. He looked out the window, his face not bearing any expression, but she could see that his thoughts were far away.

"I knew her from the first tailor shop where she worked. We were both seamstresses, and our days were colorless and bleak. We spent countless hours hemming trousers, and adjusting the lengths of sleeves. I was recently married to your father . . ." She stumbled over the words. The word "father" caught in her throat, as though after so many years of it being the truth, it was now suddenly a lie. "She wasn't married and had little means of support, and we were overjoyed to have a child to raise. Her only stipulation was that you learn the truth when you came of age." She paused and took a deep breath.

"I will not be hurt if you want to meet her. She has since become so different than I . . ." Her voice trailed away. "She belongs to another world. One difficult for me to explain."

He spent the next several days looking at the letter. He would withdraw it from his desk during breaks from studying and gaze at Marthe's full, scripted hand.

Only after he had finished the last of his entrance exams to the school of pharmacy did he decide to write her a reply.

His stationery was not as heavy, nor his handwriting as grand. On a simple sleeve of white paper he wrote:

Madame de Florian, I would like to visit you next Tuesday at four o'clock. Please let me know if you might be free. As you know, I have recently learned it is a falsehood for me to use the last name "Franeau." So I will close this letter with what Madame Franeau has informed me is in fact, my real last name.

Henri Beaugiron

When he called on her at her apartment, a housemaid opened the door and led him inside. The air was heavy with the fragrance of flowers, and the space was crowded with collections and curios from exotic lands. Even before she appeared, he felt ill at ease. There were just too many things. Too much velvet and satin. His childhood home had been a simple place: a bedroom with a wooden desk and book-shelves, and a living room with modest but tasteful furniture. A kitchen with a warm stove.

Now he felt as though he was entering a secret theater, one in which he clearly did not belong. Heavy drapes cascaded over the tall windows, which made it difficult to gauge whether it was night or day outside. His breathing began to escalate as he waited for her. He looked at the collections of Asian porcelains on the shelves, then the large portrait of a beautiful woman over the mantel painted with exuberant brushstrokes, and he was struck by its palette of sensual colors, its feeling of vibrancy and heat. He was about to move closer to examine it, when he became distracted by the sound of rustling silk and the striking of measured footsteps against the parquet floor.

"Henri," a voice emerged. There, standing before him, was Marthe dressed in a soft pink dress, her neck roped in pearls.

They stood, several paces from each other. Her gaze was one of appraisal, as if she were looking at him as an object she may or may not choose to buy.

"Well, now . . . you look nothing as I had imagined!" She let out a gentle laugh. "But I suspect neither do I."

He was unable to reply.

If my calculations are correct, she must have been close to forty when my father first met her, though it is impossible for me to know that for sure. Even when I met Marthe years later, she claimed to be an age that would have been impossible given my father's age and my own. But this was certainly not the first step in her reinvention. As I would eventually learn from her, one needn't be born into a beautiful life in order to have one.

I met my grandmother in the last months of 1938, when I had just turned nineteen years old, a few years before everything in Europe would smolder under Hitler's torch. Her existence came as a complete surprise to me, like a hidden steamer trunk that was suddenly pulled down from an attic and opened to reveal a forgotten treasure.

My father spent most of his hours running his small pharmacy on Rue Jacob. Since my mother's death, he had struggled to find ways to occupy me, his only daughter. I had finished my schooling five months before, and now spent my days dreaming of adventures and writing down imagined stories and plays.

We were mutually frustrated with each other, and my restlessness only made it worse. At night, when he returned home from work, all he wanted was solitude, while I was eager for companionship.

Our apartment was dark, the paint worn and the furniture practical. My mother's legacy was her books that lined the shelves. Every time I pulled a bound leather volume down from its resting place, a part of me ached, and my mourning felt like a fresh wound.

When I complained one evening about the lack of excitement in my life, he seemed to be on the brink of despair.

"I'm sorry I can't be more entertaining." The exasperation in his voice was apparent, and it was clear he was unprepared for the trials of rearing a daughter on his own.

For a moment we sat across from each other without speaking, his eyes focusing on the tower of bookshelves before finally settling on me. At first, I thought he was thinking of my mother. The woman who had kept his house tidy, cooked his meals, and nurtured my love of books. But then, something unexpected happened.

The light in my father's eyes shifted. It was as though he had stumbled upon an elixir in a forgotten cabinet in his shop, and he believed this tonic might have the power to alleviate the ennui that plagued me.

"I know someone I believe you'll find interesting . . . Perhaps she'll even give you some material for your writing . . . I haven't seen her in quite some time, but I will write and see if she will meet you."

Three days later he walked into my bedroom with a letter in his hand.

"Tomorrow, we'll visit someone you will not believe is actually related to me. But it's the truth," he said, as if he, too, could not quite believe the veracity of his statement.

"And who might that be?" I asked, perplexed.

"You'll finally meet the woman who bore me. Marthe de Florian."

The next day, after our lunch, we set off for Chaussée d'Antin in the ninth arrondissement of Paris, where Madame de Florian's apartment was located. On the way, he told me he never thought of her as anything more than the woman who had given birth to him, as they had been estranged from each other most of his life.

"The only thing we share is her original last name," he told me as he shook his head. "But even that is something she's changed along the way."

"And does she know about me?" I asked him.

"Yes . . . she knows. I took your mother to meet her before we married, and we later visited her again to announce we were expecting a child. But you will see when you meet her, Madame de Florian has little interest in marriages or births . . ."

I raised an eyebrow. "What *are* her interests?" I pushed him.

"Things I find tiresome . . . her own comfort and pleasure . . . her own beauty . . . her belief that she is somehow above the banality of this world."

We had nearly reached her apartment.

"She's an actress of sorts, so be prepared," he warned. "She enjoys an audience." He paused for a second and looked at me. I was dressed in my best clothes, a navy hat and wool coat, and one of my mother's dresses that I had taken in for the occasion.

"She will like you very much, Solange. You're pretty enough to fit in amongst her things."

"But you haven't seen her in so many years," I told my father. "How do you know everything will still be beautiful?"

"I don't . . . but I suspect that she has kept herself quite well preserved; that was very much her nature."

I think that upon our introduction, we both surprised each other. I know I certainly wasn't expecting to be greeted by a woman so elaborately dressed, with makeup camouflaging a face over sixty, and around her neck the most exquisite set of pearls.

And I believe she, too, appeared slightly amazed, for my face, although years younger than hers, so clearly resembled her own. I had the same pale skin and slate blue eyes, the long neck and Gallic nose.

My father introduced us coolly. It was evident by the way he stood in the hallway that her apartment made him nervous, and he had little tolerance for staying any length of time in her company.

He refused to call her "*maman*," or introduce her to me as "*grand-maman*."

"Madame de Florian," he said with great formality. "Let me introduce you to my daughter, Solange."

Our arrival appeared to delight her. She didn't bother to reprimand my father for not having visited her in what must have been nearly twenty years. I would later learn that she didn't calculate time as most people did. For her it wasn't the minutes passed, but the moments exchanged.

"A pleasure," she said to me, extending her long white hand. "Will you both be staying? I can have Giselle prepare us some tea."

"I won't be able to as I have work to do," my father said, making an excuse for himself. "But Solange will, if that's acceptable." He looked at me, then back at this tall woman who seemed wholly unrelated to him. "Since her mother died, she has been restless . . . She just finished school and tells me she wants to write plays, perhaps even try her hand at a novel . . . So I thought perhaps you might share some stories with her while I am at the pharmacy."

"But, of course, Henri," she said, reaching to touch my arm. "I am not so busy anymore, and I would appreciate having the company of a beautiful girl to share my afternoons."

I stood there, rapt at her. Her voice was melodious. Her eyes were full of life.

"Giselle, take her hat and coat." My wool coat and felt hat were given to the elderly maid in the black dress and white apron.

"I'll pick her up at six," my father said.

With that he left us, and I was led inside.

I will never forget the parlor, with the large portrait that dominated the room. It was undoubtedly of her, created in a tornado of brushstrokes. Around her neck, the same necklace she now wore, a glimmering, perfect set of pearls.

She saw me look at the painting, and then the choker around her neck.

"I have never seen so many beautiful things," I whispered.

"Why, thank you," she replied, ever so pleased. She then took a seat in one of the velvet chairs, as though it were her personal throne.

I believe she could sense my desire to study everything that surrounded us in the parlor, even though I tried hard to conceal my urge to stare. The collections of porcelain. The many objets d'art. The painting over the mantel. Even her string of pearls.

I admitted to be most taken in by the painting. I couldn't take my eyes off it.

"Who was the artist?" I asked, pointing to her portrait. The body, depicted with great, artistic exuberance, seemed to give off a pulse within the room.

"The artist?" She was bemused. "It's not the artist you should be asking about."

"No?" I answered, perplexed.

She motioned for me to sit down.

Her eyes flickered and she reached to touch her necklace. Its clasp, a small green butterfly with emerald wings, slid forth.

"No, it's the story behind it. Everything of value contains a story, Solange."

She touched the butterfly with a light caress of her fingers. I had never been in the company of someone who could so captivate me with only a simple gesture of her hand.

"You intrigue me, Solange. I know we've just met, but I sense you're a young woman who is not easily scandalized by another woman's truth."

I looked her straight in the eyes, and I again noticed their color. It was the same as my own.

"Let us have an agreement," she said. "The best people always do. You come to me once a week, and I will tell you how I, a girl born in the dark alleys of Montmartre, came to be ensconced in this apartment. It is not a tale for the prudish or faint of heart. But if you are willing, I will tell you the story of the painting as well as the one about my pearls, and everything else that happened along the way."

With that offer, a beautiful and strange smile spread across her face. It opened like a fan.

1.

Marthe

The first thing she noticed when he opened the door that afternoon was the unmistakable scent of flowers.

The fragrance was intoxicating; it pulled her deeper inside the apartment.

He took off his hat and placed it on a small pedestal table near the door

"Violets." She beamed, turning to him.

He was pleased she had noticed his gesture. He could feel her body against his own, and his fingers traveled beyond the curl of her back, reaching to grasp the tight middle of her waist. "I ordered them this morning. Cost me a small fortune . . . violets imported from Parma. I am told they are the best."

She squealed with happiness, and the sound of her joy washed over him like a bath of golden light.

He had taken great pains to decorate the apartment on the elegant

Square La Bruyère. A large gilded mirror with a small marble table flanked her on the right. Two gourd-shaped Chinese porcelains in a peach-blossom glaze and a tall cloisonné vase occupied the center. As she walked deeper into the room, she saw French doors that opened up to a small salon with walls upholstered in powder blue silk. There was a love seat with fluted legs, and two large bergère chairs with cushions that looked like nesting doves. On the mantel of the carved marble fireplace, she saw even more flowers. Topiaries created out of orchids, ivy, and moss. It was an apartment in the palest colors, a palette that would offset a woman's flush. A vault created for whispers and caresses.

"I wanted it to remind you of Venice," he said. She looked around and saw the heavy drapes on the tall windows woven in silver, rose, and Nile green.

"The city where I was reborn," she whispered into his ear. Their trip together had been her first time abroad, and its memory still stirred her.

"Indeed." He nodded as his hand slid across her bare arm.

He had taken her to a room near the Accademia, where the air was laced with the scent of wisteria and the water outside the color of jade. They had walked arm in arm across the wooden bridge and a dozen others made of stone.

At night, he had pulled down the red silk coverlet on the tall bed with its carved spiraled posts and marveled at her beauty. She closed her eyes, and her former life seemed to slip away.

The next afternoon, he took her to Florian's in Piazza San Marco, one of the oldest and most celebrated cafés in Europe. A place where the most beautiful and fashionable came to be seen.

"Mathilde Beaugiron." He said her name as though it was a dessert that gave him no pleasure. "This name . . . it is not right. It does not do you justice."

She lifted her chin and met his eyes.

"You need a nom de guerre."

She said nothing in reply. She would allow him the pleasure of renaming her. In the momentary pause between them, she merely lifted the steaming cup of hot chocolate to her lips.

He looked around the café, with its walls of painted figures, mirrors, and bronze lamps, and then again at her.

"Marthe de Florian . . ." He extended a single finger and touched her under the chin as he said it. "It's the perfect name for you . . ."

She curled her lips and smiled. The café was sumptuous and elegant. It delighted her that Charles thought its name also suited her.

"Do you like it?" he asked her.

"Very much," she answered. "Who knew it would be so easy to lose my name and start again with a new one?"

He leaned back into the deep plush of the banquette and took out his pipe, its barrel intricately carved in the shape of an eagle's talon holding an egg. She watched as he placed the mouthpiece between his lips and deftly lit the chamber. His movements were elegant and self-assured. She observed him, a student receiving a silent education. He closed his eyes briefly, and a plume of blue smoke wafted into the air. She could see how her new name, combined with the tobacco, filled him with a sense of satisfaction.

From the moment she shed her original name, Mathilde, a wonderful sense of weightlessness washed over her. "Marthe de Florian" evoked beauty and infinite possibility. She felt free.

In Venice, they steeped themselves in illusion. They soaked in a tub as deep as a Roman tomb. They ate food that tasted of the sea, and they drank wine from goblets the color of amethyst and gold.

She welcomed her new name and the anticipation of a new life. How wonderful it would be to have the opportunity to erase her past and the memories of her childhood, with its dark, cramped rooms. She would act as an artist with a brush dipped in gesso, and wash over the canvas of her previous existence. Her mother with the tired face and dusty eyes. The baskets of other people's clothes that needed washing. The one window that looked onto an alley piled with broken furniture and garbage.

For her, now there would be no more cold rooms, empty larders, or landlords threatening eviction. Never again would she have to wear dresses that needed mending or shoes that soaked through in the rain. She would now only cultivate pleasure, and she would offer it to others. She would live splendidly amidst it. Like those other girls she knew who had accepted the care of wealthy benefactors, women who were kept as secretly and luxuriant as hidden jewels.

She turned to Charles and batted her eyelashes, as her hand brushed against his cheek. Through the veil of his pipe smoke, she saw his eyes glimmer as she touched him. They would have an arrangement. He would keep her. She could see it etched into his expression, and she interpreted his smile as the seal.

They had taken the train ride back from Venice to Paris together, in a private compartment paneled in deep mahogany. During the day, she looked out through the glass windows and saw villages made of stone, and stretches of farmland with yellow rapeseed and barrels of sun-bleached wheat. In the evening, they dressed for dinner and drank champagne from tall glasses as the locomotive's wheels hummed beneath their velvet seats.

She could see how he watched her reflection, cast in the panes of the dining car windows, the heavy red curtains pulled to the side. There was now nothing of the scenic landscape of the afternoon to compete with her countenance, for outside it was as dark as ink. She took a sip of her champagne, her tapered fingers reaching for the stem. And when her lips met the rim, she caught sight of his smile in the glass.

She had a studied, deliberate way in which she moved. She had only recently learned the correct way to hold her cutlery, to ensure that her knife and fork didn't make a noise against the porcelain when she ate.

But even before then she had mastered the art of crafting her appearance. She was wrapped now in all of her elegant finery, dressed for the evening until he had her alone in their compartment completely to himself.

Draped over her shoulders was the black velvet cape lined in pink satin he had bought her in a shop near San Marco. She already knew how it would come undone. She would unpin her hair only after the porter had made up their bed. She would stand in front of him and take away each of her layers. The silk faille dress. The chemise. The corset and camisole. The petticoat. The garter with the tangle of ribbons and lace. She would remove the silver combs he had given her when they first met, and run it through her red hair, like Titian's *Flora.* She would turn to him and let him unbutton and untie her until she was completely undressed.

These were the things she would let him see. Her soft limbs, and her nipples she had rouged the palest rose. She would let him cup her breasts and let his fingers take hold of her waist. She would be his flower, opening and wet at the graze of his hand.

She was twenty-four and a student of love and touch. It was he who taught her about beautiful things. About the poetry of space, the need for pockets of solitude amongst the chatter. The need for color after a moment of darkness, or for the contrast of white porcelain and white sheets when one wanted to feast.

He had been the only one to send her orchids when she performed at the theater. Five perfect stems. On the card he wrote:

Your beauty is not like the others'. You hold the stars in your eyes, the moon just beneath your skin.

Charles

P.S. I shall be the one holding the sixth orchid outside the theater tonight, should you wish to join me afterward for a glass of champagne.

The other girls were awash in red roses. Packed bouquets with their garlands of green, with cards from men inviting them to meet after the show. Every one of these male suitors had a wife, with children asleep in their beds or in a boarding school somewhere. And all of them came to the theater for a night of entertainment that did not end for them when the curtain descended and the applause died down. Quite the contrary, that was the signal that the evening had just begun.

She was young and beautiful with a radiance that set her apart from the others. A perfect specimen to showcase in Paris, a city now famous for both its ability to illuminate and to seduce. In the past five years, the city had undertaken an urban renaissance. Streets were lined with the contrast of heavy, black ironwork and milky white globes that flickered long fingers of light far past midnight. Now gaslights brightened the stage instead of candles, as the girls took their bows and curtsies, and the men studied their programs to remember the most beautiful dancers' names. Backstage, the girls peeled out of their costumes, unlaced each other's corsets, and finally breathed again, released from the constraints of their whalebone and lace. As the endless flower deliveries arrived, the girls reapplied their white powder, their lipstick as red as crushed poppies, and their mascara with glossy coats of black.

And like them, what had first attracted Marthe to the theater was the possibility to be somebody else for a few hours a day. To leave her humble background behind. To reinvent herself with beauty and illusion.

She left her first seamstress job at the tailor shop after she had become pregnant, a part of her life she wanted desperately to forget. She tried, with great effort, to erase from her memory the man who had gotten her in such a wretched state, who had told her in no uncertain terms that he had no intention of ever making her his bride or recognizing the child as his own.

She had tried to forget those awful months when she had struggled to hide her pregnancy. She had covered her fuller breasts by wearing higher necklines. She had raised the waistlines of her dress and wore more voluminous skirts. But when she eventually became unable to cloak her condition, even in the most generous waistband and skirt, her employer, Monsieur Brunet, ruthlessly informed her he had found another seamstress to take her place.

Her friend and fellow seamstress, Louise Franeau, offered her the perfect solution. When Louise wrapped the baby Henri in her arms and promised to care for him as though he were her own, Marthe convinced herself this was the best way to put that chapter of her life behind her.

"Are you absolutely certain?" Louise had asked her as the child nestled against her breast.

"Yes, I am sure." Her voice drowned in exhaustion. She was still bedbound, every part of her body raw from the labor that had taken place only a few hours before. The midwife had been impatient with her as she cried out in pain. She still felt as if there were a fire burning between her legs.

She did not look at Louise nor the child that had grown inside her for the past nine months. She instead began to imagine a huge expanse of space engulfing them. On the ledge of the window, a small sparrow peered in from the outside.

She refused to take her eyes off the bird. She would not look at the baby that was rooting on Louise's finger in search of milk.

Her breasts ached. The baby had begun to cry, and the pull inside her became unbearable. Yet, she knew that if she took the baby into her arms and fed him, she would lose her resolve. She could already feel the steel casing around her heart beginning to weaken.

"Take him, please . . ." Her voice began to crack. "But make sure the wet nurse feeds him."

"She is already outside waiting for him," Louise assured her.

"Go, then, please," she said, her head turning away. The bird's finely boned face was still peering in through the window. Its gaze was sharp and unflinching, slicing through her like claws, releasing her milk like a river of tears.

For days afterward, she spoke to no one. She instead willed herself to be stronger. To forget. To create a tourniquet around her heart. She bound her breasts tightly with yards of muslin until all the milk dried up. She spent hours fashioning a special corset that enabled her to tighten the laces from the front. She showed herself no mercy, pulling the corset tighter each day until she had regained her former silhouette.

A week later, dressed in a simple cotton dress, her hourglass figure proudly displayed, Marthe walked in to the Gouget Brothers' dress shop on Rue Montorgueil to interview for a position as a seamstress.

She began the new job at once, but she found no comfort in her needle and thread. She had a restlessness inside her that would not leave her. Still only twenty-one, her beauty had returned to her and she was hungry for things that existed outside the store. Paris was aflutter with excitement. Monsieur Eiffel had begun constructing his impressive tower of steel. And the streets were full of the most extraordinary fashions.

She could imagine herself with great ease in these sumptuous dresses made from luxurious silks and lace. The other women who came into the Gouget Brothers' store rarely had a figure to rival her own.

But none of these women noticed the poor seamstress on her knees, who fitted the muslin patterns against their virtuous, white corsets and who hemmed their dresses and adjusted the cuffs of their sleeves.

On a whim, she decided to go to an audition for chorus girls with one of the other seamstresses from the dress shop, who had one day whispered to her about an open call at the upscale theater, Les Ambassadeurs.

"I wish I could," she had told Camille. "But I fear my dancing and my voice are rather unremarkable."

"What you might lack in your vocal cords, you make up in how you would fill out the costume," Camille teased.

She knew it was true. All traces of her pregnancy had evaporated. She had a neck as long and as slender as a tulip stem, a generous bust, and a waist that could be encircled by two firm hands. When she stood in for a fit model at the store, the other seamstresses would fawn over her perfect proportions. And her face would come alive as the silk draped against her skin.

So she went to the theater with Camille. She stood on the wooden stage with the lights radiating off her skin. She gazed out on the expanse of near-empty seats and was not afraid. On the contrary, she was thrilled by the vastness of the space. Almost instantly, she could imagine every seat filled, with all eyes on her and the other singers dressed in costumes far lovelier than anything she owned.

A man named Julian called out the names of the girls who were auditioning. He told them they could each choose what song they would like to sing. Marthe knew few songs by heart, so she chose "Vive la Rose" because it was romantic and lyrical. The range of the song was also not too challenging, so she knew she would be able to project.

When the list of those who had been selected was posted outside the theater, she huddled close next to Camille, both of them searching the list for their own names.

"Your name!" Camille cried out. "'Mathilde Beaugiron!' There you are!" Her finger tapped the line of cursive black script. Camille, who had not been selected, only showed excitement for her friend, not jealousy or envy.

"This pays five more sous a week than working at the shop!"

But it wasn't only the extra money. It was the chance to reinvent herself, to feel alive and to sparkle under the glow of lights. A sense of exhilaration came over her.

She walked back to the shop with Camille, and later that afternoon, after she put down her needle and thread for what she believed would be the last time, she gave her notice to the Gouget brothers.

"You're leaving us for the chorus in a dinner and dancing show?" one of them asked her in disbelief.

She straightened her back and looked at them with her wide, Gallic eyes.

"Why, yes. Plus, a little bit of acting, too."

She saw both of the brothers' eyes fall to her breasts one last time, as though their departure was what saddened them the most.

Seeing her name on the list had given her a newfound confidence.

"But first, I'll need this week's wages."

Her forwardness shocked them, and even she had been surprised at how quickly they went to retrieve the ten sous they owed her.

"Well, good-bye then," she said as she folded the bills and placed them inside her purse. "If you ever miss me, you can always come see me perform at Les Ambassadeurs." With that, she picked up her bag and walked proudly out the door.

In the beginning, the girls at the theater had not welcomed her. They looked at her ample cleavage, her sculpted calves, and saw their newest member as competition. Behind her back, they laughed at her demure underpinnings, her milk-colored corsets, and petticoat without an edge of lace. But they underestimated her eye for detail. Her desire to do more for herself than just dance and sing.

She had never been one for gossip or mindless conversation, preferring instead to observe. So she studied the other women as though they were their own form of education. When she was alone in the changing room, she secretly examined the labels of their clothes to discover the names of the dress shops they preferred. She took note of their festive colored corsets, the ones they wore beneath their silk dressing gowns, with the flashes of color peeking out like an invitation. She learned what exotic blooms impressed them, and what flowers were left behind.

During her first months at Les Ambassadeurs, she had not yet learned how to fully exploit her charms. She sang with her eyes straight ahead, focusing on the back door of the theater, and never played the coquette. And so evening after evening, not a single bouquet arrived for Marthe. It wasn't until one of the other dancers felt pity toward her, that she was given some advice that would change her fate.

"When you sing, search for a single pair of eyes in which to anchor yourself. So that the man believes you're singing only to him."

The girl came closer to Marthe. "And don't forget, sometimes the most sensual part of the body is the part they never anticipated seeing."

So the next performance, Marthe took those words to heart. She searched the audience for a pair of eyes that burned the brightest, finding a pair that belonged to a slender, handsome man in a dinner jacket, sitting at one of the tables closest to the stage. She took note of how his eyes lit up at the sight of her, and she immediately latched on to his gaze, directing the words of the song solely to him. When her sleeve slipped off her shoulder, revealing a globe of white polished skin, she could feel his eyes hard upon her. He smiled, even after the lights had dimmed.

. . .

Charles came to watch her every Wednesday, each time sending her orchids, and always taking the seat closest to the stage. She would anticipate the arrival of his carriage outside the theater. The swing of the black lacquered door, the quick grasp of his hand pulling her inside. She memorized the scent of the leather seats, a blend of sandalwood and hide, powerful and immediate. The Oriental perfume of his tobacco that floated in blue clouds from his pipe. She knew the sound of her skirt as it rustled under his searching hands. She knew the taste of his tongue as it touched her own.

For nearly six months, they used his carriage for their private nest, as his driver expertly led the horses through the quieter streets of Paris.

There was much one could do within the confines of polished wood and glass. She became an expert in acrobatics. Arching her back against the corner of the damask-lined walls, lifting her legs at half angles. Offering herself to him underneath the layers of her dress.

Her wardrobe was now an array of colorful silks and expensive laces. She made sure she wore his gifts—the gown from the Callot Soeurs and the black garter from the most expensive lingerie shop in Paris—both for his pleasure and for her own. Every Wednesday, she waited with anticipation until the curtain fell and she could be in his arms again, with the carriage wheels rolling beneath them and the moonlight highlighting those warm, white places of hers that he skillfully managed to expose.

The trip to Venice was the first time he had seen her completely naked. Her body released from her corsetry, her limbs finally free to move and stretch unhindered by the confines of his coach. He had gone to the bath while she lay in the bed. She waited for him without a peignoir, without even the flimsiest material between the linens and her skin. This time there would be no garter, ribbons, or lace. The surprise would be the lack of any veil; her body completely bare.

He pulled away the covers, and as the gas lamp flickered on the nightstand, she felt his eyes soaking in the sight of her. She sensed his desire in all its strength and undulations. The hunger. The thirst. The belief that she was wholly his to touch and possess.

She rejoiced to be loved, to be adored, to be touched by such gentle and refined hands. There was a new music to their passion. Beyond the breath and the small cries, emerged the unfamiliar pleasure of being two unknown travelers in an exotic city far from their own. Here, with none of his peers to recognize him, he allowed her to loop her arm around his own as they walked brazenly in the Venetian daylight. Here, he did not check his watch or leave her after his caresses had cooled from her body. Here, she was as precious to him in the day as she was to him in the night. And it thrilled her.

He had promised Marthe her own place upon their return, but she held her breath waiting to see if he would make good on his word. For she knew more than anyone that a man could take what he wanted, and then leave nothing in return.

But Charles *had* followed through on his promise. He pressed the heavy bronze key in her hand and then led her through the rooms of her new apartment. The place was even more beautiful than she could have ever imagined, with one room leading into the next.

"It's all for you," he told her. She felt his voice like a caress, a wisp of air on the nape of her neck.

She had gasped when she first arrived in the bedroom. A large headboard upholstered in silk and embroidered with butterflies occupied most of the room.

On the left, a stream of bright light poured through the tall windows. Another carved fireplace. A large mirror with a frame made of golden flowers. And, finally, the source of the perfume. On the mantel, five small vases. Each one filled with violets.

"For us," she whispered back.

She felt his hands on her shoulders, then her waist. She felt him reaching for her as he did when the locomotive had churned beneath them. She felt her head dizzy from the fragrance. And the bed was soft as he pulled her near.

2.

Marthe

Paris 1888

He came the next afternoon with a birdcage painted gold and a canary, as yellow and as small as an egg yolk, chirping inside.

"To keep you company," Charles told her. He dangled the gilded cage in front of her like a lantern.

She took it from him and placed a finger through the wire to touch the bird's downy feathers.

"You spoil me," she said as she kissed his cheek.

"It's my greatest pleasure." She watched as he removed his hat and gloves.

She was still in her robe de chambre, a gossamer silk confection edged in silver lace. Another gift he had bought for her during their week together in Venice.

She placed the birdcage down on the table, and she felt his fingers touching her wrist, the patch of skin hidden beneath her sleeve.

"My beautiful girl," he whispered into her ear. He was behind her now, his arms wrapped around her waist, his face buried in the curve of her neck. And when she lifted her eyes, she saw their embrace like a portrait moving within a golden frame.

He had placed mirrors throughout the apartment, and she wondered if this was done on purpose, so that they could share in the pleasure of seeing how they looked wrapped in each other's arms. That this was part of what enthralled him, to see the art of lovemaking unravel before him. It was part of the parlor game. To take what was hidden and expose it. Reveal it like a pearl shucked freshly in his hand.

She felt the pressure of his chest against her as he peeled her robe off her shoulders, and watched as both of their eyes met at the sight of their reflection, every one of his caresses captured within the glass.

She had known about the demimonde, that half-world that she now occupied. A world that existed in suspension, between the warmth of a jewel box apartment and the cold of the streets. A world where beautiful women existed smelling of lavender and rose. Where they welcomed men into their smooth, scented arms for a few hours, before their lovers slipped from this world to the next.

She was aware of this special world even before she had stepped onto the stage of Les Ambassadeurs. At the Gouget Brothers, where she had pinned dresses on women who were not wives, but who nonetheless had an abundance of large, crisp banknotes within the silk lining of their purses. They did not have a gold wedding band on their fingers, but they did have an independence of which she and Camille were envious.

And within a week of starting at Julian's theater, Marthe had seen how quickly the embodiment of beauty and illusion was devoured by the men who paid money to see a stage filled with girls as ripe as cherries. Girls whose job was not only to sing and dance, but to provoke dreams and desires, their mere sight inspiring thoughts of sensual possibility.

But this was how illusion was created on a small scale. Men like Charles, who had money and a title, were able to create their own private world. A world created purely for their comfort.

They became architects of their own pleasure. They financed apartments near Pigalle, where they could explore their own desires in private. Where the shadows were just as important as the light. Where they could enjoy a woman who was not afraid of their passion, but who, on the contrary, reveled in it as though it were the most delicious meal.

It was an undeniable fact that she had always enjoyed pleasure, even before Charles had named her Marthe de Florian, for she had always had a weakness for the sensual and beautiful things in life. She had learned to master sewing early, to avoid the fate of being a laundress like her mother. She had seen her mother lose her beauty in the endless washings, and watched as her hands became dry as ash. The wooden scrub boards that erased a woman's youth as quickly as if it were a simple stain. And so Marthe had learned to pull a needle and thread early on.

By the time she was ten, she already knew how to hem and mend. She was quite pleased with herself, to have a skill that enabled her to keep busy and earn some money, rather than spending hours as her mother did, washing other people's soiled clothes.

She would never forget the first time she touched silk. It was in an apartment that had curtains the color of the sky.

Her mother had dispatched her to pick up a client's basket of laundry. She was barely eight years old, but her mother had sent her proudly in a wool dress and tights to the address she pinned to the clothes.

Mistakenly, she did not enter through the servant's entrance of the apartment, but somehow arrived at the main door. The maid had been kind and neither admonished her nor taken her to the kitchen, but rather let her remain in that splendid foyer for a few moments as she fetched the clothes. Perhaps the maid acted this way because the mistress of the house was not at home, or because she sensed the wonder in Marthe's young eyes. Or perhaps it was a little of both. But regardless of the reason, as Marthe stood in the foyer waiting, she had marveled at the beauty around her. Realizing that no one was watching, she found herself unable to control her curiosity and reached over to finger the silk.

There was mystery in that first touch. As wondrous as the first time she remembered snow melting in her hand. She pulled herself closer. First it was her fingers wrapping around the cloth, then she pulled her entire body into the folds.

She had been so distracted by the sensation of the silk wrapped around her that she had not heard the maid's footsteps bringing the basket of laundry.

"Child, you must get out of there," she said kindly, but urgently. "Please . . . you don't belong there!"

She had stood frozen from the words, the material dropping from her fingers.

The silk fell perfectly back into place, but the words the maid had uttered made her grow cold. She took the basket and left the apartment in a hurry, shivering the whole way home.

It was a terrible thing to be so cold that you could never feel truly warm. This had been the way Marthe remembered so much of her childhood in the apartment on the Rue Berthe where she had grown up. That wretched place where she had awakened one morning to find her sister's body lifeless beside her. She had clasped her small body for warmth, but instead found Odette stiff and cold.

She would never forget her mother washing Odette's only white dress, the one her sister would be buried in. She watched her mother iron it through her tears. Marthe had shuddered at the sight of the large hole, and then, the soil that engulfed the tiny pine box whole. She had been incapable of erasing the image of the spray of flowers, limp from her hands, having clutched the stems too tightly, on top of the mound of wet earth. And now her heart had broken because they didn't have enough money to have her sister's name—Odette Rose—carved in stone.

She remembered the stream of men who came and stayed for only an hour at a time in the months that followed her sister's funeral. The scent of alcohol and perspiration. Her mother's desperation that stole what was left of her youth and clouded the light in her eyes.

She could mark the change in her life from the moment that Odette left them. Her mother broke the only mirror in their apartment and never replaced it. For who wanted to see their own face etched in sorrow? A complexion dull as a tin cup. Even Marthe began to look away from her mother's watery gaze.

But while her mother seemed to shrink into the shadows, Marthe's radiance began to emerge more and more with each passing day.

She grew from a thin, almost strange-looking child into a beautiful young girl. Her long, coltish limbs began to soften, and her once-concave chest grew full.

She took to adjusting her clothes to accommodate these changes in her body. She learned to taper her blouses to accentuate her waist, and to adjust the buttons to ensure they lay flat.

Every part of Marthe, every contour, every pad of muscle and every stretch of bone, filled with exuberance; an unrestrainable sense of life.

She needed no makeup. Her rouge was the clap of her hands against her cheeks. Her lipstick was the nibble of her teeth against her delicate mouth. She grew her strawberry red hair so long that when she unplaited it, it fell to the small cleft just above her lower back.

When she grew older, she would still recall that winter when she was thirteen, that afternoon when the cold had not stung her cheeks, but rather sent a thrill through her whole body. She thought of the boy who walked her home from school and told her she was beautiful when she flushed. He had offered her his hat and his red wool mittens, but she had refused him shyly. She later wished it were that boy who had been the first to touch her, to cup his hand between her legs. Not the one whose face she couldn't bear to look at. The one whose eyes burned not brightly with youth, but from the shine of alcohol. The one who offered her five sous to touch her in the dark corner of the alley, but who ended up taking far more from Marthe than a caress.

It had been so cold that night. She had returned home that evening and dropped the coins numbly into her mother's hand to pay for a few shovels of coal.

But although the fire stoked brightly that evening—for once—she found herself shivering, unable to find any warmth.

She now kept her apartment as warm as she possibly could. She had white birch delivered to the fireplaces twice a week, the bark crackling and sizzling in the hearth.

It was a delicacy to walk around with little clothing and not feel the cold breath of air. Her bathwater was sometimes so hot that she had to lower herself slowly and carefully—knees first with her arms propped on the sides—until her body was completely submerged.

The tub was porcelain with a sloped back on which she reclined. It was nothing like the barrel she bathed in when she had lived at home with her mother.

Afterward, when her hair was tucked underneath a cloth turban, she would sit down at her vanity and gaze at herself in disbelief at how much her life had changed since she joined the theater and met

Charles. Looking at her reflection, she saw the face, the familiar blue eyes, the sharp nose, and pink mouth. These features had all remained the same. But around her there were comforts and luxuries that she still had to blink twice to believe were now hers to savor.

She saw herself in the many gilded mirrors in her new home. Her new narrative cast in glass, a beautiful girl that floated through the light and dark of her own memory, and the chiaroscuro of the floating world.

3.

Marthe

S he named her canary Fauchon. She took a housemaid, an able and bright-eyed girl named Giselle.

Her mornings were spent in a succession of baths. One in milk, then one in lime blossom, and a third in scented water using either almond oil or rose petals.

The linens, too, were washed in aromatic water. So that not only were her tangles with Charles accompanied by the perfume of flowers, her subsequent dreams were as well.

She considered preparing herself for this new lifestyle to be her full-time job. She lined her vanity table with face creams made from orchid petals and dusting powder made of crushed pearls, investing part of her monthly allowance from Charles for her own beautification and care.

As a child she had scrubbed her face with a lump of soap and a rag that was twisted and torn. But now she paid attention to every advertisement and searched the shelves at the apothecaries for salves and elixirs that would one day help her defy the passage of time.

But aside from her beauty regimen, Marthe allowed a few hours a day just to daydream. To imagine different ways of pleasing Charles. She had enough experience in life to realize that she would always have to keep things fresh for him. For the same reason women had come into the Gouget Brothers' store looking for a new dress, Marthe believed if she were to continue to keep Charles's interest, she would have to maintain a repertoire of skills, the more creative the better, for giving him pleasure.

She looked for inspiration in the places she knew the best. With Giselle, she searched the fabric stalls of the bustling market of the Carreau du Temple for materials she could use to create a special architecture for their bed. She caressed the fabric between her fingers, imagining how it felt against bare skin. It was one thing to lie against a downy white pillow, but quite another to arch one's back over a velvet bolster piped in satin ribbon. Marthe imagined every detail. Colors and textures became yet another sensual language in which one could communicate in the theater of pleasure. And, still, she continued to expand her knowledge and skills.

She learned not only to secure her hair with combs, but also how to use her mane when it came undone. To sweep it against his bare chest or to use it when she kissed him, a decadent and playful veil.

But, most importantly, she learned that curiosity was never to be harnessed; it was hers to lead. She might feel uncomfortable sitting at a formal dinner, but in her butterfly bed, she was free to touch anything. To caress him with the softness of her thighs. To spread open her wings.

Marthe's own curiosity grew, like a thirst or a hunger that needed to be fed. She became fascinated with the objets d'art that were flooding Paris from the Far East. The delicate ceramics with their semitransparent glazes held a mysterious allure. She soon began to collect them.

The rooms that at first held one or two Asian porcelains, soon had ten or twelve on the shelves. She found a small shop near the Rue de Seine where the owner pulled out the long, slender vases from wooden crates lined in tea paper and straw.

Just walking into the shop brought her into a small frenzy. The air smelled of jasmine, and the interior walls were dark teak. The owner, a small, wizened man who was quiet as a crane, would cup each piece in his hands, then lift them gently for Marthe to admire, showing her how they shifted and changed in the light.

She began to collect the Kangxi blue and white porcelains that soothed her and reminded her of water and sky. She loved their inky landscapes of bamboo and pagodas. She admired the soft feathering of the artist's brush. The glazes in celestial colors like celadon and moonlight blue.

She was attracted to the contrast, the way the porcelains appeared one way in the light and another in the shadow, for it mirrored the half-world she occupied, captured in her very hands.

She purchased with increasing frequency so that Ichiro-san, the owner of the store, soon sensed Marthe's tastes and preferences. One afternoon, after he had shown her a precious vessel in the shape of a calabash gourd, its sensual hourglass shape meant to hold the liquor of immortality, he asked Marthe if she'd be interested in seeing something he reserved for only his best customers.

"Would I?" A smile flashed across her face. "What have you been keeping from me?"

"A collection of secret prints meant to inspire," he whispered. "To delight."

Her eyes grew wide as he fed her the smallest bits of information. "Come this way, Madame de Florian," Ichiro said, gesturing for her to follow him behind the curtain that separated the storefront to his personal quarters. As she passed through the curtain, she found herself in a small room with floor-to-ceiling shelves. Already, she could recognize most of the shapes and periods of the pottery. The Edo-period Imari, the yellow-glazed Tang horses, and the decorative Kangxi enamels that she so loved. But he did not reach for anything on the shelves. Instead he pulled out a portfolio and began to unwrap ties of silken cord.

What he revealed enthralled her.

"These are our images of the floating world," he told her. "The art of *shunga*." His eyes floated downward. "Literally, the pictures of spring."

There on rice paper were images of men and women in half-open kimonos, engaged in the many different acts of love.

Marthe could not look away. She saw couples with their sashes undone, their bodies entwined, their rapture caught by the wood-block artist's delicate hand.

"These prints are a window into the secret world of lovers."

Marthe grew warm as Ichiro put forth a series of prints. Each one displayed elaborate positions for lovemaking, intimate scenes of arousal and gestures of pleasure that unfolded like a dance. The prints were so different from the daguerreotypes in Europe of showgirls in corsets, with their breasts exposed and their legs slightly apart. Those images were produced only for the delight of men, but these prints appealed to her secret feminine side as well.

"Are these for purchase?" Marthe asked as her finger touched the corner of the paper. It felt like a secret, breathing scroll.

"But of course," Ichiro replied.

"I'd like these four," she said, selecting the ones that she found particularly alluring.

"Whatever you wish, Madame de Florian."

She had been so enraptured by the prints that she had forgotten to even inquire about the price.

"And how much?" she asked.

Ichiro scribbled a number on a piece of paper and turned it toward Marthe's direction.

"But that's exorbitant," she cried.

"The price for such secrets is always high," he replied.

But she wanted them desperately, and knew she would have paid any price he asked.

She carried her package home, each print carefully wrapped in several layers of rice paper and slipped into a stiff portfolio tied with a purple silk cord.

That afternoon, when she was in the privacy of her bedroom, she withdrew them and gazed at the images for clues of giving Charles pleasure that she might not otherwise have known.

She looked at the women with their broad faces, their black hair plaited with tortoiseshell combs, their robes open and their bodies welcoming their lovers' touch. As if studying a dance, she scrutinized the way their bodies entwined, their fingers grasped, discerning what they revealed and what they kept hidden.

She also noticed the sparseness of the rooms depicted in the prints. Paper screens and sliding doors. There was no evidence of a bed, just a floor with the sculpture of interlaced limbs. But it was the unabashed rapture in the lovers' expressions that fascinated her. Another world had opened for Marthe, and she was curious for more.

Every week thereafter, she would pay Ichiro a visit, never once asking to be taken to the back room.

She would instead merely admire the ceramics he displayed up front, her gloved finger caressing the pieces on the shelves. Ichiro, however, would remain firmly in place, his hands clasped in front, his eyes firmly weighted on her. He could sense her anticipation, her yearning to be invited behind the curtain. But still he waited, holding her off in order to increase her anticipation, before he finally relinquished and motioned for her to follow him inside.

Her eyes would come alive in the darkness of his storeroom as he withdrew a few more of the prints she had come to secretly enjoy.

"I have a rare print from *The Poem of the Pillow* series," he told her. The name itself was so evocative, Marthe felt a tingle run through her spine.

When Ichiro revealed the images, she was immediately struck by the calligraphic lines, the soft rendering of color added to the folds of the lover's robe, pulled up to reveal the soft contour of her thigh. The intimacy of the scene thrilled her. The woman's exposed neck, her slender fingers threading those of her lover's, the pressure of her hands revealing her delight.

"And I have something else to show you," he whispered. He removed the print he had just shown her and placed it back in a portfolio, returning it to a drawer in his desk.

He then reached for a small wooden and paper scroll on the shelf beside him and placed it on the desktop between them.

"This is from the seventeenth century. It belonged to a Samurai family for many generations . . ." Ichiro's hands grasped the ends of small wooden handles and began to carefully unroll the scroll.

The images were hand painted on the rice paper, the artist's sweeping black lines enhanced with dabs of brightly colored paint. The figures had their eyelids closed, their mouths joined in a kiss.

"Lovers in a bamboo grove," Ichiro told her. His finger pointed to the man and woman embracing in a garden of stiff bamboo and lush green leaves.

The scenes continued to unfurl in front of her. The rapture and joy discovered in the lovers' various poses made her flush.

When they had finished gazing at the scroll, Ichiro rolled it closed and tied it with a string. "A hand scroll like this was once kept in the sleeve of a robe, to be pulled out and looked upon when one needed a little viewing of pleasure during the day."

"How perfectly civilized," Marthe said, clearly amused.

"I'll take both the print and the scroll." She pulled down the cuffs of her sleeve. She smiled at Ichiro. "It's too bad, it can't fit."

She wondered if Charles could sense a change in her, for she was aware of how her secret prints were beginning to stretch her mind.

She began to dress in ways that mirrored her fantasies. Embroidered silk robes with images of exotic birds and flowers. Combs for her hair, made not of silver or gemstones, but rather of tortoiseshell or wood.

She would emerge from behind her dressing screen sometimes in a silk kimono, her body soon revealed as her loosely tied sash came undone. She closed her eyes as he embraced her and pulled up her robe, her mind transporting her from the tangled linen of her butterfly bed to the aromatic garden of a bamboo grove.

Afterward, when his body was spent and he reached for his pipe to relax in the tangles of their bed, she would bring up the need for money.

"I might need a little more this month," she said as she threw a leg over him, caressing him with the inner softness of her thigh.

She could feel his body stiffen at the suggestion of money, and he let out a sigh.

"Darling, I think you've managed to decorate every corner of the apartment. There won't be room for me if you spend any more."

"There will always be room for you . . ." Marthe adjusted her leg to wrap herself even more tightly against him.

Charles's long, slender body stretched the length of the bed. She opened her hand and placed it on his chest, feeling the rhythm of his breathing as he took small puffs from his pipe.

"And the extra money certainly wouldn't be for knickknacks."

"What then?" He took a finger and caressed the line of her neck, before circling it just above her breasts.

"It's for my education . . . ," she insisted. "I need the money for books."

Her words had taken him by surprise. As naturally curious as he found her, he had never seen her show the slightest interest in books.

"Well, pages of books, actually . . . but I promise you, the investment will pay off." She lifted his fingers from her skin and placed his palm on her cheek. "Why, you wouldn't want me to become a bore, now would you? I need to feed my mind so I can inspire you."

He grunted and stubbed out his pipe and reached to find her within the covers.

"Inspiration, hmm." He kissed her. "I suppose that's always worth a little something extra."

4.

Solange

November 1938

My visits to my grandmother increased. Now instead of visiting her once a week, I was going two or three times. I was addicted to her stories; like opium, I wanted more and more.

When I was in her company, everything that appeared bleak or mundane melted away. I could have walked for several minutes in the rain to her house, and by the time Giselle had taken my coat, umbrella, and hat, I would have forgotten all about the clouds or the puddles that had ruined my boots. I had entered a place where there would always be comfort and beauty.

After I left, I carried her voice inside my head. At night, I could see her sitting in her velvet chair, her mantel filled with vases of fresh flowers, her shelves lined with porcelains. The image of her ignited my imagination and soothed me.

I began writing down nearly everything that she told me. My

father had been right in believing she was the perfect muse. A woman, born in the dark corners of Paris, who elevated herself through her own cleverness and charm to carve out a better life for herself.

Her memory was as sharp as glass. She could recall everything with vivid detail, and nothing from her past embarrassed her. She believed me to be old enough to hear the truth. And it pleased me that she spoke so freely.

My journal became filled with every detail she relayed. I could imagine her Charles. Tall and slender. His stiff top hat. His pipe and its rings of blue smoke. I could see Ichiro's antique shop with its dark walls and its storefront filled with beautiful ceramics. I could close my eyes and envision the more alluring treasures he concealed behind the curtain.

We would sit in her living room, a tray with two porcelain cups of tea between us, nibbling a small plate of chocolates that Giselle had arranged with care. On sunny days, the shutters would be ajar, so that the daylight cast a beautiful glow over the room. Materials that I had always believed to be gray now appeared almost opalescent. And Marthe's face, too, seemed to change with the sunlight. Illuminated from the shadows, it was easier to see the faint lines by her eyes, and the softness of her skin no longer tight against her cheekbones. But, still, like a well seasoned actress, she knew her best angles and she used them to her full advantage.

During the course of my visits, she had yet to reveal how she came to sit for the large portrait. Nor had she mentioned how she came to own her luminous pearls with the emerald butterfly clasp. Yet, for weeks she had managed to keep me enraptured. I held on to her every word, anxious for the next installment of stories. She came alive when she spoke, her neck grew slightly longer from beneath her collar, and her eyes grew wider. And though she used her hands to emphasize certain elements, she never raised her hand further than her waistline and her fingers never opened. She used them a way a bird might use its feathers, to give her words flight.

When I was in her company, it was easy for me to understand how seductive she must have been at the pinnacle of her youth. But I had yet to figure how she sustained her financial independence after all these years.

She did not appear concerned about money. Somehow, she had managed to prevent the struggles of the outside world from penetrating her apartment. There were luxuries aplenty. Not just in the furnishings and artwork of her living room, but in the smaller details like the full-time housemaid, the expensive chocolates, and the abundance of bouquets of fresh flowers. Even her perfume smelled regal and refined.

In contrast, my father continued to work even longer hours as he, like the rest of France, struggled to make ends meet. On the streets, people mirrored the country's depression on their faces. Their expressions tight. Their clothes more and more somber. The newspapers screamed headlines of factory strikes and the growing rise of Facism throughout Europe.

But my grandmother's apartment offered a respite from all that. It remained my refuge, a place where I could lose myself for a few hours of the day in the cocoon of another person's life story, one that was so much more interesting than my own. Those hours were like velvet to me. Stories spun of silken thread, her own light and darkness, unabashedly drawn.

When I exited the large oak doors of her apartment building, however, the chill outside seemed even more brutal than before I had arrived. And the beauty of her apartment made the lack of ours more apparent. I began to write on the days I did not see her, in a café not far from our house. I'd bring my notebook and pen and sit beside the glass, my imagination trying to conceive a way of weaving what she told me into a book. I could envision her as a young girl with her basket of laundry, her worn gray dress and her apron. I could then see her as a young woman pulling a needle through yards of chiffon, as well as her singing on the stage, her face illuminated by the gaslights, then later cloaked in the shadow of Charles's carriage.

I had never once stepped outside Paris, yet I could imagine with ease the pale green of the water in Venice. The plush banquettes of Caffè Florian, where Charles baptized her with her new name.

And then I would return home. I'd walk up the narrow steps to our apartment on the Rue des Saints-Pères. I'd find the living room with my mother's needlepoint pillows. The small wooden dining table. I'd light the stove and boil myself a cup of tea.

In our small, modest apartment, my mother's bookshelves resembled the intricate tiles of a fortress. Each one tightly stacked against the other. And since her death, I had looked at each book as though it contained pieces of her soul, stories that had nourished her during the course of a too-short life.

My own life was rooted in that bookshelf as well. My first childhood memories were on its lowest shelves, where the picture books she had read to me were placed. And beside those were my first chapter books like *Les Aventures d'un Petit Parisien* or *Le Dernier des Mohicans* that she had encouraged me to read when we curled beside each other in her bed.

Her taste in literature was both varied and mysterious to me. She enjoyed Dostoevsky as much as she did Flaubert. But her library also contained secrets to a past that I, as a young child, had failed to understand.

On the top shelf, she had books that she instructed me, when I was no more than seven years old, not to reach for without her help. "They are rare and valuable," she cautioned me one afternoon. "If you're curious, let me know and I will take them down for you."

I had, of course, asked to see them immediately. What child wouldn't want to look at books she was forbidden to touch on her own?

I remember she smiled and that she cradled my cheek. Her eyes appeared to grow moist, as though my interest in her books, which was both innocent and genuine, had deeply moved her.

She pulled a stool from the kitchen and withdrew one of the thicker volumes from the shelf. The design on the tooled cover was worn; its fragments of gold leaf flickered in between the rivers and tunnels of the design. When she opened the book, I remember I felt as though I was gazing at something written in a magical code.

The pages were ancient looking. The parchment was yellowed. The edges were rough and in some cases torn.

The words were not written in a language I understood or recognized, but my mother informed me that it was Hebrew.

Though I would never be able to read the books, it gave me a strange comfort just to touch the pages and to think of those who had owned the books over the centuries before my mother and me.

My mother rarely spoke of her family. Her own mother had died during childbirth, and her father had never forgiven her for marrying my father, an act he believed was not only a desertion of him but also of her faith.

She had spent her early years in a small apartment on the Rue des Rosiers, her father a dealer of rare and often ancient books.

She grew up without a mother or siblings, her childhood instead spent amongst leather bindings and parchment leaves. I had heard her whisper into my ear, more times than I could recall, that a person who loved books would never feel alone. We would spread out on the carpet and she would read to me her favorites: *Les Histoires ou Contes du Temps Passé* by Perrault or the stories of Hans Christian Andersen. I can still recall the flicker of her finger as it turned the pages, and her smile as I drifted off to sleep, begging her to read one page more.

But the books with the timeworn covers, those, she did not fully explain to me until she approached the last months of her life.

I caught her looking at them with more and more frequency when her illness began to transform her. I have often wondered if, as death approached, she wanted to return to the part of her life she felt guilty for having left behind.

When I would come home from school, I would find her in bed, her slender arms emerging from the sleeves of her robe, her long fingers tracing the ancient lines of text.

She had become so thin those last months. Her black eyes were rimmed in circles. Her hair was no longer lustrous, but coarse like straw.

I curled next to her and tried to give her some of my warmth.

"When your grandfather died," she began, "I sold most of his books. All but a select few.

"The fifteen I took for myself were not the most valuable. I sold those early on in my marriage to your father, I'm sorry to admit. Instead, I kept the ones that, in my hands, felt like they had a soul."

She placed a frail hand on the cover of the book she had brought with her to the bed, and momentarily closed her eyes.

I knew the meaning of my mother's words. Old books contain a history that transcends the words inscribed within their pages. The paper, the ink, even the spacing of the words. They possess an ancient soul.

"My father taught me to read Hebrew when I was much younger than you are now . . ."

She smiled and lifted her hand off the page to reach for mine. I could feel the birdlike bones of her fingers, and her grasp was weaker than it had been just the day before.

"I should have taught you, too," she said as her voice began to crack. "I didn't resist your father when he wanted you to be Catholic. He never went to church, and I told myself that if dipping my daughter briefly in holy water could shield her from experiencing bigotry and hate, I wasn't doing anything wrong."

"Let me . . . ," she said, but her voice began to tremble.

She took my finger and pointed to one of the Hebrew letters that to me looked almost like a musical note. "That's the letter *shin*," she began. And with great effort, her lungs taking shallow and frequent breaths, she began to decode what was written on the page, guiding me through a text that had been handed down over the centuries. After her death, I read those sentences, over and over in my mind. I did not understand what the words meant. But to me, it was the language of my mother's last breaths.

5.

Marthe

Paris 1892

Instead of bringing flowers or boxes of chocolates as small gifts of appreciation, Charles now started giving Marthe books about the history of art and other subjects he thought might inspire her. It bemused him that she wanted to educate herself beyond her toilette of expensive face creams and perfumes, closets of silk dresses, and drawers of delicate lingerie.

"You might find this of interest," he would tell her as he left her a book on the history of English furniture or one on the evolution of French landscape painting. She admitted freely to him that she had many blank pages in her education, and it delighted him to help fill them.

One afternoon, he arrived particularly pleased. He handed her a dark leather volume with gilded edges.

"What's this, my love?" she asked coyly.

She took the book in her hand, looking at the cover embossed with the title: *Fables by Jean-Pierre Claris de Florian*.

"Ah, the name." She smiled and reached over to his cheek and kissed him. "Might I claim him as a relative?"

"It is not only the similarity of the name, my dove. Although it might add to your glamour to say you descended from an eighteenth-century writer . . ."

"Indeed." She ran her fingers again over the cover, smiling at Charles's most recent gift.

"What I found most remarkable was the last line of Florian's eighth fable."

She sat down on the sofa and began leafing through the pages until she found the one of which he spoke. It was entitled "True Happiness."

"I believe you will find yourself captured within the lines." He reached for his pipe and struck a match. Blue plumes of smoke filled the air.

"*A poor little cricket,*" she began, "*observes a butterfly fluttering in the meadow . . .*"

The fable continued to describe how the butterfly is chased by a group of children who race to catch the fragile insect. The butterfly tries in vain to escape them as they eventually seize the butterfly and tear off a wing from its fragile body, then its head.

The cricket seeing the cruelty of the world remarks:

"*It costs too dear to shine in this world.*

How much I am going to love my deep retreat!

To live happily, remain hidden."

She paused as if unsure she truly understood the words.

"Don't you see, little dove . . . I saw you at that dance hall, where all the unsavories threatened to tear at your lovely wings. But I have enabled you to live quietly and safely in your own elegant retreat."

He took the book from her hands.

"My dove is hidden safely. Her wings are only for me."

"Yes," she whispered into his ear as his arm now tightened around her waist.

"To remain hidden, to be protected." She softened in his embrace. "To be yours alone."

The gift of the Florian book had touched her. Now she set out to give Charles a gift that would remind him of her during those long stretches when they were apart.

One afternoon, on her way back from visiting Ichiro, Marthe came across a small secondhand jewelry shop on one of the side streets not far from her apartment. As she stepped closer to the window, she admired the display: a jet-beaded necklace, an enameled brooch, and a cocktail ring with an aquamarine stone the size of a robin's egg. But it was the gold pocket watch that caught her eye.

Marthe moved closer to the glass pane. The watch was open, displaying the guilloche dial and its dark roman numerals. But its interior casing was what intrigued her most. For inside, was the engraving of a dove.

Her heart fluttered. The watch would make the perfect gift for Charles. Like a secret between them, he could open the case in private and see the image of his *nom d'amour* for her—the beautiful wings spread in flight.

Marthe walked inside the store and asked the sales clerk to see the watch.

"I'm afraid this is a purely decorative piece, mademoiselle," the sales clerk informed her. "There is a defect with the escape wheel, and it has defied several attempts of repair."

Marthe removed her glove and took a finger to the edge of the case. The bird was etched in a beautiful fluid silhouette. Its wings a sensual V shape.

"So the only person who should own such a watch, is one not interested in keeping the time . . ."

"Yes, I suppose so, mademoiselle. That would be correct."

She smiled.

"The watch is very well priced, mademoiselle. The store owner established its value based solely on the weight of the gold."

He took a pen and wrote the price on a piece of paper.

"Well priced, indeed." She reached to open her silk purse strings and pulled out a check. "It will make the perfect gift. I'm so very pleased."

The next time she saw Charles, she waited until he was untangling himself from the bedsheets and reaching for his clothes.

"When will I see you again?"

"Ah, my dove, you know I can't tell you that now. I never know my schedule from one week until the next."

Her smile was coy as she pushed herself up against the silken headboard. Around her shoulders, coils of red hair draped languidly.

"Before you go, I have a gift for you, Charles."

Her long leg emerged from the linens, and she pulled the sheets around her as she walked toward her dresser drawer.

"A gift? Oh now, I do hope you haven't spent a lot of your allowance on me, my sweet girl. Because if you have, I'll be quite cross."

"No, in fact, I believe I bought it for a rather splendid price considering the craftsmanship involved."

From her dresser, she pulled out a blue velvet box.

"I believe you'll understand why this was meant for you."

His shirt buttoned, he slipped his coat over his arms as he began to walk toward her.

She opened the box and revealed the gold pocket watch with its solid gold casing. She took it out and handed it to him.

When he lifted the watch's cover, and saw the engraving inside, she sensed he had grasped its significance.

"How perfect." He beamed, kissing her on the cheek. "It will remind me of my favorite little bird . . ."

"It no longer works," Marthe said, taking the watch from his hand. She glanced at the bronze clock on her fireplace noting the current time. "At least not in the traditional sense . . ."

She rolled the small dial on the side of the watch so that its hands matched those of her own clock. "I'm setting the watch for this exact hour and minute. It will remain set at this time until I see you next." She handed it back to him and closed his fingers over the smooth, round casing.

"This way time will stand still until I see you again."

He took the watch and placed it inside the breast pocket of his coat.

"Then I will keep it close to my heart until we can move the hands of the dial once more."

Marthe no longer simply wanted to collect just shunga prints and Oriental porcelains, she sought to expand her mind during Charles's absence. She now began to take excursions to Paris's most fashionable art galleries and museums. As a child, she'd always been intimidated by the Louvre, an imperial stone vault that she imagined was filled with immeasurable treasures. She had felt at odds with the sumptuous surroundings, as if admittance was not possible for a girl of such low social standing. But now, dressed in her finery, she felt she could pass through its doors and wander through its chambers.

For hours, she walked through the museum's many portrait galleries. She studied the detailed, fine brushwork of the Dutch masters and the celestial-like faces painted by Da Vinci and Botticelli. She marveled at the way the Greeks captured both the contours and the sensuality of a woman's limbs. The glow of the marble. The use of light and shadow. She saw that it was as relevant in painting and sculpture, as it was in life.

But it was the large canvases filled with life-size re-creations of women through the different centuries that she loved the most. She would stand beneath their ornate, gilded frames and study their faces, looking for clues that might reveal something hidden or locked away. She wondered about their passions, what they were like after their corsets were untied and their gowns fell to the ground.

She did not look nearly as long at the portraits of the Venuses in their nude splendor, or the nymphs who frolicked in meadows of pale green grass. She knew what a beautiful woman's body looked like. But it was what existed behind the white flesh and flinty blue eyes that captivated her interest. She wondered where they hid their fire and heat.

The rooms of her apartment began to grow in complexity. Now it wasn't just an apartment created for whispers and caresses, it became an extension of Marthe herself. Her collection of Asian ceramics lined the shelves of her parlor, and her secret shunga prints were hidden in the drawers of her bedroom. She was already into her second year of living as a kept woman with Charles when she purchased her first oil painting—a young girl, no older than twelve, dressed all in white.

She did not tell Charles or Giselle, the only two others who ever entered the apartment, why she had chosen this painting above all the ones she had seen for sale. It was because the girl had the same face as Odette. And her dress was almost identical to the one she had watched her mother wash through her tears.

There was no hardship in the girl's face. And no wisdom either.

It was the face of a child, as pure and peaceful as a blanket of freshly fallen snow.

When she had saved enough of her allowance from Charles, she added another piece of artwork for her collection. This time, a small pastel of a dancer. Her body lithe and stretched as tightly as ribbon.

"You are becoming a connoisseur," Charles remarked one day as he settled into the sofa. Marthe had opened the tall shutters to the room, and she could see a small constellation of dust floating in the sunlight, like stardust illuminated in midair.

She pulled up her skirt and settled down beside him. On the side table he had left his gold pocket watch for her to turn the hands once more. How she loved this ritual between them, how they kept their own sense of time.

"It's interesting to see what you're drawn to . . . Most people gravitate to one style or period exclusively. But you're like a piece of cut crystal. A thousand prisms cast through a single set of eyes."

She smiled and reached for his hand. "I'm glad you think it's money well spent."

"Indeed, I do," he said, squeezing her fingers.

"I have this memory of you, Marthe, when we were in Venice. I took you to the church of San Giorgio dei Greci . . . Do you remember? It was pitch dark when we first entered. The place smelled so damp, like an old bank vault." He closed his eyes, lost briefly in the memory. "But then, suddenly from the shadows the paintings by Carpaccio emerged like a beacon of light. I heard this little gasp escape from your lips . . . and as I turned to face you, I witnessed your face transform. It was a revelation.

"You brought me so much joy at that moment. Just like the paintings of San Giorgio before us, you illuminated the whole room."

She was so taken by his words. It wasn't just the affectionate way Charles had remembered her that afternoon, it was also that he had recalled an intimate moment between them that had occurred beyond the bedroom. And that moved her even more.

For several seconds, both of them remained silent.

"Charles . . ." She was so touched to hear him speak so sweetly about her, she felt her voice tremble slightly.

"I remember that afternoon perfectly."

"And the evening, too." He closed his eyes and smiled. "That night when you took down your hair in that splendid bed. I wouldn't be much of a man if I failed to mention that, too."

She soon owned five paintings. The wood-paneled dining room, rarely used, now became an extended gallery in which she could display her burgeoning art collection. She placed a painting of a young woman holding a parasol rendered in soft, chalky hues over the oak mantelpiece and flanked it with two rhinoceros horns that Ichiro had somehow convinced her to buy.

She still visited Ichiro weekly. Their relationship had developed beyond client and dealer; she considered him a friend.

They were both outsiders. He a foreigner in Paris, she a woman of the demimonde. Ichiro understood, without her needing to explain, the paradox of her existence—that her life was as cloistered as it was independent. That she lived very much like the women in his scrolls, cultivated for the pleasure of others: an artist of the body, a connoisseur of its peaks and valleys, a lover of its acquired tastes. She belonged to a world as elusive as a poem. A plume of incense, as fleeting as the moonlight. And to those who understood it, a world exquisitely pure.

It had been Ichiro who told Marthe stories of the geisha back in his native Japan. Women who were desired not only for their beauty, but also for their charm. She would lose herself in the ink and parchment as his hands unfurled yet another scroll, as she saw women who were well versed in poetry, art, and music as well as the mechanics of love.

His affection for Marthe was genuine, for he had made a living out of recognizing things that were beautiful and rare. But what charmed Ichiro most about Marthe was her curiosity. She did not have a life that afforded her the ability to travel. But when she held a precious porcelain in her hand or traced her finger over the painted images in a scroll, he could see her eyes falling into a journey all her own.

"You remind me of the very ceramics you so love," he told her one afternoon as they sat in the back of his store looking at his latest shipment. "Fire within the layers of a soft cloud."

She blushed. She had never studied him too closely, as she was always concentrating on what artworks he had on hand to show her. But now she focused solely on him. He was as finely boned as a sparrow. His features small and sharp, his skin warm and golden.

"Show me more of what you have in those boxes back there," she said with mischief in her eyes. She knew he had recently expanded his inventory. He was importing not only Oriental porcelains and exotic prints now, but also pieces of ivory and amber. Even rare painted ostrich eggs, and rhinoceros horns.

A smile crossed his lips. "To you, I only show the best."

He returned with two small velvet pouches. Slowly, he untied the first one and pulled out seven miniature carvings, each rendered as an animal. A small fox carved in amber, a hare chiseled from ivory, and a tortoise carved from paulownia wood.

"These are the latest fashionable pieces to collect from the Far East," Ichiro informed her. "They are called netsuke . . . Small enough to carry on your person, and to easily gaze upon from the palm of your hand."

As he cradled one of the netsuke in his palm, he traced its delicate lines with his finger. Then, he closed his hand and made a fist, warming it. "Every person who has ever held a netsuke adds something to it. Their oils add to the beauty of its patina. Its value increases with every touch."

"May I see it again?"

"Of course," Ichiro said, pleased that Marthe was intrigued.

She reached for the small amber fox and examined it closely.

In her hand, the small object transformed. She could see how the amber changed from when she held it to the light, so it became nearly opaque in the shadow of her cupped palms. Ichiro understood better than anyone Marthe's tastes. She was attracted to things that were as elusive and as secretive as the world she occupied. Things that were not only beautiful, but also that transformed as much in the darkness as they did in the light.

"I love how small they are . . . ," she said, smiling.

She felt as though she was holding something that was a secret.

"Hidden beauty," he said, closing his eyes. "It is always the best kind of all."

6.

Solange

It was difficult to sleep, my mind raced with all of the stories my grandmother had shared. I could envision everything she told me with such precision.

I longed to return to the comfort of her apartment. There the air was always fragrant and the light soft. We drank from hand-painted porcelain, where delicate birds and flowers floated on crisp white cups and saucers, and reached for chocolates that were served on a glimmering silver tray.

My grandmother was the opposite of my mother. My mother was not a woman whose magic was rooted in elegance or beauty, but rather was one of those rare creatures whose intelligence and soul were wedded in her affection for the written word. *Maman* did not love silk or perfume as Marthe did. She adored the cadence of words and the music of poetry. She believed in the truth that every good novel holds within its pages. And though her father had accused her of abandoning her faith, I knew otherwise. For the last books my mother held to her chest were not her beloved novels by Dostoevsky or Flaubert, but those that connected her to an ancient past.

Marthe, on the other hand, had no connection to the written word, only the spoken one. On all my visits, I never once saw a book anywhere in her apartment. If she did read novels, Marthe kept them far from public view. What I sensed was that she now had little interest in stories outside her own. What she enjoyed was to sit in the silk throne of her chair, close her eyes, and remember. To recall her life when she was as radiant and as beautiful as she was in the portrait above her mantel.

She had spent a lifetime pushing the reality of the world far from her threshold. She stroked her pearls as though they were a rope leading her back into a different time. The furniture in the parlor, the porcelain on the shelves, and the silver tray on the table were unchanged. But the main character was forty years younger, and the person who sat in the chair across from her was not her restless nineteen-year-old granddaughter who hungered for her stories, but a captivated nobleman named Charles.

At the cafés near my home, a coffee and a croissant came cheaply. For two sous, I could spend several hours at a small table and begin to see the material for my book taking form. I filled my first journal. Then, my second and third. As I wrote about my grandmother's childhood, her pregnancy, and how she reinvented herself with Charles, my perspective on my family soon shifted. I began to understand not only my grandmother more fully, but my father as well.

I saw how the circumstances of their early lives had shaped them. Whereas my grandmother sought to erase the squalor of her childhood with the sweep of a powder brush, my father tried to find solace in achieving order in the space around him. While I once

believed my father to be cold and unfeeling, I now saw him resem-
bling one of Ichiro's antique boxes. He had his own hidden drawers,
many of which contained his own silent pain.

I saw when he was eighteen years old opening the letter from
Marthe, learning that she was his birth mother, as well as him standing in the entrance to Marthe's apartment, nervous and ill at ease,
waiting in the parlor as she entered the room in one of her pastel-
colored dresses.

But just as I could imagine my father in his most vulnerable
moments, I could do the same with my grandmother. I could envision
Marthe as easily in that beautiful pink gown, as I could see her, scared
and shivering, in the dark room of her apartment, years earlier, giving up her child to a woman she knew would take far better care of
him than she ever could.

I took pen to paper. And as each page filled with my words, I
came to see their humanity. As Marthe was quick to point out, light
and shadow existed within every life.

And through all of these different angles of perception, I saw a
clearer picture of myself emerging. I realized that I was now a piece
of this story, too. As my story grew, I saw not only how those around
me had lived. More importantly, I sought to understand how they
revealed different parts of themselves by looking closely at how they
had loved.

7.

Marthe

Paris 1897

Marthe detected a change in Charles. Like two dancers who knew the other's rhythm so well, she sensed that he was holding something back from her.

For nine years she had known the language of his caresses. His fingers had traveled over her skin in a thousand different patterns. She knew him as both a lover and as an explorer. He had discovered her with hands warm and curious; he had mined her every valley, every curve, every cliff.

But now he no longer encouraged her acrobatics in bed. Instead, he preferred simply to hold her tight against him, her body nestled against his own. When they lay in her butterfly bed, he would turn on his side, cup his hand around her belly, and bury his face in her hair to breathe in her perfume.

She could feel not only the change in his touch, but in his body as well.

"I'm concerned," she would tell him. "You have grown so thin." The ribs of his chest protruded like harpsichord strings.

"It's nothing," he reassured her. "You are my sustenance. My medicine. I only need to see you more." He pointed to the pocket watch he had taken out from the breast pocket. "The hours in between have been too long."

But Marthe knew better. He hardly ever ate in front of her anymore, and eschewed even his favorite meals, which she asked Giselle to prepare for him. Not only did he refuse her offers of cold duck or pheasant poached in red wine, he seemed unable to tolerate alcohol anymore as well. Marthe couldn't help but notice he barely touched his favorite vintage of Margaux.

"You need to see a doctor," she insisted the next time she saw him, but he waved her off.

"Émilienne has already arranged for me to see a specialist. So no need to wrinkle your brow worrying about me."

Émilienne. The mere mention of his wife's name felt like the prick of a needle against her skin.

Since she had known him, Charles almost never divulged the details of his familial life. She knew—and fully accepted—early on that he had a wife and a son. He spoke of them sparingly, as if they were objects displayed on a shelf she would never be able to see or touch. She was aware he had a title, a town house in Paris, and an estate at the family's holdings in Bordeaux.

On more than one occasion, Charles had complained that his wife preferred to stay in Paris rather than at their estate, when it would be easier to have her and their son safely ensconced in the country. When Émilienne was in town, it was more difficult for him to stay with Marthe for any length of time. Their meetings had to be brief, their passion often hurried. "She thinks I'm with friends," he'd tell Marthe, making sure he drank a scotch before he left so his wife would smell the familiar scent of a gentleman's afternoon.

But just as Charles expected Émilienne not to question him on
his activities outside their home, he expected the same from his
mistress. It was an understood arrangement between him and
Marthe that she would maintain a respectful distance from all matters concerning his family. She would never be invited to his apartment on the Rue Fortuny even when his wife was in the country.
She was never to ask questions pertaining to his personal life. The
life he shared with Marthe only existed within the walls of the
apartment on the Square La Bruyère.

But Marthe had never been able to completely curb her curiosity.
Early on in their relationship, only weeks after their trip to Venice,
she felt the need to know where Charles spent the main part of his
life. And so one afternoon, when she knew Charles was away in
London, Marthe set out to see his Paris home.

She chose her simplest dress and a hat that shielded her features
for what felt like an expedition in espionage. When she arrived at
the building's ornately carved stone facade, her body rushed with
adrenaline. The town house was an impressive example of Beaux
Arts architecture, far more grand than what she could imagine. She
looked at the elegant windows with the latticed glass panes. She
studied the chiseled stonework. The shell motif that scrolled in a
fanciful arabesque over the door's threshold. The glimmering brass
knocker with the golden ring.

Marthe had been caught by surprise when the door opened and
a young woman, around her age, stepped outside, her fingers clasping the hand of a little boy.

Émilienne was impeccably dressed. Her coat was hyacinth blue,
her skirt a creamy duchess silk. She did not appear at all like the
mouse-like creature Marthe had imagined, but rather exuded a
youthful radiance and innocence. Her hair was flaxen, her features
sharply defined. With her long, elegant neck and small shoulders,
the trimly cut coat nipping her tightly around the waist, she reminded

Marthe of one of the perfectly coiffed women illustrated in the ladies' fashion magazines, with their narrow hourglass frames, and hair in compact chignons. Charles could not have picked a more striking contrast when he chose Marthe for his lover. His son, on the other hand, was Charles in miniature. He had the shock of black hair, the marble white skin. Even his smile was just like his father's.

The boy began to sing the lyrics of a nursery rhyme that Marthe remembered from her own childhood.

Ah, vous dirai-je, Maman
Ce qui cause mon tourment?

His voice filled the air with such a sweet innocence that Marthe felt something inside her threatening to crack.

From her rough calculations, the little boy appeared close to four. Her own son would by now be nearly the same age. An image flashed in front of her eyes of Louise Franeau holding a baby no more than a few hours old.

Marthe was suddenly struck by that same dreadful feeling she had experienced when she had just given birth. That pulling sensation that made her breasts leak with milk. But now there was no moisture, only the same throbbing pain. She grew dizzy, as if the sidewalk was falling beneath her. She had suppressed the memory of giving away her child like a bad dream she could will herself to forget, but now a violent flood of emotions swept over her.

She stepped back from the edge of the sidewalk and tried to steady herself without success, even though Émilienne and the boy had slipped from view.

Marthe could barely raise her arm to call a coach to get her home that afternoon. In the confines of the buggy, she tried to regain her composure. She closed her eyes and rested her head against the leather seat for a moment, concentrating on taking deep breaths. But her normal breathing still did not return to her. If anything, it escalated. And despite her efforts, a slight whimper escaped from her lips.

She fumbled to open her purse and reached for a small vial of Ricqlès that she kept tucked inside for emergencies. Once a few drops were dabbed onto her handkerchief, she pressed it to her mouth, inhaling the calming vapors.

By the time the coach arrived at her apartment, she felt a familiar sense of numbness overtake her. It was the same sensation that had come over her when Odette died, or when she had seen her mother trying to cover the bruises above her eye after one of her "visitors" had left. Marthe tried to cloak her emotions, just as one would roll a glove over a shivering hand.

When Marthe returned to her apartment that afternoon, she said little to Giselle after the girl took her coat and hat from her. She only asked her to draw a bath. There, under the blanket of soothing waters, she tried to forget the sight of Charles's elegant wife and child, and her own painful memories the sight of them had reawakened.

Just as she had done years earlier when Louise Franeau had walked out the door of her apartment carrying her son, she shut her eyes as tightly as she could and willed herself to push all of them out of her mind.

That Christmas, Charles grew weaker and there was little doubt in Marthe's mind that he was gravely ill. Her own health began to be affected as well. She lost her appetite and found it difficult to sleep. She did not want to burden him with her own fears, but it was frightening to imagine her life without him. It was hard not to see herself like Fauchon, a canary in a gilded cage. Every bit of food, every bit of conversation—even every touch—came from Charles. At night, she looked around and imagined everything she had grown accustomed to, vanishing. A sense of powerlessness came over her and she struggled with how to balance her genuine concern for Charles's health with her own fear of returning to the hardships of her former life.

As much as she tried to get more information from him, Charles never spoke again of the specialist that Émilienne had arranged for him to meet. Nor did he even mention any medical diagnosis. It was as if his illness was like his wife and son, yet one more thing of which she was not allowed to speak.

And although his declining health was not a permissible topic of conversation, she could see how his waning strength had caused him to seek pleasure in other ways.

He had ordered a tall standing mirror to be sent to the apartment and instructed Marthe he wanted it brought into the bedroom, so that when she disrobed for him, he could gaze upon her from every angle.

A few days before the holiday, he arrived holding another present for her.

"Marthe . . ." The expression on his face was more serious than usual. "I have brought you your present early."

In his hand, he grasped a beautiful red bag, its handles tied with a stiff red ribbon.

In the parlor, they sat side by side. He took a small leather box out of the bag and handed it to Marthe to open.

"This is the first part of your present." She noticed his eyes were glassy and his hands seemed to shake as he gave her the package to open.

"Mellerio . . . ," she said breathlessly, recognizing the insignia on the package. "This must have cost you a fortune."

"It did, in fact . . ."

"I can't take the anticipation anymore, Charles . . ." She knew Mellerio dits Meller was the oldest and most prestigious jewelry shop in Paris. The store on the Rue de la Paix had been the jeweler to the aristocracy for centuries. Whatever was in the box, Marthe knew it was going to be something extraordinary.

"Can I open it now, Charles?"

"Please." He made a small gesture with his hand. "I would prefer you wasted no more time."

She withdrew a black leather box with a gold crown embossed in its center. When she opened the box, a small gasp escaped from her lips.

"Now that's the sound I'd been hoping to hear all day. Almost as good as that enchanting little cry you made when you saw the paintings at the church of San Giorgio dei Greci."

"Better," she said as her eyes fell again to the interior of the satin-lined box. There inside was a glimmering set of pearls with a clasp in the shape of a butterfly set in emeralds.

"Oh my goodness, Charles." She covered her mouth with her hand. She could hardly believe her eyes.

"Try them on," he insisted. "I want to see them against your skin"

She lifted them slowly from the satin interior, placing on the table the index-size parchment from the jeweler that gave the necklace's details and vouched for its authenticity.

"That paper is essential, should you ever sell it," he told her.

She was careful to keep it secured in the box as he leaned toward her to lift her hair.

"Oh, I would never sell something so beautiful, Charles . . ." She could smell the lingering scent of pipe smoke on his neck as he leaned into her.

Once she had latched the clasp and the pearls fell against her skin, he pulled back to admire them both.

"I wanted you to have some security after I'm gone, Marthe. These pearls will ensure that you are taken care of. They're worth over one hundred thousand francs."

She felt her throat tighten. Even though she had never voiced her insecurity, he must have understood and had taken precautions on her behalf. A hundred thousand francs was enough money to live on for the rest of her life if she was careful.

"Do you know why pearls are more valuable than even diamonds, my dove?"

She shook her head no.

He took his finger and hovered it slightly above the necklace.

"Because it takes a single grain of sand to cause a blister in an oyster. And from that blister a pearl might—just might—begin to grow inside. And this doesn't happen overnight. The whole process could take years, just to grow one pearl the size of a pea." He took a deep breath.

"And all of this happens in the secrecy of the oyster shell. A shell that is hardly transparent . . ."

She shook her head in agreement. She had first tasted raw oysters at Maxim's with Charles one night after he had picked her up after one of her performances. She had held the heavy gray shells in her hand and slipped her lips around the wavy edge, drawing the mollusk inside her mouth. The taste had been exhilarating to her, as though she was drinking straight from the sea.

"For every oyster that is shucked, only the rarest ones even contain a pearl at all . . . And then the search becomes even more challenging . . . One must find enough pearls that are the exact size, color, and radiance to start composing a single necklace." He smiled at her.

"Can you imagine how extraordinarily difficult such a feat is, Marthe?"

She shook her head.

"And yet, there you have it. Around your beautiful neck are sixty-five natural pearls, harvested from the bottom of the sea, that are all the same size and have the same luminosity.

"If anything were to happen to me, you should sell this necklace back to Mellerio's . . ."

"What nonsense are you talking?" she interrupted, reaching for his hand. "You're not going anywhere . . . are you?"

The expression on his face suddenly shifted. He patted his breast pocket in search of his pipe.

"Your health . . . you must tell me!" The thought of losing Charles terrified her.

Again, he remained quiet.

"But what did the doctor say? Surely there is some cure you can take?"

Her fingers were trembling. The necklace suddenly felt cold against her skin.

"Let's just say that I've been told to put my affairs in order."

He tried to force a smile. "You are my great love, Marthe." He reached to pull her hand into his. "Consider the necklace a gift of insurance."

That afternoon they tucked themselves inside her bedroom as though it were a raft adrift at sea. She undressed for him slowly, as though it were the last time. She tried to make it a gift to him. To see her cast against the mirrors. Her long white limbs. Her full breasts. The pink nipples that he reached to touch as though they were rose petals meant only for him.

After her silk dress fell to the ground, her corset untied and placed on the chair, and her stockings rolled down over her knees, she stood before him wearing only the pearl necklace.

"It is just as I imagined," he said as he closed his eyes. She crept onto the bed as quiet as a kitten, and she fell asleep in his arms.

8.

Solange

September 1939

A light drizzle was falling when I left my grandmother's apartment. The hours had evaporated between us as I listened closely while she took me back nearly forty years, to when she first had held the priceless strand of pearls in her young hands.

But now, as I stepped outside her building and walked toward the Métro, I noticed an unfamiliar amount of commotion. Men and women were huddling on street corners, and gripping newspapers. From the cafés I could hear the radios blaring. I stopped for a moment and bought a paper from a boy on the corner. The front page, in large black and white letters, announced Hitler's latest advancement. Germany had invaded Poland. A photograph of him on the pulpit, his hand raised and his face twisted with rage, cemented my feelings of dread. Grandmother's apartment slipped away from me as I hurried home.

I ran up the stairs of our apartment and found refuge inside, quickly taking off my sweater and placing my bag and newspaper down on the kitchen table. Outside, I could hear the patter of rain striking the iron balcony.

I had just walked to the stove and lit a match under the burner to boil some water when my father came through the door.

"Solange?" He had not been as lucky as I with the rain. He stood there, drenched. Hanging from his hand was a newspaper, the pages soaked through.

I could hear how worried he was just by the sound of his voice.

"Yes, I'm here . . ." I walked toward him. He was peeling off his wet suit jacket.

"So you've heard, then . . ."

"Yes. But what does it mean?"

I watched as he considered my question. His eyes were closed. I could see the pink circle of skin where his hair had thinned.

"It means Hitler has his eyes on far more than just Austria and the Sudetenland." His face looked ashen and I felt a shiver run through me.

He gestured toward the radio and I went at once to turn it on.

We pulled out our chairs and sat down at the dining room table.

That evening we ate with hardly a word between us. The radio broadcast the news that Germany had violated its previous agreement and had invaded Poland.

"This will mean another world war." Father shook his head. "All those lives lost in the last one, and now another with hardly a reprieve." His eyes darkened and sorrow washed over him. "I don't think France can endure another battle against the Boche," he said, his voice barely a whisper. "But I think the next headline we will hear shall be that we have no other choice than to declare war."

The brutality France had endured during the last war had been so extreme that there wasn't a Frenchman in the country who didn't fear the possibility of another conflict. The German army had brought us to our knees. The trench warfare had been horrific. Many of my classmates were born never knowing their fathers or having one who was maimed.

I knew little about my father's experience in the Great War except for a few bits and pieces, most of which were told to me by my mother. I knew he had spent the last months of his deployment in a military hospital near Verdun administering morphine to hundreds of wounded soldiers. He never spoke of these men, whose wounds and amputations no doubt required his constant attention. But I knew, having heard him cry out from nightmares during my childhood, that he carried his memories of these shattered men deep inside him. And it was on those nights when these men and their wounds returned to him, that *Maman* did her best to soothe my father back to sleep.

In some ways, I believed my mother had saved him from his secret pain. That she had brought light back into a life that would have remained shut and otherwise dark.

She had told me the story of their courtship in various chapters over my childhood. I knew they had met in the months just after the war in a small bookshop off the Boulevard Saint-Germain. She was holding a copy of *Madame Bovary* when his shoulder struck against hers. She had been so caught off guard by their collision that she lost her grip on the novel and it came tumbling to the ground.

"Beware of rat poisoning . . . ," he said, referencing the novel as a shy attempt to make light of an awkward situation.

It seemed her laughter bolstered his bravado, and they spent the next hour looking through the labyrinth of bookshelves together. My mother, for popular nineteenth-century novels. My father, for treatises on natural remedies and cures.

It wasn't until after her death, when I studied my notebook and tried to see beyond their quiet courtship and marriage, that I searched for clues that would reveal his true feelings for my mother.

I closed my eyes and recalled how, shortly after my mother's death, I had found him standing in front of her bookshelf, his hands deep within his pockets. He stood there staring at the apparent disorganization, never once trying to reconfigure anything on the shelves. He simply left her collection just as she had maintained it, embracing what was left of her spirit in the varied bindings on the shelves. And as that memory came flooding back to me, I saw clearly the depth of his love.

Neither my father nor I spoke as the radio blared news of Germany's latest invasion.

My father's face was grave. I watched as he placed his head in his hands. For much of my life, my head had been crowded with words. But now they escaped me.

When I left him to go to my room, he was still sitting at the table listening to the broadcast be repeated time and time again.

That night, when I went to bed, my thoughts wandered back to my grandmother. I had never seen a radio in her parlor. Nor a newspaper on the table. I wondered if she had even heard the news about the invasion. And if she did, whether it would affect her at all.

9.

Solange

At my next visit, I came in and immediately scanned Marthe's living room.

"Do you not have a radio?" I asked.

"Of course I do. It's in here."

She stood up and brought me to another room I had never been in before. It was paneled in wood with a coffered ceiling. In its center was a large dining room table with matching Edwardian chairs. To the right stood a breakfront filled with china, and on a pedestal table next to the ornate fireplace was a small horseshoe-shaped radio.

"You see, I do have one, Solange."

"Well, when did you last actually turn it on?"

"Not recently," she admitted. Yet her skin did not flush with embarrassment. If anything, she seemed almost defiant, if not proud, of this fact.

"Have you heard about Hitler's invasion of Poland?"

She tilted her head slightly, as if she were studying me.

"Giselle did mention something, I believe . . ."

"And does it not concern you?"

I could feel her spirit rustling, like the feathers of a bird considering flight.

"Solange . . ." She said my name slowly and the light changed in her eyes. "Does it appear as though I'm concerned?"

In fact, she only seemed concerned by the judgmental tone I used to question her.

"Don't we know each other well enough by now for you to realize that I've lived a lifetime blocking out every unpleasant thing from outside these walls?

"That is what my artistry was, Solange. And why my visitors always came back to me, time and time again."

"Visitors." So she had more lovers than just Charles. I felt a small shiver run up my spine.

"But what if there's another war?" my voice challenged her. Even with her evident displeasure, I knew I could still ask her anything. We had a relationship far more open then the one I shared with my father.

"Solange . . . I've lived through the war with Prussia. Not to mention, the French Empire's pursuit of Africa from Djibouti to Dakar." She took a deep breath and pressed her shoulders back into the velvet of her chair.

"And of course the Great War, too. So you can see why this latest news does not cause me alarm. I've seen wars waged over things ranging from the price of rubber trees, to the archduke being shot in Sarajevo.

"But in any case, I'm old enough to realize that men will always have two needs. To make war and to make love." A smile formed at her lips. "And I've never had much of an interest in war."

. . .

I wished I could have shut out the rest of the world like my grandmother did. But as I left her apartment, the threat of the looming
war with Germany immediately washed back over me.

It would not take long for my father's prediction to be proven correct.
Two days later Great Britain and France would declare war on Germany.
The news traveled like lightning through the city. It spread through the
telephones, the newspaper headlines and household radios, but also in
the cafés and on street corners. The following morning when I went out
for my coffee and croissant, every conversation I overheard was about
the war. Would we be bombed? Should women worry about their sons
being drafted? Already every grocery and butcher shop had lines forming down the block. I was sure Giselle had been the first in line. Within
a matter of minutes all the shelves and glass cases would be empty.

My father and I now spent every evening at the kitchen table, the
wooden radio between us, as we waited for the latest news reports.

We began to care for each other more gently. Each day, I left
Marthe's a little earlier than I had in the weeks before, accepting
Giselle's offer of some provisions she had procured on the booming
black market. I took the bits of chicken wrapped in butcher paper or
leftover soup she served for lunch. When Father arrived home, I would
have something warm and nourishing waiting for him. I also attempted
to keep my papers contained and not scattered all over the table. And
I stopped complaining as I so often did in the past or pick petty fights
with him. Instead, I strived to be grateful, to be more kind.

The radio reported not only the latest advances of Hitler's army, but
also the anti-Jewish laws being passed by the Reich in Poland. I had

no Jewish friends but the news pained me. I began to dream more and more about my mother. I pictured her long black hair, her thin face, and her gray eyes. I saw her hands fluttering over the books that were written in Hebrew. I imagined her fingers tracing the inky black lines and turning the pages of the crisp yellow parchment. Yet still her family's history remained a mystery to me.

The Jewish Section of Paris was full of winding streets and small family-run stores, tailor shops, and kosher butchers. Eastern European immigrants who had fled their own countries after enduring years of pogroms and vehement anti-Semitism had flooded to Le Marais, bringing with them traces of the countries they had left behind. The air was laced with the strong, briny scent of vinegar and garlic from the pickle barrels outside the delicatessen shops and the sweet fragrance of cinnamon and dates coming from a bakery next door. I had walked there on occasion, curious about the people among whom my mother had once lived, and from whom I had become so far removed.

I took my grandfather's books from *Maman*'s bookshelf, hoping that I'd learn more of a still-emerging story. One that was as intricate as the one I was learning from Marthe, inspired by a portrait and a strand of pearls.

I wrapped the books carefully in brown paper to protect them from the outside world, and then set out from the apartment. I went on a Thursday morning, knowing that many of the shops would be shuttered the following afternoon as the Sabbath approached. I took the Métro to the Saint-Paul stop and began to walk the cobblestone streets, my eyes wandering over the storefronts and their signs. I saw the occasional men in dark coats, black hats, and long beards who filled the streets, but I also saw young women who looked just like me—some even wearing the wide-cuff trousers that were now the latest style. I wasn't sure where I was going or what I might discover here. But I knew I had to learn more about the books that connected my mother to her past.

It was right in the center of the Pletzl, the heart of the Jewish quarter, on the Rue des Écouffes, that I found a small shop with a sign outside that read: *Rare Jewish Books and Manuscripts.*

I pulled my books close to my chest and opened the door.

When I entered, I was struck by the comforting smell of paper and ink. Books lined the shelves, and I noticed two in a special glass display case. But it wasn't as crowded as the other bookstores I had frequented in the past. An older man with an apron tied around his waist moved past me.

I heard him holler toward the back of the store that he'd return later in the day. His accent sounded slightly German.

In the back sat a young man, his shoulders hunched over a desk, the green dome of a brass lamp obstructing his face. All I could see was his thick shock of black hair, like the pelt of a black miniature poodle, illuminated by the light.

He must have heard the door close behind me, for I was only a few steps into the store when he moved his head to see more clearly.

"May I help you?" he asked politely. He placed a small piece of note paper between the pages he was reading and closed the book shut.

I felt slightly bewildered as my eyes scanned the shelves lined with old leather volumes.

"I must tell you, mademoiselle, we're not a regular bookshop. We specialize in rare books and manuscripts . . . specifically rare, Jewish books . . ."

I smiled. "Well, then, I've come to the right place."

I approached him and pulled the package of books from my chest. "Is there a quiet place where we can open these?"

The color of his complexion changed at my suggestion, as if someone had added another layer to his coloring. His blush bolstered my confidence.

"Yes," he said. "Come this way, please."

In the store's back room stretched a long wooden table. A lightbulb dangled from the ceiling, and he flicked on the switch.

"Why don't we take a look at them here? But first I should introduce myself," he said, with a shyness I found endearing. He extended his hand. "I'm Alex. Alex Armel. I work with my father."

"And I am Solange Beaugiron," I returned the introduction. "Was that your father who just left?" My curiosity had gotten the better of me. While there were many immigrants that had flooded the Marais in recent years, Alex spoke French like a native.

"Oh, no, that's Solomon . . . he does amazing work restoring old bindings," Alex explained. "He used to do restoration work in Berlin. We're lucky to have him here with us now."

I smiled and began to slowly unwrap the books. When I had taken away the paper and string, *Maman*'s two volumes, each with its own distinct leather cover and binding, rested on the table between us.

"I never get tired of seeing what people bring in," he said as he moved closer to the books. "May I take a look?"

"Yes, of course . . ." I stepped away from the table so he could see the books more clearly. He approached cautiously as if assessing them visually before he began to touch them.

I watched, mesmerized, as he examined the outside leather binding before carefully opening the first book. Just as my mother had, he opened it from left to right.

"The rag paper is in good condition considering the book's age," he said. "And look at this filigree motif." He pointed to the design printed around the border of the title page. In the center, Hebrew writing was printed in dark calligraphic type.

"It's quite old and very beautiful . . . printed in Venice in the sixteenth century by Giovanni di Gara, one of the great printing houses in Europe during that time. Even though di Gara wasn't Jewish himself, he printed many books in Hebrew."

He took the book and now held it up closer to the light. "Whoever has had this in his possession over the years certainly took great care of it."

"Thank you," I answered softly.

"Have you had these books for very long?"

"They belonged to my late mother. Her father had a bookshop much like yours, I believe on the Rue des Rosiers."

"How strange," he said. "It's not familiar to me . . . but my father will surely know of the store. He should be back shortly.

"In the meantime, let's take a look at the other treasure you have in your possession." He let out a small laugh. "This one looks even more special than the first. I've been eyeing it anxiously ever since you unwrapped the paper. If I'm seeing correctly from afar, you've brought in something very rare . . . and I suspect quite old."

He reached for the larger book, the one that was as heavy as an old Bible, and opened it just as carefully as he had the last one. This book was the one my mother had read from during the last weeks of her illness. Since then, I had looked at it on several occasions, fascinated. I had not been able to remember any of the words she had once sounded out for me, but I spent hours poring over the many illustrations dispersed throughout the book. Animal and bird motifs, all painted in a bright palette of blue, red, and gold, created intricate borders. A few of the pages contained illustrations that depicted people. A man sitting at a table with his family. Another of a figure holding a staff.

Alex squinted over one of the pages and then turned to study a few more. "This is a very, very old Haggadah, a prayer book used by the Jewish people for Passover." His voice seemed to drop to almost a whisper. "It's an amazing example of craftsmanship." He turned another page and looked again at the calligraphic lines. "It's all inscribed by hand on vellum . . . parchment made from calfskin."

He began to study the pages portraying what appeared to be the patriarch of a family telling the story of the slaves in Israel.

Just as he reached to show me something else hidden within the illustrations, the bell above the store's door chimed and we heard footsteps walking toward us.

"Alex," a voice wafted into the back room. "Has Solomon gone for the afternoon?"

"Yes, Papa. I'm in the back . . . with a customer."

The store was quite small, so within seconds a man who appeared as an older version of Alex was standing at the threshold.

"What have I missed in the thirty minutes since I've been gone, besides the only pretty girl to walk into our store all day?" Other than his graying hair, the father's resemblance to Alex was uncanny. They had the same features. The chiseled face, the strong nose, and lively green eyes.

"Well, let's see . . ." Alex let out a small laugh. "You missed the same beautiful girl walking in with what I believe to be a sixteenth-century copy of the *Zemirot Yisrael* by Najara, and what appears to be a rare example of a fourteenth-century Haggadah under her arms."

"Are you joking, Alex?"

"No, Papa. Not at all. Here, come take a look."

His father could hardly contain his excitement. He extended his hand for me to shake. "Let me first introduce myself, Bernard Armel, bookseller and Alex's father . . . and you are?"

"Solange Beaugiron."

"A beautiful name, for a beautiful girl," he said as he approached the table where the two books were laid out. Immediately he began examining them with careful hands.

I watched spellbound as Monsieur Armel made great effort to minimize how much he touched the pages and how he handled the book delicately, to prevent placing any unnecessary stress on the binding. He squinted as he looked over the mysterious Hebrew writing and made a few grunted sounds, as if he were confirming something to which only he knew the answer.

He spent only a few minutes looking at the book that was printed in Venice. It was the Haggadah that had evidently captured his interest.

"Where did you get these two books?" I noticed right away a change in his voice, like a musician's note that had slipped off-key. It no longer had even the slightest hint of playful flirtation. Rather, a sense of suspicion now threaded through his words.

"They were my maternal grandfather's," I said, and my voice surprised me with its air of defiance. But I suddenly felt on the defensive.

"Your grandfather was Moishe Cohen?"

He stood silently for a few seconds before I responded.

"Yes," I answered again firmly.

"Incredible."

I watched as Alex's eyes focused on me. The energy had now shifted within the room. I felt like I was no longer a stranger, but someone with a connection to them and their community. Like a lost suitcase that had miraculously washed ashore.

"I knew him."

"You did?" My heart leapt inside my chest.

"Yes, quite well, in fact. It's a small circle of people who are in the business of selling rare books, and even smaller with rare Jewish ones.

"Your grandfather had a gift for discovering many hidden treasures scattered throughout Europe. He was immensely respected within the field and within our community here."

I held on to Monsieur Armel's every word as he spoke, for I knew almost nothing about my maternal grandfather.

"After Moishe died, I bought his whole collection. Or at least I thought it was his entire collection . . ." Alex's father said. "Actually, I bought everything directly from your mother.

"Your grandfather showed me this Haggadah only once, and I always wondered who had bought it . . ." He pointed to the book that Alex and I had just been looking at together. "It's so rare and valuable, I knew he was offering it for a price few people could afford. But I would have taken great pains to buy it as an investment."

"Well, he didn't sell them," I said, my voice now softening. "My mother took them for herself when he died."

"Your mother . . ." His voice again changed to another key. This one almost wistful.

He looked up from the table and began to study me, scanning my features as though he recognized something familiar in them. "You have her eyes. That beautiful gray-green that shifts in the light." His voice drifted for a moment.

"She was a beauty like you, and when she married your father, she shattered your grandfather's heart."

He closed the Haggadah and placed the other book beside it. "Let's return to these in a bit . . ."

I smiled at him. Within only minutes of meeting him, I could see both the clinical expert and the warm father he was to Alex.

"Alex, why don't you prepare a pot of tea for us. Bring over those little cookies Solomon's wife baked for us this morning."

"Yes, Papa," Alex said. He smiled as he stood to oblige his father's request.

Until that moment, I hadn't noticed the discreet counter with the single burner and sink tucked into the far side of the room. I watched out of the corner of my eye as Alex filled the kettle with water and began to prepare the tea.

"Come." Monsieur Armel motioned for me to go to the desk where Alex had first been sitting when I arrived. "I'll clear these papers and bring two more chairs."

I followed him as he arranged the desk into a makeshift table with chairs. Then I sat down.

Alex arrived with a tray containing a plate of cookies and a pot of tea.

"At your service," he joked as he placed down the tray. He poured the tea into three ceramic cups and then took a seat himself.

"Please take one, Solange," his father said, moving the plate of cookies closer to me.

I smiled. They were the type of cookies I had always associated with my mother. In better times, one could always taste the luxurious taste of butter running through them. But the thumbprint of plum jam in the center was something that was typical in her baking. Now I wondered if there were other small things she did that had gone unnoticed by me, gestures she did privately in order to keep the connection to her past alive, even if only for herself.

Alex's father smiled as I nibbled at the cookie.

"May I ask, Solange, did your mother share any stories with you about your grandfather, or her life in the Marais before she married your father?"

I shook my head no.

"I suspected as such . . ." A small sigh escaped from his lips. "It was probably not easy for her to talk about her family, after what happened once she married your father.

"The last time I saw your mother, she was pregnant with you, and she had sought me out to sell some of her father's inventory. She was his only heir, and even though he had disowned her while he was living, he left everything to her at the time of his death."

He studied me. "She couldn't have been more than a few years older than you are now."

I bit my lip. It was a bittersweet thought to imagine *Maman* at the cusp of motherhood.

"She came to me first, because she knew I had been your grandfather's friend for years. And I told her I'd buy everything from her . . . How funny she didn't answer me when I inquired about the Barcelona Haggadah. Now over twenty years later, I know why. She had kept it for herself all along."

"I don't think she would have sold it for any price," I said in her defense. "My mother kept things that were precious to her for reasons that transcended money." I lowered my eyes. "Though I'm sure she knew it was worth quite a bit of money . . ."

"I would have paid handsomely for it," he told me. "The *Yisrael Zemirot* is valuable, but certainly not as much as the Barcelona Haggadah. It's priceless for many reasons. It's not just the age and rarity of the book, it's also the story of the people who created it."

I raised an eyebrow.

"It's absolutely extraordinary to be able to see this book resurface again after all these years. As I mentioned before, your grandfather showed it to me only once. I had heard a rumor that he had somehow come to own it, and I hounded him for months before he finally agreed to show it to me. That said, he always kept the story on how he acquired the Barcelona Haggadah shrouded in mystery."

I gazed at the table with the two books I had brought to the Armels' shop. I had always suspected they were worth a bit of money, but I was even more grateful to learn more about my mother.

"You have no idea how interesting the story is about how this book was created. It wasn't just conceived as a prayer book for Passover, but as a project between two people in love."

Alex turned his head and looked at me. I could sense that both of us were about to hear a story that even he had never heard before.

"This particular Haggadah was written by a Sephardic rabbi and illustrated by his wife in the fourteenth century. The couple produced only one book in their lifetime, and it's the one in your possession." He paused for a moment before continuing.

"Rabbi Avram had a master calligraphic hand, and his wife had considerable artistic talent, particularly in painting. Early on in their marriage, they conceived of an idea of doing a Haggadah together. Rabbi Avram would write the story of Passover and the prayers as they were handed down over the centuries, and his wife would paint the illustrations. It took them over twenty years to finish it."

He opened it to one of the pages with the painted border of birds and lions. The heavy parchment was stained in places, and some of the gold leaf that had been used was almost completely gone, but the wife's talent was clear.

As Alex's father told the story of this Haggadah's unique conception, I imagined the rabbi writing with his wife working alongside him, doing the illustrations with her brushes and paint, so many years ago. It was a magical and mystical image.

Monsieur Armel closed the book and then carefully lifted it. "Can you imagine working on a single book for twenty years?"

I shook my head.

"Well this book is almost four hundred years old. So when you think of it, twenty years is not so long to make something that has withstood all these centuries of turmoil, wars, and the perpetual threat of floods and fire," he explained.

"But it's like the Jewish people. It continues to go on, even though each century threatens to extinguish it."

I felt a shudder pass through me.

"Did your mother ever tell you that she was Jewish, Solange?"

I felt my stomach turn inside.

"She only told me a few months before she died," I answered, my voice almost inaudible. I knew I had nothing to be embarrassed about with the Armels, and yet a sense of shame flooded over me.

Alex's eyes fell downward. "With Hitler, now perhaps it's not very good timing . . . to learn this news."

His father made a look of disgust. "Hitler." He shook his head. "He is what we now must fear, more than the bombs and trenches of another war. He wants to extinguish every last one of us."

I made a pained face.

"I'm sorry . . ." Alex's father tried to smooth over my obvious discomfort. "It's just that Solomon tells us terrible things. Things he hears leaked out from Germany." He let out another loud sigh.

"I suppose we must just try to be hopeful that France really does stand by *liberté, égalité* and *fraternité*," I said.

Alex took the last sip of his tea. "It's nice to be surrounded by a woman's optimism, right, Papa?"

Monsieur Armel smiled.

"My mother passed away some time ago. So it's just the two of us now."

"Just like me and my father," I said.

Alex nodded. "It's good to have someone in our shop that is not telling us to prepare for gloom and doom. Unfortunately, as my father alluded, Solomon has told us that we have much to fear if the Germans enter France."

I shuddered. It wasn't solely the Jews that feared a German occupation. All of France feared it. Even those who were not alive during the First World War heard stories about the cruelty and barbarity of the German army.

"I have to think the French army will do everything in their power to stave off an invasion. Plus, we've spent all these years preparing the Maginot Line of defense," I offered. "Surely that will help us."

Alex opened his hands. "We can only pray that you are right, Solange."

The talk of Hitler had unnerved each of us. Despite Alex's filling both his father's and my cups with more tea, none of us touched another cookie or took another sip.

I could feel a growing knot in my stomach after our discussion and decided it was time to return home. I thanked both Alex and his father, then walked back toward the worktable and let Alex rewrap the books in fresh brown paper.

"We assume you are not interested in selling these," Monsieur Armel said with understanding.

I nodded. At this point, I would not sell them for all the money in the world. My mother had her reasons for not selling them, and I would honor her wishes. And although I could not read the Hebrew or understand the layers of history that Alex and his father saw in these two rare books, for me it was still a thread that bound me deeply to her.

As I walked home that afternoon with the sunlight on my hair and the books clutched even tighter to my chest, I felt my mother's spirit deep within me. I heard her voice, and saw her face fluttering before me. I had learned another chapter of her life today by bringing her books to Alex and his father. And her words, that "every book has a journey all its own," echoed in my ears.

10.

Marthe

Paris 1898

They never spoke of his illness. Charles had made it clear to her that, no matter how much time remained for him, he did not want to spend it dwelling upon his declining health.

Marthe had now spent a decade with Charles as his exclusive lover. She had become an expert at maintaining the beautiful illusion he so loved. But whereas it was easy to re-create herself with silks and satins, or further refine herself with the collection of art and porcelains, it was far more of a struggle for her to silence her growing concerns about him.

His malaise had become the white elephant in the room. And although Charles refused to discuss it, his physical deterioration was undeniable. Marthe felt it constantly—whether they were sitting in her parlor or wrapped in each other's arms in her bed. His illness was overtaking him.

He no longer possessed his insatiable hunger for her. He moved more slowly and she sensed his need to conserve his energy. Where there had once been athleticism in their amorous entangles, now there was a palpable fatigue.

His illness proved a challenge to Marthe. Her entire adult life she had cultivated ways to banish life's unpleasantries from her mind. But Charles's sickness was not something that could be forgotten by shutting one's eyes tightly. It remained a shadowy presence that, as much as she tried, she could not keep from penetrating the walls of her apartment.

His eyes were jaundiced most of the time. His lips chapped and cracked. Even his beautiful skin now appeared ashen to her.

Sometimes she felt herself unable to remain muted, no matter how much he insisted it wasn't something he wished to discuss.

"I come here to forget the outside world . . . to be with you."

"But it's not the outside world when it concerns you . . . your health." She was trying desperately not to cry, but her voice was cracking.

"What will happen to me when you go?"

"You still have your youth, my sweet girl," he said, though Marthe was approaching her thirty-fourth year. "You only need to walk on the Champs-Élysées or by Eiffel's tower of steel, and some rogue will snatch you up for sure."

"I don't want just any rogue." She lowered her eyes. "I only want you." Around her neck was his necklace. She almost never took it off.

His finger reached for the butterfly clasp that had fallen forward, and touched it lightly.

"You already have the best of me, Marthe. You own my heart."

She could feel herself starting to unravel. The first sign was the tears. She would do anything not to come undone in front of him. She had bitten her lip so hard when Louise Franeau had carried off

Henri, she had cut right through her skin. And now she could taste the blood again on her tongue.

She was afraid if she spoke any more, her voice would betray her. He had treated her more kindly than perhaps anyone ever had. Marthe knew that her situation could have turned out very differently with him, when she first came under his wing. She was aware of men who simply paid by "the visit" to certain women of notable beauty and charm. Paris had a whole hierarchy for women of pleasure from the highest-paid courtesans to the girls at the lowest brothel. Marthe was lucky she hadn't ended up like so many of those poor girls, for most of them had childhoods much like her own.

But Charles had treated her as generously and as kindly as he possibly could. He had denied her nothing. The only thing he had asked in return was for her to respect their arrangement. To not interfere with his life with Émilienne. And to open her arms for him when she needed her love.

The thought of losing Charles plagued her. Even with the pearl necklace as financial security, she could not imagine her life without him. She needed him to get well.

"The pocket watch," she whispered. He reached into his coat, handing it to her as he did with each visit. The gold casing was now worn with its own patina. Clutched between her own fingers, she wondered if Charles often held it in his closed palm, the memory of her washing over him as the metal warmed in his hand.

She opened it to reveal the dial, the hands locked in the position from the last time he lay in her arms. "Are you going now?"

"Yes, my dove. Émilienne is already waiting for me."

She fought back her tears to look at him with clear eyes. She saw past the yellow in his eyes, the sallow of his cheeks. Without a sound, she began to turn the small dial to adjust the watch's hour and minute hands to the time of the clock on her mantel.

"Time will stand still until then." She placed the watch down on the table and, softly, brought his hand to her cheek, before kissing it and closing it shut. How she wished he could keep her kisses contained in the well of his clenched hand.

11.

Solange

September 1939

The three of us continued to meet around the dining room table every night: my father, myself, and our radio.

The radio held a position of honor between us. After I had dished out the evening meal and poured a little wine in our glasses, we'd listen to the broadcast to learn what either Germany or the Soviet Union would do next. Two weeks after France and Great Britain declared war on Germany, the Soviet Union invaded Poland from the east. The country had now been attacked from both sides.

"Do you think that France will be invaded?" I asked my father.

"I pray that won't happen, Solange." He looked older, more tired in the past few weeks. "But, it's not impossible."

I poured more wine into his glass.

"What I believe is that the Germans will not stop with Eastern Europe. Hitler will want all of it."

I felt a shiver run up my spine.

"I'm afraid." I uttered the words so quietly it almost sounded like a whisper. "He's blaming almost all of Germany's problems on the Jews." I did not mention to him about my afternoon spent at the Armels' bookshop, the stories I had learned about my maternal grandfather, or the worry I had seen on Alex's and Monsieur Armel's faces when Hitler's name was mentioned. But I needed to know what my father would reveal when I mentioned my concern for the anti-Semitism that Hitler was inciting across Europe.

I watched as my father lifted the wine to his lips. His spectacled gaze was now straight upon me. There was a sudden lapse into silence. From the way I returned his gaze, he seemed to understand without me uttering another word that I had come to learn I was part Jewish.

"*Maman* showed me some of her books written in Hebrew, before she died." I took a deep breath and continued to look at him. "I know I'm half Jewish."

I heard a deep breath escape from him. He placed his empty wineglass back on the table.

"I must tell you . . ." He pushed himself into the back of his chair. "It's a relief to me that you finally know the truth . . ."

"But why did you both keep it from me for so long?"

My father looked down at his half-eaten plate. One of his fingers traced the rim of his glass, as if he was considering the right words for his reply. I could see how it pained him not to have had more time to formulate his answer to me, having always had such a deep need to be precise.

"Of course, you realize that the Jews have not always been treated kindly by the French people, Solange. Consider what happened to Captain Dreyfus, for example. We are still very much a country that considers itself French, very much Catholic, and quite suspicious of anyone else . . ." His eyes drifted upward. "And as much as we claim to be a tolerant nation, that's not always the case . . ."

"So you both made this decision to protect me?" It was hard to mask my disappointment that they had kept the information from me for so long. "Even if you chose to raise me as a Catholic, I still don't understand why *Maman* felt she had to keep the truth from me. She hardly seemed like someone who would be ashamed of her past."

He shook his head. "No, she wasn't ashamed of her roots, Solange. She was hurt by them."

I raised an eyebrow, questioning.

"Your mother's story was a complicated one . . ." His voice trailed off. I watched as he took another sip of wine before placing his glass on the table.

"She grew up with more privileges than a typical girl in her community. It was just she and her father for so many years . . ."

I nodded, knowing that my maternal grandmother had died when my mother was barely three years old.

"And those books"—he lifted a finger and pointed in the direction of her bookshelves—"were such a comfort to her. For most of her life, anyway."

The tenor of my father's voice shifted. His tone always had a trace of hardness to it, perhaps out of an innate need to always be clinical in how he revealed information. But now it had softened, as though just the thought of recalling my mother had the capacity to somehow soothe him.

"Your grandfather had a rare book and manuscript shop on the Rue des Rosiers. I believe he thought your mother would one day assist him there . . . or perhaps more realistically, that she'd marry someone Jewish to whom he could bequeath the store."

He lowered his eyes.

"But she brought me home, instead."

Father cleared his throat. "I think you can imagine his disappointment . . . I was a struggling pharmacist, a Catholic, and someone whose family background was anything but clear."

I looked at my father with empathy. Even now, so many years later, I could see that he blamed himself for what happened between my mother and her father.

"I was never going to be the Jewish boy who could take over the family business, their traditions, or maintain their place in the community that they had created over the years."

I nodded, knowing this to be true. My mind kept returning to the memory of Alex and his father working side by side in their small shop. The respectful way in which the son deferred to his father's expertise.

"Your grandfather reserved his respect for those books he believed to be precious and rare. And his circle of friends were all people who understood their value.

"But even though your mother was what he prized most in his collection, I was never going to be someone that belonged to his world." He raised his glass for another sip of wine and steadied his voice again. "He might have thought I was common as newspaper, but what he didn't realize was that we both loved her more than anything in the world."

"But if he loved her so much, why did he disown her?"

My father shook his head. "Shame is a terrible thing, Solange." He pushed away his plate to the side. "He felt she had betrayed him. They had a huge fight just after I proposed. He didn't want her to marry me. He told her there were at least a dozen potential suitors in the neighborhood that wanted to court her, all of whom were worthy of being his son-in-law. I don't think he could believe that she actually wanted me."

I tried to envision my mother engaged in such a fiery row. She was so gentle, with such a soft-spoken voice, that this was almost impossible to imagine.

"He threw her out. He told her she had shamed him and dishonored their family name."

I shuddered.

"We married a few weeks later in the town hall."

The rest of the story I knew. I had learned during my mother's last months how my grandfather had died of a heart attack when she was pregnant with me, and how she had returned to close his store and put the remaining inventory up for sale. The only things she had kept were those two books, and perhaps the regret of not having put aside her differences with her father before he died.

"I just don't understand why this was all kept from me for so long. To find out so late . . . It just seems wrong."

My father shook his head. "You have to understand, your mother was shattered when he told her she could never come home again if she married me."

I had never considered my mother as being so strong or even defiant. Father was now revealing a side of her that, for me, was previously unknown.

For a few moments, a silence lingered between us. But the lack of words did not feel uncomfortable. If anything I felt closer to my father than ever before. I appreciated his finally telling me the truth. As I sat quietly at the table beside him, my mind raced with questions.

"These past two years have been full of many unexpected things for you . . . Don't think that I don't see that." He took a deep breath. "It has been difficult for me to raise you without your mother. I miss her so much." His voice nearly broke at the last three words. "I was nearly the same age as you when I learned a secret had been kept from me, that my mother was not in fact Louise Franeau, but the woman you now visit weekly, Marthe de Florian."

My eyes slid down to my lap. I had not made the connection, but what my father said was true. He, too, had been kept in the dark about his ancestry. And the **contrast** between the woman who raised him and the woman who bore him must have come as a complete shock to him.

"We have both learned that women are capable of keeping secrets . . . and that both our mothers were far more complicated than we initially believed."

"Yes," I agreed. "Still, it is strange to only learn now that I am part Jewish."

"I suppose you are Jewish in so much as your mother's blood runs through yours. But the woman who raised me, Louise Franeau, who died two years after your birth, took you in her arms and had you baptized at the local church. She couldn't sleep without knowing you had been bathed in holy water."

"But Mother's religion is not listed on my birth certificate?"

"No," he said. "I don't believe religion is ever stated on the French birth certificate. But I will check to make sure." He stood up and went to his bottom desk drawer where he kept all of his important papers locked in a small metal safe. He took out a key and unlocked it, retrieving an envelope with my birth certificate inside. "It only says your mother's maiden name: Cohen."

"Well, the name will certainly give me away if they search through the records."

"I don't think we should worry ourselves about such matters now, Solange. There are no Germans marching down the Champs-Élysées just yet."

"Not yet," I said as I turned up the dial of the radio. "But I can't help but imagine if they did."

12.

Marthe

Paris 1898

Marthe had not quite believed Charles when he promised her there would be a second present to follow the pearls. She couldn't imagine anything that could possibly top what he had already given her. But less than a week later, as they lay in bed with his finger tracing the length of her body, he turned to her and said: "I've commissioned a portrait of you."

She grabbed the sheet around her and sat up. "A portrait?"

"Yes." Despite his fragility, she could see the pleasure in his eyes. "I've taken note of all of your little collections . . . all of your objects scattered throughout the apartment and all of those paintings in the dining room, too. Now, I want a large portrait of you to hang over the mantel in the parlor. I want to be able to see two of you whenever I'm here."

"For such an ascetic these days . . . you're becoming quite greedy, aren't you?" She took her hand to his cheek. "Really, two of me?" She feigned a sense of modesty at his generous suggestion.

He reached out to kiss her. She closed her eyes. It was hard to see him so thin. He resembled one of those wire armatures that sculptors used to create the skeleton before they began applying the clay.

"I really wish you'd save your strength, instead of squandering it negotiating with artists."

"Come now, Marthe . . . I know you far too well. Doesn't the idea absolutely thrill you? To sit for one of the most fashionable portrait painters in Paris?"

"And who might that be?" she teased.

"A man named Giovanni Boldini."

Marthe's face went blank. She didn't recognize the name.

"Why, he's the biggest name in society portraits these days, my darling. He's a good friend of Sargent's."

Marthe raised an eyebrow, intrigued. She had certainly come a long way from the first time she had heard the name John Singer Sargent mentioned while strolling the halls of the 1884 Paris Salon with her fellow seamstress, Camille.

Camille had always been full of ideas and was interested in making any spare time outside their workshop an adventure.

They had agreed to meet just outside the Palais de l'Industrie. Marthe had been so excited, she arrived early. She had never seen so many people crowding the streets. The day was beautiful. The chestnut trees were in bloom. A steady stream of horse-drawn carriages pulled up to the entranceway. Marthe watched as the city's most fashionable women stepped out into the daylight, their pastel parasols opening like cabbage roses in the sun.

She and Camille walked together into the first salon rooms, their lungs filled with the strong, foreign smells of varnish and linseed oil. They wandered through the enormous hallways, clutching their Salon catalogs. They walked past the enormous mural by Pierre Puvis and then stood for a few minutes contemplating the nude figures drinking wine in Bouguereau's *The Youth of Bacchus*.

But it was Sargent's portrait of Amélie Gautreau that she remembered most clearly. It had been the scandal of the Salon. Displayed in the final room of the exhibition halls, the large portrait stood out in haughty defiance. The painting was nearly life-size, taking up almost the entire hall, and dwarfing the other paintings that surrounded it. Marthe could close her eyes and still recall how Sargent had painted Gautreau's creamy white flesh and swanlike neck, her chiseled features as sharp as glass.

Marthe and Camille had walked past countless rooms of nudes that afternoon, but this portrait of the fully clothed Gautreau had been the most provocative of all. The nudes rendered in the other paintings all looked like sexless cherubs, most of them cast in idealized landscapes. Madame Gautreau, or Madame X as she was identified by the small plaque beside the portrait, appeared far more sexual than any of the other paintings exhibited. Sargent had painted his subject with her head turned in profile, wearing a plunging black bodice with one strap over her shoulder and the other dangling over her porcelain white arm. It was as if the dress could slip off of her at any moment. The painting had struck Marthe like a dare.

All these years later, Marthe had never forgotten the painting. Gautreau's body, though sheathed in black velvet, had left little to the imagination. One could see every line and curve. This was a portrait that lit up the room like a match.

While everyone gasped and whispered at its inappropriateness, it had secretly thrilled Marthe.

Now, she could hardly believe that Charles was suggesting a contemporary of this great artist to paint her portrait. "I do like Sargent," she said, curling up closer to Charles. "But I've never heard of this Boldini . . ."

In her mind, she started imagining how an artist might portray her. Already, she could envision herself sitting with her head turned, her body dressed in one of her most beautiful gowns. It was comforting to also know that even in his illness, Charles had not tired of seeing her from all points of view.

"I've made an appointment for him to visit the day after tomorrow," Charles interrupted her from her reverie.

"Let Giselle prepare something nice for him. He's small, but he's known to have an enormous appetite."

He smiled. "You'll see what I mean when you meet him."

She took his hand and brought it to her lips. "I am not too concerned, my darling. I've never been known to starve a man."

Boldini arrived at half past noon. Marthe was already seated, waiting for him in the parlor. A pale lilac dress fell languidly over her long body. Around her neck, she wore the pearls from Charles.

"Monsieur Boldini," Giselle announced as she ushered the painter into the room.

Marthe could hardly believe her eyes. The man did not look like anything she had imagined. He was short and balding, with a long mustache and goatee. His eyes were framed by thin wire glasses, and above their rims emerged a pair of thick and pointed brows.

Marthe rose from her chair and extended her hand. She was nearly a half foot taller than the artist.

"What a relief to discover I'll have such a beautiful subject to paint," he said as he kissed her hand. "You will make my job here a pleasure."

She smiled, pleased that the artist made up in charm what he lacked in good looks and height.

"And I am grateful to be painted by such a talent. Charles has spoken incredibly highly of you."

He was still standing in the center of the parlor. Against his waist, he held a large sketch pad tied closed with black cord.

"Please, Monsieur Boldini, make yourself at home . . ." She made a small gesture, encouraging him to sit down.

He nodded, taking a seat across from her. She noticed how his eyes were scanning the objects around the room.

"I see you like Oriental ceramics."

Marthe smiled, delighted that the artist had taken note of her collection. Her porcelains had become a source of great pride for her. "Yes, very much. They were the first precious objects I began collecting . . . and once I started, I couldn't get enough."

"How interesting . . ." His expression suggested he was genuinely surprised that Marthe had chosen something so exotic as her first collection, for Asian porcelains were appreciated by a rarefied few.

"I must confess, I'm a bit of a collector myself." Again, his eyes scanned the room. "I admire what you've managed to get your hands on."

Marthe beamed. She was happy to have impressed him with something she had cultivated by herself, something beyond her own beauty.

Boldini pointed to one of the gourd-shaped vases on the shelves. "Moonlight glaze. One of my favorites." He closed his eyes briefly, as though the pale blue glaze had triggered something in his mind.

"The Asians have such a delicacy of palette," he continued. "It's as if they can pinpoint the exact shade of breath, of water, of ice . . . Elements we think of as being clear, they find in that perfect shade of blue."

She felt a slight flutter inside her as he spoke, a feeling wholly unexpected. She wanted him to keep talking, for she was immensely curious about what else he had to say.

"And that one . . ." He pointed to another one of her porcelains, one of the famille rose variety. "How easy it would be to imagine one of the blooms in my hand . . . the velvet petals between my fingers." His voice lowered in pitch as though he wanted to intensify the almost erotic nature of his words.

Marthe's skin grew warm underneath her dress.

"The lines of the artist's brush fired to a perfect high relief. The contrast of the hard against the soft." He turned from the porcelain and then focused his eyes on her. "There's something quite sensual to it . . . don't you think?"

She smiled back at him, pleased that they had something in common. She could feel herself becoming entranced by him, despite his impish appearance. Marthe studied him again. The small face, the pinched features. The balding head. Nothing was handsome about him at all. He lacked what had first attracted her to Charles: the height, the head full of thick black hair, the sharp, straight nose and cupid-bow lips. But when her eyes fell upon Boldini's hands, she saw the one physical feature in which nature had been kind.

The fingers were long and tapered. The skin white and smooth, not a blemish or hair to be seen.

How beautiful his fingers were indeed. She could easily imagine him holding a paintbrush and palette.

"Yes," she said, trying to reignite the conversation after her momentary distraction. "It's not only the lines of the enamels that are so remarkable . . . it's the shape of the porcelains as well . . . There's something so feminine about the hourglass ones . . . even the melon gourds have a certain female robustness to them . . ."

"You have an extremely good eye." He smiled. "I am impressed."

"There is no need to be impressed," she answered. "It's refreshing to discover someone else who speaks the same language . . ."

"This is a rare thing, madame. To be able to speak to a woman so freely about beauty and art . . ." He opened his hands above his lap as though he were releasing an imaginary bird into the air. Marthe watched him intently, listening to every word. She could feel herself becoming almost hypnotized by his movements and speech.

"The glazes inspire my own work . . . You can't imagine how many times I've tried to replicate those shades. Yet it's impossible to achieve that kind of transparency with oil paint . . ."

"Yes, I *can* imagine." Her body rushed with adrenaline. Their conversation was a form of flattery that thrilled her. The artist spoke to her as though she were an equal, a woman who understood the unique language between artists.

"But I do have other talents," he said, again gesturing with his hands. "So don't fret. I can promise you, your portrait will be beautiful."

"I have little doubt," Marthe answered with a beguiling, feminine smile. "I've been told that if one is to have her portrait done, you're the top choice of those in the best circles."

"My patrons have made Paris a very hospitable place for me, that is for certain."

Again, she saw a certain flash in his eyes. He possessed a unique sense of vitality, and she realized that she had missed being in the company of someone with such physical and mental energy since Charles's illness had made him a faint shadow of his former self.

Boldini reached down the leg of the chair, where he had rested his sketch pad. He took it and began to untie the black ribbons that were wrapped around the stiff canvas book.

"May I?" He tapped his sketch pad. "It might help to get a few quick drawings of you sitting here before I leave."

"Of course," she said, readjusting herself in the chair so her posture was straighter and her chin was slightly lifted. Then, like a huntress, she focused her gaze squarely at him.

"You seem to have done this before," he mused.

"No. You will be my first."

He smiled. "At some point that's convenient for you, I will need you to come to my studio on Boulevard Berthier so I can start the portrait. My easel, paints, and brushes are all there." He opened up his sketch pad and smoothed over one of the blank pieces of paper with his hands. "And I certainly wouldn't want to sully your apartment with all of my supplies . . .

"But if you don't mind, today I'd just like to do a few sketches of your face . . . your features . . ."

His pen had already started to fly over the paper. He began capturing her in a flurry of rapid black strokes before she even had a chance to respond.

"What a queer little man!" she told Charles when she next saw him. He lay against the pillows of her bed, the barrel of his eagle and talon pipe nestled in his hand.

"But quite talented, I assure you. I saw his portrait of Madame Veil-Picard at the Paris Salon last year . . ." He sucked in his pipe again. "It was remarkable. He caught the mischief in her eyes . . ." He placed a finger underneath Marthe's chin and tickled her. "I wouldn't want just some stale portrait of you. I want someone who can bring you to life."

"I wish you had commissioned a portrait of yourself, too." She turned and whispered into his ear, "You're the one we should be immortalizing."

He smiled. Two paper fans of wrinkles lined the corners of his eyes. "I'm afraid I'm no longer worthy," he said with a small laugh. "I'm in, as they say, a state of decline." He took her hand and brought it to his chest. "But you . . . you're at the peak of your splendor."

"But you seem better, my darling." She had thought in the past week his pallor had seemed much improved. He had even eaten some of the small sandwiches that she had asked Giselle to prepare.

"Let us just enjoy ourselves right here, at this moment," he said. By now, Charles had become an expert in changing the subject anytime Marthe tried to discuss his health.

He took a hand and placed it between her thighs. "Never mind this Boldini," he said playfully. "He might paint those lips of yours." Charles kissed her on the mouth. "But I get to see you at your most beautiful."

She felt his fingers enter her.

He touched her so deftly. A smile came over her, and she closed her eyes.

13.

Solange

October 1939

That autumn in Paris proved to be the last months of mass delusion about the impending war. I had never seen so many lines at the cinema as movies had become the perfect two-hour tonic for those who wanted to forget reality. Instead of sitting in my favorite café with my journal, even I would take my two sous and spend it on a movie ticket instead of a cup of coffee.

By the end of September, Warsaw had surrendered, and Germany and the Soviet Union divided Poland between themselves, forcing the former government to flee to London.

As the headlines blared the latest news of the Soviet troops arriving en masse in Latvia and the French troops retreating to the Maginot Line in anticipation of a German invasion, the average French person seemed more concerned with the emptiness in their stomachs. We all dreamt of butter and sugar ever since the glass cases in the local boulangeries appeared nearly barren. In one bakery, only baguettes and a few rustic *boules* of bread lined the wicker baskets. Gone were the trays of tarts and chocolate cakes. Instead of sweets, the baker had only a basket of bruised fruit to offer. Overhead, we saw the silver wings of airplanes, though not yet the iron cross of the Luftwaffe.

My father had begun to stockpile penicillin, a new drug he believed would be as valuable as gold as the war progressed. I watched as he brought a few precious vials home to the apartment and stored them in the medicine cabinet in the bathroom.

"All the boys your age will now be drafted, Solange," he informed me over dinner one night. "Conscription begins at nineteen."

I shook my head. It was terrible to imagine that so many of the boys I had attended school with would now be sent off to fight. I could only imagine the pain in their mothers' hearts.

"How horrible for the families of these boys, who are expected to become men and soldiers overnight," Papa went on.

I nodded. My mind wandered to Alex and his father. Alex had to be at least nineteen.

"You'll be safe from the draft, though . . . won't you?" I asked. Papa was no longer a young man, and I couldn't imagine him being asked to fight.

He didn't answer me at first. His eyes seemed to be focused elsewhere, perhaps remembering when he was drafted decades before when he was only in his twenties.

"I doubt I'll be called to fight, but there will be a great need for pharmacists on the front to help administer medicine. Or I could be called to assist in one of the military hospitals. It's hard to predict what will happen."

I knotted my hands together. The anxiety of the unknown was a burden that nearly everyone in France now shared. Everyone except Marthe. I had started seeing her nearly every day, and when I left our apartment to visit her, I took note of the changes of the people around me. Women wrapped themselves in the protection of their shawls, and men reached into their pockets only to retrieve a few coins for the latest newspaper edition. The hands of children were clasped tighter in their mothers' grasp. Under the gaslights, lovers pressed against each other, their kisses frantic as though they might be their last.

I found my own life to be without interest, while the lives of those around me I could ponder for hours. I saw everything through the lens of someone perpetually on the outside. And I wondered if this was the curse of those who aspired to write.

So I continued to pass through the streets with my notebook pressed to my chest, my eyes firmly focused on my surroundings.

I now walked through the doors of Marthe's apartment knowing she was expecting me with my pen and paper in hand. The chapters of her story were beginning to accumulate, the characters now forming themselves on the page. My head was spinning with anticipation, as I waited to hear her tell about Monsieur Boldini and the creation of Marthe's portrait.

14.

Marthe

Paris 1898

The artist had handed her a small card just before he left her apartment that stated his address.

Giovanni Boldini
41 Boulevard Berthier
Paris

She clutched it, staring at the black embossed print before turning it over, where she discovered the painter had left her a small surprise—a quick drawing of her in profile. In a few deft strokes, he had captured her long neck, her straight jaw, and a few tendrils of her hair. His departure that first afternoon had left her intrigued. They had discussed so much more than just her portrait, and she was eager to see him again and learn what else they might have in common. Perhaps he even shared her secret love of the erotic shunga prints. Marthe secretly tucked those thoughts into the back of her mind.

He had suggested she visit him at his studio on Wednesday, and she had waited anxiously for the two days in between. But the day had finally arrived, and she awakened full of excitement. Being that the space was owned by John Singer Sargent, Marthe wondered if the artist had painted his scandalous portrait of Amélie Gautreau within the same walls in which she herself would now be depicted.

Sargent's portrait had captured both the light and the darkness of its muse. Gautreau's luminous white skin was in stark contrast to her dress's black bodice. But this effect had given Gautreau a severity— a cold beauty—and Marthe imagined herself being portrayed with more softness.

She now stood in front of her wardrobe pondering what dress she should wear in her portrait.

Her fingers reached out and touched the long skirts of her various gowns. There was one in particular that she loved and which she thought Boldini might enjoy painting. It was one of her most sumptuous dresses, her first and only one purchased from the famous Callot Soeurs—four sisters who had created one of the most fashionable couture shops in Paris. Marthe had coveted their dresses since her own days as a seamstress. She pulled the bodice and skirt from her armoire and pressed it against her body. The color of the silk was a deep rose. It seemed like yesterday she had visited the store on the Rue Taitbout and discussed the details of the dress with the most talented of the four sisters, Marie.

Marie had suggested the silk charmeuse. The elder sister had taken the bolt of fabric from the shelf, and pulled out a length of the fabric for Marthe to examine.

"It has what we call an iridescent," Marie informed her. "It's semiopaque . . . Think of it like the sun and the moon." She placed her fingers under the fabric and showed how the color changed from dark to light when she moved her hand.

"It's especially beautiful when you walk," Marie went on. "The fabric has its own vitality . . . a certain magic, shall we say?"

Marie remained completely unaware that her client had been a former seamstress herself and knew very well the gifts such a fabric would lend to a dress.

"Come near the window," she had sweetly instructed Marthe. "You see how it has its own shimmer? The warp and the weft of the silk are woven in opposite directions to create the effect."

Marthe touched the fabric between her fingers and nodded. "Yes, it will make a magnificent dress."

Marie then showed her a pale seashell pink organza for the sleeves. Marthe touched the stiff silk fabric and knew right away the dazzling effect it would have as the material stood away from her shoulders. "We'll make them voluminous—like two sunbursts—to accentuate the narrowness of the bodice and skirt," she said, her voice flush with creative excitement. "Let me go get some paper and a pen to show you."

The drawing had been unnecessary, for Marthe could envision the gown with ease. The contrast between the two fabrics, the feather-like effect of the sleeves, and the lines of her body revealed through the lines of the dress.

Now as she brought the gown up against her body, Marthe smiled. Just as Marie had promised, the dress possessed its own magic. The sleeves were extravagant with several tiers of ruffles, the pigeon-breast bodice tight and plunging with two rows of lace sewn down its front. When she moved, the fabric reflected a thousand different shades.

That's what she wanted Boldini to capture with his paintbrush, not just the curves of her figure or the angles of her chiseled features. Marthe wanted to show how she could become transformed—

shifting from opacity to transparency—a woman emerging from the shadows, resplendent when the light struck her. She imagined the portrait to have the capacity to illuminate an entire room.

The Callot Soeurs had charged a small fortune for the gown, but now the cost would be well worth it. Already she could imagine herself walking into Boldini's studio, his eyes capturing her even before his brush touched his palette. She knew he would react to the first sight of her in the dress, that his imagination would immediately be stirred. He would bring her to life on the canvas. He would show her as she saw her collection of porcelains. A woman comprised of a thousand different glazes. A woman of both fire and softness, one filled with her own shadow and light.

15.

Marthe

Paris 1898

Now that she had chosen the perfect ensemble, Marthe was determined to perfect the rest of the finishing touches. So after Giselle had fastened the dress and wrapped the jeweled sash around her waist, Marthe sat down at her vanity and applied a little rouge to her cheeks and a deep shade of pink to her lips. She piled her long sheets of auburn hair high above her head, pinning it so her slender neck was revealed, and then reached for her priceless strand of pearls.

The coachman helped her down from the carriage when they arrived at the Boulevard Berthier. It was a rather unremarkable street with little splendor or luxurious facades unlike the Rue Fortuny, where Charles lived with Émilienne.

She pulled up the hem of her dress and walked toward the door.

Outside she heard a newspaper boy screaming the most recent headlines about the Dreyfus trial. *J'accuse!* the newspaper blared. Earlier that morning on her way out, she could have sworn she heard an older boy scream, "Death to the Jews! Death to the traitor!"

Marthe cringed at the outbursts. Like most other political events, she had not concerned herself with the details of this latest scandal and, not knowing many Jewish people herself, she had little feelings toward them one way or the other. But the ugly words offended her sensibility. She loathed brutish behavior. She hurried toward the entrance and pressed the doorbell, anxious to enter the artist's oasis, away from all the unsavory noise outside.

"Madame de Florian," he said as he ushered her in. He was wearing a smock over his suit, and two paintbrushes emerged from one of its side pockets. "I'm so delighted you've come."

"The pleasure is mine," she said as she extended her hand. She watched as his lips hovered slightly over the skin of her glove, the kiss barely perceptible.

"May I take your cape?" She had selected an oyster gray silk velvet capelet with pink satin ribbons to wear over her upper body. As he slipped it from her shoulders, she smiled and fluffed up her sleeves. "Perhaps your hat, too?"

She reached above her head and unpinned the small marabou leather hat she had put on just before she left her apartment.

"You look pretty enough to paint, Madame de Florian."

"Why, thank you." Her voice revealed how much delight she took in his attention.

He placed the cape over his arm and made a sweeping gesture with her feathered hat. "Now please . . . if you'll come this way."

As she entered the large room with canvases set against the walls, the smell of oil paint and varnish struck her immediately. The strong vapors made her feel light-headed, but at the same time a renewed sense of vitality flowed through her.

"You've painted all these?" She gestured to the works around the room.

"Yes, they're in different stages of completion . . . I move between paintings. So often when I return to one, I see it with fresh eyes."

"It would be nice if we could do that with people . . . ," she mused. "The distance might do us all some good."

He paused for a moment as if studying her, gauging whether he should answer with a polite "indeed," or to answer her more fully as though she were his artistic peer. He chose the latter. "Perspective is a tool used far too infrequently. If people had the courage to alternate their lens every now and then, the world would be a far more beautiful place."

Marthe eyes met Boldini's. "You're quite right. We have magnifying glasses to read our letters, and opera spectacles for when we attend the theater . . . but we rarely look at our lives from another point of view."

He remained quiet before answering her, but his momentary silence only served to increase Marthe's adrenaline. She hadn't realized how much she missed the tête-à-têtes she used to have with Charles before he became ill. Her life inside the apartment had been insular even before Charles's sickness, but in recent weeks she had felt her mental energy might tire him, so she tried not to share every thought that raced through her mind. But now that she was in the company of Boldini, the chance to speak about art and the painter's creative process made her feel more alive than she had in months.

"I think beneath that beautiful gown, the pearl collier, and the tumble of strawberry hair, you're really an artist, Madame de Florian . . ." His green eyes narrowed behind the glass of his spectacles. "What you've just said to me now is something one of my painter friends would have expressed."

She smiled. "Monsieur Boldini, you flatter me too much." Marthe's hand lightly touched her pearls. She could feel the clasp, which she had tucked beneath her hair, slide slightly around her neck.

"If I wanted to flatter you . . . I need only remark on your beauty. I wouldn't have to bring art into the equation."

Marthe flushed at his words.

"Now the challenge for me is to somehow convey all of this with my oil paints and brush. I cannot simply create a portrait that merely shows your likeness. I must also reveal your fire, your intelligence . . . your exuberance for life," Boldini said, breaking the silence. "And that, Madame, will be a formidable challenge."

This short man with the balding head, wire glasses, and narrow eyes had just taken her breath away.

"Well, let us begin, then," she said as her eyes sparkled like two brightly colored stones.

"Why don't you sit down?" Boldini suggested as he guided Marthe to a less crowded spot within the studio. In the corner, she noticed a pale taupe-colored love seat with scrolled white edges. A matching chair was positioned just across from it.

"I don't have a servant to fetch us some tea, but I am capable of boiling water."

"You are what they call a man of the modern age, then . . ." She laughed, then turned around to face the few bits of furniture. The light streamed from the tall windows that flanked one side of the room. Marthe could feel his eyes on her as she moved. She knew the fabric would play with the light as she walked.

"And you'd be equally welcome at home in any era, madame. It was obvious that it was that artistic eye of yours that led you to choose a fabric so evocative . . . The color shifts with each footstep."

"Does it now?" she said, her voice feigning surprise at his remark.

She paused by the love seat before reaching for skirt and train. She deftly shifted the abundant material to the side, so she wouldn't be encumbered by the fullness.

"Should we *even* have tea?" He stopped himself for a moment. "Do we need such a formality between us? It would only be wasting time . . ."

He sat down across from her and leaned in. "What I really *want* to do is begin sketching you in that dress . . ." He raised both eyebrows. "Would that be quite wrong?"

"I think you already know, Monsieur Boldini, that I'm quite happy to forgo tea."

A smile flashed over his face.

"I do believe it's better we spend our time on the portrait than idly sipping tea."

"You are a great sport, madame. Sacrificing the niceties for the sake of a painter's insatiable appetite. Let me get my sketchbook."

She watched as he proceeded to the far corner of the room where, amidst lots of papers, a stack of sketchbooks in varying sizes was piled high. He took one of the larger portfolios and a few stems of vine charcoal out from a long slender tin.

As Boldini walked back to where she was sitting, Marthe could feel her adrenaline escalating. He sat down and opened the pad on his lap.

"Turn your head to the left, please," he instructed.

As she turned, the ruffles of her sleeves fell beneath her shoulders, and she could feel the cool air of the room strike her breasts.

He had not yet put the charcoal to paper. Instead, his head remained lifted slightly above the sketchbook, and he studied her as though he were making an appraisal of something of considerable value.

She lifted her chin to ensure the lines of her profile were as sharp as a knife's edge. But instead of the expected sound of his charcoal hitting the paper, she heard him placing his sketchbook down on the floor.

He stood up. "I just need to make a few adjustments." He came closer to her and she could feel his hands adjust her necklace. He slid its clasp to the back of her neck and then pressed his hands on the ruffles of her sleeves, pulling them deeper over her arms and revealing more of her bare shoulders.

"There," he said as he placed a finger underneath her chin. His hand felt like a lit match. "That's much better."

He went back to his chair, opened his sketchbook, and began drawing. The sound of the charcoal finally moving along the paper was thrilling to her—like the wings of a bird first taking flight.

16.

Marthe

Paris 1898

Charles now appeared ghostlike to Marthe. In the three months since she first noticed his illness, he seemed to have transformed from a tall, elegant figure to one shrunken with pain. Even though it was now April, he shuddered from the cold. Marthe had to ask Giselle to keep a fire going in the parlor just to keep him warm.

His complexion was no longer gray or ashen, but yellow. She suspected jaundice, for even the whites of his eyes now also appeared the color of custard. And perhaps even more alarming, he no longer had the appetite to even disrobe and lie in her butterfly bed.

They instead settled into a quiet routine of companionship. He would arrive wrapped in a long coat and hat, his pipe clutched between bone-white hands. Her skin would still be warm from her morning bath as she embraced him, his cheeks cold as she cupped them in her hands.

Despite his illness, Charles's ability to absorb Marthe's beauty had not diminished. He savored the sight of her in her transparent silks. He inhaled her perfume as though she were his own rose garden.

Sometimes she caught him staring at her in such a way that it reminded her of the way Boldini now studied her.

He had surprised her the last time he visited, when he confided to her that when he was a young boy, his governess had told him he had considerable artistic talent.

"I used to draw birds," he told her as he threaded her fingers into his own.

"We had so many at the estate. And even though the larger birds, like the pheasants and the hawks, were the most majestic, I always gravitated toward the tinier ones, like the wrens and sparrows. I loved that they were so small you could hold them in your hands."

She had smiled and closed her eyes, imagining Charles as a little boy with a sketchbook. She envisioned him looking like his son when she had seen him that day outside his home. The thin legs poking out of wool shorts, the white shirt and suspenders. What an endearing image of him sitting cross legged in the garden of his family estate drawing birds.

"So now you know why I thought of you as my little dove." His eyes looked at her softly.

It hadn't surprised her that Charles had exhibited artistic talent when he was young. She knew that he had decorated her apartment, the scattering of objets d'art, the mirrors, and the furniture that was upholstered in the softest, most sensual hues. Those were not skills of a banker, but of one with a keenly trained eye.

"Why did you stop drawing if it brought you so much pleasure?" She tightened her fingers around his. They were both so relaxed now, she didn't want him to fall asleep.

He let out a deep sigh and she felt her hand fall with his sinking chest. "My father, I suppose. He started taking me out to shoot. Never the small birds, but the pheasants and the grouse on the property. My life became less tranquil after that . . ." His voice trailed off. "By the time I was sent off to boarding school, I no longer had the peace of mind to lose myself in drawing."

"How sad," she said. "I would have very much liked to have you draw me."

He laughed. "I've hired the best to do that . . . and a painting, not just a little pencil sketch!"

Now, a week later, he was even more fragile than at his last visit.

"How is the portrait developing? Will I be seeing it anytime soon?"

"Oh, but he's only just begun sketching." She reached for Charles's hand. "You must get stronger so you can visit his studio. It really is the most marvelous place."

He smiled. "I would enjoy that. I have the address already." He patted the pocket of his suit. "There's little difference between bankers and artists. In the end, they're both crystal clear in giving instructions to where you must send the checks."

She laughed. "Really, Charles, I think you're going to be quite pleased when it's done."

"I'm sure I will . . . I only hope I can last long enough to see it."

She realized that he had stopped avoiding any discussion of his health, as he had when he first took ill. He spoke openly of his decline, and even sometimes alluded to his own death.

Their roles had reversed. It was now Marthe who didn't want to speak about the ugliness of his illness, or the painful truth that he would not get better, only worse.

"You will recover, my darling," she said, squeezing his hand. "Why, it's been a long winter, and spring has only just arrived. By the time you see the first roses in the Bois de Boulogne, you'll be feeling so much better . . . I just know it."

"I have set my goal not on seeing the flowers, Marthe. But on seeing you within a gilded frame."

"Stop that . . . you will see it so many times over the years, you'll grow bored with it." She took her hand and ran it over his hair, then leaned over and kissed him. His once-soft lips were now cracked and dry.

"My dove," he said, looking at her. His eyes were soft. "To be six years old again, so I could draw you with my own hand."

She said nothing. She simply rose and walked out the French doors of the parlor to the small side room where she kept her stationery, her notepads, and her pens.

She opened the bottom drawer and searched until she found a pencil. She almost never used the red cedar sticks, but they were helpful when she had to go over the household budget with Giselle.

Marthe returned to the parlor. "Here," she said, handing him the pad she had found and the pencil stick.

"Master Boldini won't be done for several weeks, so yours will be the first portrait of me."

He lifted his hand and took the pad and placed it on his lap. Then he took the pencil.

"I can't remember the last time I did this," he told her.

"I suspect it's not something you lose completely . . ."

'Well, if my memory serves me correctly, I drew blue wrens, and gray sparrows . . . but never a dove."

"There is always a first time, my darling."

"Indeed," he answered. "Why don't you go stand by the mantel." He gestured in the direction of the white alabaster fireplace.

"It would be my pleasure . . ." She was happy to oblige him.

He took the pencil and began to sketch her head, the length of her neck. But soon he stopped.

"Please forgive me." His voice broke into a cough. "I'm getting a bit tired." He laid down the pad on the sofa. She had only been posing for a few minutes.

When she walked over to sit beside him, she lifted the pad to see what he had drawn.

He had rendered her in profile; the face was half done. He had drawn a few wisps of hair around the curl of her ear.

But still she could see he had talent.

"I should be getting home. Émilienne will be expecting me."

She nodded, her heart stung at the mention of his wife's name. She placed the pad down on the sofa and walked him to the door. She cupped his cheeks in her hands just as she had greeted him hours before. This time planting a kiss on his dry lips.

He kissed her back. Then, as was the familiar ritual between them, he reached inside his breast pocket and handed her the pocket watch to set with the exact time they were separating.

"Until next time," he whispered, placing it back in his jacket and kissing her on the cheek.

"I will wait until the hands move again," she whispered in his ear.

After she saw him to the door, Marthe went over to the sofa to retrieve the unfinished drawing, tearing it off the pad. She went to her desk and placed it amongst the first love letters Charles had written to her. She knew he would never complete it. But she was happy to have herself captured even incompletely by his hand.

17.

Marthe

Paris 1898

Charles canceled his visit the following week. And then the week after. A letter arrived, which read that as much as he longed to see her, he was having trouble getting out of bed. Émilienne had insisted he convalesce at their estate in the country, where she thought the air was better for him.

The following week, Marthe awakened to an ominous sign. As she walked down the hallway, passing the pedestal table where she always kept Fauchon, she discovered the little bird lying at the bottom of his gilded wire cage, his legs pointing upward. When she peered closer, she noticed his eyes were like two hard, black stones.

Giselle tried to soothe Marthe, wrapping the dead bird in some waste silk, telling her that the bird had lived far longer than most, and promising her mistress that she'd make sure he was properly buried in the park.

"He was one of Charles's first gifts to me," Marthe lamented as she watched her maid tuck the bird in its makeshift shroud into a biscuit tin. "He bought him to keep me company, to provide me with birdsong."

But what disturbed her more than Fauchon's unfortunate passing was the feeling that it foreshadowed something terrible to come. She tried to push it out of her mind, but a dark cloud engulfed her. She feared Charles's death would be next.

With Charles away from Paris and little else to distract her, Marthe looked forward to her visits to Boldini's studio more than ever. Charles's illness had reduced him to such a frail state that she yearned to be in the company of someone who had as much energy as she did. She soon learned that he not only shared her love of Asian porcelains, but also of Venice.

Early on in her sittings, he had asked her about her name. "De Florian?" He raised one of his eyebrows as he appraised her for one of the early sketches. "Is it French?"

"I wouldn't say that," she answered coquettishly.

"What would you say, then?"

"Venetian."

"You mean like the café in San Marco?"

"Exactly."

His eyes came alive again.

"*Bellissimo.*" She knew he was Italian, but to hear him suddenly switch into that language instantly delighted her.

"I fell in love there. So I took the name."

"And your real name?"

She hesitated. "Beaugiron."

He made a face. "Yes, you were right, *carissima*. De Florian is much better."

"I thought Venice was the most magical place. The water. The light. The palazzos with those beautiful colors . . . I felt as though I reached the end of the world, where there was only beauty . . . and the impulse to make love."

He laughed and placed his sketchbook down.

"You always speak of colors. I'm thinking I should give you your own set of paints."

She smiled, her skin warming beneath her dress, its yards of organza and chiffon now felt too tightly wrapped around her. She wished she could instead be free of her corset and in her robe de chambre, reclining on one of Boldini's divans.

She arched her back slightly to relieve a cramp. "It's not easy to hold a pose for so long . . . I would rather be like you, moving about and clasping a stick of charcoal in my hand."

"I think you'd find that it's too dusty," he laughed. "It's easier to imagine you with a palette."

"I would like that . . . to mix paints, create colors," she mused. But I'd also like to go back to Venice . . ." She closed her eyes and spoke as if dreaming aloud. "To walk down the serpentine streets, and gaze at the palazzos with their tall windows and pastel facades . . ."

She could still hear his charcoal against the paper. "To lift my head in those dark churches and see the splendor painted above."

"Your heart beats like an Italian." He looked up from the pad and smiled from beneath his mustache. "Perhaps one day we will make a trip there together, and I can show you my beloved Ferrara."

Her mind leapt. Charles had never mentioned another trip again after Venice. It had been the grand seduction, the place where they first tested out their arrangement. Even if the artist wasn't serious, the suggestion of making a journey excited her. "Ferrara?" she cooed. "Is it close to Venice?"

"Not too far. A simple enough trip to make." He pulled slightly at his mustache, his eyes still firmly planted on her. "Less than a day's journey."

"And do you go back often?"

"Not often at all. Rarely, as a matter of fact. Italy's a place of the past for me. Just like you did on your trip to Venice, I've reinvented myself here in Paris." He motioned to her that she no longer needed to keep the pose.

Marthe, relieved to no longer be forced to remain in one position, softened immediately against the velvet upholstery of the settee.

"When I left Ferrara, I felt . . . How should I say? Free . . ."

The artist reached for a pipe and struck a match. Marthe detected the scent of oak leaves as she breathed it in—a far earthier fragrance compared to the Oriental flavor of the one Charles preferred. There was something intoxicating about the perfume as it laced the air. She closed her eyes and savored Boldini's words.

"For the first time in my life, I felt liberated from my father's shadow. I was no longer the son of Antonio Boldini, the great religious painter of angels and saints."

He puffed a few more clouds of smoke in her direction. "Perhaps I was *un piccolo diavolo*, a little devil," he laughed. "I preferred to paint a beautiful, real woman over God.

"That isn't to say I wasn't grateful for all the training my father gave me . . . In some ways, those early lessons on painting the human form made me years ahead of my fellow students at the academy. And my fondest childhood memories are those I spent in his studio. The smell of turpentine and sawdust. Unfinished canvases leaning against the walls . . ."

"A little like here?" She took a light finger and playfully stroked her pearls.

"It was more cluttered. More rustic . . . Imagine wooden cross-beams exposed like an old barn . . ." Boldini pointed to the ceiling. "And imagine ten times more canvases in a far smaller space. One thing I learned early on was to be a better businessman, though. It pained my father to ask for money, no doubt because he dealt with the church. I make a point to get most of my money up front."

"So my Charles has paid you handsomely already," she laughed.

"Indeed," he said.

"I would expect no less from him. Always the perfect gentleman . . ." Boldini leaned forward. "And I am always the perfect rogue."

She let out a little squeal. "You really are far more entertaining than I ever imagined! You've made this hour holding a torturous pose a pleasure!"

"And you, my dear, are a magnificent model. I've filled my sketchbook with enough drawings to start the portrait."

"So my work here is done?" Her voice lilted ever so slightly. Marthe had missed playing the coquette and, as much as she loved Charles, the attention Boldini showered upon her soothed her.

"Hardly. I will need a few weeks to start the preliminary bones of the painting . . . Then you will have to return for another sitting." He closed his sketchbook. "May I write to you when I've managed to create something worthy of your approval?"

She flushed. "I would like that very much."

"Then that's another thing we have in common, Madame de Florian."

She left Boldini's studio flooded with excitement. The artist also considered himself reinvented. Instead of judging her as an imposter of sorts, he had revealed his own vulnerability. As her coach pulled through the bustling Paris streets, she felt a need to thank him for this gift of kindness.

"Thirty-one Rue de Seine," she ordered the driver. It was the address of Ichiro's store.

She hadn't visited in several weeks, but she knew it would be the perfect place to purchase something to show Boldini her appreciation, as well as cement their friendship. *A gift of beauty*, she thought to herself, something that would communicate her feelings far beyond a simple note card filled with a few polite words.

18.

Marthe

Paris 1898

Ichiro stepped forward from the dark purple curtain and greeted her with great warmth.

"Madame de Florian, it has been far too long." His head dipped into a deep bow. "You have missed many beautiful things that have come in and out of the store in the past few weeks."

She could see immediately as his eyes, so expert in appraising things beautiful and rare, fell upon her neck, encircled in her priceless set of pearls.

Marthe raised a finger and touched them lightly. "You notice everything, don't you," she said sweetly. "These were a gift from someone with the most exquisite taste."

"Indeed," Ichiro said. "They are Japanese, too," he said as he came closer. "How beautiful for me to have the opportunity to see something that has come from my native sea."

She smiled. "I was told how difficult it is to find these many pearls that exactly match in color and size . . . That's what makes the necklace so rare."

"Yes, whoever told you that is right." She could see how he was unable to take his eyes off the pearls, and it delighted her to have their roles reversed. Ichiro now coveting something that she possessed, instead of the other way around.

"It is a shame I wasn't trained in the pearl business," he said with a smile. "I think it's far more lucrative than antiques . . ."

She laughed. "But I would be lost without your help. Just today, when I was thinking I needed to purchase a gift for someone with a strong artistic sensibility, I knew I couldn't find what I needed at La Samaritaine. I needed, instead, to come to you . . ."

"That is most kind of you." Ichiro clasped his hands in front of him. "So, how can I help you?"

"I have a new friend who shares my love of Asian porcelains. Perhaps you have a few things to show me?"

He nodded knowingly, and his eyes brightened with a liveliness she hadn't realized how much she missed.

"I do. I have quite a few things to suggest." He brought his hands together and gestured a small bow. "Give me a few moments to bring them up from the storeroom. In the meantime, please let me prepare you some tea."

He excused himself and disappeared behind the curtain.

The store still retained its magic for Marthe, as she walked carefully around the small pedestal tables where Ichiro rotated his various collections. He had two Zhou vases on display that were quite beautiful, and a large dish in a chrysanthemum pattern that she thought she might like for herself. But nothing called out to her as something that befitted Boldini.

Ichiro returned with a lacquered tray and two ceramic cups of steaming tea.

"Come sit . . . I have a few things downstairs that I will bring up and show you in a moment."

He pulled out a chair by the small viewing table he kept for his customers, and Marthe sat down.

Ichiro joined her at the table and took the tea to his lips.

"This friend, he has his own collection like you?"

She smiled. "I am unsure how vast his collection is. But I know from our conversations he has a particular affinity for the translucent glazes."

Ichiro nodded. "He must be quite a gentleman to be so learned about such matters." He placed his palms on the table and stood up. "Now, let me bring you what I have in mind."

Moments later he appeared with two bamboo boxes tied shut with twine.

"These two vases arrived only last week . . . They belonged to a Samurai family in Nara."

He removed the lid from the first box.

"Although I acquired these from Japan, they were actually fired in an imperial kiln in Korea. They are very rare."

She watched as he lifted the vase from the nest of dry grass that protected the porcelain, and held it to the light.

The glaze was a soft, milky blue.

"It's beautiful," she whispered as she cupped her hands around the base and lifted it slightly toward the light. She proceeded to turn it around from all sides, examining it from different angles.

"The next one is also quite unusual." He bent down and retrieved the second box, placing it on the table.

Ichiro repeated his actions, again carefully removing the box's lid, dipping his hands into the dry straw, and withdrawing the vase so Marthe could examine it more closely.

As soon as she saw it lifted to the light, she felt her adrenaline rush. The vase was gourd-shaped, its glaze an opaque celadon with a crazing of thin black lines floating over the surface.

"This is an especially rare piece. I almost don't want to sell it . . ." Ichiro placed it carefully on the table. "It is from an imperial kiln, just like the last one I showed you, but the glaze is quite unique. We call it 'cracked ice' because the glaze lends itself to the appearance of shattered ice."

She leaned over and looked at it closely. She had never seen anything like it before.

"It's breathtaking . . ." Her finger reached out to touch its glimmering surface. "It looks like a spiderweb has been caught within the glaze."

"Exactly." A small smile crept over his lips. She could see he was delighted that she immediately responded to its delicate beauty. "It's a very difficult process for the potter. He must apply several coats of the glaze and fire it several times in order to achieve the distinct crackle. Many pieces are lost during the process . . ."

"Extraordinary," she whispered. "May I hold it?"

"Certainly." He gently lifted the vase and placed it in her hands.

Again she brought the vase up to the light to examine the glaze more carefully. This one captured her heart and imagination. She loved the atmospheric green color. It reminded her of the color of the water in the Venetian canals, but with the effect that the surface was breaking even though it remained intact. She knew Boldini would be drawn to something that was both so delicate and complex. Marthe again closed her eyes, the surface of the hourglass vase warming in her hands.

Immediately she knew this was what she wanted to give to the artist.

"I think my friend will find this one particularly inspiring," Marthe said as she placed the vase down on the table.

"It's a bit more expensive than the first one I showed you," he said softly. She knew he had always found the discussion of money distasteful.

He wrote down the price on a piece of paper.

She saw he had written five hundred francs. It was far more than she liked to pay even for something for herself.

She took a finger and stroked her pearls, considering the steep price.

"It is more than I'd imagined, but I do think my friend will appreciate the beauty and rarity of the piece . . . ," she answered, trying to justify the purchase.

"Madame does have the most exquisite taste."

Marthe smiled. "Will you put it on my account, Ichiro. I will settle it at the end of the month."

She watched as he slowly put both vases back in their boxes and gently repositioned the straw around the vessels so they would not break.

"I will wrap it in the back for you, Madame de Florian, so it appears like a proper *cadeau*."

"Thank you." She nodded as she replaced her gloves.

She began to imagine the scenario of presenting the vase to the artist. But then she reconsidered, deciding it would be far more elegant to have Ichiro send the package directly to Boldini's studio. In that way, she would avoid any embarrassment if he didn't like it as much as she hoped.

Marthe reached for one of her cards in her purse and wrote in her careful, elegant handwriting:

Giovanni Boldini
41 Boulevard Berthier

When Ichiro returned, she pressed it into his hand.

19.

Solange

Late October was a difficult month. The tension between those in Europe who would surrender to Hitler's demands and those who would fight him had begun to intensify. Not only had France's prime minister Édouard Daladier, refused Hitler's "offer" for peace, but so too had Britain's Prime Minister Chamberlain. Over several radio broadcasts we had heard that Jews from Poland were being deported.

My mind kept returning to Alex and his father and their shop, which could have easily been my maternal grandfather's shop had he still been alive. Although I had no intention of selling my mother's rare books, I still had a strong desire to visit them again.

So on a Monday afternoon, the day I typically reserved for my writing, I returned to the Rue des Écouffes.

. . .

On the Métro that afternoon, passengers clutched their newspapers as though they were Bibles. The front page of *Le Monde* blared the headlines that the first air attack occurred at the Firth of Forth in Scotland. How much longer, I wondered, until my father and I were crouching under our kitchen table as bombs shattered through Paris? Already children were being instructed to use gas masks in school, and air raid drills were becoming routine.

As I came up from the Métro station, I paused momentarily to reacquaint myself with my surroundings. The neighborhood of the Marais was filled with so many small streets that it was easy to get lost, even for someone like me who was a Parisian. I walked down the Rue Pavée and headed toward the Jewish quarter, my arms feeling empty without the security of my mother's books I had held the last time I visited. When I walked past one of the bakeries, I went inside hoping to buy a small gift to bring Alex and his father, even though I had only a few francs in my purse.

If the bakeries in our neighborhood held little selection since the war began, the bakeries here had even less. Weeks before I had seen several delicate pastries with nuts and dried fruits, and miniature breads with chocolate rolled inside. Now, nearly every basket in the bakery was empty. Only a small tray of cookies dusted lightly with cinnamon and a few loaves of bread remained.

I asked for a box of the cookies and left the bakery with a heavy heart. The custom of bringing something sweet when visiting friends was part of the French soul, but the cookies I purchased looked lifeless, hardly something that one would consider a special treat. Still, it felt comforting to hold something between my nervous hands.

In the crisp autumn sunlight, the area's labyrinthine streets held a special magic to them. The mezuzahs on some of the doorways reinforced the bridge between two worlds within the city. And the men who in their heavy black coats and hats made me feel as though I had entered a place exotic and unfamiliar.

Yet, at the same time, I was unmistakably drawn to it.

I wondered if some of the men or women I passed there were people who had once known my mother, or perhaps had even visited my grandfather's store.

When I finally reached the Armels' storefront, I hesitated for a moment before entering, trying to think what I would say when I saw them. I could no longer rely on the excuse that I wanted my books appraised. I saw my reflection in the window, my hat pulled to my eyes, my coat buttoned over my skirt and blouse, and I realized that I was returning to a place where I was still very much an outsider, despite my curiosity to learn more about my connection to this place and its people.

I turned around and saw a few more people walking past the store, none of them taking notice of me at all. Then, I took a deep breath and walked inside.

The smell of the store immediately soothed me. The scent of paper and ink. There is nothing else like it for those who love books. It was the fragrance of my childhood, what I considered my mother's perfume. Immediately it brought back the memory of her turning the pages of my nursery books, her breath sweet and warm against my neck.

"Solange?" Alex had seen me as soon as I walked in, and as he started toward me, he opened his hands to greet me.

"I was in the neighborhood, and I couldn't pass by without saying hello," I said quickly. "You and your father were so kind and generous to me during my last visit, I wanted to bring you something to show my gratitude."

I handed him the box of cookies.

"This wasn't necessary . . . I know my father was happy not only to meet you, but also to see your grandfather's Haggadah again."

I smiled. "And I was glad to learn more about my grandfather."

"Come . . . ," he said, making a small gesture toward the back. "My father isn't here today, but we could have some tea." He tapped the box from the bakery. "And I wouldn't want to be left alone to eat these all by myself."

"They're only a few cookies, I'm afraid. The selection in all the bakeries now is quite sparse . . ."

He nodded. "One of the first casualties of the war," he answered playfully.

"My grandmother somehow always manages to still get the best pastries, but I'm not sure how she does it."

"How lucky you are to have such a grandmother . . ."

"Yes, she is rather remarkable." I let out a small laugh. "You'd probably find her quite charming. She lives as if time has stood still."

"And what time period has she maintained?"

"The Belle Époque." I smiled.

"The peak of decadence, then." He was clearly amused.

"Yes. Originally I thought I was going to write a play about her. But now I'm thinking I have enough material to write a book about her life."

"So I'm about to have tea with a budding novelist?" He pulled out one of the chairs for me to sit down.

I lowered my eyes, slightly embarrassed that the discussion had turned toward me. "Writing her story gives me a distraction from the war . . ."

"You are full of surprises. The last time you came, you showed us a priceless Haggadah, and now you tell me you are at work on a book yourself. May I ask how old you are, Solange?"

"I'm nineteen." I felt myself blush when I answered him. I had never had someone flirt with me before. "And you?"

"Far older." He returned my smile. "Twenty-one in fact."

"A veritable older gentleman . . ."

"Indeed." He placed his hands on the table. His fingers were white and slender, more delicate than I had imagined. I remembered how my grandmother had said it had been the moment she saw Boldini's hands that she first discovered the artist's beauty.

"And now this gentleman must get the lovely lady some tea."

He stood up and went back toward the storeroom, returning minutes later with the tray.

I must have stayed with Alex for well over an hour. He went back at least twice to refill the teapot with more hot water, and the box of cookies I brought were soon finished to nothing but a few remaining crumbs.

We talked about our favorite books and the writers we most admired. I also told him about my grandmother and how she had begun life as the daughter of a laundress yet was now ensconced in an apartment of silk and velvet. "You have the material of a nineteenth-century novel there, don't you?" Alex said, impressed.

"Yes, I suppose I do," I laughed.

"You have my utter vote of confidence, Solange." He smiled. "I can't wait to read it."

"I have to finish it first," I laughed. "That's the hard part. I've been taking my notebook to one of the cafés near our house and trying to work there. Somehow it's easier to work there than when I'm at home."

"You can always work in our back room if you'd like. I'm sure my father won't mind. As you can see, we have almost no customer traffic these days."

I looked around. It was true. Since I had come into the store, there hadn't been a single customer.

"How will you manage, if no one is selling or buying rare books?"

"Oh they're selling. My father just went to look at a private collection outside the city. Everyone is selling because they need funds. Everyone is nervous because of the war . . . It's the lack of people who are buying that's the problem for us."

I felt a sudden flicker of pain in my heart. I hated to think of Alex and his family struggling to make ends meet.

"But we are not your responsibility to worry about . . . How sweet you look with that expression of concern."

I flushed.

"I've embarrassed you. I'm so sorry." He stood up and began to clear the dishes and put them back on the tray. "I'm not an expert in conversation, as you can see . . ."

"Oh, not at all." I rose to my feet and tried to help him with the cups and saucers. "I'm really the one who's clumsy and poor with small talk." A wisp of hair fell over my eye and I pushed it behind my ear.

"It's so much easier when you're writing," I said. "You can rewrite the sentences a hundred times until your character says just the right words . . ."

He stood only inches away from me now, his hands holding the handles of the tray. "What would my character say if he knew a beautiful young girl was about to bid him good-bye?"

"He'd say something hopeful, I'd think . . ." I smiled. "Perhaps something like . . . 'It would make me so happy if you'd visit me again.'"

"Well, then," he said as he walked toward the door. "Solange, I hope one day I'm able to hold the novel you've written in my hands." He stopped and pulled the door open. "But until then, I hope you'll visit me again."

20.

Marthe

Paris 1898

Two days later, Marthe received a letter in the midday post with her name in a voluptuous scripted hand. The return address on the envelope was *41 Boulevard Berthier*, Boldini's apartment.

Madame de Florian,

Your beautiful porcelain arrived this afternoon. You cannot imagine my delight when I opened the box. But first, I must tell you how the package itself arrived. Whoever prepared it must be an artist himself. Around the bamboo crate, a wrapping was created not with paper, but with a large silk scarf. The silk itself was extraordinary, a dark aubergine with a motif of pale blue cranes printed across. I was able to unknot the scarf and see the light wood box with the Asian markings. Who could have sent me such a beautiful and mysterious gift? I thought to myself as I

began to remove the top. When I reached in and discovered an
exquisite porcelain from the Far East . . . I knew it had to be you!

Madame, it is rare that I am a recipient of a gift so reflective
of my personal taste. The glaze is unlike anything I have ever laid
eyes on before. Firstly the color . . . it is no ordinary celadon. It
reminds me of the jadeite waters of our mutually beloved city,
Venice, but captured in a state of thaw. I know this must have
been intentional on your part.

This was far too generous a gift, and I cannot imagine the
price you must have paid for such a rare piece of pottery. Know
that this beautiful vase will be prominently displayed in my studio
and will contribute a dose of daily inspiration.

I cannot wait for your next visit, so I can show you the
beginning strokes of your portrait.

With great respect and
admiration,
Giovanni Boldini

For several minutes she held the delicate writing paper in her
hand. It was not the heavily bonded paper she had for her own personal stationery, or the one with the aristocratic coat-of-arms
embossing like Charles's. Boldini's was as thin as rice paper. Nearly
translucent, it reminded Marthe of the paper that children used to
make kites. If she opened the window, it was so light it could have
blown away.

Each time she reread the letter, she could vividly imagine her gift
arriving to his door. It felt like a secret indulgence as she envisioned
Boldini unknotting the kerchief, peeling away the first layer, and
then opening the box carefully to reveal the porcelain. How it
delighted her that they both reacted to the vase in the same way.

A thrill ran through her, for her gift had communicated her

thoughts not by the use of words, but through the shades of a potter nearly three hundred years before and a world away. Boldini had seen the waters of Venice in the ancient Korean glaze—just as she had—a glaze that was like a current caught between stillness and imminent fracture.

The new, unexpected discovery that she and Boldini had a unique connection reinvigorated her. Marthe had no intention of betraying Charles, but she also couldn't deny that the artistic language she shared with Boldini boosted her spirits. She couldn't wait until she saw how this added layer might be revealed when he sat in front of his easel and continued her portrait.

In the drawer of her vanity table, tied with pink satin ribbon, Marthe kept the letters Charles had written to her over the years. The ones he wrote when she still danced at the theater, and the ones he penned after they had enjoyed a particularly rapturous session in her butterfly bed. But his letters had grown more infrequent over the years. Lately when he wrote, it was typically only to inform her of his current health or a change in his plans.

Now, she relished the chance to return Boldini's letter, to write more about art, beauty, and the beginning stages of her portrait. She had been unable to see Charles for weeks, ever since his wife had insisted they now take a cure together in the mountains. "She thinks the waters there will help," Charles had told her as gently as he could. "At this point, I'm not particularly hopeful, but I've promised her I'd try." At first, she felt a pang of jealousy. But Charles was no longer the robust gentleman he once was, so she did not consider it a betrayal when she sat down to return the artist's letter. After all, it was Charles's wish to see the portrait completed as soon as possible. *I'm only making him more motivated to finish*, she told herself as she took out a leaf of paper from her drawer and withdrew her pen.

Dear Monsieur Boldini,

How delighted I am to hear you enjoyed the gift I sent. I hope it will inspire you for many more years to come. When I saw that particular piece, I knew you would recognize the same beauty that it stirred inside me. The man from whom I bought it told me they call it "a cracked ice" glaze, and that the potter must fire the porcelain several times, each time applying more coats of pigment in order to achieve this effect. How extraordinary is the result . . . to hold something in your hand that looks as though it has shattered, yet it remains firmly intact. I knew you would appreciate this paradox.

I do hope my portrait is coming along and that I'll be able to see how it's progressing. Should you need another sitting, it would be my pleasure to slip again into the same dress and pay you another visit.

With deepest respect,
Marthe de Florian

She couldn't admit to being surprised when two days later she received another letter. On the thin, translucent paper Boldini had written:

Madame de Florian,

As usual, you anticipate my own thoughts even before they have registered inside me. Yes, if possible, it would be wonderful to see you for another sitting. May I be so bold as to suggest tomorrow, at three o'clock? And, yes, please wear the rose-colored dress. It is perfection.

With great anticipation,
G. Boldini

. . .

Charles had been away with his wife for several weeks. And although she still kept part of her mind engaged in thoughts of what he might be doing with Émilienne, Marthe was grateful for her burgeoning friendship with Boldini.

The dress now became almost a uniform to her. No longer did Marthe see it as an example of the Callot Soeurs' masterful dress-making skills, or a testimony to feminine extravagance. Instead, the pink confection was firmly connected to her portrait. Marthe reached for the gown and began to get ready.

When Giselle pulled the laces of her corset tight against her back, Marthe instructed her to pull harder.

"It's as tight as I can make it," Giselle told her.

"Tighter," Marthe insisted. "I want him to feel as though my waist is as small as a wren in his hands."

She could feel all of Giselle's strength tugging to bring the laces toward her.

Against Marthe's torso, the whalebones of her corset felt like knives.

"But how can madame breathe?" Giselle shook her head as she next helped Marthe get into her dress.

When the girl bent down to retrieve Marthe's kidskin boots, she noticed Giselle's hands were red from the exertion of tying her corset.

"I'm afraid I've made you suffer as much as I do for the sake of this portrait."

"What is that saying? *'Il faut souffrir pour être belle.'* 'It hurts to be beautiful.'"

Marthe smiled. "Yes, my mother used to say that when she tugged a comb through my hair."

"Mine, too," said Giselle wistfully, as if touched by the intimate moment between them.

Marthe wondered if Giselle suspected that they had more in common with their childhoods. She always tried to be kind to Giselle, never taking on any airs of superiority when it was just the two of them alone in the apartment.

The girl was pretty. Straw-colored hair. Wide blue eyes. Her only shortcoming was her figure, which was as straight as a ruler and lacked any natural feminine curves.

"The pain of beauty," Marthe mused as she looked at her reflection in the full-length mirror. "Every woman suffers in her own way . . . ," she said as she fluffed up the ruffles of her sleeves. The faces of the two women floated in the glass like a portrait within an oval frame. "But to be born ugly . . . ," Marthe said more to herself than to Giselle.

"Can you imagine how wretched that would be?"

21.

Marthe

Paris 1898

The first thing she noticed when she entered his studio for the second time was not the scent of varnish and paint, nor the sight of his other paintings. It was the vase she had given him. Boldini had prominently displayed it on a pedestal table near his desk.

The vase shone with a beautiful intensity as the light streamed in through the tall windows behind it. It reminded her of one of those small Dutch paintings she had seen on her occasional trips to the Louvre.

He had been watching to see her reaction, and she could feel his eyes on her.

"How wonderful you've placed the vase in such a position of honor," she said, turning to him.

"I wanted to be able to see it from every corner of the room . . . and the light there strikes it just perfectly." He extended his arm toward the wall of floor-to-ceiling windows.

She smiled. "I can see the effect immediately . . . the beauty in which the sunlight bathes it half in light, half in shadow."

"Exactly." He beamed.

As she moved through the room, Marthe caught sight of a small watercolor study on his desk. It was of the vase. Three small renderings were done on the same piece of paper. She could see how delicately he had applied the soft touches of pale blue and green to the sketches.

She walked over and touched the edge of the paper. "I'm so pleased to see it's inspired you . . ."

"You didn't see the other sheets, which ended up in the fire. It's impossible to re-create that glaze! It's pure madness to even try!"

She let out a small laugh. "I wasn't intending to send you to the madhouse."

"Then perhaps you should have worn another dress today . . ."

She laughed again. He was flirting with her, and it amused her.

"But I wore the dress for the portrait's sake, not yours . . ."

This time, he laughed.

"Yes, Madame de Florian, I suppose you did. Then let's get started for the portrait's sake."

In the corner that faced the settee where she had sat during her last visit, now stood a tall wooden easel with a canvas set on top. The canvas was primed, but not a single brushstroke had been applied to it. It was as blank as a new sheet of paper.

"But, monsieur, there's nothing on it." She could hardly hide her disappointment.

"Underneath that coat of gesso are about a hundred brushstrokes that couldn't do justice to you. Just like that vase you sent me . . ." He shook his head. "It's easy to recognize the surface of beauty. To see it with your two eyes. But the challenge to the artist is conveying the many layers underneath."

She stood there bewitched by his words.

"If you only show one top layer of beauty, it remains flat and two-dimensional." He walked toward the blank canvas and pinched the corner.

"With some models, I can work directly from my preliminary sketches . . . but with you, I simply cannot."

He took her hand and ushered her to the love seat.

"I want to begin with you in front of me."

She watched as he returned to his easel and took his bladders of paint pigment and applied them to his palette, blending them with a knife.

"Now, show me how you want to be seen for the next one hundred years," he said when he had prepared his paints.

She laughed, and one of her ruffled sleeves fell over her shoulder. She reached to pull it up, while she placed her other elbow on the arm of the settee.

"Don't move," he quickly instructed her. She was still in profile as she had been the last time he had sketched her, but now her chest was precariously revealed. She could feel the tension between her body pushing forth from the dress and the contrast of her tight skirt and her cloudlike sleeves.

"Charles will want it to be inspired . . . ," she whispered, afraid to let go of the pose.

"Charles will be delighted," he insisted. She could hear the rapid application of paint. The swirl of his brush. The energy that erupted between his imagination and his mind.

The heat inside her was unbearable. "I feel like I'm coming out of my dress. The only thing keeping me in place is my bodice and the corset beneath."

"Such tension is a good thing . . . ," he said, a brush gripped between his teeth. "There cannot be pleasure, without knowing the sensation of pain."

She knew this all too well in her own life. A woman of the demi-monde, the half-world. Caught between beauty and darkness. In some ways trapped, but in other ways completely free.

22.

Marthe

Paris 1898

He painted the first brushstrokes using a neutral shade of gray. He began with the top of her head, painting the outline of her profile, the sharp line of her nose, the edge of her lips, and the soft curve of her chin.

His brush was no longer just an extension of his hand, but also his mind and his imagination. He had fallen into the dreamlike state of painting—his own private séance with the canvas and the paint.

He drew the length of her neck, the expanse of her broad shoulders. He painted in a few feather-like strokes to suggest where he would later create her voluminous sleeves. In long, quick gestures he articulated the elegant, slim length of her arm that rested on the side of the love seat, her tapered fingers opening like a fan.

He applied these first brushstrokes with a robust energy, solely to capture the curve of her body. Even though he had yet to apply the colors that would come later—the pink of her dress, the flush of her skin, the opalescent pearls glimmering around her neck—the rough outline of Marthe's portrait captured her essence. She appeared swanlike, with one bared shoulder and a plunging neckline that revealed her full breasts. The pose was not so much a statement as it was an invitation to touch her, caress her. To feel the heat that Boldini would create when he began to actually paint her skin.

23.

Solange

November 1939

What I learned from Alex during my last visit with him was that his family's apartment was not above their shop on the Ruc des Écouffes as I expected, but actually in the sixteenth arrondissement.

"Like many of the Jewish middle class, we've since moved out of the Marais," he told me. "It's just too crowded now with families like Solomon's who've just arrived. Belleville is the same . . ." He looked into her eyes realizing that she was probably unfamiliar with the changes the community had undergone in the past few years. "But we've kept the shop there. The rent is inexpensive, and for our wealthier clients, we take the books to their homes so they can view them privately.

"It's a bit inconvenient to meet near us, but perhaps we could find a place in between. Do you know the Café Saint Georges? It's across from the old Adolphe Thiers estate. It might be a good meeting place since it's not far from your grandmother's."

"The one with the large red awning?" I asked. I was certain I had passed it on occasion. "Doesn't it look right onto the square?"

"Exactly." He smiled.

Just before I left the store, he gathered enough courage to ask me if I might meet him at the café.

"Perhaps next time you visit your grandmother, we could meet for a coffee before I go to work . . ." I felt his hand graze lightly over the sleeve of my coat. Even through the cloth, his touch penetrated into my skin. I shivered, as if he had nearly ignited something inside.

"I would like that . . . very much." I could feel my face becoming flushed. "I plan to visit her on Wednesday. Finally I'm learning about the artist who painted her. I've been waiting for months to hear the details."

He laughed. *"The Picture of Dorian Gray . . ."*

I smiled. "I think Oscar Wilde would have been deeply amused by my grandmother. She's certainly witty enough to have entertained him."

"In all matters but love . . ."

"Yes, I fear he would have preferred you in that regard," I teased.

"Well, Solange, I look forward to Wednesday." He walked me out the door.

"Wednesday," I said.

He came closer and kissed me on both cheeks, and for the rest of the afternoon I held on to the sensation of his lips brushing against my skin. Like a girl holding a butterfly between cupped hands.

On Wednesday morning, I found Alex already at a table outside the café. It was November and although the air was damp, nearly all the tables were occupied. He was wearing a dark navy suit and a gray cap pulled over his black hair. A copy of *Le Monde* was spread out over the table. His face was buried in the newspaper.

"Alex?"

He looked up and quickly shuffled the paper.

"I'm sorry," he said. "I got caught up in the headlines . . ."

I pulled out a chair and sat down.

He folded his newspaper and looked up at me again. "Well, I'm glad to see you. You're far better for my eyes than what I was just reading in the paper."

I smiled and began to unfasten the buttons of my coat.

"Thank you," I laughed. "That's fine praise, indeed."

His eyes brightened, amused.

I looked around the café. The tables were filled with men in gray overcoats and caps. Some were already smoking their first cigarette of the morning, now that their coffee cups were empty.

"Do you come here often?" I asked.

"Yes, I like the fact that it's far enough from home. I rarely run into anyone I know, and I can sit and read without any distraction." A small sigh escaped from his lips. "It's not pleasant to have to share the paper with my father and constantly hear all his thoughts of what might happen next with Hitler. The war has made everyone on edge."

"I understand," I said as I readjusted my scarf. "My father and I spend most of our time together glued to the radio."

"You don't hear the worst of it on the radio . . ." He took a sip from his water glass. "Solomon is my father's true news report. He received a letter the other day from his brother back in Berlin. They write in code to each other to fool the censors. What he wrote was alarming."

I looked down at the table, quietly.

"They rounded up a whole street. Men, women, and children, all carted away somewhere."

I grew pale. "That's horrible, Alex."

"I know . . ." He stopped and shook his head. "I'm sorry. I shouldn't tell you these things. If you find the radio upsetting, this is so much worse . . ."

He shook his head. "What do you say, we make a promise not to talk about the war this morning. Let's try to forget it for at least an hour . . . I'm so tired of all the energy I spend imagining what's going to happen tomorrow, next week, in a month's time . . . What a joy it would be to have a coffee with a pretty girl and imagine nothing except how nice it would be to hold her hand."

I could feel my cheeks grow warm.

"And now I've made you turn the color of your scarf!"

I laughed.

"I like you in red." He smiled. "It becomes you."

My fingers touched the edge of my scarf. "Thank you." This morning I had made a concentrated effort on my appearance. All of my grandmother's talk about her makeup and clothes had inspired me to make the most of my features. I thought the red of my scarf would be a striking contrast against my dark hair and eyes. I was glad it seemed to have pleased him.

"What would you like?" He motioned for the waiter's attention.

"Just a coffee . . ." I wasn't particularly hungry. I had felt butter-flies in my stomach since I had gotten up that morning.

"And another cup for me," he told the waiter before the man vanished inside.

"So . . . ," he said as he leaned into the table. "You go to your grandmother's a few times a week?"

"Yes." I smiled. "The strange thing is, I only met her for the first time last year. Before that, I didn't even know she existed . . ."

"Really?" His eyes widened. "How unusual your family is, Solange. You arrive at our bookstore holding two rare and valuable Jewish books, and you tell Papa and me that you only recently learned you were half Jewish. And now an unknown grandmother appears in your life . . ." He leaned closer. "I wonder what will be revealed to you next?"

"I don't know . . ." I was amused that he saw any part of my life to be of such interest. I had always believed it to be rather dull.

"Well, my grandmother is certainly a character . . . I think that's why my father waited so long to introduce her to me. He kept her hidden because he was embarrassed by her, but since my mother's death, he was at a loss on how to keep me occupied." I touched my napkin briefly. "I suppose knowing that I wanted to be a writer, he thought she might provide some good source material for me . . ." I laughed. "It does sound crazy, though. There is so much more to my family than I had previously known."

"It's all rather fascinating to me, really. I know too much about every member of my family . . . not just my father, but my aunts, my cousins . . . their husbands and wives. Your family is far more interesting."

I looked at him and smiled. Hours before, I could hardly button my coat or tie my scarf around my neck, I was so nervous Alex would find me boring and that I'd have nothing to say. But here I was sitting across from him with his eyes bright upon me.

"Tell me about your grandmother, Solange . . . Tell me about your writing . . ." A big smile swept over his face. "Why, just tell me everything about you!" He placed his hands around his coffee and laughed.

"How much time do I have?" I asked as I lifted the cup to my lips. Small puffs of steam floated between my breath and the coffee. And as I raised my eyes, his own were staring back at me.

24.

Solange

November 1939

I told him everything Marthe had shared with me so far. The story of her bleak childhood. Her relationship with Charles. And now the beginning seeds of the Boldini painting.

"A woman of the night, how wonderfully scandalous." An impish grin crossed his face.

"Hardly," I said.

"A courtesan, then?"

I laughed. "She doesn't seem to have kept her dance card quite that full over the years."

"I'm intrigued." He leaned in closer. "Another one of your family's many secrets."

"Isn't that the truth?" I nodded my head, agreeing with him.

"Yes . . . but I think I'm still going to insist that owning the Barcelona Haggadah to be the biggest."

I smiled. "Who knew that my mother was in possession of something so rare and valuable. I suspect it's worth more than all the other contents of our apartment."

"I've never seen your apartment," he teased.

"One of these days I should invite you, and if you're very good, I'll even take down the Haggadah and show it one more time."

His eyes flickered. I had never flirted before, but I was surprised how naturally I took to it. Perhaps it was my grandmother's influence.

"I'd like that very much," he said as his fingers reached out and grazed my own. Just the slightest touch of his skin against mine made me tingle from head to toe.

My mind traveled to Marthe and the butterflies embroidered in the silk above her headboard, the emerald clasp around her neck. The feeling of the first signs of attraction, I was beginning to recognize, was always accompanied by the sensation of wings.

We made a date to meet again a few days later. I gave him the address of our apartment and told him to come by after ten a.m. when I knew my father would already be at the pharmacy.

That morning I had tried not to appear suspicious to my father, as I knew I could not tell him I was inviting a young man back to our apartment even if it was just to give him a second opportunity to look at a very rare and valuable book.

I said good-bye to my father and began to straighten the apartment so it appeared as neat as possible. The day before, I had attempted to do some dusting, but I still needed to fluff the couch pillows, hide the piles of paperwork on my father's desk, and run downstairs to the florist to buy a fresh bouquet.

With only fifteen minutes to spare before Alex was to arrive, I arranged the roses I had bought and quickly went into the bathroom to fix my hair, apply a little lipstick, and slip into my favorite blue wool dress.

It was ten fifteen when I heard him buzz the main door down-stairs.

His footsteps sounded like the most beautiful percussion. We were on the fifth floor, and with every landing I could hear him getting closer.

But it was only after I could hear his escalating breath that I stepped out from the open door.

"Solange," he said. He was clutching a bouquet of violets. "No elevator?"

I laughed.

"You are worth the climb," he said as he tried to catch his breath. I was now standing in the hallway in my favorite dress, my hair tied back. At the last minute, I had tied a black silk ribbon behind my hair. I had never bothered with such a feminine detail before.

"I'm so sorry, and we're on the top floor," I apologized.

"There is no need for regrets," he said, smiling at me. I saw his eyes take note of the nice shape the dress made of my figure, as well as the ribbon in my hair. "How lovely you look."

"Thank you." I blushed. I pushed back against the door. "Please, Alex, our apartment is very modest, but come in."

My mother's bookshelves were in the first room when one entered our apartment. An extensive wooden tower took up the entire wall.

"It's wonderful to be greeted by books," Alex said sweetly. "Your home looks very similar to ours."

I smiled. "That makes me happy to know we have something else in common.

"Would you like something to drink?" I offered.

Alex shook his head and I came closer to him.

"The Haggadah is safely tucked away on the highest shelf. Let me get a chair."

He chuckled. "I like your form of security, Solange. Hardly the most foolproof . . . yet I doubt there are a lot of thieves that would know you're in possession of a rare fourteenth-century Haggadah." He looked at me and smiled. "I think the biggest risk of that would be my father, but I doubt he could make it up the five flights of stairs to read it."

I laughed. "I'll just get a chair from the kitchen."

"Let me help you." He followed me to the next room. The smell from the bouquet of violets he had brought still lingered on his clothes.

I gave him a chair to take back and place closer to the shelf so I could climb on it to reach the top shelf.

"I'll hold it for you, so you're steady," he offered sweetly.

After thanking him, I stood on top of the chair to retrieve the book. It was heavy, and I knew I had to be careful. Alex's father had treated it with such care and respect when he was handling the pages. I wanted to make sure I treated it the same.

"Are you okay?" he asked. His hands were tight around the seat of the chair.

"Yes, I just want to make sure I have a good grip on it."

Slowly I came down from the chair, clutching the centuries-old Haggadah in my hands.

We did not speak as I brought it to the dining room table and laid it carefully on the flat surface. It was as if the object itself demanded a reverent pause before we opened its pages.

It seemed strange to look at it now, knowing the backstory of the couple who had created it. The Haggadah had only looked ancient and mysterious to me before, but now it also contained a love story. Two people who had spent decades together working to make something that was not only a testament to the longevity of the Jewish people and their exodus from Egypt, but also their own relationship. The book now appeared more beautiful to me than ever.

I could sense he wanted me to be the first to touch it. So I reached delicately for the far left corner of the old book and opened it again.

The vellum had yellowed to the color of wheat. I could almost hear the whisk of the scribe's feather quill against the parchment as I looked at the care with which each letter was applied.

"It's difficult to imagine how painstaking this all was before the printing press," Alex said softly. "We are so spoiled now."

He touched the edge of the page as if connecting with something he knew had a soul.

"Back then, the vellum had to be lightly ruled and the layout ensured before the quill nib ever touched the parchment. Any mistake was costly because the materials could only be procured at considerable expense."

"I can imagine," I said softly.

"But whereas Rabbi Avram's skill inscribing the prayers took time and patience, truly it's his wife's talent that makes this so unique."

He turned a few pages until he found one of the illuminated paintings.

"She not only knew how to paint. Even more incredible, she knew how to work with gold. Very few people possessed that skill then, much less a woman."

"Really?" I had noticed that a few of the pages had gold applied sparingly, but I had never thought much about it.

"Yes. A person had to not only have access to gold leaf, they also had to know how to prepare it for application. There were two ways to do that back then: either to apply gold specks very, very carefully with a brush, or to hammer the leaf and burnish it, dusting it onto the page after first applying glue. Rabbi Avram's wife was able to do both."

The book now took on yet another layer of interest for me.

"How would she have mastered this?" I couldn't even begin to fathom where she might have learned to use gold like this.

"Funny you should ask that, Solange. That was exactly what I asked my father after you left that first afternoon."

"Did he know the answer?"

"Yes. He said it was believed that her own father was a master illuminator and in private, he taught her everything he knew."

"It makes the book that much more meaningful." I took a deep breath. "To think how many relationships needed to be nurtured just for this book to exist and eventually make its way to Paris."

"Yes," he said quietly. "Even your mother's relationship with her father."

I felt a shiver pass through me.

"And now your own connection with your mother."

What he said was true. What I chose to keep to myself was that the book had also brought Alex into my life. I felt my mother in the room as we spoke. And I had never been more thankful that she had kept it safely tucked away on her shelves.

It had been quite a few days since I had the chance to go see my grandmother. I had to reschedule my last visit, on two separate occasions. For over a year, I had tried to see her at least twice a week, so this amount of time passing was something I knew would not go unnoticed by either of us.

While by now I considered myself to be quite close to her, it was still difficult to gauge her emotional connection to me. We existed as storyteller and audience. Even though she knew I was working on a novel based on her life, she never asked to see what I had written or expressed much interest in what I did outside our meetings. It was easy for me to see how she created a world for her and Charles that had no connection with the outside. And I could also understand how someone like her could have little interest in the fact that another war was raging throughout Europe.

I knew I would find her as I last saw her. A tall, slender woman who hennaed her hair and powdered her face. A strand of pearls around her throat. Sitting down to tell me about her dying lover and the painter who did not see her only as a commission, but also as a muse.

To soften what I suspected would be a chastisement, I brought her an extra-large bouquet of flowers. It was impossible to find good chocolate or coffee anymore, but one could always find flowers in Paris. I had spent the last two nights sleeping with the combined scents of the roses and violets, and it had made me think of Marthe. It was her apartment's perfume.

I buzzed the main doorbell and walked inside the marble interior. To my left, the door to the apartment of the concierge who lived on the ground floor was open. I had never noticed anyone there before, as that door was always closed. But today, I could see a young gentleman and his family bringing in their groceries. A few bags were left outside by the threshold, waiting for a pair of hands to carry them inside.

As I stood there with my bouquet waiting for the elevator to land, the young man came outside to retrieve the last remaining bags.

"Hello," he said, looking up at me kindly. "Who are those beautiful flowers for?"

"My grandmother on the eighth floor."

"Your grandmother . . ." I could see him mentally trying to place which of the apartments on the eighth floor had an older woman in it.

"Madame de Florian?" His voice sounded perplexed "I had no idea she had a granddaughter. Why, I had no idea she actually had ever been a mother, in fact."

I smiled. "I can imagine your surprise." I let out a small laugh. The elevator's cage had descended to the ground floor, but the man had now placed the bags down on the floor and couldn't resist asking me a few more questions.

"My father was the original concierge for the building, and I inherited the position from him. And I must tell you, as a young boy, the few times I ever saw Madame de Florian leave the building, it left me breathless."

I smiled. "I can imagine so."

"Even now, when I catch the rare glimpse of her, she still looks beautiful. It's as if she's impervious to time."

I knocked on the door of the apartment, holding the flowers in one hand.

"Madame is waiting," Giselle said coolly as she opened the door.

"I apologize. I met the concierge in the lobby for the first time. He was quite friendly, and it was hard to break free."

Giselle smiled now. "Ah, Gérard, a lovely boy."

"He didn't say his name, but he said his father had been the concierge before."

"And his father was even lovelier," Giselle said softly. "God rest his soul."

"But how nice the position was maintained within the family . . ."

"Yes," Giselle answered quickly. "And it appears Gérard has inherited his father's discretion, which is a good thing. One never really wants a nosy concierge."

I laughed. "No, I suppose not . . ."

Just as I was about to ask Giselle more about Gérard and his father, Marthe's voice fluttered through the air.

"Solange? Is that you?"

"Yes, I'm so sorry I'm late . . ."

She always waited for me in the parlor, and it was a shock to see her standing in the threshold, in a long lilac dress, her white fingers grasping the edge of one of the open French doors.

"Giselle and I were just discussing that you have broken your pattern. You have never once been late, an attribute I've always admired."

I tried to readjust my eyes at the sight of her. It had been a week since I last saw her. Yet somehow she now looked very different to me. Was she thinner? I focused on her face for a second, trying to pinpoint the exact change. It had grown considerably colder in Paris over the past few weeks, and the radiators in the apartment hissed steam to maintain a sense of warmth through the rooms and halls. Perhaps the sudden change in climate had caused her delicate skin to slacken a bit.

But it was hard to deny that her eyes looked tired in a way I had never seen before.

"Mademoiselle Solange got distracted downstairs talking with Monsieur Gérard," Giselle offered up my excuse to Marthe.

"Ah." Marthe smiled. "She has a good excuse, then. Such a good man. Just like his father, Pierre."

I had never witnessed these two women bonding about anything. But both of them clearly had a soft spot in their hearts for Gérard and his father.

I looked at Marthe with an expression that could only have shown how perplexed I was. I could not imagine her fraternizing with Gérard or his father, the concierge. From what I had heard so far, she hardly had left the apartment except for her shopping excursions to buy her porcelains or her outings to see Boldini.

"One never forgets someone who helps you out in a time of need. And Pierre was just that man."

As Giselle took the bouquet from me to put in a vase, I followed Marthe back into the main room.

The silk curtains had been tied back, and crisp sunlight poured through the windows. Now that most of the leaves had fallen from the city's trees, the light seemed sharper than ever. Marthe sat down, and I settled into the same chair I always did, directly across from her, and my suspicion that something had happened over the last several days was confirmed.

"Solange." She said my name slowly and carefully as her hand touched her pearls, which I now sensed was the way she calmed herself when she was slightly unnerved. "It's been some time since I last saw you . . . We had grown use to a certain rhythm, as they say . . ."

"Yes." I smiled. "We have."

"Did you bring your little notebook with you?" Her hand now fell to her lap and she smoothed down the pleats of her dress. The gesture was somehow automatic with her.

"I did." I reached into my purse and retrieved my leather notebook and pen.

"And do you remember where we left off?"

"Yes, of course." I opened up the book to a blank page. "Charles was ill and Monsieur Boldini had just begun your portrait."

She smiled. "Exactly right."

I couldn't help but turn my head and gaze at the large portrait of her over the mantel that had captured my attention since our very first meeting together. Now, I could visually re-create every line, every brushstroke from its original conception.

"So where do I begin today?" She closed her eyes and breathed in deeply, her tiny nostrils quivering slightly. "I suppose we should begin with Charles . . ."

I rubbed my forefinger against my pen and waited for her to start. But she was looking out at the window, the light illuminating her face as her memory traveled back in time.

"November 1898. He had come back from Switzerland with Émilienne."

As she uttered the date, I was struck by the coincidence. It was now November 1939, and here she was forty-one years later, still able to recall those events as though they were yesterday. Her memory was extraordinary.

She looked at me, and her eyes were moist with tears.

"It's never easy to remember a person's last time with you," she said wistfully. "We always want the chance to press those final moments into our mind. To remember every detail."

She stopped for a minute, and I suspected she was trying to catch herself before her voice broke.

"I was so excited because my portrait was being delivered that day. You know I barely looked at Charles. And I should have been savoring every last moment between us."

25.

Marthe

Paris 1898

The painting, wrapped in a protective layer of cotton sheets and a second covering of brown paper, was delivered to Marthe's apartment by two very large men in smocks.

"Feels more like marble than a portrait," one of the men complained as he settled the portrait down in the hallway. The weight of the painting seemed to surprise him. "Must be the frame . . ."

Two weeks before, Charles had agreed to the added expense of the gold frame that Boldini insisted would best offset the portrait.

"I'm sparing no expense," he had informed Marthe. Charles's face was pale and gaunt. "And I'm determined to live until I see it delivered to the apartment and hanging over that very mantel." He pointed to the fireplace in the parlor. "I want to be able to see the two of you whenever I'm here." He let out a small laugh. "I've been conserving my strength just for that moment."

Marthe took his hand in hers and brought his fingers to her lips.

So much had changed in how they interacted physically. Charles was now so thin, so fragile, he appeared almost translucent. When she touched him, she felt she had to be as careful with him as though he were as fragile as glass.

"I am curious to see if he's truly captured you. In our correspondence, he said you had inspired him to push himself even further than with his other portraits . . . that you were more than just a beautiful young woman. That your intelligence and taste set you apart."

Marthe felt warm at the thought of Boldini praising her.

"I had no idea he was writing to you about the portrait."

"Of course, my dove. It was a considerable financial investment on my part . . ." He stopped for a moment. "And it was the first time I've let myself share you with anyone."

"Share me?" Marthe's voice sounded surprised.

Charles laughed. "Not like that." He patted her hand. "I'm fully aware your devotion to me has always been as pure as snow."

She smiled.

"I can't wait for you to see it. I do feel that if there was ever a painter to capture me in canvas and paint, it is Boldini. You chose the right artist, darling Charles, and I'm forever grateful."

What she didn't tell Charles was how much she had enjoyed her time with the artist. It gave her the opportunity to once again make herself beautiful for a man, and it buoyed her spirits. She was a woman who savored preparing herself to meet a gentleman. She loved the baths, the creams that made her skin soft and supple, and the spray of perfume that left a hint of her in the air, even after she'd departed from the room. She enjoyed the clothes, the application of her makeup, the arrangement of her coiffure. She even relished the laces of her corset being tightened through the metal grommets. All of these rituals were part of the feminine world she so cherished.

She knew, like any great actress or dancer, which audience would appreciate her most. And Boldini befitted that role, a man who loved and appreciated beauty as much as she did.

The few times she had appeared at his studio, she had seen how excited he was as he brought her to the divan to pose for him. She had delighted in his wit, his flirtations. It was the same titillating sense of pleasure she had first experienced with Charles. And yet, she and Boldini had hardly even touched.

She would never confide to Charles that his desire to see her painted by one of Paris's most celebrated portraitists had given her a well-needed distraction during his illness.

But perhaps Charles, who she believed knew her better than anyone else, had done this on purpose. That this was yet another one of his gifts to her.

"I can hardly contain my excitement!" Marthe remarked as the men brought the painting inside.

"Take it inside the parlor," she said, bringing her fingertips up to her lips. "We can unpack it in there."

She turned to Charles, who had remained on the sofa waiting for the painting's unveiling, and rushed back to him. "Just a few minutes, darling, and then we will finally see it!"

Marthe had not even seen the finished portrait herself. She had asked Boldini if she could visit his studio and see the final rendering first, but he had insisted he wanted her, too, to be surprised.

Once inside the parlor, the men cut the string around the portrait and began to tear off the brown paper and then removed the protective cotton sheet. While the packing paper had sounded like fireworks to Marthe's ear, the fall of the white sheet had hardly made a sound.

But what was finally revealed underneath took her breath away. For a second she forgot it was her own image she was looking at, and instead sensed that she was experiencing that flicker of astonishment a man must feel the first time he witnesses a beautiful woman disrobe.

There, in the middle of her living room parlor, she emerged through Boldini's brushwork like a starburst. The curve of her body and the length of her neck all contributed to the swanlike sensation of the pose. Even the exuberant ruffles on her sleeves, pulled down to reveal her glimmering white shoulders, looked like feathers.

But it was the contrast in colors, the sharp relief of her profile against the sunset of pale hues in the background, that made her feel as though he had captured more than just her figure and her features.

She turned back and looked at Charles, who had used all of his strength to lean forward and look more closely at the painting being held up at each corner by the two men.

His eyes traveled across each inch of the canvas. He began at the top of her head. The pile of auburn hair, then down along her profile. The aquiline nose, the proud chin. The sensual mouth, painted in a red as deep as a ruby.

She watched as his eyes grew even wider as he came upon the white of her throat and the delicate rendering of her priceless strand of pearls, each one painted like an opalescent tear.

Boldini, like a provocation, had painted her bodice precipitously low, as if its silk had dropped any lower, the nipples of her breasts would be bared.

But there were no traces of her pink rosebuds that Charles had once kissed so often. It was simply the expanse of her broad, white bosom, its creamy flesh an unblemished landscape all its own.

His eyes softened as they came upon the dress. The panel of lace over the bodice, the silk skirt that hugged her hips, and the satin belt with its embellishment of sparkling crystal beads.

"My God," he whispered as he turned to her. "It's as though you're breathing right in front of me. Your flesh, your radiance, it's all there pulsing beneath the paint."

She sat next to Charles, her fingers clasped around his, as the men took down the mirror that had been above the fireplace and replaced it with the portrait of Marthe.

"Is it as beautiful as you were expecting?" she said, turning and then gently nesting her cheek against Charles.

"More so than I was expecting." She could sense he didn't want to speak, as his eyes still focused firmly on the painting now hanging above the mantel.

"Are we done, madame?" the larger of the two deliverymen asked.

"Yes. Thank you." She stood up and walked them toward the door.

"Quite a painting," the other one said as he turned to leave. "Almost makes a grown man like me blush."

She reached into her purse for the men's tip. "I'll tell the artist you said that," she said, smiling. "He'll be quite pleased. It means his painting is truly a success."

26.

Marthe

Paris 1898

That afternoon they sat in the parlor, hand over hand. The din of the city outside had long since faded in their ears. They watched transfixed as the painting seemed to transform in the changing sunlight.

Neither of them was hungry, so they dismissed Giselle when she inquired if they would like a meal brought in on a tray.

The portrait provided them with sustenance. He had waited for months to see the completed painting, and it had not disappointed. It was his beautiful Marthe forever captured in paint, her body emerging from the canvas in all its sensual glory.

But it struck Marthe in a way that she had not been expecting. Her emotions at seeing her own portrait surprised her.

She placed her head on his shoulder.

"I used to think no one beyond these walls would ever know I existed. My name is invented, my past all but erased. I always believed once I was gone, I would leave little trace of myself in the world. But you've given me a gift, Charles . . ."

She grasped his finger tightly into her own.

"This painting has immortalized me. Part of me will always remain, captured by Boldini's brush . . ."

Charles turned to her, and she lifted her head to meet his eyes.

"Anyone who sees your portrait will know that your beauty had the power to warm an entire room."

He lifted his free hand toward the portrait.

"Whether it's now or in a hundred years, anyone who looks at that painting will be struck by your splendor."

He kissed her. "But I am the lucky gentleman to have actually savored it."

The sun had now almost fully descended and the room and the painting had taken on new shadows.

"Tell Giselle she can leave. Émilienne is not expecting me this evening. The last part of my gift to you is that we can spend the night together."

They had rarely, if ever, spent a whole evening together since Venice. For years she had learned to make the most out of only a few fleeting hours with Charles.

She put herself into motion. She went to the kitchen and told Giselle to go home and not return until ten the following morning.

Once Giselle had departed, Marthe began to search for as many candlesticks and tapers as she could find. Only then did she return to the parlor, where Charles remained quietly, still fixated on the painting.

With the last threads of natural light hitting the room, she heard Charles remark about the color of the sky outside the window. *"Entre chien et loup,"* he whispered. The expression referred to the color between a dog and a wolf, but the word had a second meaning: when one slipped from the safe harbor of the day into the mysteries of the night.

Marthe looked back at him and smiled. She began to arrange the candles around the perimeter of the room. Then she struck a match, lighting every wick without uttering a word.

She left Charles sitting there watching the portrait flicker amongst the candlelight as she went to her bedroom to change out of her dress and into something they would both always remember.

In her bedroom, she unbuttoned her tea gown and stepped out from the silk. Then she began to open the front eyes and hooks of her corset, freeing her body from the tight confines of the whalebone and laces. She let out a deep breath, her rib cage delighted to now have nothing against it. Her breasts felt the frisson of the air. In the standing mirror, she caught sight of herself in profile. She admired the cleft in her back, the roundness of her derriere. Her vanity didn't shame her; quite the contrary, it gave her immense pleasure.

She opened up her wardrobe and found the silver lace robe de chambre he had bought her in San Marco Square, with the satin pink ribbon, the color of a conch's shell, that tied at the waist.

She wore nothing underneath, just the lace over her body. Her white skin glowing underneath like the pearls around her neck.

She wore no shoes. No earrings. She took the combs out of her hair, and let it fall over her shoulders and her breasts. She walked down the hallway, to the room they had happily sat in over the years for so many hours.

He turned to face her, his eyes finally leaving the portrait, to instead now gaze at the actual woman whom he had maintained as his private and precious jewel.

Even in illness, he felt himself stirring, the sight of her still setting him ablaze. The room, illuminated by the orange glow of candlelight, was warmed a thousand times more just from the heat she brought into it.

"Come," she said, and lifted his arms from the sofa.

She walked toward him, her footsteps as light as a butterfly's wings, making hardly a sound.

Her fingers reached to untie the satin ribbon of her robe, the material loosening around her body before falling to the ground.

She watched as his eyes widened at the sight of her body, white as milk. She ran her fingers through his hair, and embraced him.

Hours later, their bodies remained entwined in front of the fireplace, the portrait above them radiant as a star. Charles in her arms, his body nearly weightless, his cheek pressed like a leaf against her skin.

She tried for a moment to savor every sensation. They were knitted together far beyond their bodies now, and this gave her a strange sense of comfort. She could hear his breathing, and feel his heartbeat rising beneath the thinness of his chest. What floated between them was far different than when their love affair had first begun. Then, they had read each other's bodies like maps. They had navigated each peak and valley, and discovered secret places that came alive only by the other's touch. But now, theirs was a dance of simple gestures. She took her finger and caressed his arm. Marthe had no wish to ignite his passion, only wishing to soothe him, even as he slept. And she knew this would be as close to marital sweetness as she would ever come. She closed her eyes, careful to lift her face away from his, not wanting him to feel the moisture of her tears.

She pulled herself away from him, covering him with the blanket she had brought from the bed hours before. Resting, he looked like a young boy as a peacefulness washed over him, and she wondered what sweet things he dreamt of that caused such a smile to curl at his lips.

Her mind was still fresh from the memories of the evening. She recalled how he had reached his hand into her robe and how his hand traveled upward to find the curve of her breast.

"I have lived well," he whispered to her. He looked up at her portrait. "I have lived a full life, I have known love and experienced true beauty with you. I have been blessed."

Afterward, she wrapped herself in her silk robe and helped him to the bed. She wanted him to sleep comfortably with the halo of butterflies circling above them. To rest against down pillows and beneath a silken coverlet. To sleep like a pasha, with his dreams scented in rose.

The next morning, she awakened early, just so she could watch Charles sleep beside her. She had fallen asleep with him in her arms, not even leaving him to close the curtains. Now the first fingers of morning light filled her bedroom. She stretched out her limbs, the white sheets twisted over her calves and her chin nestled against the inside of her arm. She felt strangely removed from Paris, even though the morning bells had begun to toll in the distance. Yet an unfamiliar bliss came over her. Her eyes lifted toward the colorfully embroidered headboard, and even the butterflies seemed to flutter off the silk.

As he slept beside her, she imagined they were someplace in the countryside. On a vacation far removed from the city. She dreamt of grapes on the vine. Tall blades of grass. A warm breeze against their naked skin.

In his slumber, Charles's face appeared more flushed than

normal. And his forehead appeared moistened with beads of perspiration. She placed a hand on his cheek, and a sense of alarm gripped her.

His eyes opened at her touch.

"Marthe?" His voice was hoarse from sleep and, no doubt, fever.

"Darling, you're burning up!"

She could see him struggling to focus on her.

She took her hand and held it on his chest. She could feel his heart beating rapidly beneath his skin.

"We need to get you to a doctor."

Those few moments she had lost in early morning reverie had fallen away as quickly as they had arrived. Marthe jumped up and retrieved her robe, tying the sash tightly around her waist.

"I will get a basin and cold compresses."

She looked back toward the bed. His eyes were wide upon her, and his skin looked aflame.

Marthe returned with a porcelain pitcher and a basin of water. Through her sash, she had tucked a tea towel.

"Let me cool you off," she said gently as she pulled the sheets away from his body. The towel, which she had dipped into the water, she now firmly wrung with her hands.

"My dove," he struggled to say.

"Shhhh," she whispered as she dabbed the towel over his skin. "Save your breath."

As she struggled to cool off his skin, her mind began to race.

"I think we need to get you into a carriage and to your doctor at once." She looked around the room to find his clothes.

She brought his underclothes, white shirt, and suit to the bed.

"Let me help you," she said as she tried to dress him.

He swung his legs over the side of the bed to show her that he could manage by himself. But as he stood up, Charles fell to the ground.

It was Pierre, the concierge, to whom she now called for help, as there was no one else nearby that could come to her aid. Giselle lived nearly an hour away, and would hardly be able to carry Charles to the street with her. No, Marthe needed someone who was strong enough to lift Charles, and the only person she could think of was Pierre.

She dressed quickly, putting on one of her simpler wool dresses and buttoning it as she raced toward the door. She did not wait for the elevator to get to her landing. She simply lifted the hem of her dress and rushed down the stairs to the ground apartment.

"Madame de Florian," Pierre said, shocked to see her without her hair done, nor a single stroke of makeup on her naked face.

Young Gérard was by his knee.

"I need your help," she blurted out to him.

His eyes seemed to register how distressed she was. "Gérard," he said as he gestured toward the back of the apartment, "go find your mother. I need to help Madame de Florian." The little boy looked up at his father with wide, curious eyes before scampering toward one of the interior rooms, dragging a little toy boat behind him.

Pierre closed the door of the apartment and came outside to the vestibule.

"What has happened, Madame? You are white as a sheet." His hand reached out to touch her shoulder, and the warmth of his gesture surprised her.

"I have a friend who is in desperate need of a doctor." Her breathing was rapid.

He didn't ask another question. He saw Marthe ignore the elevator, and he followed her as she raced up the stairs.

. . .

She opened the door of her apartment and ran down the hallway toward her bedroom, Pierre keeping pace behind her.

Charles had pulled on his clothes and somehow managed to get himself back to bed. But just looking at his face and hair matted with perspiration, it was clear how important it was that he get to a doctor at once.

"Come." Pierre lifted him off the bed. "In two minutes I'll have you downstairs and into a carriage. Just tell me the address of your doctor."

She heard Charles say, "Seven Rue du Chevalier."

Pierre lifted him to his feet, wrapped Charles's arm around his neck, and began dragging him toward the hallway.

Just before they reached the door, Pierre paused to gather his breath, and Charles took every ounce of his remaining strength to lift his head in the direction of the parlor. Marthe knew instantly that Charles was peering through the French doors to take one last opportunity to look at the portrait he had commissioned of her.

"My painted dove." His breathing was labored, but Marthe still made out his words.

She came closer to him, kissing him on his forehead and then on his mouth.

"Yes . . . I'm here," she said, fighting back the urge to cry. She would not permit his last image of her to be of a blotchy, tear-streaked face.

When she squeezed his hand, it was as cold as wax. She gripped tighter, hoping she could transfer her own heat back to him. To somehow heal him with her touch.

She followed Pierre outside her apartment and into the elevator. When a carriage pulled up to the side of the street, Pierre hoisted Charles into the coach. Marthe only expected Pierre to inform the driver of the doctor's address. But he surprised her by doing something more than she expected. He pulled himself into the coach, insisting that he travel beside Charles.

She ran beside the coach for a few yards, before stopping from exhaustion. Slowly, she returned to the steps of her building and began to make her way back to the apartment. Stepping inside the vestibule, she saw something glimmering on the floor and knelt down to pick it up. The gold watch had slipped from Charles's pocket. She tightened her fingers around it and then opened the casing, her eyes first meeting with the image of the engraved dove. She checked the clock in the parlor. It was 6:14 a.m. Marthe adjusted the dial, and silently prayed that she would have the chance to move the hands once again.

27.

Marthe

Paris 1898

It was Boldini, not Charles, who arrived at her door two days later. Seeing him dressed in black, she knew immediately why he had come.

"I am sorry to be here under such unfortunate circumstances," he said as he stepped into her apartment.

"It's Charles . . ." Her words were barely audible. "He's the reason you're here."

He lowered his eyes and nodded.

"A few weeks ago, he wrote to me and asked that I be the one to tell you when the time came. He wanted to make sure you were informed as promptly as possible."

She pulled her arms around herself. Her skin now felt terribly cold.

"He passed away last night. I was informed by a mutual friend."

She remained quiet for a moment as she tried to gather her words.

She felt the floor falling beneath her, and she struggled to regain her composure.

"He had been ill for some time." Her voice faltered as she spoke. "I suppose he was holding on just long enough until you finished your portrait of me."

Boldini nodded. "Yes, he wrote me saying that was the case. I painted it as quickly as I could, while still ensuring that you were captured with all the beauty and radiance you deserve."

She looked at the floor, not wanting to show Boldini her eyes. She knew he would read her immediately, that he wouldn't be fooled by her stoic expression. He was a master of seeing what lay beneath. One glance at her, and he would penetrate every emotion she hoped to conceal.

"Please," she said softly. "Why don't you come into the parlor and see how beautiful your painting looks now that it's been properly hung. It made the delivery men blush; I knew you'd be pleased."

She motioned for him to follow her, pushing through the French doors and into the room where only days before Charles and she had spent their last moments together.

"It is even more magnificent outside the walls of my studio." He reached into his breast pocket for a cigar and lit it. The smell contrasted with the Oriental blend of Charles's pipe, a fragrance she now missed more than ever.

She tried to force herself to smile, but it felt false. For the first time since it had been delivered, she felt at odds with the way Boldini portrayed her in the portrait. In the painting, she was depicted so full of life and warmth. But now, in her grief, a glacial coolness ran through her veins, just as it had when her sister died. It was the same feeling, the sensation that nothing in the world could ever make her warm again.

Giselle, who had overheard the news, brought tea and a plate of biscuits into the room, hoping the tea would calm her mistress. But even as Marthe poured the tea for Boldini and filled a cup for herself, she continued to shiver.

"You are a beautiful and clever young woman, Marthe. You will continue to have a good life, I'm certain of it."

She could see his eyes looking around the room. Even though he made an effort to appear discreet as he exhaled blue circles of smoke into the air, she could see him absorbing all of her little collections that lined the shelves.

"You are not frivolous or stupid like so many other women I've met in Paris. Even your collections reflect a great intelligence, a keen eye. To me, this demonstrates you will always land on your feet."

"I am flattered you have such confidence in me." His words had a temporary soothing effect on her. "Thank you."

"I have complete confidence . . . ," he said as he extinguished his cigar in a crystal ashtray. Marthe winced slightly. That crystal bowl was where Charles had also always emptied his pipe.

"You must let me help you in any way you need. I hope it doesn't sound disrespectful during this time of mourning, but I believe we speak a similar language. And that we share a love of beautiful things, too."

She finally raised her eyes toward him. His honesty and ability to treat her as a peer touched her deeply. "Yes, I do feel we share similar tastes."

"It's a shame you can't openly partake in the rituals of mourning Charles. The Mass is at Notre Dame d'Auteuil this evening. The funeral is the following morning. Émilienne is in perhaps a state of greater shock than you."

A splinter of pain coursed through her at the mere mention of Émilienne's name.

"Surely she knew Charles was gravely ill." Marthe's voice cracked. "I know she was the one to suggest they take the cure in Switzerland. So his death couldn't have taken her by surprise."

"Yes," the artist agreed. "But it is always terrible to be the one that discovers the body."

Marthe flinched.

"I was told she'd gone into his bedroom that morning, thinking he had only slept late. In what she mistakenly thought to merely be a deep slumber, she said he so resembled their son."

Marthe knew she would never be allowed to attend the funeral. She would never have the opportunity to receive the mourners nor partake in the public rituals of grief. But she could still wear black and grieve privately for Charles. They could not rob her of that.

She had Giselle move all of her soft, pastel-colored dresses to an alternate wardrobe and had her replace them with only black ones. Now, the carved armoire in her bedroom was filled with black taffeta dresses, dark silk faille skirts, and silk chiffon blouses that were the color of smoke.

Her world felt emptier than ever. She saw traces of Charles everywhere. The furnishings, the original objets d'art, were like fingerprints he had left behind. She looked at the sparkling crystal ashtray, since cleaned of Boldini's ashes from the day before. She would never again smell Charles's tobacco or the scent of his cologne.

She ate little and spent most of her afternoons sitting in the parlor staring at the portrait. Her mind tried to re-create every minute of the last evening they spent together before he had collapsed.

She imagined him there beside her. Conjuring up every detail of him: his soft hands, his chiseled profile, the fine gabardine of his suit that he had tailored to fit his lean frame. She felt him sitting there beside her, a ghost. She tried to fill her head recounting every one of his last words. He had called her his "painted dove," and she had clutched his hand trying to stave off the cold.

. . .

If it hadn't been for Boldini, she would have stayed inside her apartment alone, never leaving for even a stroll in the park. She had no desire for anything. She had even lost interest in her love of collecting.

"Come outside with me," he implored her one afternoon when he visited her a few weeks later. "The cherry blossoms are in bloom. The women are wearing the colors of spring. Put on one of your dresses . . . perhaps the lilac one. It offsets your blue-gray eyes."

She decided to indulge him. She was beginning to feel like a vampire with the curtains drawn for so long. She saw how grateful Giselle looked when Boldini had insisted, and the girl had gone to the other wardrobe and laid the lavender silk dress on her bed.

In the mirror, with her black silk faille skirt draped over the divan, she saw how her muscles had slackened over the weeks she had indulged her grief. The sculpture-like quality of her physique, the dancer-like muscles that had always defined her shoulders and back, and the tautness of her derriere, all of that had softened.

When he suggested later that evening they go to a dance hall, she agreed. She needed to start moving again. To be alive. And to fill herself again with light.

Under candlelight they drank. He ordered abundantly from the menu, and she drank the brine from the oyster shells and ate small toasts with wedges of foie gras.

The energy from the dance hall permeated her body. She looked at the young girls kicking up their skirts, laughing with their heads back and their mouths open, and she felt like she was her twenty-something self, back again at the theater.

"You've breathed life into me," she whispered in Boldini's ear as he pulled her into another dance.

"If only I were taller and more handsome," he answered. "I know you'd fall in love with me."

Marthe did not answer. She knew better than to say anything that might hurt him.

Her heart had become like a piece of furniture over the years. While most people imagined their hearts with chambers that kept the blood flowing through their veins, Marthe imagined hers as a cabinet of secret drawers. In one she kept the memory of her family, in another she kept the only image she had of her infant son. Only Charles was kept in a sacred space for romantic love.

"It does not become you to play the widow, when you're not, my dear. Charles would not have wanted you to dress in black for the rest of your life."

"One cannot force these things," she said as she sat down again at their table. A small votive flickered between them, bathing her face half in light and half in shadow.

"We speak the language of art and friendship," she finally said as the music came to an end. She took his hands in her own and squeezed them. "I will always be indebted to you. Your painting has graced me with eternal life."

28.

Solange

December 1939

"Charles's death was a turning point in my life, Solange." Her voice sounded sadder, more reflective than it had in previous visits.

"At some point, each and every one of us will pass from this earth, but still it's so difficult to comprehend . . ."

What I didn't say to her was how hard my mother's death had been for me. We hardly spoke of my mother when I was in Marthe's company, and I didn't think I could forgive her if she showed any disinterest in her or possibly even said something unkind.

"I realized a lot about myself after Charles died." She took a deep breath. "I learned how to be resourceful. I learned that I was lucky I had people who still looked out for me, even though when he died, I thought myself to be completely alone at first." She looked away for a moment, her eyes gazing past me and toward the direction of the tall living room windows.

"That's the thing about death or illness. It reveals who your true friends are. The ones who remain after everything else slips away."

She rose unexpectedly, and I saw her grip the side of the armchair as if to balance herself.

"I want to show you something, Solange." She lifted her other hand and gestured a small wave for me to follow her. "I'm sure you're tired of sitting in that chair. Come."

I stood up and followed her. I watched as she straightened herself like an egret, pushing her shoulders back, lengthening her neck, and lifting her chin. Her slender arms fell against the pale gray of her dress. And when she floated down the hallway, I understood why Charles had always affectionately called her his dove.

At the end of the hall, to the left, was another set of white French doors. She placed her two hands on the doors and pushed them open. As she walked inside, the hem of her dress fluttered behind her, lifting like wings.

The bed was enormous with a carved Louis XV headboard in walnut wood. Its central panel was upholstered in a silver-colored silk that was embroidered with butterflies of almost every color—red, blue, gold, and malachite green.

I had never seen such a magnificent bed. It seemed to rise from the ground, and swell with its sensual curves.

But Marthe did not look at the bed, nor the mirrors placed around the room. She went directly to her vanity table and pulled the handle of one of the small drawers.

Inside were what appeared to be several stacks of letters, each tied with a different colored ribbon.

She pulled one out that was wrapped in a pink satin ribbon.

"These are the ones from Charles." She sat down on the velvet stool, her slender finger touching the corner of one of the faded envelopes.

"And these are the ones from Giovanni."

"Giovanni?"

"Yes," she said, and closed her eyes. "Giovanni Boldini. Even though I refused his physical advances, he still wrote me several love letters hoping to change my mind." She took a deep breath.

"You are too young to understand, Solange, but there are many different types of love in this world. There are lovers of the flesh, lovers of the mind, and love sustained by family." Her eyes softened.

"Until recently, I have only known two of those loves."

She brought the letters over to the bed. Each of the piles was still firmly tied with its ribbon. Pink for Charles. Pale yellow for Boldini.

I stood over her, seeing our reflection in the mirror of the vanity. Her expression was softer than I had ever seen it before. Her slate-blue eyes looked to meet mine in our reflection in the glass.

"Does your father ever ask about your visits with me?"

A feeling of unease washed over me. I wasn't sure how to respond.

She reached her hand into a second drawer and pulled out two additional stacks of envelopes. Each one of them was tied in pale blue ribbon, the color of the sky.

"These letters are from Louise Franeau." She placed her hands on both stacks of envelopes.

"Do you know who she is, Solange?"

"Yes," I answered her softly. I would never forget the name. She was the woman who had raised my father after Marthe gave birth to him.

"I kept every one she wrote me."

"Did you ever write back to her?"

A long sigh escaped her.

"It was so hard for me, Solange." She shook her head. "For all these letters she wrote describing your father's accomplishments, I wrote back only twice."

29.

Solange

December 1939

Alex met me near grandmother's apartment, his neck wrapped in a blue wool scarf.

"Did you get more material for your novel?" He smiled as he leaned over to kiss me on both cheeks.

"Yes," I said. "She showed me a more sensitive side of her that I wasn't expecting." I made a face. "And she seemed more fragile this time, too . . . I hope she's not ill."

"I hope so, too," he said. "After reading today's headlines, I'm not sure I could take any more bad news."

He showed me the newspaper he was holding. The Soviet Union had invaded Finland, so now those two countries were also at war.

I shook my head in disbelief. Part of me wanted to stop reading the newspaper. Every day the headlines seemed to worsen, and I always felt sick to my stomach afterward. "It was just sad to hear her tell how she learned her lover had passed away." I didn't think I could mention the latest revelation, how Boldini had showered her with love letters, too.

"Lover." The word felt strange and mysterious on my tongue, like a secret.

"One of these days I hope you'll introduce me to this grandmother of yours. She sounds completely different than mine was!" He laughed. "What I remember of mine was that she was missing a tooth, and spent all her time either knitting or baking. Certainly not one to have had a lover!"

I smiled. "I think she'd probably like you." My eyes ran over him. Alex was tall and slight with dark hair and green eyes. No one would deny that he was quite handsome.

"I have to be back at the store by three p.m. Solomon has finished restoring two books, and Papa has miraculously found two collectors who are interested in purchasing them." Alex glanced at his watch. "So that leaves three hours to be with you."

I smiled and his eyes flickered back at me.

"Let's go to the Bois de Boulogne," I said. "The grass will be covered in frost, the trees will be bare, but at least we'll have the whole place to ourselves."

It was true. December had made everything gray. The sky was the color of pewter. There wasn't a flower in sight. But the thought of walking through the park with Alex thrilled me.

"Very well," he answered. "You shall have your wish. But we should be quick. It's not so close."

I felt his hand reach for mine, his fingers tightly grasping my own.

As we raced to the Métro, I had never felt more alive. The striking of our heels against the pavement sounded exuberant. It was the music of youth, excitement, joy all wrapped into one.

We rode the Métro like young students. Our chins nestled in scarves, my bag with my notebook and pen slung across my coat, and our hands entwined. For the first time since I could remember, I wasn't absorbed in observing the faces of those who crowded into the subway car around me. My world consisted at that moment of only Alex and me.

At the park, we strolled through the winding paths. Little clouds formed from our breath as we spoke, and I clutched his hand even tighter.

"I haven't been here in years," I said. "My grandmother told me that the highest-ranking courtesans used to take their carriages out here for their illicit rendezvous. Can you imagine?"

"In their carriages?" Alex smiled. I thought I saw the color deepen in his cheeks. "Well, that's a morsel I'm going to be mulling over in my mind tonight."

I closed my eyes and tried to savor just how wonderful it was for us to be in the middle of the park with hardly another soul in sight.

Alex pulled me closer, and my body suddenly felt weightless.

"Solange," he whispered.

I didn't answer. I simply let him kiss me.

30.

Solange

December 1939

On the radio that evening, almost everything we heard became lost in static. Father smacked the dial out of frustration. I barely noticed. I was still thinking of Alex and our kiss.

"Are you all right?" my father questioned.

"Yes," I answered. I tried to think of an excuse for my obvious distraction. "Grandmother just told me something unsettling today."

He looked at me, then down at his food.

"I hardly think she could have told you anything sadder than another world war only twenty years after the last one." He shook his head.

I felt my stomach suddenly fall. Although I mentally fought to cling to the memory of Alex's kiss, I could feel it dissolving in the face of my father's agitation.

He stood up and went into the pantry in search of a bottle of wine. I heard the glass being placed on the counter, then the sound of his pulling out the cork. He took a long swallow and came back to sit beside me.

"I don't mean to be cross, Solange. I just never thought I'd be alive to see another war like the last one. Every one of those boys whose last dose of morphine I administered, died fighting to free France from occupation by the Germans."

He shook his head and took another swallow of wine. "I feel like a dog that senses a storm is coming."

"Don't say such a thing," I said. "I feel it will only bring bad luck."

But the words had already been let go into the air, and they floated heavily like dark clouds between us.

I slept fitfully, vacillating between the sweet memories of Alex's kiss and the ominous predictions made by my father.

But in the end, his sixth sense was confirmed. Two days later a letter was delivered to us with an official government letterhead. I placed it on the kitchen table. When I returned home that afternoon after a morning of writing and a brief coffee with Alex, my father was sitting at the table with his head in his hands.

"What is it, Papa?" I asked.

"I've been conscripted, Solange."

At the sound of his words, I immediately felt my stomach twist in knots.

I picked up the letter and read it. "You are to report to duty as medical pharmacist, to the army hospital with the Sixth Army Regiment just outside Caen."

My heart was pounding. How was this possible? Papa was fifty-three years old, and yet Alex hadn't even received draft papers. At least, not that I knew of.

"Papa, can they really make you go?"

He nodded. "I'm afraid so. I'd be arrested if I refused."

"But there is still the medical test, Papa. Maybe you have a weak heart."

"I don't, Solange." His voice, almost always clinical, now had a traceable sense of fear in it. I could hear it like an out-of-tune musical note.

"I'm not thinking of myself now, I'm thinking of you . . . I don't want you to live in this apartment by yourself. It won't be safe. I'll worry constantly not knowing if you're all right."

"I'll be fine." I shook my head. "Please don't worry about me."

"It's not an option, Solange. I want you to move in with Marthe."

I was incredulous. "But that would be impossible. She would never have me. I would be like a piece of mismatched china or broken furniture in her apartment."

"You are quite wrong, Solange. I paid her a visit late this afternoon, after I received my letter from the army. And she said she'd be delighted for you to stay there."

My father explained that he could think of no one better than Marthe to make sure I was taken care of while he was gone.

"She has survived at least one great war in that apartment," he told me. "She'll surely know how to survive another one."

"But how did she react when you asked her?" My mind was racing to put together my prior afternoon with her, when she showed me her private letters from her vanity. So many things had happened within the last twenty-four hours, and I was struggling to put all the various pieces of information in order.

"Perhaps I shouldn't have been as hard on her as I was the other day. She seemed different to me when I visited," he said softly. "I suspect you're having a beneficial effect on her . . . That said, I don't think she's all too concerned about the war."

"No, I don't think so, either . . ." My voice floated into his.

"As I suspected, she merely reacted as though I was going on a long journey, not understanding I had received orders to report to a hospital for wounded soldiers."

"That does sound like Marthe," I agreed.

"I am not one to show my emotions, Solange. You know that about me. But I must say, I'm grateful she's pleased to have you live in her apartment. No one knows more than I do that she's not maternal . . . but she truly seems to have real affection for you."

I nodded. "I know, Papa. I know."

The truth was, I had noticed a palpable change in Marthe over the course of my last few visits. She not only seemed more fragile, she seemed to reveal more of an internal softness as well. A sensitivity I had not seen before. I had visited her for over a year and a half, and for much of that time, I felt like she was happy just to have an audience to share her stories. But after my last visit, I felt there was a deeper need for her to share more than just her past.

Outside, a fire alarm wailed in the distance.

"We're all feeling so vulnerable now," Papa said.

"Some more than others," I whispered. I shook my head and thought of Alex and his father.

My father was given less than one week's notice before he had to report to the military hospital in the northwestern part of France. He arranged for a retired pharmacist to take care of the shop while he would be away on duty.

One week was not very much time to get everything in order, but my father packed very little.

"Unlike me, you can always come back to the apartment fairly easily," Papa said, "so you needn't feel that you must take everything with you now."

I nodded. On the bed, he had folded three white shirts, four pairs of pants, and two small, framed photographs. One taken of me on my first day of school. And the other, a photograph of my mother in her wedding dress.

I walked over to the bed and picked up the black-and-white portrait of my mother. They had married at the town hall, and she had not worn a veil or headpiece. Just a long, white dress with a high neck, edged in lace that she had made herself after taking apart an old wedding dress she had bought at a secondhand shop. In the photo, she clasped a nosegay of delicate flowers between her hands.

"She was so beautiful, wasn't she . . . ," I whispered.

"Yes." He picked up one of the shirts and began to refold it, his eyes not lifting as he spoke. "You know, you're the same age that she was when I first met her, and you look exactly as I remember her at that time."

Now looking at the portrait, I could see our resemblance more than ever.

My face had changed over the years. The soft face of my adolescence had been replaced by features that were in sharper relief. When I was a child, people always told me I had my mother's features. We had the same high forehead, a similar slender nose. And although our eye color was different, we shared the same gaze. A look that people said went right through you.

"If you're not taking the larger wedding portrait of both of you, Papa, may I take it to Marthe's now?"

"Of course." He was now preparing his toiletries. In a small canvas bag, I watched him put in soap, a tube of dentifrice, a razor, and shaving brush, all things I knew he had taken from his store.

From his bedside I took the larger portrait of both of them. I had stared at this particular portrait countless times while my mother lay ill in bed. But now, I did not focus on my mother. Instead, I looked at my father in his dark black suit and vest. He was probably close to Alex's age in this photograph, and it made me look at the portrait with a new perspective. I didn't just look at them now as my parents, but as a young couple first setting out on their own. Only now could I imagine how full of hope and love they were then.

My father insisted that I move into Marthe's a few days before his own departure. On that afternoon he carried my small leather suitcase to her apartment, and again tried to tell me he thought the situation was for the best.

"You don't know how relieved I am that someone is looking after you while I'm away, Solange," he said as we walked toward the Métro.

I had brought little with me, as I didn't want to upset Marthe's apartment with any unnecessary clutter. In my suitcase, I packed only the necessities: a few everyday dresses, my toiletries, my writing notebooks that contained my working novel, and my parents' wedding portrait. And of course, I packed the two precious books from my mother, carefully wrapping them in brown paper and placing them between the layers of my clothes.

"I understand," I told him. Although I wasn't sure how comfortable I would feel sleeping in Marthe's apartment, I knew my father would rest easier knowing that I was not alone while he was at the army hospital. I was also concerned that Marthe seemed frailer than she had in past months. Seeing her every day would now give me the opportunity to make sure her health was not deteriorating, and it would enable me to hear more of her life story.

This time, it was Marthe, not Giselle, who answered the door.

"Solange and Henri . . . ," she said, and waved us inside. "Such a rare treat to have you both here at once." She kissed me on both cheeks as Papa put down my suitcase.

"Hopefully, I'll get some leave in a few months," Papa said as he straightened his back and walked over to us.

"I'm still surprised they'd conscript a fifty-three-year-old man for the war," she said, shaking her head.

"There's a dire need for pharmacists at these army hospitals. The nurses can administer the medicine, but they need someone there to do the compounding. Not to mention, the dosing of the morphine . . ." His back stiffened. "These are matters of science that need to be in the hands of those with pharmaceutical training."

Marthe nodded. Her face was heavily powdered today, and she was wearing a long gold necklace in addition to her pearls.

"Well, at least at the military hospital you won't be in the line of fire . . ."

"No, I'll just see the men with their heads blown off."

I shuddered.

"Sorry," my father apologized. "It's just that I haven't forgotten what I saw in the hospitals twenty-one years ago with the Great War . . ."

"Well, it's good Solange will be safe here away from all that . . ." Her fingers gently touched my arm.

"Yes, we are all in agreement on that."

Marthe nodded, pleased to hear him grant her at least one concession.

"I'm very thankful you're allowing her to stay with you."

"It's my pleasure, Henri. I feel a real kinship with Solange."

I smiled, touched by her words of affection. I had been visiting my grandmother for over a year and a half, but it was only in the past few visits that I felt she had truly shown a more human side of herself.

"Giselle has made a cot up for Solange in the small room next to mine. There's even a desk she can use for her writing. I think she'll find it all very comfortable."

"Thank you, *Grand-maman*."

I saw my father's face register that I had called her "*Grand-maman*."

"Shall we go into the parlor and have some tea?" I saw her glance over to my father, and there was a look in her eyes that I hadn't seen before.

It was as if she was seeking something from him. And I wondered if it was the need for forgiveness.

Father did not accept her invitation to tea. "I must go over the store's inventory with Monsieur Cotillard this afternoon. I have at least a dozen loose ends to tie up before I leave."

"I can only imagine." She went over and kissed him gently on both cheeks. It was the first time I had seen them touch.

"Let me give you a moment to say good-bye to Solange, then," Marthe said with a maternal kindness that surprised me.

Papa and I now stood in the hallway alone.

"Solange, be good and take care of yourself." Papa clasped me around each arm. "Hopefully now you'll have the chance to finish your novel."

His expression was soft, his eyes slightly wet.

"Perhaps this is how all families are in the end. Imperfect, but still able to offer a helping hand when it's needed . . ."

"Yes." I smiled. "Please don't worry. I'm in very good hands, and the accommodations couldn't be better." I gestured toward the parlor with all of its beautiful furniture and objets d'art on the shelves. The portrait of Marthe pulsed over the mantel.

"You're right," he said as he leaned forward to kiss me good-bye. "I'll write when I get to the military hospital."

"I'll write you, too," I promised.

"Finish your novel, daughter." His words floated through the air as he let himself out. "Your mother's bookshelf is incomplete without it."

. . .

When he shut the door, I turned back to find Marthe standing at the end of the hallway.

"Are you all right, Solange?"

"Yes," I whispered. I wondered if she could hear the crack in my voice as I answered her.

"When a door is closed," she said as she began walking toward me, "it means another chapter is about to unfold."

I nodded as I struggled to fight back my tears. My sorrow at Papa's departure had taken me by surprise.

"Why don't we go look at where you'll be staying for the next few months? Giselle and I tried to make it as pleasant for you as we could."

31.

Solange

December 1939

The room could not have been more perfect for me. A rosewood desk. A side table with a pitcher and basin. A small cot made up in crisp, white linen. Above the bed, cut into the plaster, was a diamond-shaped window that reminded me of a kite. Its panes capturing a view of the changing sky.

"I hope it's to your liking," Marthe announced as she waved me inside. I walked into the room while she remained standing at the threshold.

"You've made it so comfortable, thank you. I couldn't ask for a lovelier room." In the corner, I saw Giselle had brought in my suitcase. She always moved so stealthily, her every movement nearly imperceptible as she navigated through the apartment.

"There's a small dresser for your clothes." She pointed to a three-tier chest. "But I knew you'd enjoy the desk . . . I used to write all of my letters on it."

A small sigh escaped her.

"Now I don't have the need to write as many . . . ," she said as she stepped into the center of the room.

"I'm looking forward to having you here, Solange. I haven't had a houseguest in so long . . . ," she told me as her fingers caressed her strand of pearls.

"And I'm grateful to you for your obliging my father. I would have stayed alone back at our apartment, but he wouldn't hear of it."

"There's no reason for you to be alone. I have more than enough room for you." She paused. "And I enjoy your company."

I was surprised by her compliment. "And I enjoy yours. I'm glad Papa thought we'd make a good match."

I lifted my suitcase onto the bed and unlatched it. On top was the wedding portrait of my parents.

I saw her eyes fall upon the photograph, her gaze weighted down by it like an anchor.

She looked up at me. "You look just like her, Solange."

"Yes." My voice softened. "Everyone says so."

"I only met her twice . . ." Her voice was softer, gentler than I had heard it before.

"She must have been just a little older than you are now when she and your father last visited me here. She was pregnant with you."

I felt a lump in my throat. I turned away from the portrait.

"Yes," I answered her. "Papa told me."

She lowered her eyes. "I suppose he must have."

There was an awkward pause between us. I didn't know how to fill the air with a response.

Finally Marthe broke the silence.

"I don't believe in regrets, Solange. I believe in starting new chapters . . ." Her eyes were no longer somber, but filled with sparkle.

The writer in me appreciated the line.

"Let's eat out tonight," she said, her eyes alight. "I'll tell Giselle she needn't prepare us dinner."

"A restaurant?" I couldn't remember the last time I had dinner out. I was used to only nursing a cup of coffee and a croissant for hours when I took my notebook to write in a café. And Alex and I had met only a few times at the café near Place Saint Georges.

"And not just a brasserie. A real restaurant!" She clasped her hands. "We can mark our new start together with a glass of champagne!"

Marthe spent the next hour preparing for our little sojourn into the city. As I finished unpacking my case, I heard the water run in the bathroom. Then the patter of her footsteps across the floor.

I waited for her in the parlor, which gave me the chance to finally study the portrait of her without her being there. Nearly all of my prior meetings with Marthe had taken place with me seated in one of the velvet bergère chairs directly across from her. I hardly ever moved from that spot, as I had been invited to the dining room just once, and only recently had I gone into her bedroom when she showed me her letters organized by ribbon color. I desperately wanted to look at the portrait more closely, but always had found it difficult to take my focus away from Marthe when she was telling her story.

Now that I was alone, I treaded closer to the painting, my heartbeat escalating with each step.

I approached it cautiously. It appeared even larger with no one else in the room. Within the carved gilt frame, Marthe's energy and sensuality seemed to burn off her skin. I noticed how Boldini had her fingers pulling slightly on one of her sleeves, thus revealing her bare shoulder, and exposing her broad décolleté as though it were its own white canvas. Around her slender neck, he had painted her pearl necklace in exquisite detail, leaving the butterfly clasp hidden behind her hair.

I studied the brushwork. The swirls of pink and apricot paint. I looked at her face in its pinnacle of youth. The flirtatious glint in her eyes. I traced her profile with my eyes, trying to see if there was a marked change in how she now looked forty years later.

Even now, one could see the sharpness of her cheekbones, her straight nose, her long white neck. Her skin was certainly more feathered, and the jawline not as taut, but the beauty was still evident.

"Solange." I heard her voice coming from the doorway. She stepped into the parlor. I turned to face her, but I was so surprised by what I saw I hardly recognized her.

Marthe was standing in the parlor wearing a pair of wide-legged trousers and a cream-colored, silk blouse, with her hair twisted back in a tight chignon. I had never seen her wearing anything other than her flowing silk dresses that went down to her ankles that echoed another time. But now, the woman standing before me looked thoroughly modern.

"Do you like them?" she said, patting down the placket of her pants.

"I sewed them myself." She gleamed with an understandable sense of pride. "I was intrigued after I saw you wearing a pair during one of your visits. I sent Giselle out in search of the gabardine and the pattern." She laughed. "I'm still handy with a needle and thread, aren't I?"

I walked closer. "You look smashing. I'm impressed."

She had painted her mouth not in the rose pink she typically preferred, but a soft red.

Again my eyes ran over her.

"Really, *Grand-maman*, the trousers suit you so well . . ."

She let out a small giggle that made her sound far younger than her years. "Thank you, Solange. I've been looking for the opportunity to wear them." She shook her head back, and the delight on her face was clear.

. . .

At the last moment, she had gone into a hall closet and retrieved a long fur coat. We took the elevator down, she and I. This was the first time we had ever left the apartment together.

She slipped it on as easily as if it had been one of her silk robes de chambre.

We walked through the streets, the sky heavy and gray. The air as crisp as apples. Both of us inhaled the night as though it were perfume.

"I can't remember the last time I walked in the snow," Marthe said. "It brings life into my old lungs."

She stood for a moment outside an awning and looked up. The ground was dusted with snowflakes, the soles of our shoes damp from the moisture on the pavement. Marthe's cheeks were pink and flushed like a young girl's. She looked so happy, her eyes bright, and the night full with abundant possibility.

32.

Solange

December 1939

We entered the restaurant crowded with couples smoking cigarettes and drinking wine. All the things every Frenchman needed to help forget the war.

The maître d'hôtel gently pulled the fur coat off Marthe's shoulders, and she slipped a crisp note into the host's hand. If it were true that she hadn't been out on the town in a long time, she hardly seemed to show it. She knew exactly how to navigate the room.

She smiled as we were shown to a corner table with a semicircular leather banquette. Positioned against the red upholstery, she looked out onto the restaurant as though she were on a stage.

"Perfect," Marthe said, smiling as she took the tall paper menus from the waiter and put them down on the table without a second glance.

"Two glasses of champagne and a dozen fresh oysters. We'll share, my dear."

. . .

We sat facing each other, each of our reflections caught in the mirrored panels of glass.

It was strange and marvelous to be with her outside the apartment. To see her come alive against a new backdrop.

Even after all these years, she still moved like a dancer. Her neck stretched, and her shoulders pushed back, she took in the crowd as though she were appraising them from afar.

When the waiter had placed the pedestal of oysters in front of us, Marthe lifted her arm to retrieve one as elegantly as a swan.

She sipped her champagne with relish and slid the oyster into her mouth, drinking the brine. Once the waiter returned, she ordered two cassoulets for us and a bottle of wine.

"I never imagined you enjoyed being outside the apartment much," I confessed to her as I washed down my oyster with champagne. "Of course I knew you went to Boldini's studio and to Ichiro's shop, but . . ."

"In the beginning, I didn't, Solange," she interrupted me. "Certainly I never dined out with Charles. It was always his wish to keep me a private affair . . ." She smiled. "But after his death, Boldini enjoyed taking me out, and I can't deny I took pleasure in all the attention."

She took her fork and moved the oyster shells to the side of her plate. The waiter arrived with two small bowls of warm lemon water for us to soak our fingers. Then, the waiter returned with two fresh glasses and filled them with wine.

Marthe lifted the glass and took a sip.

"I didn't feel the passion toward him that I had with Charles, you know. But I craved our exchange of ideas, the ability to discuss art with him . . . and he was not ashamed of being seen with me. He introduced me to so many of his friends . . . artists, even a few politicians."

I nodded. I could only imagine how thrilling it must have been for her to enter his artistic circle.

She took another sip of her wine.

"I've been lucky, Solange. I had three men who took good care of me in my lifetime."

I knew two of them, Charles and it appeared Boldini did as well . . .

But who could be the third?

"Three?" I questioned her.

"Yes," she said wistfully. "Charles, Giovanni, and my dear Ichiro."

That evening after we returned home, our shoes leaving footprints in the path of white snow, Marthe came upon the steps to her apartment building and stopped, her head turning to me in the moonlight.

"I've lived here for so many years now . . ." She looked up. The sky was now filled with a spray of stars.

"To think where I came from, it's rather amazing. I still can't quite believe I'm here."

It was true. It had always perplexed me how she was able to sustain herself after all these years. The money Charles had left her surely would have been spent by now.

"You've been able to maintain it all these years all by yourself. Not an easy feat."

Marthe smiled.

"That's the next part of the tale, Solange. But we'll save it for another night." Marthe had an incredible ability to always make one feel as though she had a secret up her sleeve.

"As you wish," I said, smiling. I stood next to her as she fished into her purse for the key to the building.

She jiggled the contents and peered deeper into the little silk satchel with a golden handle.

"I think I've forgotten my key." A girlish laugh escaped from her.

I glanced at my watch. It was half past ten.

"I'll ring Gérard," she said. "He'll let us in."

She went over to the call box and pressed the ground floor apartment's buzzer.

"'Gérard, it's Marthe de Florian. I'm sorry to disturb you, but I've misplaced my key."

"I'll be right there, madame." His voice sounded gravelly through the intercom.

Within a few minutes he was holding the door open for us.

"Thank you, Gérard," Marthe said. "I apologize that it's so late."

"I was up with the children . . . They don't want to go to bed tonight, and Francine has a cough and went to bed early. It is not a problem at all."

I could see he was slightly bleary eyed and was trying to readjust his gaze on Marthe. Probably, like me, he had never seen her in trousers.

Marthe read his look of bewilderment.

"Yes, I'm not in chiffon tonight . . . ," she said, smiling. "I was in the mood to experience a night out with my granddaughter as a modern woman."

"I hardly recognized you," he laughed. "And it's been some time since I saw you out for the evening. Always it's Giselle out doing your errands."

"Yes." Marthe nodded. "You know, better than anyone, I've always been a creature of habit, staying in my apartment with my things most of the time."

He nodded and his eyes were soft and kind as they looked at Marthe.

"But every time I do see you, it's hard for me to reconcile this young gentleman with a wife and family of his own. To me you're still Pierre's little boy."

He smiled. "And you're still the glamorous woman upstairs that Papa told me not to stare at when you came through the lobby. You always reminded me of a cherry blossom . . . floating by in your pale pink silk."

In the elevator, Marthe looked pensive.

"I should add one more to the list of men who have enabled me to stay in my apartment as long as I have. And that is—without a doubt—Gérard's father, Pierre."

33.

Marthe

Paris 1917

The morning they executed Mata Hari, Marthe had risen early. She lay in bed, the first rays of sunlight stretching across her silken coverlet like golden branches. Her slender calves peeked out from her peignoir. Her auburn hair, which she now maintained with the help of henna, flowed over her shoulders. A woman of fifty-three, she looked at least ten years younger.

She did not know about the execution until Giselle had brought in her breakfast tray. The newspaper was ironed and placed next to her pot of coffee. Giselle always took such care with her morning service. The porcelain cup and saucer painted with birds, and, on a plate no larger than her palm, a single croissant.

The headlines blared Mata Hari's crime as treason, accusing her of spying for the Germans. Her death had taken place at sunrise, an execution by firing squad. Marthe shuddered, recalling all those years before when Boldini had taken her to one of the dance clubs to see Mata Hari perform.

She had been enthralled when she first saw the dancer. They sat at small tables, she, Boldini, and his coterie of artist friends, their faces illuminated by the flickering votive candles. Those were the years when she was still gay and beautiful herself. Boldini had accepted the fact they would never be lovers and had pretended not to notice when one of his wealthy friends flirted with her. She never knew how he came to learn about the bouquets that were sent to her apartment in the days that followed. A select few, she took to her bed over the years. But they were never long-term lovers like Charles had been. And she always sold the rings and bracelets she received as gifts from those men. They were a form of currency that in the end brought her a source of well-needed funds.

When Marthe had performed as a dancer during her early courtship with Charles, she wore black taffeta and silk stockings, her petticoat sometimes edged in red. But in 1905, Mata Hari cultivated her own sensation, dressing and dancing to evoke the Oriental fantasy of the day. Her blue black hair was coiled above her head and threaded with pearls. Her breasts were covered by a brassiere sewn with glass beads, her midriff was bare, and her legs were encased in silken pantaloons that were slit up to her thigh. She undulated like moving water as she danced. She hid and emerged through a sea of colorful veils.

Mata Hari was a girl after Marthe's own heart, a woman of reinvention. She had created a glamorous life for herself by harnessing her beauty and imagination. At the time, Boldini told Marthe that Paris's most fashionable dancer did not, in fact, come from some exotic land, but had instead been born in a rather bleak village in Holland. Just as Marthe had shed her name so many years before and stepped into another world of fantasy, so too had the mysterious "Mata Hari."

However, a decade later, Mata Hari had suffered the fate of every other dancer in Paris. She began to age. Her body softened and her face became feathered with lines. Even as her income decreased, her appetite for beautiful clothes and glittering baubles never waned. Marthe wondered if Mata Hari had been drawn into the world of espionage as a means of digging herself out of debt or whether she had fallen in love with the wrong man, perhaps a German officer who led her down a treacherous and treasonous path.

The description of Mata Hari preparing for her execution felt eerily familiar for Marthe. She prepared herself for death just as a courtesan did when meeting a lover. After the guards woke her, she rose from the prison bed and slipped on a silk kimono, tied the satin ribbons of her shoes around her ankles, and put on a long black velvet cape trimmed at the collar and hem in ermine fur.

She next adjusted a felt hat on her head, wiggled her fingers into kidskin gloves, and looked straight ahead as she was led away by the guards who took her to the Caserne de Vincennes, where twelve waiting soldiers formed a firing squad.

For a woman who had always danced with a veil, Mata Hari defiantly refused a blindfold. She fell backward from the impact of the gunfire, her eyes directed toward the sky.

Marthe no longer had a stomach for breakfast after reading of the dancer's execution.

She was grateful that she had the security of her apartment. Paris had become a labyrinth of suspicion and fear. The war was now in its fourth year with no end in sight, and already a generation of young men had been left wounded or dead. Certain parts of Parisian society were still in denial, these places where under a veil of cigarette smoke, one could pretend the war was far away rather than only one hundred miles to the west. But one now had to seek these places out, and Marthe no longer had much interest in going to the cafés or the nightclubs like Musée Cuvée, where she had first seen Mata Hari perform. After Charles died, she had enjoyed those nightly distractions with her friend Boldini, but now she preferred to spend nearly all her time at home.

"You love art and you love collecting. Why don't I invite a few of my friends over to your place and we start our own salon?" Boldini had suggested. "It will give me the chance to show off my portrait of you, and also allow you to meet some new people."

The thought of entertaining in the comfort and privacy of her home intrigued Marthe, and she soon agreed.

The guests were handpicked by the artist and predominantly male. Most of them were married, and every one of them was happy to share a few hours of escape in her parlor.

At first she had been skeptical, thinking no one would attend. But she sat down at her rosewood desk and handwrote the invitations anyway.

She used her stationery embossed with the gold-leaf butterfly, and she wrote in her best scripted hand. A few days later, Marthe was proven wrong when her apartment on the Square La Bruyère was filled with guests.

They ranged from Boldini's wealthy patrons to his fellow artists, and even the occasional politician looking to lose himself for a few hours under the haze of candlelight and canapés.

She even invited the Japanese painter Foujita, through her connections with Ichiro, who brought his cat and sat on her divan as though he were an emperor holding court.

She always kept the gatherings small. She spent the days before creating the menu and selecting the flowers she would place around the apartment to create just the right ambience. She did not serve the most expensive food or the best wine and champagne. Instead, she watched her bank account as best she could. On her small painted plates, she served things people could pick up with their fingers. Smoked salmon on rounds of toasts, oeufs mimosa, and chicken legs roasted in rosemary and thyme.

She never knew how Boldini managed to charge an admission fee for her parties. But, at the end of the evening, the large Chinese urn she had on her sideboard in the vestibule was always filled with envelopes of money. With the night air filling the hallway, the banknotes strewn on the table fluttered like a hundred paper birds.

But as many guests as she had entertained in the years since Charles's death, a particular young man had surprised her. One evening, she noticed a new name on Boldini's suggested guest list. A Major Antoine d'Angelis.

"I knew his mother well," Boldini informed her. "He will be a nice addition to the evening."

He couldn't have been more than thirty years of age. He did not smoke cigars or boast about himself, as did so many of the other aristocratic men Boldini enjoyed inviting to their soirées. The major instead had a surprisingly deep desire to talk about art.

He stood in front of Marthe's portrait for several minutes when he first arrived. The cognac in his glass hardly touched his lips.

"A marvel of a painting," he said as Marthe approached him. Dressed in chiffon, she floated through the room like a water lily.

"Thank you," she said. "It was commissioned by a dear friend."

"Well, Boldini certainly has captured you."

"It was ten years ago," she said. "I'm no longer so young."

He smiled at her, and Marthe sensed that by the way he looked at her, she must have reminded him of someone from his past.

"A beautiful woman never ages . . ." His mellifluous voice was soothing to her. "I'm not sure if Master Boldini told you, but my mother was also a painter."

She shook her head. "He alluded to the fact that you were more than just a military man, but, no, he did not mention that your mother was an artist. Would I know her name?"

"Marie d'Angelis," he answered proudly. "She was an extraordinary woman."

"The name doesn't sound familiar . . . Not that that means anything other than that I'm revealing my ignorance." She laughed.

"I look around your apartment and I see you are anything but ignorant, madame." He took a sip of his cognac. "You clearly have a keen eye for beauty."

She lifted her hand toward her collection of porcelains. "I started collecting Asian ceramics years ago. The glazes comfort me. They remind me of the fog rising off the Seine, or the sky before it snows."

"Again, you remind me of my mother, Madame de Florian. The same words might have come from her lips."

She smiled. "I believe that is the first time, Major, that someone has told me I remind him of his mother." She let out another small laugh to show him she was pleasantly amused.

"I assure you it is an enormous compliment. One I have not bestowed upon any other woman before."

"Well, in that case, I'm quite flattered," Marthe said, placing a hand over her heart. It was a challenge for her not to flirt with the young man, who was clearly at least twenty years younger than she. But with great flair, she reanchored their conversation back to art.

"And do you paint as well, Major?"

"Please call me Antoine." He smiled. "Unless you are planning on enlisting in the reserves."

Marthe laughed. "Well, Antoine, I'm curious if you have inherited your mother's artistic skill."

"I have been known to pack a sketchbook in my rucksack." His eyes were merry. She could see it brought him pleasure to discuss things he probably rarely had a chance to talk about in his military life.

"Your mother," she asked as she stepped closer to her portrait. "When did she begin painting?"

She saw the light change in his eyes, as though his mother's image had now washed over him. "Quite honestly, I can't remember a time that she wasn't."

34.

Marthe

Paris 1917

With the Great War still raging throughout Europe and terrifying many of his patrons, Boldini was traveling far and wide in order to obtain new commissions. He found himself even as far as America, where he had first achieved prominence a decade earlier with his portrait of Consuelo Vanderbilt.

Though she was relieved her artistic companion had left London, where she knew there had been a series of air raids, he hadn't returned to Paris since her last salon, and Marthe felt his absence profoundly. She missed their conversations about art and collecting. She missed the gossip he loved to share. So, the handwritten card she received one morning from Major d'Angelis couldn't have come at a more opportune time for her.

Dearest Madame,

It has been three weeks since your elegant salon, and still the memory of you lingers like a rich and complex perfume. I must confess that it has been some time since I was able to converse so deeply with someone about art and painting. The career of a military officer is rather black and white, with little room for nuance. While I take pride in my service to our country, there is still a part of me, nurtured by my late mother, that relishes the opportunity to discuss life's most beautiful treasures. So I thank you for allowing me to speak freely with you.

I will be returning to Paris for a short reprieve next week, and wonder if I might have the opportunity to take you to dinner for I miss your intelligence and the beautiful shell that encases it. Please say yes.

Cordially yours,
Antoine

Marthe read the major's letter several times before folding it and placing it in her desk drawer. A well-written letter, particularly one with an undercurrent of flirtation, was one of her great pleasures in life. How many times she had reread those first letters from Charles during their early courtship, or even the ones Boldini showered her with shortly after Charles's death. It was too many to count. The major's letter now sent a frisson through her entire body, and she couldn't help but be flattered by the attention.

Time was a woman's mortal enemy, and Marthe knew that each day that passed would make it more difficult to resist its ravages.

Her monthly cycle had nearly ended, and she dreaded what all women her age feared: that the dewiness that had made her so desirable would soon evaporate. It was only a matter of time before her face would begin to resemble one of those old master paintings where the once creamy white complexion on the subject's face was cracked with a fine web of lines.

Her body was still lithe, soft in the places that it should be, though her neck was no longer taut, and that saddened her. But that was the beauty of a high collar or a strand of pearls. Like a clever chameleon, a smart woman could camouflage nearly any physical fault.

In the same way Boldini had first served to bolster her spirits when Charles was ill, allowing her a safe arena in which to flirt and talk with someone who shared her love of the arts, the major's invitation provided Marthe the same boost. She could hardly contain her excitement to go out to dinner with him.

She went to her desk and pulled out a sheet of her heavy bonded stationery with the gold butterfly embossed on the top.

My dear major, she wrote in her perfectly scrolled hand. *How lovely to hear from such a busy man . . .*

She was giddy at the prospect of seeing him again. It was a far better tonic then any rosewater bath or expensive face cream. The adrenaline of their anticipated meeting had restored her youth. The day before they were to meet, a second letter arrived, shorter than the first, simply stating: *Meet me at eight p.m. at Maxim's. And wear your very best dress.*

When the evening arrived, she chose her wardrobe as carefully as a soldier prepares for battle. She knew what parts of her body could still be exposed, and what was now in need of a shield. Hardly anyone still wore the tight-fitting corsets of the Belle Époque, and she was probably one of the rare few who missed the cinched waist. The pain had always been connected to pleasure for her. The untying of the laces, the ability to finally breathe freely as you slipped into your lover's arms. Now the fashions were more diaphanous, the waistline higher. No longer was there a need to bind oneself to create the most exaggerated hourglass figure.

Still, she would not forgo a beautiful undergarment. A woman must have a secret she kept to herself. Beneath the first layers of wool or silk chiffon, the lingerie she chose was the second layer of the flower. The skin beneath, the sacred petal, only a chosen few would ever get to touch.

She chose a corset that slimmed her hips and elevated her ample breasts, one in deep navy satin and pale blue flossing. Over the years she had never tired of her colorful collection of corsets, even though the styles had changed to accompany the latest fashion. While virtuous women wore only white to bind them, a woman well versed in the cultivation of pleasure knew how to communicate through the language of color. Marthe smiled, remembering how when she wanted to be demure with Charles, she chose a corset in tea rose edged in ecru-colored lace. When she wanted to accentuate her passionate side, she chose one that was strawberry red.

Now, as she prepared for her evening with the major, she stroked the satin panels of deep midnight blue. She reached for a black chemise edged in lace before putting on her corset. After Giselle tied the laces in back, only then did she begin to apply her perfume.

The dress she selected to meet Major d'Angelis was peacock blue. The collar was high and trimmed in silk satin. The décolleté was of a matching blue chiffon, showing off her breasts, like a beautiful face beneath a veil. The shoulders, too, were capped in sheer fabric, thus highlighting the softness of their shape without the glare of bare skin.

Marthe believed only a few women understood how important the right clothes were in the art of seduction. She considered herself an expert.

The fashionably high waistline of her dress was gathered at the center and marked with a circle of glass beading. The skirt, made of hammered silk, fell in soft, fluid folds as she walked.

She had always loved how fabric changed when one moved within it. The ripple of shadows, the shimmer of light, as the female contour shifted beneath the silk.

Marthe walked over to the long mirror to admire her silhouette.

The color of the dress offset her red hair and slate blue eyes. Her eyes sparkled. And having rested with ice-cold compresses on her face since early morning, her skin was as taut and white as an artist's canvas. On her vanity table she arranged her makeup brushes, then slowly and carefully, she began to add color to her face.

In the oval frame of her mirror, Marthe appraised herself. The only thing missing was a comb for her hair and her strand of pearls.

Marthe took a cab to Maxim's, where the velvet capes were lined in ermine and every woman's wrist sparkled with diamonds except hers. Still, she felt beautiful. A young woman in her twenties wearing a gray silk-georgette gown with feathers at the sleeves, stopped to marvel at the color of Marthe's dress.

"Major," she beckoned, as she approached his table. The light was soft and flattering.

He stood up and looked at her with his dark, fawnlike eyes.

"Come sit down, I've been waiting." The waiter in the white jacket pulled out the chair for her.

"I wasn't sure you'd come. Finally I can breathe easier." He snapped his fingers in the direction of the waiter and ordered a bottle of champagne.

She laughed and he smiled. A full set of broad, white teeth she hadn't remembered when they had spoken so intimately in her apartment.

"You must realize by now, women find flattery hard to resist," she teased.

"I was not lying when I wrote that our first encounter restored something in me. It is not easy to find such scintillating conversation in the military."

"Don't your brothers-in-arms speak adoringly of the wood and shades of varnish of their pistols? I've heard some are quite beautiful, with inlays of amber and tortoiseshell . . ."

"Ah, and now you tease me, Madame de Florian."

Again, she laughed. "I don't mean to mock you. I'm happy to have the chance to have dinner with a gentleman and an officer."

He smiled.

"Well, I'm equally delighted. It's a rare occasion that I have the opportunity to dine with a woman, much less one of such beauty and sophistication. And one that obviously selects the colors of her dress the way a painter chooses his pigments."

He reached underneath the table, to touch her thigh through the silk.

"Peacock blue," he said. "A perfect choice to offset the red in your hair."

How she loved that he shared her language of color. Their flirting was a dance with all the right artistic notes, just as it had once been with Boldini. But this time the romantic chemistry was as strong as it first was with Charles. As Marthe sat across from the young major, her imagination took hold of her. She saw in her mind's eye her fingers running through his dark, black curls. She saw him unbuttoning her dress. She saw him sliding her black slip from her shoulder, before unlacing her corset and peeling off her final layer, her chemise. She could see herself standing naked in front of him, waiting for his touch. All this while sitting across from him sipping champagne.

"I am nearly old enough to be your mother," she whispered, her lips coming closer to his ear. Beneath the table, she now squeezed his hand.

"Beauty is infinite. It has no age," he whispered as he leaned in to her.

She felt the heat of his fingers, and her skin tingled at his touch.

"How long are you in Paris?" Marthe asked. Her hand now moved toward his trousers.

"Sadly, only the weekend." She could see him struggling to maintain an expression of control. "As you know, we are in the middle of a great war."

She closed her eyes. She wanted desperately to pretend the war did not exist. She wanted only to focus on the pleasure, no matter how fleeting it was.

"A short reprieve, then?" She smiled.

"Yes, too short, I'm afraid."

"Then we must make the most of our time together, Major." Her eyes came alive, and beneath the table, she caressed him yet again.

Their flirtation escalated as the hours passed. Marthe circled around him, not knowing whether to unleash herself or bridle her passion deep inside. How wonderful it felt to be desired by someone so much younger and with such dark, handsome looks.

She could hardly believe he could desire a mature woman who was closer in age to his mother than a lover should be.

So, after they shared a plate of oysters, dined on roast chicken, and ended with two pots de crème so dark and sinful, she knew there would be no better way to end the evening than to take him back to her butterfly bed.

He stood there undressing her in her bedroom, just as he had in her imagination hours before.

The dress was unfastened. The slip was removed, the satin laces of her corset untied, and finally he took off her chemise. Only then did the major take two firm hands around her waist, and lift her toward the bed.

. . .

Later on, when she traced a line down his chest with her finger, she felt as though she were stepping back in time, to a period in her life when she had Charles beside her. But, as was often the case with intense sessions of lovemaking, a sadness crept in afterward that was hard for her to shake off.

Before finally going to sleep, Marthe had drawn the curtains and kept the bedroom bathed in shadow so he would not see the fine lines around her eyes and mouth. But she knew it would be difficult to fool him when the light changed in the morning.

"How beautiful you are, Marthe," he said, kissing her fingertips. It was as if he had read her mind and sensed her vulnerability.

She took her hand to his face and brought her mouth close to his, inhaling his sweet breath as though its youth and vitality had restorative powers. "I am grateful we spoke so intensely that evening at my salon . . ."

He smiled. "Isn't that where all great seductions begin? With the mind?"

She felt her skin coming alive as he spoke; the connection between her intellect and her body was an intricate web.

"The mind is the gateway for desire, for that is where all our secret fantasies are stored."

"How did such a young man become so wise?" she asked as she roped her leg over his. "Did they teach you such things in military school?"

He pulled her closer to him.

"No, it was my mother. She encouraged me to keep a dream journal. Every morning she told me to write down what I remembered from the night before." He looked up at the ceiling, then closed his eyes.

"When I was little, it was difficult to retain the exact details. I might remember a single image. A dragon or a paper pinwheel gifted to me in the park. But soon my mind trained itself to recall the images more clearly."

"Do you still keep one?" she asked as she stroked the inside of his knee.

"I no longer write them down, but every morning I pause for a few minutes and try to force myself to remember before I start my day." He sat up and now faced her.

"In fact, just last week you appeared in one of my dreams like an empress, your body wrapped in a silk kimono embroidered with silver cranes."

"How marvelous," she chimed, her pleasure was evident.

"You dropped the robe from your shoulders, and the material pooled around you like a frozen lake. I stood transfixed as you raised one foot after the other, stepping over the fallen silk and walking toward me with outstretched arms."

He lifted a hand and ran it through her heavy hair. The tortoise-shell combs lay on the bedside table, and now her hair ran over her shoulders and breasts.

"It was after recalling the vividness of that dream, that I decided to write you."

"I'm so happy you did."

"I only regret that I won't have time to buy you something beautiful before I leave tomorrow."

"Don't give it a second thought," she laughed, kissing him again. "It will be nice to have a handsome young major in my debt."

She pulled herself on top of him, his body a saddle beneath her. And her hair fell against his skin, the sensation as delicate as fallen rain.

35.

Marthe

Paris 1917

Over the years, Marthe had been forced to become creative in order to supplement her dwindling income. She had modeled for Boldini on a few occasions for his own personal studies, though never nude.

But when he asked her to pose so he could experiment with different positions of the body, she always obliged. He always showed his appreciation by leaving an envelope of money by the pedestal near his door.

She had also sold a few of her ceramic pieces to Boldini as well as back to Ichiro, who had told her when she first bought them from him that they would retain their value and he could always resell them. Marthe had already sold back to him most of her shunga collection and three of her celadon bowls and a famille rose vase.

But nearly twenty years had passed since Charles had died. Marthe realized that she was starting to run out of money, as much of her savings had dwindled. And now that she was older, the opportunities to model, as well as her list of new suitors began to grow sparse. The major had been a rare opportunity, one that would likely not repeat itself. He had written to tell her that he was now in western France, but she knew he could not say too much with all correspondence censored due to the war.

She thought it unlikely she would see him again, and she knew he was not in a position to financially support her as Charles had. If he survived the war, he would come back and marry a woman his own age, as she believed he should. The only men who'd take her as a mistress would be ones close to seventy with failing eyesight. Marthe understood that the same affliction that had caused Mata Hari to turn to espionage was now threatening her. The next step to stretching her finances further would be to let Giselle go.

When she met with Boldini now, Marthe was too embarrassed to admit she was having difficulty making ends meet, though she suspected the artist realized something was amiss when she informed him she could no longer afford to hold her monthly salons.

"With the wartime rations now, one needs to buy nearly everything on the black market." She shook her head. "The cost for everything is just exorbitant."

"I am in the same position, *carissima*. I've had to lower my commission price, but the cost of all my supplies is inflating. Canvas is now particularly high because they need it for the war."

She smiled at him. "And I was going to ask if you'd perhaps like to buy another one of my precious ceramics," she laughed. "I suppose I'll need to pay another visit to Ichiro instead."

She dressed in chiffon for her visit to Ichiro. The dove gray that had always been a favorite of Charles's, the color that offset her eyes. She also put on the strand of pearls from Charles, the ones she swore to herself she would never sell unless her situation became dire.

By this point, she had little of her remaining ceramic collection left. That afternoon, she placed her melon gourd vase in its original bamboo box and brought it to the shop.

Typically whenever she returned to Ichiro's, a calm came over her. With its dark wood interior and shelves that were never overcrowded, but instead were maintained to showcase the beauty and rarity of the objects displayed.

But this time, when she arrived at the store, Ichiro looked as though he was not setting up new inventory, but was rather packing it all up to be shipped someplace else.

"Ichiro," she gasped, unable to mask her surprise. "Where is all of this going?"

"Back to Japan."

"But for heaven's sake, why?"

He reached behind his neck and untied his smock, placing it on the ladder in front of him.

"I'm afraid, Madame de Florian, I will be returning there as well."

"I don't understand." She stepped closer to him. "You always seemed to do so well here, and you have your clientele that deeply appreciates you . . ."

"Paris is not the best climate for a Japanese anymore. The war has taken a toll on business. And things from the Far East are no longer in fashion as they once were."

"Oh . . . ," she murmured. She held the bamboo box that she had wrapped with a silk scarf closer to her chest. "I'm not so sure you'll be interested in buying this back from me, then . . ."

He smiled at her. His face, like hers, had changed over the twenty years since she had first come through his door. His once-black hair was now nearly white. His skin reminded her of the porcelain she had gifted Boldini years before, the one with the cracked ice glaze.

"Let's have some tea in the back, like old times . . ." He gestured with his hand for her to follow, and together they walked behind the curtain.

"What have you brought me today?" he asked her, after he returned from putting the ladder away and came over to his desk with two steaming cups of tea.

"The melon gourd vase . . . ," she answered forlornly. "I've held on to it as long as I could . . ." She had placed the bamboo box on the desk while she waited for him. Now she rested her palm on its lid.

"I am certain you will find it another good home."

Ichiro's eyes met hers. They had known each other for so long that he sensed without her having to explain further that she had reached a point where she could no longer survive without selling something worth a lot more than just a vase.

"I will buy back the vase. It's a rare piece and I know several collectors, both here and in Japan, who will be happy to have an example from an imperial kiln. But I feel I must give you some advice about something else."

He looked first into her eyes, then down at her neck. His eyes rested on her strand of pearls.

"I must tell you, as a good friend, some information I have recently learned from some acquaintances back in Japan."

He took a deep breath and placed his hands on the table.

"I am aware there are ongoing efforts to cultivate pearls. The trials now are in their beginning stages, but I have heard that they are making great progress.

"I believe it would be prudent for you to now consider selling your pearls."

Marthe lifted her fingers and touched the necklace.

"But these were from Charles . . ." Her voice began to tremble. "His last gift to me."

Ichiro lowered his eyes, then cleared his voice. "I am sure he gave them as a gift so that you would always have security. A single strand of natural pearls of that quality and radiance must have cost him a fortune few men could even hope to earn in a lifetime."

"Yes," she said softly. "And he bought it at Mellerio's."

"We've known each other a very long time . . . I would not guide you wrong. You really should sell them."

The necklace, with the only substantial weight carried in the emerald butterfly clasp, had always felt like little dewdrops around her neck. It had been a part of her for so long, she couldn't conceive of parting with it.

"I'm not sure I understand . . ."

"Your pearls are priceless because thousands of pearls needed to be harvested from the depths of the ocean to find ones that match in size and color . . ."

"Yes, Charles said the same thing when he gave me the necklace."

"But the day will soon come when pearls are cultivated by a man inserting a grain of sand into an oyster and waiting for it to grow under his own careful eye. When that happens, the natural pearls around your neck will be worth a fraction of their original cost.

"Sell them now," he advised. "If you are wise, you will take that money and live on it quietly for the rest of your life. But if you wait any longer, Mellerio's will hear whispers of what's going on in the Far East with the pearl market." He took another deep breath and shook his head. "And then, my dear Madame de Florian, even they will want nothing to do with your necklace."

36.

Marthe

Paris 1917

The next afternoon, Marthe walked into the bejeweled storefront of Mellerio's dressed in all her finery. The dark silk faille dress with the covered buttons. The hat bought from Madame Georgette's, the gloves from La Samaritaine. And although it wasn't as elegant as one of her silk purses, she carried the red leather case that contained her precious necklace in a black satchel she made just to ensure she arrived carrying the box in something tasteful and discreet.

The store was on Rue de la Paix, and the most celebrated names in fashion shared the street as its address. The famous couturier Charles Frederick Worth had his atelier and salon nearby, as did the esteemed fan maker Duvelleroy. The venerable Cartier was further down the street.

She entered the store with her heart in her stomach. She was selling something that was not only dear to her because it had been a present from Charles, but also something she had always known to be her most valuable possession. Selling it meant that she would no longer have it as a security blanket.

"Madame." A man in a dark suit appeared from behind the glass table of glimmering stones. "May I be of assistance?"

She took a seat on one of the velvet chairs and withdrew the red case from her satchel.

When he saw the box was Mellerio's own, he too sat down, but this time across from her. The glass display case became a resting table for her to open the box.

She heard a small breath escape from him. The pearls, and the butterfly clasp, were dazzling in the light.

"Whoever purchased these, chose well."

She felt a lump in her throat. "Yes," she managed to say. "His taste was always exquisite."

His hands reached to touch the box on each side. He searched under the satin cushion of the box and retrieved the certificate of authenticity and description for the pearls and clasp. "And how can I help you today, madame?"

"I wish to sell them. I was told that at any time, you would buy them back for at least what he had purchased them for." She paused.

"I have one request, though," she said, her voice surprisingly calm. "I would like to maintain the clasp."

He nodded and closed the box.

"One moment, madame. I will need to check our records to verify the purchase."

She folded her hands in her lap.

"And the name of the person who gave you these pearls?" He cleared his throat.

"Charles de Montagne," she said. Again her voice was unflinching.

He lowered his eyes and nodded again, before vanishing behind a velvet curtain the color of a dark sky.

. . .

An hour later, she was given a bank check for an amount of money worthy of a pasha, while inside her satchel was a little velvet pouch with her emerald butterfly clasp tucked inside.

"Monsieur de Montagne must have had great affection for you, madame," the sales clerk informed her. "The patriarch of our store himself sold them to him. They were one of the most prized possessions in our vault when he bought them for you."

"Thank you," she answered as she placed her hand over her bag.

"No, thank *you*," he said, clearly oblivious to the knowledge that Ichiro had shared with her about the burgeoning cultivated pearl trade in Asia. We are happy to have them back in our collection."

Around her, the mirrors and the glass cases with sparkling gemstones were blinding. She had always loved to be surrounded by reflections of beauty. But now she wanted nothing more than the soft shadows of her apartment.

Marthe met the eyes of the sales clerk before departing.

"It is a comfort to return them to where they were first bought," she told him. She did not look at a single jewel under the store's glimmering lights. She simply adjusted her gloves and gathered her skirt, making her way swiftly out the door.

37.

Solange

March 1940

My grandmother now sat across from me, a strand of pearls encircling her neck, the glimmering butterfly clasp resting just above the nob of her collarbone. Having relayed the story of how Ichiro convinced her to sell the pearls, and of her success in having sold them before the cultivated pearl market reduced them to a fraction of their original value, a deep satisfaction came over her. Just retelling the story had clearly pleased her.

"But then what are the pearls you're wearing now?"

She touched her neck; a sly smile emerged on her lips.

"These," she said with a soft giggle, "are actually cultivated pearls. I bought them years later and had them strung with my butterfly clasp that I could never part with."

I was speechless. Had it not been for the guidance of Ichiro, who knows where Marthe would have ended up. It was no secret that many women under similar circumstances could easily have landed in homes for the impoverished. Or worse.

"You were very lucky your friend gave you such good advice."

"Yes, and I received enough money that I was actually able to return to his store and buy back many of my favorite porcelains just before he set sail to Japan."

I pushed myself back into the chair; my mind was still spinning from her story.

"I hope you have enough to fill your notebook, my dear. I've now divulged all the high points of my life . . . Do you think I've given you enough inspiration?" A throaty laugh escaped her.

"I think enough for at least two novels, *Grand-muman*."

I placed down my pen and pad. How different the air now seemed between us. In the beginning of our relationship, I sat in Marthe's parlor intimidated by her elegance and in awe of her apartment. Now, a true friendship had developed between us. She had shared her life story with me and, now more than ever, I was inspired to craft the material into a novel. With Father away and the war forcing most of us to stay indoors, it seemed like the time was ripe to begin.

"You know, Solange, since I've been spending so much time with you, I've begun to reflect on my own mortality. I look at you, a girl at the peak of her youth with her life ahead of her, and instead of making me feel older, you bring me a surprising sense of comfort." Her gaze traveled toward mine and then lifted toward the window. Outside, the sky had turned a chalk blue.

"I suppose because I never had children around me, ones that I could mark time by the way they grew or the milestones they achieved, I didn't feel the passage of time like most women." She reached over to pour water into the small drinking glass Giselle had left by her side. With Marthe's recent coughing spells, Giselle had been vigilant in making sure there was always a filled pitcher nearby.

The water slid down her throat, and the sound of her swallow was slightly perceptible.

"It has been strange for me to look at a young and bright girl across from me for the past year and a half. It's made me feel more alive to have someone visit me and hear my stories, but it's also forced me to recognize that I am not eternal. I won't be around forever."

I lowered my eyes. Marthe had never appeared sentimental with me before, and I was unsure how to respond.

I shifted my gaze toward her painting.

"Your portrait will be here forever," I said as my eyes focused on the image of Marthe captured in the gilded frame. In the sideways glance of young Marthe, her image seemed omnipresent, as if Boldini had painted her knowing this. He had, in fact, made her immortal.

"Yes, the painting." She let out another small laugh, and now she, too, focused her gaze at herself captured on the canvas.

"Will I always remain above that mantel . . . even for years to come?" She turned toward me, almost as if asking me to seal some sort of promise.

I stole one last look at the portrait and then at Marthe. "Well, if it's within my power. I will do everything to keep it that way."

"It is a wonderful thing to be able to believe in another person's word, and I certainly trust you," she confided. Her eyes closed for a moment and a sense of peace washed over her face. "I am so grateful for that . . ."

"Of course," I said, hoping to reassure her.

"I made mistakes with your father, I realize that. But I don't think I would have been a good mother even if I had kept him." She took a small breath. "Sometimes life gives us a second chance to redeem ourselves."

"Yes," I agreed, "I would like to believe it does."

"And who would have ever thought I'd have a third role in my lifetime. '*Grand-maman.*' I wonder if Charles and Boldini would say my new title suits me?"

I smiled. "I think they'd both say you wear it regally, as you do everything."

"Thank you, my dear," she said, the last word catching in the reverberations of her cough.

"To think now, I'm ending my evening with a glass of water instead of wine or champagne . . . Indeed, Solange, I'm getting old!"

"Well, I must be as well, as I'm off to bed now, and it's only nine thirty," I said, getting up from my chair.

"Beauty sleep is very important . . . Especially if a young woman is intending to meet a gentleman the next morning."

Had I told my grandmother about Alex? I didn't believe I had.

"I'm not sure I know what you're talking about." I was trying to see if she'd reveal her hand.

"Oh, Solange," she said, shaking her head. "I'm an expert on these things." She laughed.

"I could fill an entire notebook of yours on how I am able to read all the signs concerning love."

38.

Solange

March 1940

Marthe had read me correctly. I had made a date with Alex to meet him at his father's store the next day. That morning, I dressed deliberately, inspired by Marthe to make myself look as fetching as possible. I reached for my red dress, instead of my blue one, and fastened a belt around my waist. In the mirror, I pinched my cheeks and applied a little lipstick. Having spent so much time with Marthe, I now understood just how much color could communicate. I gave myself one final glance in the mirror and decided something was still missing. Searching through my drawer, I found a navy scarf edged in white piping. I knotted it around my neck and suddenly felt infinitely more elegant. Only then did I reach for my coat, hat, and gloves.

On the Métro, every person appeared buried in a different newspaper: *Le Monde. Le Figaro. Le Temps.* Each man hid his head behind one like a fan.

Women held the hands of children, their eyes averted, their gaze focused on the ground. When the doors opened up at the Métro stop, I hurried outside, my adrenaline increasing as I knew I was that much closer to seeing Alex again.

It had been a few weeks since I had visited the Marais, as Alex and I had met the last two times at the café in Place Saint Georges. The same winding alleys that had seemed so exotic for me the first time I went to the Armels' bookstore now seemed much more familiar. As I approached Rue des Écouffes, two dark-haired children crouched near the doorway playing with marbles.

I circled around them and pushed through the door.

The bell chimed, and as I entered, the scent of old parchment permeated my nostrils like a familiar perfume. In the back, I could see Alex engrossed in conversation with his father and a man who appeared to be the book restorer, Solomon.

Alex turned and saw me as the door closed.

I saw him motion to excuse himself and he walked toward me, a big smile crossing his lips.

"You're the best sight I've seen today."

"No rare Haggadahs coming into the store this afternoon, then?" I teased.

He leaned closer to me. "What does it say for my future career that I couldn't concentrate on work all day? All I could think about was seeing you."

I felt my temperature warming at his words. "I think it means you might consider another career option," I laughed.

"The shy girl who first came into this store holding her priceless books, has since become emboldened, I see."

"Indeed." My eyes flickered. "Shall we go near the Place des Vosges and have a coffee?"

He smiled. "There isn't anything I'd like to do more."

． ． ．

We left the store and his hand reached for my fingers, his own folding into mine. "Those children are Solomon's," he said as he turned back to look at the children still at play. "His wife has been crying all day. A gentile neighbor back in Germany wrote to him in some sort of code they devised, saying that police had rounded up his brother and sister, along with their families."

He turned to me, his face illuminated by the winter light. "Papa thinks we may have to leave Paris sooner rather than later."

My heart sank.

"But where would you go?"

"North America or South America, I suppose. Isn't that where every European Jew wants to go right now?"

I bit my lip. I felt the desperation wash over me, fearing I was about to be abandoned by someone I had just come to love.

I didn't know how to respond. The mere mention of the word "America" from his lips made it feel as though the floor had been dropped beneath me. Only seconds before, I had felt a light flood through me. Being in Alex's presence, the proximity of his body near mine, filled me with a warmth that had penetrated my skin. But with the news that his family might be emigrating, I felt as though we were engulfed in a dark shadow. Instead of feeling the heat of young love, I felt terribly cold.

"But immigration is incredibly difficult. Do you have family there that can sponsor you?" I was trying to mask my despair by sounding practical. "Are passenger boats even leaving now?"

The papers had already reported about torpedoed ships. I worried it would not even be safe to travel at this point in the war.

"Yes, the waters are more dangerous than ever, but boats are still being chartered. My father has a second cousin in New York. Also a

book dealer. We've written to him, asking if he will sponsor us. If
we can't get the entry visas, there's always South America."

I said nothing. All the excitement I had kept inside my heart for
the past two days, and the happiness I thought I would feel when my
eyes saw Alex again, had vanished.

"But who knows if he can even sponsor us? And the amount of
paperwork needed before anything can actually happen is daunting,
to say the least." Alex sensed my nervousness.

"And I don't want to leave *you*."

My heart lifted at his words.

Before I had a chance to respond, his hand grasped my fingers,
and the sensation that I had felt the first time his skin brushed against
mine, again flooded through my body.

He did not speak. He did not even offer any expression on his
face for me to interpret. He simply pulled me to his lips. His kiss
telling me far more than words ever could.

Alex and I now began to see each other daily. We tried not to speak
about the possibility that he might be leaving for the United States.
Everyone knew how difficult it was to gain sponsorship and to get
a visa, so part of me genuinely believed it was unlikely to happen
soon, if ever. We spent the remainder of the month finding ways to
see each other.

I would bring my journal and write at our favorite café on Place
Saint Georges until he arrived. And it was in those stolen moments,
when our knees touched beneath the table or his hand clasped my
fingers, that I felt I understood the words of my grandmother, that
the touch of one's beloved could resurrect you.

In mid-March, however, Alex received a letter from the French
army announcing his conscription.

It was another moment when words failed us.

The letter was very similar to the one Papa had received. It gave instructions for him to report for his physical, and provided the address where he needed to go register for his unit.

"I was surprised it took them this long to call for me," he said, his voice clearly numb from the news.

"How is your father taking it?" I could only imagine how upset Monsieur Armel must be.

"He's of course blaming himself that he did nothing to prevent it.

"I think this is the first time in my life I ever wished a doctor would tell me I was in poor health, so I could fail my physical." He attempted a forced grin.

My mind raced. Were there things one could take that could help fail a medical exam? If my father were here, I'm sure he would know of drugs that could cause complications.

"There has to be something we can do," I said, my voice cracking. If Alex reported to duty, I knew I'd never see him again. It was one thing when Father had to report to a military hospital. I knew he wouldn't be fighting. But if Alex was right, the French army would treat him as little more than disposable military fodder.

"We must find a solution to get you out of this."

"I told my father he should maim me by dropping his heaviest books on my legs." Alex reached for a way to make me smile.

"No. There must be another way," I said.

He lifted his hands.

"When do they say you report for duty?" I asked him.

I pulled the paper from his hands and studied the date. *March 25, 1940,* was written in typed block letters.

"That gives us five days," I said, counting on my fingers.

"There is nothing we can do, Solange. Half the boys in my class were drafted more than a year ago. I should consider myself lucky I've had this extra time with you."

"Nonsense," I said. "We'll devise a means for your escape." My voice now sounded defiant and full of energy, its strength surprising even myself.

"I would like to believe you could save me," he said as he leaned over the table to kiss me again. This time his fingers ran through my hair, and I could sense that his fear of having just been conscripted made him even more desperate to live as fully as possible before he had to go.

"At least now, I know if anything were to happen to me, Solange, I've experienced love." He paused and lifted his eyes toward mine. "I have you to thank for that."

My own eyes were fighting back tears.

"We have five days, Alex."

He placed his hand on my knee and cupped it through the cloth of my skirt.

"I have the rest of the day just to be with you, Solange. Let's fill it with light."

I placed my hand over his, sealing his invitation with my answer to join him for whatever time we had together.

We rose and headed straight to the Métro. Without either of us speaking, we both knew where we wanted to go.

In the Bois de Boulogne, where courtesans used to ride their carriages and where lovers for centuries found seclusion off the beaten paths, we found shelter under the budding almond trees.

I lay down with Alex in the damp grass. I let his hand travel beneath my skirt. His body pressed against mine. I inhaled his breath between kisses. I ran my fingers through his black, wavy hair, and let him touch every curve of my body without protest.

With my eyes closed, I surrendered under his caresses. I let the young naïve girl melt into the grass, and I allowed my own longing to awaken.

Mapmakers record every cliff, every plateau, with their drafting pen. But lovers use their hands to mark the topography of flesh and bone.

Under the canopy of fragrant trees, my hands memorized the strong contours of Alex's chest through the cotton of his shirt. My thumbs traced the cleaving of his shoulder blades.

Afterward, we wandered toward the pond. Lilies floated softly, and a family of swans navigated the gentle green water.

It was dusk when we finally walked back toward the Métro, our hands laced together. I did not look at Alex in profile. My mind was already full, and I saw him more clearly than if I had used my eyes.

That evening, I did not tell Marthe about any of these passionate moments. But I did go to her and ask her if she knew of any way she could help us.

I was surprised when she eventually asked me for the details of the letters. Alex's name and his address, where and when he was to report to duty.

She could sense my despair even though her own cough and health seemed far worse than the week before.

"This Alex," she said. "I would like for you to bring him to the apartment so I can meet him.

"Time is of the essence," she said. "See if he can come by tomorrow at four o'clock."

39.

Solange

March 1940

Knowing Alex would be coming seemed to reinvigorate Marthe. I watched how she acted buoyantly the following morning as she rose and took her bath. I could see she was taking multiple cups of tea and honey to calm her persistent cough.

In midmorning, she was still in her dressing gown, giving Giselle orders about the menu. Giselle reached into the tin for the extra money she would need to obtain such delicacies in the midst of the war.

By the time Alex arrived, Marthe had transformed back to the way I had first seen her. The beautiful dress. The rope of pearls. A sparkling comb set into her chignon of thick hair.

Her face, which had been gaunt for months, was dusted in powder. Her cheeks were rouged and her eyes glimmered. I had given her something to look forward to, and the sight of her appearing somewhat restored made me immensely happy.

Alex was wearing a suit and tie. He looked older in his elegant clothes. He had smoothed his black curls with pomade and smelled of sandalwood soap and night air.

"You must be Alex," Marthe said, extending her hand. With great politeness, Alex kissed the space just above her fingers.

"*Enchanté*," he said. His slow, deliberate pronunciation delighted my grandmother; for a moment, I could imagine her extending her hand to gentlemen such as Charles or Boldini who arrived at her door.

"My granddaughter has spoken so highly of you." She smiled. "To the salon, shall we?"

He followed her as she gestured in the direction of the parlor. She opened the French doors, and I nearly gasped at the sight of how beautifully Giselle had prepared the room. It wasn't just the array of small tea cakes and petits fours that Giselle had placed on a tiered serving dish. The tall famille rose vase from Marthe's porcelain collection had also been filled with fresh flowers. Roses and lilies of the valley were bursting forth in great abundance from the vase's mouth. The room smelled of the most beautiful perfume.

"Now I know why Solange has said your apartment seems as though time has stood still . . . Why, I would never leave if I lived here." His eyes glinted first toward Marthe and then me.

But soon I saw his focus travel toward the mantel then to Marthe's portrait. I glanced over at her. I now realized this was part of her ritual with every new visitor who walked through the doors of her parlor for the first time. They would meet her first, but the largest impression she would make was when her guests' eyes fell upon Boldini's painting of her.

It was Alex's turn to discover the painting. He stood in front of it, entranced.

"Madame de Florian," he said, prying his eyes away from the sensual portrait. "What an incredibly stunning rendering of you."

Her smile was one of a coquette, even in her seventies. "Well," she uttered, beguiled. "I'm quite flattered you can still discern it is me."

'There is little doubt," he replied, his eyes returning to the portrait. "It's captivating."

"Thank you." I could hear the satisfaction in her voice. Alex had passed her first test, and I was relieved.

"Let's take a seat and have some tea," she said as she gestured for him to sit on one of the bergères.

She rang a small bell to signal Giselle to bring in the tea.

We sipped dark, fragrant tea from porcelain cups and saucers decorated with butterflies and birds, the winged creatures that Marthe so loved. We spoke of Alex's love of rare books, his apprenticeship in his father's shop, and Marthe's passion for Asian ceramics.

It wasn't until the end that she asked Alex about his conscription.

"It is wrong to draft such a cultured young man into the army." She shook her head. "Many men are built for fighting brutes who are natural warriors. And then there are those who have minds suited for wartime strategy. But you are gentle and blessed with an artistic eye."

She looked as though she was appraising him as she spoke. "I can see why my granddaughter has taken such a liking to you."

I felt myself redden with embarrassment.

"*Grand-maman* . . . ," I protested, but she raised her hand to silence me. She would have the last word.

"You seem like a delightful young gentleman," she told him. "And when I look at you, I can imagine you making my granddaughter quite happy. To an old woman like myself, this is a gift."

That evening, as I went to say good night, I saw her at the dining room table.

"Good night, *Grand-maman*," I said sweetly. I came over to her.

"Thank you for today." In her peignoir set, her face naked and without makeup, she looked more vulnerable than she typically appeared. She seemed to be writing something, but she covered her hand to shield me from seeing what it was. I inhaled the scent of flowers from the cream she used on her skin. And I realized that I didn't just love Alex. My heart had also made room for this woman who smelled of rose.

40.

Solange

March 1940

I went to Alex the next day at his father's store. When I arrived, it looked as if half of the inventory had already either been packed away or sold. The shelves were nearly empty, as less than a third of the number of books remained compared to my previous visit.

Standing in the back were Alex, his father, and Solomon. I could hear the faint sound of German being whispered. I knew that Alex's father's family had originally come to Paris from Alsace and it was probably easier for the German-born Solomon to converse with them in his native tongue.

I walked closer to them, my eyes traveling again to the sparse shelves. An ominous feeling washed over me. What if Monsieur Armel had decided he had no other choice but to flee Paris, even at the risk of Alex being imprisoned for ignoring his draft notice?

"Solange." Alex looked up. I could immediately sense the strain on his face.

Monsieur Armel, too, looked far wearier than the last time I had seen him.

"Have you met Solomon Weckstein?" I shook my head. "We're very lucky to have him. He does amazing work with restoring our most delicate manuscripts and books." Monsieur Armel gestured with his hand toward the thin man in the ill-fitting black suit. He was taller than both Alex and his father, but he stood with his shoulders sloped and his neck bent forward as if he were afraid to take up too much space.

"A pleasure to meet you," I said, extending my hand.

Solomon, clearly uncomfortable with my presence, did not take my hand. He only nodded politely. I let my hand fall to my side.

"We have been discussing the need to close the store," Alex said.

"At this point, most of our former clients have no interest in buying anything for their collections. If anything, they want to sell what they already have." Monsieur Armel's eyes fell to the ground as Alex spoke on his behalf.

"And Solomon here is telling Papa that we should just sell everything we have and try to get visas to the United States before it's too late."

I remained quiet.

"But as you know, leaving is impossible for me unless I'm first released from my military service." Alex looked exhausted. "And I don't see that being possible."

"There's no point in me still working without my son at my side." Monsieur Armel's voice sounded shattered. "I built this business to be able to provide for him, with the hope that one day he would take it over," he sighed.

Solomon muttered something in German to Alex, and I saw both he and his father shake their heads no, as if saying whatever he was suggesting was hopeless.

"What does Solomon think?" I sounded desperate.

"He says Papa should do something harmful to my eyes, so I'll fail my medical exam."

"What?" I was incredulous. "What could he possibly do to your eyes?"

Alex shook his head. "He said in Poland, teenage thugs threw acid on the most beautiful Jewish girls' faces, and it not only scarred them, it blinded them, too."

I shuddered at his words, and my fingers instinctively floated to touch my own face. The image of the young girls was horrible and hard to put out of my mind.

We left Alex's father and Solomon. Monsieur Armel had insisted that Alex leave the remainder of the packing to him, as he had only a few more days of freedom left.

"Where will you store everything?" I asked as our hands reached for each other's.

"We'll move the boxes to our apartment. It will be crowded, even with me gone, but the books will be safe there . . ." He seemed confident that his father would be able to manage.

The day was warm and the sky was delft blue. "Let's go somewhere we've never been together before . . . If I have only a few more days with you, I want to see you next to as many different landscapes as I can . . ." He leaned over and kissed me.

This time his kiss was firmer, more passionate. When our lips parted, I could see he was savoring every moment between us.

Although I loathed how time was slipping away so quickly, Alex's kiss felt like a magical box opening inside of me. I now felt beautiful and desirable. And it was as intoxicating as perfume.

We ventured toward the Luxembourg Gardens. We would save our money by forsaking the Métro, and instead walk hand in hand toward the park. On the streets, people clutched their belongings to their chests. Packages wrapped in brown paper. Newspapers that bore the latest Nazi advancements. The looming threat of a German invasion felt like hovering storm clouds, even though all around us were the first signs of spring.

Like the rest of the Parisians, we distracted ourselves with what simple pleasures we could find. On the street, we found a man selling crêpes. Alex reached into his pocket and bought one for us to share.

Our fingers touched as we traded the crêpe between us.

The taste awakened our senses, warm and sweet against our tongues, and inspired us to forsake our shyness.

"Tell me," he said. "Do you write every night?"

I smiled. I felt my eyes dancing as he asked me about the thing I loved to do most in the world.

"I have written every night since I was twelve. My mother was the one who gave me my first leather journal. And I've filled the pages of a dozen others ever since."

"I've always loved to read," he said, sneaking another glance at me. "Not just the classic novels, but the French philosophers, too.

"Voltaire, Montaigne, Rousseau . . . I grew up believing the French valued the rights of the individual. I'm not sure I have that same confidence now. Solomon tells us that, in the end, we will be considered Jewish before French."

I lowered my eyes.

"I suppose I should read some Dumas now. It would provide a well-needed diversion."

"*The Count of Monte Cristo* would be perfect . . . just in case we need to escape from prison," I replied, trying to match his ability to use comic relief. I knew he was trying to return our conversation back to less gloomy waters. Alex could shift between darkness and light. It was a pattern with him. He could be grave one minute talking about the war and flirtatious the next. I enjoyed the undulations in our conversation. He always kept me on my toes.

We were now at the entrance to the gardens. The grass was green, the palace in the center cut majestically against the sky.

Around us, apple blossoms lifted off of their branches floated in the wind like snow. Pigeons landed on the pebbled pavement and then took flight again as our shoes crunched on the sandy taupe-colored gravel. The walk from the Marais had been lengthy, and now we looked for a place to sit.

I pointed to a park bench under one of the many elm trees that lined the grounds. With his hands now free, Alex reached for my fingers and pulled me to where we could finally sit down.

He kissed me again. "Will you write in your journals about my kisses?" he said as he reached now to touch my hair.

"I will write about everything," I said, closing my eyes. I lifted my lips toward his once again.

What I didn't tell him was that when I sat down to write, it wouldn't be only his kisses I would remember, but also the ache in my heart that he was leaving. It is a terrible thing to feel so powerless. I wanted to rewrite our destiny in my journal. I wanted to believe that I wouldn't lose yet another person I loved.

41.

Marthe

March 1940

My *dear Antoine,* Marthe wrote as she pulled out her stationery. Over the years, she had written countless letters of correspondence on the paper with the gold embossed butterfly, but now she paused as to what to write next. She ran her hand over the heavy bonded paper. She pressed her finger to the butterfly. This one needed to be drafted with particular care.

> *I am not sure if you will remember me, as so many years have*
> *passed since we last saw each other. Then, you were a young major,*
> *and I have since learned you are now a general. I write not because*
> *of our mutual love of art and painting, but because of something*
> *even more personal. I do not like to ask for favors. It is also not my*
> *nature to interfere with the government or matters that concern*
> *men of power. But if you remember that evening we spent in front*
> *of my Boldini portrait, our discussions of your mother's art and*

talent, and that one night we shared thereafter, you will recall that
what fueled me both then and now as an old lady, are the things in
life that keep our hearts aflutter and our blood warm. And so you
must realize, I am writing about love . . .

She continued crafting the letter, her pen rolling over the paper
as smoothly as a skate on ice. Her words were well chosen, and her
emotions pressed deeply into every sentence. She remembered how
powerless she had been to save Charles. But her heart was now
flooded with a different type of emotion. It wasn't the physical, amorous love that besotted the young. She instead saw herself on the
outside, a voyeur to both her granddaughter's burgeoning happiness
and the potential for it to be destroyed.

She did not know if the letter would reach the officer, or if what
she wrote would ultimately have any effect on what she was attempt-
ing. But she wrote anyway. For even when he had been a young major,
Antoine d'Angelis had surprised her with his sensitivity, and she
knew she had to try. She had to believe that even if their connection
was brief, it had been unique. She had even sent him a wedding gift
when she read in the newspaper that he was engaged.

That afternoon, Marthe did not ask Giselle to post the letter. She
vowed to do it herself. As her fingers let go of the envelope in the
mailbox, she turned to hear some rustling in the linden trees behind
her. There on the branch were two stock doves, their beaks pecking
at each other playfully. She took it as an auspicious sign. All her life,
something in the constellations changed for the better whenever she
was in the company of birds.

42.

Solange

March 1940

Time became a form of currency. We counted days, hours, even minutes together as though they were precious coins.

He told me he had written a letter to his father and one to me should he not return.

"Don't think like that," I told him. "You will come back."

"I am hardly a soldier," he said. His eyes were bloodshot. "And even if I were, the Germans have the superior army."

"You haven't slept. You're not thinking clearly," I insisted.

"I am not worried about myself. It's my fear for you and my father that keep me up at night."

"We will be fine. Perhaps my grandmother will let your father come live with us, too," I said, hoping to soften his angst with humor, a trick I had learned from him.

I succeeded in making him smile.

"Now *that* would be worthy of a novel." He laughed, and I realized at that moment, the sound of his happiness restored me.

We reached for each other's hands again. The touch of his skin. The warmth of his blood. Our fingers searched for each other, the roots of two trees entwined.

"Let's get lost again today," he urged, looking at his watch.

I thought of my grandmother. First, her life in the shadows with Charles, and now still ensconced in an apartment where time stood still. How I wanted to shut its doors and retreat there from the world with Alex by my side.

"Yes, let's . . . ," I whispered to him. I yearned for the security of the shadows. I didn't want either of us to ever be found.

In those five days, we had become experts in finding the most secluded wooded areas in Paris. In every garden that had once belonged to a courtier, we found the hidden canopies and discovered each other with our hands and lips.

I now knew the language of caresses, the music of escalated breath. I understood that kisses could leave their own imprint. That skin retained the memory of a lover's touch, like a fossil pressed into stone.

When he left, I felt his fingers still around me. His palms that had mapped my thighs. His warm mouth on my neck. I discovered his fragrance in the perfume of freshly cut grass. His voice was always in my ear, even after he had departed. It was like a song I carried inside my head.

When I returned to my grandmother's apartment, my face betrayed my anguish. Two days remained, and then Alex would be gone.

I went straight to my room. I had brought Marthe's radio to my bedside so I could listen to the news reports at night. And now I wanted to smash it to the floor. I hated the war. I hated how little control we had over our lives. I flung myself on the bed and began to cry.

"Please invite Alex and his father for dinner tomorrow night." I sat at the long dining room table with Marthe. She was wrapped in her dressing gown, her face without makeup. She looked almost translucent, as her weight loss had made the angles of her face more pronounced. Her eyes were hard upon me.

"I don't think it will be possible, *Grand-maman*. It will be his last night before he has to report to his military training. I think he'll want to spend the evening alone with his father."

"Nonetheless, you will need to find a way to get them both here." She took a deep breath, and the sound alarmed me. Her breathing sounded raspy, her chest as hollow as a drum.

"Have you seen your doctor about that cough?" I asked, changing the subject. "I'm concerned." In front of her was a plate of poached chicken and julienned vegetables that Giselle had prepared. Since we sat down, Marthe had hardly taken a forkful.

"Don't avoid what I just asked of you, Solange." A cough escaped her. She quickly tried to muffle it with her hand, but it intensified. Her face became a painful shade of red.

"Let me get you some water." I reached over for the pitcher and refilled her glass.

She shook her head. "All I want is for you to find a way to get them here for dinner tomorrow night. You must, Solange. I insist."

I had no idea how I would manage to get both the Armels to come, but the next morning I put on a dress the color of marigolds and tied my hair back with a white satin ribbon I had found in Giselle's clipping basket.

Only a few days before when I walked into their shop, there were still a few volumes on the bookshelves. Now, every shelf was empty.

The bell on the door that announced my arrival left a chill in the air. Without anything to sell, the store seemed like an empty tomb.

"Alex?" My voice sounded nervous. The door had been open. I knew someone had to be in the store.

"Alex?" I repeated.

I waited for several seconds, although it felt like several minutes. Suddenly I heard a rustle. It was Monsieur Armel.

"Solange." He said my name softly. "You're a sight for weary eyes."

I stepped closer. He looked so tired. His pale eyes were dim and watery. His hair was out of place. Fatigue and sadness had aged him in a matter of days.

"You must be looking for Alex . . . not me." He forced himself to smile.

"It's always a pleasure to see you, Monsieur Armel."

He reached for my hand and pressed it between his two cupped palms. I was used to the sensation of Alex's skin against mine: warm and soft. The cool papery sensation of Monsieur Armel's saddened me, while Alex's touch had always made me feel alive.

"He will be back shortly. He needed to do an errand for me." He let go of my hand and motioned for me to sit down.

In the same chairs where I had discovered the story of my grandfather and his rare books, I now sat with Monsieur Armel, with hardly a word between us. The glimmer in his eyes that had once ignited when he saw my rare Haggadah was now replaced with a sense of defeat.

If my heart was heavy because of Alex's imminent departure, his father's heart was drowning.

"I am sorry," he apologized, lifting his chin. "I don't even have tea to offer you. Everything is already packed. Today is the last day left on our lease here."

"It's quite all right," I said, forcing a smile. "I already had some this morning."

He nodded and I noticed he was wringing his hands.

"So many of us are losing our sons just before Passover. The irony has not been lost on any of us."

"I am so sorry . . ." It was hard to find any other words.

"The Jewish Telegraphic Agency reported this week that over sixty thousand Jewish boys are in the French legion. And now the army is taking boys like my son."

He took a deep breath and raised his head in my direction.

"I have lived my whole life coveting beautiful treasures from centuries past. I've held books in my hands that have withstood flooding, fires, and raids. But nothing is more precious than a child. I would do anything in the world to save my son and yet, I am completely powerless to help him."

Monsieur Armel's voice broke off.

I walked over to place my hand on his back. I felt his bones beneath the tweed and was struck by how fragile he had become.

"I, too, wish I could do something." The words broke in my throat. I swallowed them, painful as bits of glass.

"He should be here any moment." I felt Monsieur Armel's back straighten beneath my palm. "We will do him no favors if he sees we are already mourning him.

"So please, no tears, Solange."

I nodded.

Just then we both heard the jangle of the bell and Alex's voice fill the air.

"Papa?" The sound of his voice made my heart flutter.

I could hear his approaching footsteps.

When he reached the back of the store, his face brightened at the sight of me.

"Solange?" A smile formed across his face. "What a wonderful surprise."

"I knew today would be hectic for you." I stumbled out an apology. "It's almost unfathomable to imagine that tomorrow you'll be getting your uniform."

I struggled to continue. "I have no idea if you've even begun to pack . . ."

Alex's eyes softened. "I packed this morning. I probably have too many socks." He tried to make a joke, but neither Monsieur Armel nor I could bring ourselves to laugh.

"I must confess the reason that I'm here. In addition to wanting to see you before you leave, my grandmother has put me up to some unexpected business."

Alex pulled off his jacket and placed it on the chair. "And what sort of business might that be?"

"It's a social request on her part." I blushed.

Alex's face suddenly turned curious.

"I know my timing must seem callous considering how precious every last moment with Alex is for you . . ."

I took a deep breath. "But my grandmother would like to extend an invitation for both of you to come to dinner tonight."

I was so confident that Monsieur Armel would politely decline, that I had already imagined his voice conveying their regrets. It took me by complete surprise when I heard him say: "I think we will all be grateful for the distraction, dear Solange. So please tell your grandmother we are very appreciative of her request."

They arrived at half past seven. Monsieur Armel and Alex both in dark suits. One could see their resemblance now that they were both dressed in their best clothes. Monsieur's white hair was smoothed back in pomade, his glacial blue eyes piercing. It appeared he had undertaken great lengths to camouflage his mental anguish.

That afternoon we had heard that Hitler was directing his troops toward Norway. Their footsteps were pounding across Europe, boots striking against pavement and arms raised in Fascist salute. Food was increasingly scarce in Paris. Giselle had to bribe the butcher to get even a few scraps to make a pot-au-feu. But Marthe was at her finest when it came to creating a stage of beauty out of almost nothing.

My grandmother, who had looked fragile for weeks, had transformed herself from the last time I had seen her, just as Alex's father had from this morning. She stood in front of her painting, her hair perfectly coiffured, her face radiant with the arrival of new guests.

I saw Monsieur Armel take a step back, as though he had walked into something wholly unexpected. Grandmother opened her arms like a great actress greeting an audience from the stage.

"Monsieur Armel . . . Alex . . . I'm so delighted you've come."

She came alive that evening. Her arms danced as she spoke. Her eyes glimmered. I saw her as a coquette, as a hostess, and as a femme fatale, who used every word, every movement, to charm.

Monsieur Armel softened under the gentle haze of candlelight. The man who only hours before had sat forlornly in an empty storeroom now seemed rejuvenated in Marthe's presence. He began to speak of his love of books, and illuminated manuscripts, passions that Marthe knew all too well could inspire the spirit and imagination.

And Marthe spoke of her own love of collecting. Her porcelains. Her foray into paintings and being an artist's muse. Although she did not collect books and certainly nothing connected to Judaica, both she and Monsieur Armel soon bonded over their mutual appreciation of all that revealed the imprint of the artist's hand.

Giselle served chocolate mousse for dessert, and I saw how slowly Alex ate each spoonful. I could sense how he savored the sweetness of the cream, as though each mouthful might be his last.

"You must be on good terms with your dairy," Monsieur Armel said after he had made sure nothing remained of his chocolate mousse.

Marthe laughed. "We do our best." I noticed, however, she had not lifted her own spoon.

As the hours ticked away and it seemed clear that midnight would soon be upon us, I heard Alex's voice come softly into the chatter.

"I think we should be going, Papa. I must leave in the morning." His voice, although quiet as a child's, sliced through the air.

Marthe placed her hands on the edge of the dining room table. "But I have not served the last course yet, Alex."

His eyes widened and his mouth opened as though he was about to apologize for what appeared to be a misjudgment in manners.

Marthe rose and walked toward the console. Next to a bowl of fruit was an envelope.

"It's a letter from an old friend of mine. General Antoine d'Angelis," she said as she pressed it into Alex's hands. I could see that the red seal on the back of the envelope had already been broken. "Open it, Alex. I think you will like very much what it says."

We all fell silent. I looked over at my grandmother, who now stood next to Alex. The official white stationery from General d'Angelis fluttered slightly in his fingers.

Alex read the letter to himself before reading it aloud. And when he realized the words indicated he would be dismissed from serving in the French army, he stopped midsentence and put the letter down.

"Can this really be?"

"Sometimes a woman can manage to call in a favor," Marthe said as she returned to her seat. She folded her hands in her lap and smiled. I hadn't ever seen her look so pleased.

"Can what be?" Monsieur Armel's voice was impatient.

Alex turned to Marthe. "How did you manage this? It cannot be true."

"Oh, but I assure you, dear Alex, it is."

"But what does it say, Alex?" I reached across and touched Alex's wrist and squeezed it.

"It says I have been dismissed from duty."

My eyes darted to Marthe, who was now beaming. Enthroned in the tall wooden dining room chair, she appeared triumphant.

Monsieur Armel, however, looked as though he was in a state of disbelief. Even I struggled to believe the contents of the letter were true.

"I have no words," Monsieur Armel's voice rattled. "I have never been one to believe in miracles."

Marthe smiled. "No one is asking you to believe in miracles." Marthe's eyes looked over to me, then to Alex. "Instead, I ask you to believe in love.

"I am an old lady now. And Solange is really the only connection to family I have. It is a gift to see her and Alex together."

"I don't know how we will ever repay our gratitude." Monsieur Armel still looked as if he was in shock.

"There is no need to thank me." Marthe raised her glass. "It has been a gift for me in my old age to witness my granddaughter falling in love."

My face warmed as she looked over to me. I had never believed my grandmother to be sentimental, but once again she had surprised me.

I met her gaze and at that moment we both exchanged a look of gratitude, communicated solely through our eyes.

She took another sip of wine and pressed her fingers to her chest, stifling her cough.

In the few seconds we waited for her to speak, I focused on Alex. He was still studying the letter, as though he couldn't believe what it said.

With her voice returned to her, Marthe lifted her glass again in the gesture of a toast. "Let young love be our lantern in times of peril."

Monsieur Armel lifted his glass and looked in the direction of Alex and me.

And for a moment, everything seemed perfect. Time stood exquisitely still. Marthe had managed to give us a gift of unexpected possibility. We savored it as though it were something that was connected to the magic of her apartment and the woman who lived as though the unrest outside did not permeate her silk-upholstered walls. I pressed it deep within me. I saw life return to Monsieur Armel's eyes, and relief wash over Alex. And my own heart was restored, the worry temporarily alleviated. I saw it all as though it were a moving painting, captured within a golden frame.

After Alex and his father left later that evening, I found my grandmother sitting alone in the parlor. She was ensconced on the sofa, her dressing gown wrapped tightly around her, her face without a trace of makeup.

She sat in profile, her body slightly twisted, with her legs curled beneath her and her chin titled upward toward her portrait. It would have made a striking painting, the dual images of Marthe. The first when she was at the zenith of her beauty and youth, hovering over the second, older image, which struck me as somehow more pure.

I stood at the threshold for several seconds watching her, careful not to make a sound so I could continue to observe her from afar. A sheaf of moonlight streamed through the window, and a single candle burned at her side. The setting reminded me of an old master painting. The quiet repose of a fragile, aging woman, wrapped in oyster gray silk with the painting behind her, as bright as a burning star.

After a few seconds, I walked toward her. "*Grand-maman*," I said as I sat down beside her. I had never before joined her on the small love seat where she perched herself, instead always preferring the chair positioned across. But now I made it a point to settle in next to her.

Her white hands were clasped in front of her. I reached and lifted one, taking it into my own.

"Thank you so much." I did not whisper. I said the words plain and straight, to emphasize how much I truly meant them.

She turned and met my eyes. Her fingers grasped my own.

"I never expected you, Solange. I assumed I would live out my life alone in this apartment surrounded by my things. With just a few words each day uttered between me and my maid."

"I did not expect you, either," I said. My eyes were betraying me, as I felt the onset of tears. "I suppose we have Papa to thank for our union," I said, forcing a smile.

"Henri . . ." She said his name as though he were something that had slipped through her fingers. Something that would never be hers to own.

"Yes, he did bring us together. I will always be grateful. Though he has no love for me, he gave an old woman a gift, even if it wasn't deserved."

She shook her head. "I understand his hurt that I gave him up, but I had no way of supporting a child then. Louise did me a great favor, and she loved him and gave him a good home."

I nodded. I understood, even if my father did not. I remembered the details from when she first shared them with me.

"Now that I'm old, I am more reflective of what I am leaving behind." She lifted her eyes toward her painting. "I once told Charles that when I died, all that would be known about me was my painting. That I was an illusion otherwise." Her eyes returned to me. "But now you know my story, and you still didn't leave me after you heard it to the end."

"But it's not the end, *Grand-maman*," I interjected. "There are so many more chapters to be written. And, hopefully, they will include me."

Her fingers squeezed mine again. This time even more tightly than the last. "Yes," she said softly.

"This is what makes a story beautiful . . . more poignant . . ."

Marthe's gaze suddenly shifted inward, as though she was searching for something that eluded her grasp.

"If I can leave behind more than a painting, if I can ensure that you have love in your life and someone beside you, then I have redeemed myself a bit, no?"

"Of course, you have more than redeemed yourself. You've saved Alex's life."

She closed her eyes as I lowered her hand to her lap.

And we remained still. Our heads tilting toward each other, a warmth floating between us. And no longer was there a need for words.

43.

Solange

April 1940

The next morning, I awakened refreshed and happy. With the gift of General d'Angelis's letter, it felt as though a heavy brick had lifted from my chest. I no longer imagined Alex dying alone in a trench or in a far-off military hospital. I pulled my legs out from beneath the white linen and stretched my toes. Sunlight poured in through the little diamond-cut window above my bed.

I slid my arms into my robe, knotted the sash, and walked toward the kitchen. I could hear the sound of water running and suspected Giselle was already hard at work cleaning up from what remained of last night's dinner.

"Good morning," I said when I saw her. She was bent over the sink scrubbing a pot with some soap and steel wool. Her apron was spotted with water.

She lifted her head toward me, then pulled out her hands and dried them on her apron.

"You are up earlier than I expected, mademoiselle. I'm sorry I haven't yet prepared your breakfast tray."

"Don't worry," I said, walking over toward the stove to retrieve the kettle. "I can do it myself. We left you with extra work after last night's dinner."

"I was glad to see madame so happy," she said as she removed the pot from the sink so I could fill the kettle.

"Still, I'm glad she is sleeping in today . . ." She placed the pot to the side and began drying it. "She tires so easily now."

It was true. It wasn't just the cough and weight loss I had noticed; Grandmother was retiring to her bedroom right after dinner.

"And I'm sure you've noticed, madame no longer seems to have an appetite."

I nodded. I had noticed that Marthe hardly ever touched her food anymore.

"You can imagine how much difficulty I have trying to get the right ingredients for her menu, and when I see she doesn't eat a morsel . . . well I know something must be wrong, mademoiselle."

I had been aware that something was ailing Marthe for weeks now, and I was relieved that Giselle had brought it up.

"Has she seen a doctor?"

Giselle stepped back from the sink and reached behind her back to unknot her apron strings.

"Madame *has* seen the doctor." She looked down at the tile floor. "She made arrangements for Dr. Payard to visit her here when you go out on your errands."

I looked puzzled. "Why would she feel the need for such secrecy? She knows I would only show concern for her."

"Madame is most private about things. But I am ashamed to say that I eavesdropped while he examined her in her bedroom."

I said nothing, waiting for Giselle to relay what she had heard.

"He told her that he wanted her to come to his office for some further tests. That he had reason to be concerned."

"Did she agree to go?"

"No. She told him she didn't want a diagnosis. She said even if he were to tell her she was dying, it wouldn't change a thing. She was going to live out her life as she always had."

"This is ridiculous . . . If there is something we can do to help her, we must encourage it."

"Madame is modern in some ways, and wholly old-fashioned in others. Surely, you realize she intends to keep her illness a secret. She is a very proud woman, Mademoiselle Solange. She will do everything in her power to hide it behind her face powder and lipstick."

I knew what Giselle said was true.

"I always believed it would be just the two of us here at the end. But now I am bolstered by the fact that you've come into her life. That she has managed to forge a connection with someone who shares her blood.

"She has been good to me." Giselle's eyes were now moist. "When my husband died, she paid for his funeral. Two days later, a basket of the most beautiful children's clothes arrived at my doorstep and a basket of food from Fauchon's. She could have sent both from a middle-of-the-road merchant, but she sent the best. Even for me, her maid."

I helped Giselle finish drying the pots and waited there hoping to hear Grandmother stirring from her bedroom.

"Let her sleep, Giselle," I insisted. "You go out and enjoy your day."

I was anxious to see Alex. I wanted to be alone with him and talk freely. I wanted to feel his hand in mine and walk through the park; I wanted to breathe in the fresh spring air. But I felt conflicted knowing that Marthe was in her room suffering.

I walked out of the kitchen, down the golden parquet floors in the hallway to the far room where Marthe slept. I slowly opened the door to catch a glimpse of her.

Marthe was asleep with a silk mask over her eyes. Her long hair was let out from its combs and flowed over her shoulders. At the crown of her hair, I could see the roots coming in all white.

She appeared majestic as she slept. It was my second time seeing her in bed, and her silk upholstery with the embroidered butterflies once again enthralled me. I wondered what she dreamt of now that she no longer had suitors calling her, the salons she had hosted years before were now a thing of the past. I wondered if when she dreamt she saw herself as that young, beautiful being that Boldini had painted above the mantel, or if she ever dreamt of me.

44.

April 1940

As Marthe slept, I left the apartment in search of Alex. Outside, the almond blossoms covered the pavement in a blanket of white petals. I tried to savor the gift that Marthe had given us, the knowledge that Alex would not be sent to war. It amazed me how each day could differ from the next. Only yesterday, I believed it might be the last time I would hold Alex's hand. Today, I was given a reprieve. But I also suspected Monsieur Armel would now be working as hard as possible to secure a way for him and Alex to leave Europe.

I knew better than to look for Alex at the shop in the Marais, as the Armels had given up the lease. I suspected the two of them would be at their residence on the Rue Chardon-Lagache. I took the Métro close to their address and then searched for a phone box on the street to let him know I was in close proximity.

"I'm near your apartment," I told Alex from the phone box.

"You're welcome to visit us here," he said. "But don't be surprised if Papa hugs you. He is still floating from all that happened last night."

I laughed. "I'll be over in just a minute."

Once outside their building, I pressed the buzzer and pushed the door open. It was a beautiful classical building much like Marthe's. A checkerboard of marble stretched across the lobby floor. The walls were painted in an opaque chalk white. In the center of the lobby was an iron-caged elevator, but I opted instead for the stairs. By the time I reached the fifth-floor landing, Alex had already opened the door.

"Good morning." He kissed me on both cheeks. "Now when I see that smile on your face, I realize yesterday evening wasn't a dream."

"No, it wasn't." I stepped into the apartment. "I told you my grandmother possessed a bit of magic."

"You weren't joking, were you?"

"I hardly ever joke," I teased.

"Come, let me tell Papa you're here. He's in the library sorting through some boxes from the store."

I followed him down the hall and through a set of French doors. The room opened and revealed an extensive library. If Grandmother's apartment smelled like a garden of flowers, the Armels' was rich with the fragrance of books. The perfume of ink and wood pulp. The smells of leather and hide.

I breathed in deeply. How I loved the scent.

"Solange!" Monsieur Armel stood up from his desk to greet me. "After last night I should call you my angel." He opened up his arms and embraced me.

"Please pardon our appearance. Alex and I live like woodsmen here," he laughed, releasing me from his arms. "The books are our trees."

"I only wish my mother could have seen all this," I said as I gestured to the floor-to-ceiling shelves. My eyes took in the old bindings in red Valiant leather with gilt-embossed titles. In the corner of the room was a movable ladder that slid across the shelves. "She would have been amazed."

"Your grandfather's apartment was equally as filled with books just as ours. Perhaps he had even more . . ."

I scanned the room again and tried to imagine my mother living in an apartment just like this one. I had always thought her bookshelf in our living room was formidable, but to live amidst all these works, some of them priceless in value, seemed incredible.

Monsieur Armel's eyes traveled over his crowded shelves and the stack of books on his desk, and he shook his head. "We've acquired too much over the past two years. So many families left, and I bought their inventory. I hedged my bets incorrectly, it seems. I thought they were all foolish for leaving Paris. But now I'm here writing urgent letters to America, buried in a tomb of books, while they're all safely across the Atlantic."

He came over and squeezed Alex's shoulder. "But I still consider myself a lucky man after last night."

I smiled. I, too, was thankful. "It was an extraordinary evening. I still can't believe it all happened."

"Come." He gestured for me to follow him deeper into the room. "I want to give your grandmother a gift to show her Alex's and my gratitude." He walked toward the far side of the library and began to climb the ladder.

"Careful, Papa," cautioned Alex.

"I have been climbing ladders for years, Alex. This is the least of my worries."

From the top shelf, he pulled down a slender volume.

"Perhaps she'll enjoy this one." He placed his palms on the dark brown leather cover. Around the perimeter was a floral design that had been tooled into the leather and rubbed afterward with gilt. "It's a book of poetry from the Ottoman empire. The illustrations reflect an Oriental influence, so I suspect it will appeal to her artistic sensibility." He closed his eyes as if he were conjuring up an image of Marthe before him.

"Even though your grandmother won't be able to decipher the words, I think she'll enjoy the illustrations and calligraphy."

"How thoughtful of you," I said, as I gently traced a finger over the cover's sensual, arabesque design. "I'm sure it will delight her."

"Please tell her how grateful we are for what she's done for me," Alex added as he locked his eyes with me. "I'm still in a state of disbelief . . ."

"We would also like to reciprocate with a dinner at our apartment . . . ," Monsieur Armel interrupted. "It is the first night of Passover in a little over two weeks' time. Solomon's wife, Rachel, will make dinner at our apartment. Do you think you and your grandmother might wish to come?"

His invitation touched me in its warmth and intimacy. But as much as I wanted to go, I did not think Marthe would join me.

"My grandmother seldom leaves her apartment, as her health has been rather fragile lately. But it would be my pleasure to come."

"Well, still, please ask her," Monsieur Armel insisted. "The meal will be simple and the accommodations far less sumptuous, but we'd be honored to welcome her into our home."

I promised them both that I would ask her.

I left the Armel residence shortly afterward and entered the warm early afternoon light. I decided to use my extra time to return to my old apartment and retrieve a few lightweight dresses and some additional notebooks. I knew I still had quite a few empty ones stored away in my desk.

Although the Métro would have been faster, I opted to walk through the Gardens of Avenue Foch. With Alex no longer heading off to war, I wanted to savor this rare pause of calm. I knew Alex's father would continue making plans to leave France. But this afternoon my heart felt as if it were a tightly petaled flower that was finally opening to the warmth of spring. I wanted to walk amongst beauty, under the shade of protective elm trees, and feel the joy of being alive.

Along the winding paths lined by the canopy of foliage, I watched young children ride their tricycles, and a nanny as she stretched out a large blanket and offered two little girls and their dolls tiny ceramic cups of tea.

My attention softened as I walked the quiet path. I hadn't written in my journal for several days, not wanting to waste a single moment of those hours I could spend with Alex. But now I felt the familiar urge to once again return to my writing.

Less than an hour later, I emerged from the gardens and set off to the closest Métro station to take me closer to home. Once in my own neighborhood, I passed by Augustin's grocery shop, the Alsatian baker, and the crèmerie where my mother and I had always shopped. When I reached the doorstep of our old apartment building, I stood outside for several seconds, surprised that I felt the need to adjust my eyes to what I saw. For well over a year and a half I had traveled between my grandmother's apartment and my own, slipping seamlessly between both worlds. But now the modesty of our own building felt somehow jarring.

I turned the key and pressed open the heavy door. Once inside, I immediately noticed that the lobby didn't smell of marble and brass as in Grandmother's or the Armels' building. Rather, a vague mustiness clung to the air. Beneath my feet, the linoleum tile was worn and in need of replacement. The walls were not chalk white, but rather the color of yellowed, faded paper. Although my father had

stopped the mail, I took the newsprint flyers from the box, and slowly
began to mount the stairs.

Our apartment looked like a dollhouse when I entered. The wooden
furniture. The dishes in the cupboard that were white and functional.
On the kitchen table sat the radio with the Bakelite dials. If the books
on the living room shelf reminded me of my mother, that radio connected me to my father. Immediately, I felt a void when I saw it, a
palpable longing to see him again. I yearned for that hum of the radio
as we searched for a station on which we could hear the news. I
wanted the comforting sight of his mustache, his eyes framed by his
wire-rimmed glasses. The security of his measured voice, his unflap-
pable ability to never appear frightened or alarmed. It felt strange
that the onset of the war had brought us closer, only to take him
away from me just when we were beginning to form a connection.

I moved through the apartment, I felt my father's absence
profoundly, and it seemed almost like trespassing to be there without him. I could see traces of his last movements as I glanced around
the apartment. The icebox had been defrosted, the door left open.
The toaster had been unplugged. On his desk was an open-faced
ledger with the list of utility companies and a notation showing they
had been contacted and knew to forward the bills to his new address
at the military hospital. His last gestures were like a marble frieze,
every action showing his careful and meticulous nature in high relief.

I entered my bedroom and looked at it with fresh eyes. It was
darker and more crowded than I had remembered it. I had grown
accustomed to my small room at Marthe's—the elegant rosewood
desk and the diamond-shaped window that cast a kaleidoscope of
colors during the different hours of the day. I scanned the shelves
filled with not only my books and journals, but also my many knickknacks and souvenirs: the porcelain rabbit where I had once stored

the coins of my weekly allowance, and the milk jar that contained my vast marble collection. Tucked in the corner was a Mickey Mouse doll that my father had uncharacteristically bought for me after taking me to the cinema to see *Steamboat Willie* when I was still young enough to hold his hand.

I knelt down and reached for my mother's old carpetbag from underneath my bed and pulled it open. I knew I could place my two remaining spring dresses and a few notebooks inside its deep vault of black-skinned leather. I went to my wardrobe and took out my dresses. Both were the same A-line flattering cut with a nipped waist and flared skirt that hovered just over the knee. One was in navy crepe and the other in a red chevron stripe. I put the notebooks on the bottom of the bag and carefully laid the folded dresses on top. On the way out, I was overcome with wanting something from my father. I reached for the Mickey Mouse doll and squeezed it inside the bag.

45.

April 1940

A Seder?" Marthe said the word as though it was the name of an exotic fruit she had never tasted before. "Why, it sounds intriguing. I actually think I would like to go, Solange."

She held the book of Turkish poetry that the Armels had gifted to her between her paper-white hands.

"I haven't been out since that night with you a few weeks ago, and of all the salons and parties I've participated in over the years, I've never once attended a Passover meal." Marthe looked out the window. "Perhaps I'll wear my trousers." She grinned mischievously. "The occasion does sound rather exotic."

"And you would look quite smart if you did . . ." I laughed. I was pleased she was considering their invitation.

She shook her head. "You might find this surprising, but I have a great affinity for the Jews. They're a smart and cultured race . . .

"And when your mother came here that first time, when she and your father were announcing their engagement, I immediately sensed she was a *Juive*."

I felt a little stab in my heart when she spoke and I stiffened, bracing myself to hear something that would shatter the warm and protective feelings I had recently come to have for my grandmother.

"She was beautiful. An oval face with almond-shaped eyes. Her skin was slightly olive. And her last name, Cohen . . . it was a telltale sign of her ancestry." I could feel Marthe looking at me and contrasting the memory she still had in her mind of my then twentysomething-year-old mother.

"You have her eyes, her dark hair, and the same exotic beauty. And, of course, her intelligence . . ."

A sense of relief washed over me. I had been fearful Marthe might say something anti-Semitic in relation to my mother. Had she done so, the affection that had grown in my heart for her over the past year would have been tarnished.

"I feel guilty that I didn't embrace your parents more fully when they arrived brimming with their young love. When I reflect on it now, I realize I was threatened by your mother. It was clear she possessed a great deal of wisdom behind those beautiful eyes of hers." Marthe's words sounded almost as if they were uttered as a confession.

"I was haughty and narcissistic that afternoon, Solange. And when they came a few months later to tell me about the pregnancy, I barely acknowledged it."

She took a deep breath.

"It was an error on my part that I've come to regret . . ." Her eyes looked out toward the window, never once looking at her portrait as she normally did. For several minutes neither of us said a word. The quiet between us filled the room.

. . .

We spent the next two hours together. I sat beside Marthe on the gray sofa, looking at the pages of the book that Monsieur Armel had given her. Marveling at the illustrations, our fingers carefully turned the parchment pages together.

"Have I ever shown you the two books I have from my mother's collection?" I asked, though I knew full well that I had never shared them with her.

"No," she answered. "But I would love to see them."

I excused myself and walked toward my new bedroom and pulled out my suitcase, where they were protected in layers of brown paper.

I returned, holding them protectively to my chest. Then I unwrapped them in front of her.

"These belonged to my mother's father, Moishe Cohen," I said.

I lifted the dark brown Haggadah and the *Zemirot Yisrael* from the paper and brought them over to her.

I placed the Barcelona Haggadah in her hands, and set the slender *Zemirot* book to the side. As Marthe touched the outer cover, I could see the collector in her come alive before me. She pored over every detail, appraising the outside before entering its inner pages.

"See how the book opens from left to right . . ." I reached over and lifted the left corner of the cover to open the first page. Her eyes widened and I watched as her finger delicately touched the vellum corner.

"Is this Hebrew?" she asked. I watched as her eyes scanned the calligraphic lines executed in dark black ink.

"Yes, the text is written by a rabbi and the illustrations were painted by his wife."

"It's extraordinary," Marthe said in a hushed tone. I could see she was transfixed, just as I had first been upon seeing it.

"The slender volume is a book of poetry by Israel Najara, printed in Venice in the sixteenth century. But, this one," I said, touching the heavy brown cover of the Barcelona Haggadah, "Monsieur Armel says is an extremely rare fourteenth-century Haggadah from Spain."

My voice floated through the parlor. I was now the storyteller to Marthe. For well over a year I had listened to her tell the story of her life, of her ascent from the alleys of Montmartre to this treasure-filled apartment in the ninth arrondissement. But now we had switched places, and it was she who was listening to my every word. Under the hush of the room, in the comfort of the velvet furniture, I began to tell Marthe the story of my mother's family and these two priceless books that now rested between us. The very books that had initially brought me to the Armels' store.

I spoke slowly and in a carefully measured voice, just as Marthe had always done when she shared her stories with me.

"The book was in my grandfather's collection, and it was one of the few Mother saved upon his death. According to Monsieur Armel, the Haggadah was written and illustrated by a rabbi and his wife. The rabbi's wife possessed a rare gift that few people, let alone women, had at that time. She knew not only how to paint, but to work with gold leaf. Her collaboration on the Haggadah is one of the reasons it is so unique. It is one of the only prayer books known to have been illustrated by a female hand."

Marthe listened quietly. I watched as she turned another page and marveled at the deep red and lapis blue design around the perimeter.

"It took them nearly twenty years to complete it."

"I can imagine." Marthe paused over the illustration of the family at the Seder table. The patriarch with his arms open and children seated around him.

"I've been told the book is priceless not only because it's several hundred years old, and the only one made by their hands, but also because it is symbolic of the love between them."

"How beautiful to think their love continues to exist through the ancient pages of the text," Marthe said as she carefully examined each page.

"Yes. It's become the second story that's woven through the book," I added. "But only known to those who are privy to the information about the rabbi and his wife."

Marthe was quiet for a moment and I could tell she was reflecting upon what I had just said.

"It's like your painting, *Grand-maman*. One sees the beautiful portrait. But when you share the story behind it . . . your friendship with Boldini, it has even deeper resonance."

"Yes," she said, her eyes lifting toward her portrait. "There are those who can look at something and only see the outer beauty, but it's always the story behind it that renders it priceless."

I nodded.

"Still, I wish you could translate a little of what is written here. It looks as though it's in a secret code." A cough suddenly broke into her words.

"Can you read any of it?"

"Sadly I can't." I looked down again at the page, admiring the artful hand of both husband and wife. "My mother sounded out only a few letters for me before she died."

"How unfortunate. I would so love to hear a translation."

I was happy I had piqued her interest. "Yes," I agreed. "So would I."

That afternoon I asked Giselle to prepare something for us to bring to the Armels'.

"We can't bring anything made with flour."

Giselle wrinkled her brow. "That eliminates all my cakes, then . . ."

"Perhaps we could get some marzipan?" I suggested.

She pulled the tin down from the cupboard and examined the

folded bills inside. "It only costs triple what it was before the war, not five times like cigarettes or chocolate. We could manage that."

"We need to have some before we leave in a few hours, so perhaps if you . . ."

"I will go ask Jean-Luc this afternoon, Mademoiselle Solange. You needn't worry. You'll have your marzipan in time."

"Thank you. I'm sorry to be so nervous." I forced a smile.

Giselle placed a hand on my arm. "You only want everything to be perfect." Her eyes looked at me knowingly, and I could see a maternal warmth that I hadn't experienced before. "It is most natural when you're in love."

We dressed for our first Seder, Marthe and I. She in a tasteful gabardine suit, the cultured pearls around her slender throat. In her hair she had placed a tortoiseshell comb.

"No trousers, then?" I said as I stepped closer to her in the hallway. I was in the navy blue dress I had brought from the apartment.

I could see Marthe appraising me as we stood across from each other, our reflections cast in the hall mirror.

"It is interesting to see that you have no powder, hardly a trace of lipstick, and not a single accessory on your body. And yet I have never seen a more radiant-looking young woman."

I looked down at the floor.

"There is no need to be embarrassed, Solange. I have never given a compliment that was not sincere."

My eyes met hers. "I'm sure you haven't."

"Now, shall we go?" She gestured toward the door. "Giselle mentioned the marzipans were on the counter."

I went into the kitchen and found a gilt-colored box with a red satin bow.

Returning to the hallway, I asked Grandmother how Giselle

always managed to find the best provisions, when nearly every shelf in Paris was bare.

"Jean-Luc," she said, and a sly smile appeared on her lips. "It's convenient to have a brother in the black market."

It was nearly five o'clock when we arrived at the Armels' apartment. Marthe had shunned taking the Métro, and so we arrived by taxi.

"It's hardly a coach," she said as I shut the door behind us. "How times have changed."

"Indeed, not a horse in sight." I laughed as we both stepped onto the curb.

I looked up at the tall stone facade of the Armels' apartment building. The carved pillars that flanked the large wooden door.

"I've never even been outside Paris," I said softly.

I paused in front of the buzzer to their apartment, hesitating for a moment before I announced we had arrived.

I was slightly embarrassed by my lack of worldly exposure, in contrast to my grandmother.

But Marthe took the opportunity to show me that the space between us was not as wide as I imagined. She touched my wrist slightly, saying: "And I have only been to Venice, the city where I first took my name."

46.

April 1940

As we stepped into the Armels' apartment, I no longer inhaled the smell of books, but rather the warm scent of simmering onions.

"I'm so pleased you both could join us," Monsieur Armel said with great exuberance.

I saw Grandmother's eyes travel inside. Sitting at the table were two little children, a boy no older than six and a girl that looked a few years older, perhaps nine.

For a moment, I was seized with a sense of alarm. In all of the excitement of the past two days, I had forgotten to tell Marthe that we would not be the Armels' only guests.

I could see Grandmother stiffen at the sight of the children. The playful excitement that had laced the air since we had left her apartment suddenly vanished.

Monsieur Armel noticed Marthe's look of bewilderment.

"Didn't Solange tell you?" He smiled warmly. "We're being joined by a colleague of mine, Solomon Weckstein, and his two young children, Eva and Leo. His wife is in the kitchen trying to help save my poor attempt to make a chicken." He laughed. "I'm lucky the butcher couldn't get me a lamb, as who knows how I would have ruined that."

"You must pardon me, Monsieur Armel. Suddenly, I am feeling quite unwell."

I looked at Marthe. She was shaking.

"She has been a bit under the weather recently," I apologized as I took my grandmother's arm. I felt its thinness beneath the silk material of her blouse, and her fragility sent a pang through my heart. I suddenly regretted that I encouraged her to leave the house.

"Come, please sit down . . ." Alex took Marthe's arm and ushered her to the living room.

She was white as a gull. She turned toward me as Alex escorted her across the hall. I read the expression on her face as though she was hoping I might be able to save her from something.

"Can we go?" she whispered. "I thought it would only be us this evening . . ."

I was still holding the box of marzipan. The red ribbon had come undone against my nervous hands.

"Of course," I said as I struggled not to meet Alex's eyes that I knew were searching for mine.

"Perhaps we shouldn't have come," I apologized. "Grandmother's health has been rather delicate lately and I think she overestimated her strength today . . ."

"Don't rush off yet," Monsieur Armel pleaded. "The table is set. The food is nearly ready and we want you to share our Seder."

I looked at my grandmother and saw that her eyes had suddenly drifted in another direction. Solomon had suddenly emerged and joined the Armels in the hallway. I almost didn't recognize him. Instead of the typical shabby clothes he wore the few times I had seen him at the shop, he was now dressed in a pressed suit and a crisp shirt and tie. He also wore a black skullcap on his head.

"A pleasure to see you, Mademoiselle Solange." He nodded in my direction. "And your grandmother as well."

"Unfortunately, Madame de Florian is not feeling well. Can we ask Rachel to make her some hot tea?"

"Yes, certainly." He looked at Marthe sympathetically and then retreated back into the kitchen.

Alex motioned for me to bring Marthe into the library, and he helped her to one of the upholstered chairs.

"Perhaps being in the comfort of my collection will soothe you," Monsieur Armel said as he gestured at his shelves of books. "I know I so enjoyed seeing your porcelains."

Rachel brought in a cup of tea. She was far younger than I had imagined, as she looked only a few years older than I. Petite with a kind face and dark brown curls, she appeared genuinely concerned with Marthe's well-being.

"Drink it slowly," she advised kindly. "And let me know if you'd like anything else. I've made some macaroons and they might restore your energy."

"Thank you, you're most kind," Marthe whispered as she took the tea and sipped slowly through the clouds of steam.

"I've brought some marzipan," I said, offering them to Monsieur Armel. "We so appreciate you inviting us."

"It is the least we could do . . . We are forever indebted to your grandmother." He looked over to her with affection in his eyes. "She saved Alex."

"You exaggerate, monsieur. I only wrote a letter."

Monsieur Armel laughed. "Has anyone told you, Madame de Florian, that your modesty is utterly charming?"

Grandmother lifted her gaze from her teacup. Her color had fully returned to her. "No one, my dear man, has ever called me modest." She gave him her most beguiling smile. "But I must say, I like it."

Perhaps having a few moments to process the addition of children to the dinner enabled Marthe to return to her jovial self. After all, she had always been someone who could adapt quickly. When we returned to the dining room and sat down next to the children, she hardly even seemed to notice them whereas I could hardly peel my eyes away from their sweet faces. One could see they had been dressed in their holiday best. Eva wore a simple cotton pinafore with lace trim, white socks, and shiny black shoes. Little Leo was in dark suspenders and a shirt that was half untucked. They sat with folded hands, their eyes peeled toward the center of the table where there was a large round dish flanked by a set of silver candlesticks. Upon the platter, arranged like a constellation, was a selection of curious things that I knew had symbolic meaning. An egg, parsley, a bone, a bowl of salt water, and a brown mixture of what appeared to be mashed nuts were placed on top of it. Beside it was a basket of covered matzo.

With everyone now seated and Monsieur Armel at the end of the table, the scene looked almost identical to the one in my fourteenth-century Haggadah.

"Shall we begin?" Rachel stood just behind the children.

"Yes, please," said Monsieur Armel as he gestured to Grandmother and me to sit down.

Rachel reached into her apron and withdrew a box of matches. I heard the strike against the carbon, and then the room was bathed in a soft, mysterious light.

. . .

Grandmother had been placed at the far edge of the table as a gesture of respect. And with her straight back, trim figure, and fashionable dress, she added an old-world glamour to the setting.

I could see how little Eva's eyes kept darting to steal glances at Marthe. I recognized the girl's wonder at seeing someone who seemed to possess such a preternatural elegance.

Perhaps Marthe noticed it, too. For as the night wore on and Marthe warmed from the red wine and the storytelling done by Monsieur Armel, I believe I even saw Marthe smile at the little girl.

But for the entire evening, she kept her eyes firmly away from Leo.

With his dark hair and pale skin, the suspenders and knee socks, I'm not sure whether he reminded her of my father, the son she never had the chance to raise. But she avoided him as if he were a ghost.

We stayed quite late. After the candles had Medusa-like curls of wax over the rim of the silver candlesticks, we said our good-byes. The children had fallen asleep after looking for the hidden pieces of matzo. And both Solomon and Rachel each carried one of them home in their arms.

"Thank you for inviting us," I said as I kissed Monsieur Armel on both cheeks. Grandmother extended her hand for him to kiss.

"A pleasure," she said. "I'm so delighted I was able to stay."

Alex stood in the background looking at me with a smile curled at his lips. He mouthed, "Tomorrow. Place Saint Georges. Eleven o'clock."

And I nodded my head. What I didn't say was that tomorrow couldn't come soon enough.

47.

April 1940

Grandmother did not take her breakfast the next morning.

"The cough seems to have returned," Giselle told me in the kitchen as I sipped my tea. "Perhaps she stayed up too late and only needs to get some rest."

"I don't want to leave her if she's feeling unwell." As much as I wanted to see Alex, it seemed wrong to leave her in a weakened condition.

"I think she is hoping you'll leave for a few hours, Solange. That way I can call the doctor and she knows she can have her privacy."

I shook my head. "I would like to meet the doctor. Discuss what is ailing her. See how I can help. It is the least I can do."

Giselle shook her head. "I don't know, Mademoiselle Solange." Perhaps just come back to the apartment earlier than expected. I will try to have the doctor come around two o'clock. Come then and it will look unplanned."

"A good idea," I said, impressed with how clever Giselle could be.

I was relieved that I could still see Alex for a few hours, but still find out more about Grandmother's illness.

I finished my tea and went to my room to get dressed.

My room in Marthe's apartment now felt completely as though it were mine. The desk was full of my journals, my books. The Mickey Mouse doll from Papa was placed high in the corner. I pulled out one of the dresses that I had folded in the bureau since there was no room for a wardrobe and looked at myself in the mirror. I brushed my hair and smoothed it with my palms, before tying it back with ribbon.

My body began to warm. In less than an hour, I knew I would feel Alex's kiss.

I was to meet Alex that afternoon at our café at Place Saint Georges, for it had become our special place.

Alex didn't seem to see me at first. His back was turned and he was deep in conversation with another gentleman at the table next to him. He was significantly older than Alex, and he was gesturing with his hands as if to emphasize his words.

As I came closer, I heard Alex say: "Everyone has their head in the sand, but it's only a matter of time . . ."

The other man shook his head as if disgusted. "I agree with what you say. And I don't think we can count on Reynaud at all," he said, referring to our new prime minister.

I came closer and the two men lifted their eyes in my direction.

"Solange . . ." Alex seemed surprised not to have noticed my arrival.

"I hope I'm not disturbing you. We did say eleven o'clock, didn't we?"

Alex's face flushed. "I apologize, Solange. I was just deep in conversation with Monsieur Clavel."

He motioned toward his acquaintance and introduced us to each other.

"Solange is an aspiring writer and also the owner of a very rare Haggadah . . ." Alex smiled. "And Monsieur Clavel is one of my father's best clients."

"It's a pleasure to meet you." I extended my hand before accepting the chair that Alex had pulled out for me. He gestured and encouraged me to sit down.

"I'm afraid your description is far more intriguing than mine. A writer? How unusual for a young woman to have such interests."

I smiled. Monsieur Clavel displayed none of the impassioned gestures or animated speech patterns I had witnessed minutes before. Now he simply appeared intrigued.

"What are you writing? A piece for one of the ladies' journals?"

"No," I said, shaking my head. "I'm working on a novel."

"A novel?" He smacked the edge of the bistro table. "Now, that's not the answer I was expecting!" He chuckled.

"I admire your tenacity. I aspired to write, too, when I was about your age . . . But now I just collect other people's old books." He took another sip of his coffee. "But there's something to be said about centuries-old books. We are only here a limited time, but it's the books that are eternal."

"I like that thought," I said. "The immortality of books."

Our conversation about books soothed me. With all of the uncertainty the war had brought and, on top of that, Grandmother's failing health, it was nice to be able to talk about books for a change.

"So now you've unlocked the secret between booksellers. Shame on you, Alex," Monsieur Clavel teased. "But this brings me back to the rare Haggadah in your possession, Solange. I'm incredibly intrigued. Perhaps you'd be interested in selling it to me?"

Alex shook his head. "Always the aggressive collector . . . But if she won't sell it to my father, I doubt she would sell it to you."

I laughed. "Yes, I'm not planning on parting with it just yet. But thank you for the offer."

Monsieur Clavel placed a few francs on the table for his coffee before extinguishing his cigarette.

"I'll have to ask your father more about this mysterious book of hers . . . I'm leaving France soon, and it might be time to give your book one more journey all its own."

Alex cut him off. "I think she'll be keeping it close to her. But safe travels if I don't see you before you leave Paris."

"I hope you'll also consider getting out before it's too late, Alex." He stood up and patted down the front of his pants.

"Things are only going to get worse here."

Alex squeezed my hand. "Then Solange and I had better make the most of today."

Later we walked toward the opera, the sunlight hitting my face as Alex's hand threaded through mine. We breathed in the fresh air. We ignored the newspaper boys selling their headlines of doom. We didn't look into the store windows whose empty shelves made me sad. Instead, we looked toward the birds and the stretch of blue in the sky.

He asked me a few questions about my childhood and my favorite memory. He searched for stories about my mother and shared with me his memories of his own, whom he had lost when he was barely three.

"I remember the sound of her heels on the tile of our apartment. The scent of her perfume. I remember she wore a sterling-silver comb in her hair. And that when I kissed her, my lips felt the veil of powder on her cheeks."

I confided to him that I believed my mother's bookshelf still contained her soul. That I only needed to breathe in the paper from one of her novels to find her again.

"I love hearing your stories," he said as he pulled me into his arms and kissed me.

It felt like there were a thousand fluttering birds beneath my feet as his lips pressed against mine. I cupped his face with open palms and closed my eyes as I kissed him once again.

After we came up for air, he pulled away from me slightly and looked at me straight in the eyes.

"Solange, I want you to know I realize your association with me and my family exposes you to danger. There's nothing I can do to help with the uncertainty of war, but I want you to know one thing is certain and absolute." He took me again into his arms and kissed me. "I love you."

48.

April 1940

It felt like a painful wound, pulling away from Alex that afternoon, but I knew it was imperative that I be at the apartment when Marthe's doctor arrived. By the time I finally reached the front door, my heart was pounding and I was nearly out of breath.

Once inside the vestibule, I could see the doctor's overcoat draped on the brass coat stand in the corner, where Giselle always hung hats and umbrellas. In the distance, I could see that the door of Marthe's bedroom was closed.

I turned toward the kitchen and found Giselle there. At the small walnut table where I sometimes took my breakfast, she was sitting having a cup of tea with Gérard. Between them was a small, half-eaten cake and two plates with crumbs.

"Mademoiselle Solange." Giselle stood up immediately. "I'm so glad you came back in time." She glanced over to Gérard, who was quickly dusting the crumbs off his lap before standing to greet me.

"Monsieur Gérard stopped by to make us aware that we will be having another air drill. He is as kind as his dear father, always thinking of us."

Gérard shook his head. "Papa made me promise I would take special care of Madame de Florian. He always had a sincere concern for her well-being."

"That is most kind of you to keep his concern close to your heart," I said, impressed by how he had kept his word to his father. "I'm sure my grandmother will be touched by your kindness."

"There are several apartments in this building, but your grandmother is one of the few owners that almost never asks anything from me. So many call for a leaky faucet or peeling plaster wall, something that should be handled by a repairman, not a concierge, but your grandmother troubles me with almost nothing. It's the least I can do, to check up on her, especially now with the Germans advancing."

"Let us hope they come no further," Giselle said. "That the Maginot Line is as strong as they say."

Gérard shook his head. "My father felt one must always be prepared for the worst. That is why I wanted to make sure you and Madame de Florian know I am here in case you need anything."

"You're a gentleman, just like your father." Giselle came over and squeezed his shoulder. "Let me wrap this cake up for you. Your children will enjoy it."

He took the cake that Giselle had wrapped in a cotton cloth. "Thank you."

"A pleasure to see you again, Mademoiselle Solange." He nodded to me and then took his leave not through the front exit, but through the pantry's back door.

"The doctor's been with her for over an hour," Giselle said as soon as Gérard left. "I do hope you'll be able to get some information from him." She turned the faucet on over the plates and began washing them. "Madame looked so pale when I brought him in to see her. And her lips looked almost blue." She shook her head. "It is terrible to see her looking so weak."

"I will sit in the parlor now and wait for the doctor." I touched Giselle's arm. "I know you're moved by Gérard's gestures of concern. But I'm also grateful for yours."

She looked up and smiled. "I've been with your grandmother since I was sixteen, Solange. I've been employed by her for over forty-five years now. Longer than many marriages. It would be impossible not to worry about her."

"Still," I said, genuinely touched by her dedication, "I want to thank you."

"Just promise me you'll tell me every word the doctor shares with you. I need to know."

"I promise," I assured her.

I walked toward the parlor and sat beneath Marthe's portrait, waiting quietly until I heard the doctor's footsteps coming down the hall.

49.

April 1940

His footsteps sounded like a metronome as he walked down the hallway's parquet floors.

"Dr. Payard," I said as I emerged from the open French doors of the parlor, clearly catching him by surprise. "I was hoping for the chance to speak with you about my grandmother's health."

"You must be Solange," he said, his eyes lifting to meet mine. "Madame de Florian has spoken about you quite often."

"Unfortunately, she has not spoken of you as often to me. I feel I'm in the dark about her recent health problems. I was hoping you might illuminate me . . ."

He fidgeted slightly in front of me. My forwardness had clearly caught him off guard.

He placed his dark satchel down on the floor and then reached for his overcoat. He began to button it up as he spoke.

"Your grandmother is resting comfortably now. I gave her a syrup with codeine to help her rest. She complains that it's almost impossible for her to sleep through the night with her cough."

"Yes, this cough . . ." The words darted from my mouth. "She's been suffering from it for several months now, and it appears to be worsening. How serious is it?"

Dr. Payard shook his head. "Please step out into the hallway with me for a moment, mademoiselle."

I followed him outside, shutting the door behind me.

"Your grandmother wants to maintain her privacy regarding her illness, and, as her doctor, I must respect her wishes. That said, without divulging too much, I'm sorry to say that I expect her time is limited. You should try to keep her as comfortable as possible and to spend as much time with her as you can. I will come by in another few days to see if she needs more syrup to help her at night."

He looked at his watch, then left me alone outside the door, his words still ringing in my ears.

The morning's joyfulness of walking through the park with Alex—sharing our most intimate experiences and the thrill of his embrace—was now lost to the devastating news that Marthe's illness was far more serious than I had believed. All my life I had prided myself in my ability to truly gauge my surroundings. Yet somehow I had failed to sense how much Marthe was ailing. I felt that I had let her down.

Dr. Payard said she would be sleeping for some time due to the codeine in the syrup. I walked slowly down the hallway and turned the doorknob to her bedroom. Tucked within her damask sheets and lying underneath her upholstered headboard with its spray of birds and butterflies, Marthe slept like an empress. Her slender white fingers were clasped in front of her, and her titian hair, now white at the temples, was piled atop her head. Even her pale eyelids looked like perfect half-moons.

I pulled up a chair and sat down at her bedside. The mirror above her caught the reflection of the two of us within its frame. It was a touching image. Two women who had come into each other's lives unexpectedly. I had first come to her simply to learn more of her story, not realizing that together we would create a new one that was uniquely our own.

I looked around the room. The vanity that I now knew contained her old love letters from Charles, along with a handful from Boldini, and, more importantly for me, the ones from Madame Francau lovingly detailing my father's childhood. I admired the free-standing mirror before which she had so often dressed for Charles, and where she had prepared herself prior to being painted by Boldini. I had imagined her bedroom almost like a stage as she described all the events in her life story, and all of the furniture seemed eerily familiar to me despite only having been inside her bedroom on a few occasions. I walked over to her oak wardrobe, which housed her collection of silk dresses. I could hardly help myself as I pulled the small brass knobs to reveal what was inside.

In the front were the black silk faille, the lilac dress she loved so dearly. To the left were more contemporary dresses made from wool gabardine, a single skirt in midnight blue velvet, and even the wide legged black trousers she had sewn herself. But at the far end of her wardrobe, behind the black velvet cape and the silver one with the pink ribbons, hung the one gown that had provided the signature look of her beautiful, sensual life: the pink silk charmeuse and organza dress she had worn when Boldini painted her. I reached to touch it. I felt the fluid silk between my fingers and could imagine her before my eyes. As I examined the bodice, I could see the detail more clearly than Boldini had depicted it in the painting—the two plackets of lace on the bodice and the gray belt with the horseshoe-shaped buckle of crystal beads. I marveled at the delicacy of the cloudlike sleeves, and the sheer beauty of the pink-tourmaline-colored silk. The gown felt forbidden, something that was reserved only for Marthe's skin and certainly not mine.

As exquisite as the dress was, it needed Marthe to bring it to life. Boldini's brush had rendered more than just a portrait of a woman in a sumptuous gown; he had captured Marthe's sensuality and exuberance. It made me pause to think how the final portrait had so many layers that contributed to making something so beautiful.

Sadly, Marthe now looked far from the robust femme fatale Boldini had captured in his portrait. Gone was the voluptuous figure and the blush of youth. Her body seemed half its size now. Her shoulders seemed to cave in, her breasts far smaller. She appeared almost childlike sleeping.

Next to her bed, inches away from her water pitcher and glass, I noticed two things I had not expected to see there. The first was the old leather volume of the fables of Jean-Pierre Claris de Florian, which Charles had given her so many years before. The second was the gold pocket watch she had mentioned during the course of her storytelling, but had never once shown me.

Unable to stop myself, I reached for the watch. The casing was now dull with age, and the metal slightly scratched. I carefully used my fingernail to open it and, there, just as she had described, was a winged dove engraved on the inside. The hands were stopped at 6:14.

I held the watch in my palms, hoping that I had the capacity to make time stand still. Marthe was fading. She conserved her speech. She mostly kept herself tightly wrapped in her layers of sheeting, the covers and blanket pulled up to her narrow chin. Her eyelids were pale lilac. Her skin, the color of rice paper. As she slept, I grasped her hand.

The memory of my own mother on her deathbed returned to me. At the time, I had thought the same thing I did now sitting beside Marthe. That we leave this world the very way we arrive. Our bodies shrunken and our eyes sealed shut.

50.

April 1940

I wrote furiously to my father, but with letters censored, all I could say was this:

Please take leave. Grandmother is gravely ill. Come at once.

Over the next few days, I did not abandon Marthe's side. I listened to her labored breathing, heavy from the medication. She murmured words underneath her breath, as though she was revealing something from her dreams. Once she asked for candied oranges. Another time she cried out for Charles.

I felt her deflating within my fingers. I noticed the contrast from when I clasped Alex's hands, the warmth and pulse that pushed forth from the inside of his veins outward toward his skin. His vitality was palpable. But when I held Marthe's fingers, I had the sensation that it was only a matter of time before she was completely lost to me.

. . .

I fell asleep with my head pressed to the edge of her bed, my fingers numb from holding Marthe's hand in my own. Moonlight streamed into the bedroom when I awakened from my slumber. Marthe's eyes were now open. I heard her voice, barely audible.

"Solange." My name seemed to catch in the back of her throat. She wiggled her hand from mine and reached for the glass of water that was on the nightstand.

She pushed herself up from toward the back of the bed.

"Please go to my dresser and open the top drawer."

I did as I was instructed and walked toward the back of the room, where her wooden dresser with the ormolu handles and marble top was located. Perched on top were more Chinese vases and other painted figurines.

I opened the top drawer, but saw only folded corsets and other delicate undergarments.

"There is a leather folio underneath."

I reached beneath the underpinnings and felt the straight edges of the folder and pulled it out.

"Good, good," she said hoarsely. "Bring it here."

I carried it over to the bed and placed it between her open hands. She closed her eyes for a moment and patted it with her palms.

"This contains essential information for you, Solange. Inside are all my important papers and a few select things that are precious to me. You'll find the deed for the apartment, and now also my last will and testament. It's all been notarized by an attorney."

She struggled to undo the cord tied over the folder. A cough escaped her.

"Here, let me help." I gently took the envelope from her and unknotted the cord.

The folder was thick with papers. As she searched to find certain legal documents, she placed the other contents to the side.

I saw old black-and-white photographs and smaller scraps of paper, and my eyes strained to glimpse a better view.

"We can look at those afterward, but this is important, Solange. I don't know how much more time I have," she said in a hoarse voice.

"This describes the contents of my estate. You'll need to bring the deed to my attorney, whose name is listed at the bottom of my will. He has drawn up the paperwork so you and your father will inherit everything that I own."

"Grandmother," I protested. "You shouldn't be speaking about these things . . . You'll be fine. You just need to rest."

"I have always been realistic, Solange. That is why I sold my pearls all those years ago. And I was lucky enough to receive some excellent advice from a banker at one of my salons, who told me to put the money in rubber factories in South America. That is why I still have savings in the bank, even now." She smiled weakly.

"I am happy to be leaving you and your father something to make your lives a bit easier . . ."

My eyes began to water.

"I have never had an easy time with children. When your father was born, emotionally I was almost a child myself." She placed the folio to her side and a yellowed, faded envelope slid out from the pile of legal documents and bank forms.

Marthe saw my eyes gravitate toward the envelope. Two black-and-white photographs peeked out from the open flap and a small, unfinished pencil sketch.

She turned her head to see what had captured my interest.

"Ah, yes, the pictures."

Marthe reached over and pulled the small formal portraits out of the envelope.

"This is Charles," she said, handing me a photograph of a man in a black wool coat and top hat. He was as handsome as I had imagined, with sharp aristocratic features and dark eyes.

"It is hard to believe he's been gone now all these years." She pressed a fingertip to his faded image. "He was only forty when he passed away. I became old but he never did." She placed the photograph down and reached for the pencil sketch.

"He never had the chance to finish this . . ." Her voice broke off. "But I kept it all these years."

It was the half-finished drawing of Marthe, her profile captured in a few shaky lines.

"You were fortunate to be captured by two wonderful men." I placed my hand over hers.

She smiled and I could see she was forcing back her tears.

"And the other photograph; who is that one?"

She lifted the second portrait from the bed. This one was not of Charles, but rather of a couple with a small child. The woman, dressed in a somber black jacket and long skirt, held her hand over the child's shoulder. The husband, heavyset with light hair and a full beard, looked wholly different from the elegant Charles. But as he stared into the photographer's lens, his eyes appeared kind.

I studied each of the faces. And I knew as soon as I looked into the little boy's eyes exactly who he was.

"This one is of Louise Franeau and her husband. The boy . . ."

I interrupted her before she had a chance to answer. "The boy is Papa."

Some people claim the dying can sense when their end is near. And clearly this was the case with Marthe.

"I was not a mother to your father, Solange, but hopefully in my death I can afford you both some financial security. The money in my bank account will ensure you have a far more comfortable life."

I clasped her hand tightly. I hated to hear her speak of her death like this.

"But I must ask you something, and I know it will sound terribly selfish . . ." Her voice broke off and she reached for a glass of water from the nightstand.

"This apartment . . . the portrait above the mantel . . . promise me you'll never sell any of it . . . that you'll keep it the way I've always maintained it." Her eyes wetted. "I know it must sound foolish, but it's important to me."

I was puzzled. "You want me to keep everything the same?"

"Yes, in this way, the best parts of me will still exist as I had lived." She reached for the book by her bedside. "*Pour vivre heureux, vivons cachés.*" She whispered it as though it was a motto she had often repeated to herself. "To live happily, live hidden," and a palpable sense of calm came over her as she said the words.

What I realized at that moment was that my grandmother believed that as long as the apartment remained the way she had created it—her portrait above the mantel, her collection of porcelains, and the other pieces of art she had hand selected—she was convinced her memory would also not be extinguished.

But what she failed to see was she had already ensured her immortality. She had shared her life story with me, and her words were pressed into me forever.

My grandmother died two days later, with Giselle and me by her bed after the doctor had arrived and given her a final dose of morphine.

I did not let go of her hand until after her body had grown cold.

Afterward, I wrote to father notifying him of Marthe's death and imploring him to let me know if he was safe.

But again my telegram remained unanswered.

Giselle said she didn't trust the undertaker to prepare Marthe as she would have wished for her burial. So she packed a small satchel full of Marthe's favorite lipstick, her dusting powder, and her tortoiseshell combs.

She did not ask me to join her, and I was glad for that.

I was grateful for Giselle's offer. She asked if she could use one of Marthe's better dresses, and we both agreed it would be beautiful to send her off in the one of pale lilac that she had worn so often. We also placed Charles's gold pocket watch between her folded hands.

But I noticed her pearls were missing from her neck.

"What happened to the pearls, Giselle?" I had never seen Grandmother without them, and I grew immediately concerned.

"I removed them and put them away for safekeeping." Giselle walked over to the bureau and lifted a leather box from the marble surface. "Here, I was saving them for you. She would have wanted you to wear them."

A wave of sorrow passed through me. Knowing that the pearls were in the case made Marthe's death that much more real to me.

I reached for the box and gently opened the lid. The necklace's original emerald-and-diamond butterfly clasp twinkled as if it were communicating a bit of Marthe's mischief.

"Let me help you put them on, mademoiselle," Giselle offered. "Now you'll always have a part of madame close to you."

I brought my hands behind my neck and lifted my hair. Giselle draped the necklace around my collarbone, and then fastened the clasp behind my neck.

The pearls felt cool against my skin, and the weight of the small butterfly clasp took me by surprise. Grandmother almost always hid it behind her hair, as though it were her little secret.

The memory of my grandmother's unique and independent spirit flowed through me as I touched the pearls. The necklace, even though not the original strand Charles had bought her, was a tribute to Marthe's strength and resilience. I would carry her memory proudly as I wore her elegant pearls. I would even keep the emerald butterfly behind my hair, a secret of my own, its jeweled wings resting against the nape of my neck.

It was Gérard, the concierge, who helped make the arrangements with the undertaker.

This gentle man, who had lived in the ground-floor apartment and whose father had once helped bring down a gravely ill Charles from Marthe's apartment, now assisted me with Marthe. The irony did not escape me.

"Anything I can ever do to help you, mademoiselle," he said as he lifted his hat.

"You are too kind," I told him. "You are so much more than a concierge, I can see why both Giselle and my grandmother held you and your father in such high esteem."

"My father always said that the concierge was the gatekeeper to the building." He paused. "Being a concierge is not just receiving packages. I have a sense of responsibility to be aware of who enters and exits the building. Knowing I could help your grandmother one final time is not only my duty. It is my honor."

Three days later, as it poured sheets of rain, a dark funeral cortege escorted Marthe to the Père Lachaise Cemetery.

When I called Marthe's attorney, as she had instructed me to do immediately upon her death, I was informed that she had bought a graveside plot for herself several years earlier. But what came as even more of a surprise to me as Alex, his father, Giselle, and I arrived at the gravesite and stood there waiting for the casket to be lowered into the ground, was that there was already another engraving on the polished headstone.

I walked closer and made out the name. *Odette Rose Beaugiron 1869–1874.* Marthe had never mentioned to me that she had secured a plot in Paris's most elegant cemetery for her sister, or that she had the girl's name etched on the headstone that one day would also be engraved with her own. But now, as I saw Odette's name incised into the dark, wet granite, the gesture struck me deeply and my tears began to flow.

I felt the touch of Alex's hand on my waist. I turned to face him, and just seeing his eyes soft with compassion soothed me.

"Come," he whispered as he ushered me around the hole of earth that had been excavated in anticipation of receiving Marthe's casket.

I had arranged with the undertaker for a secular burial. Since Marthe had never been married, explaining my own relation to her would expose that she had given birth to my father out of wedlock, making it difficult to secure a priest.

So we stood there, Giselle, Alex, Monsieur Armel, and I. Marthe's final companions, waiting to say our final good-byes, as two men in work clothes hovered close in anticipation of when they would be needed to lower the casket into the earth.

Giselle had arranged to bring the flowers. Clasped between her hands, she held two bouquets. One with roses, the other a tight cluster of violets.

I took the violets, knowing it was Grandmother's favorite flower, and placed them on top of the casket; then Giselle followed, placing hers. We stood there for several minutes before departing, the petals quivering in the rain, and tried to push out of our mind the sight of her casket being lowered by ropes into the wet earth.

However, it wasn't until we made our way to the car that Monsieur Armel had kindly arranged that I saw Gérard standing in the distance. I almost didn't recognize him standing in his overcoat. In one hand he grasped an umbrella, and in the other he clutched a wreath of white roses.

After the funeral, I politely refused Alex and his father's invitation to come home with me.

"Let us take you to lunch, or at least we can sit with you for a few hours," Monsieur Armel suggested, playing the role of the patriarch since my own father was absent.

I hadn't arranged a reception after the funeral, so there were no mourners to receive. I was incredibly tired, having not slept well for several days. "Thank you," I answered as politely as I could. "But all I want to do is go home and sleep. I've told Giselle to go home and do the same."

Alex squeezed my arm. "At least let us make sure you get home safely."

I let them take me as far as the door of the apartment building.

"Go," I said, kissing them on both cheeks. "It has already been quite a long day."

Once inside the door, I went toward the elevator and pushed the button. I had no strength to climb the stairs. I felt as though I could only manage the simplest movements. I reached into my purse and pulled out the key to open the door.

My footsteps sounded hollow against the parquet floors. It was impossible to believe I would never again see her floating down the hallway in one of her beautiful dresses, or hear one of her colorful stories or her laughter. I walked past the mirrors and the French doors to the parlor, and headed straight to the small room that I had claimed as my bedroom over the past few months.

I closed the door and fell on the bed. Only then did I allow myself to cry.

Over the next day and a half I moved through the apartment warily.

I felt as if I were walking into a painting in which I did not belong. Every room had been created by Marthe's unique brushstrokes. The oyster gray. The celadon pieces that lined the shelves. The curtains and upholstery, with their deliberate contrast between velvet and silk.

I stood for a moment and searched the air for her perfume. I half believed that if I looked into one of the gilt mirrors, I would see her standing beside me. I could hear her voice in my ears, the throaty sound of her laugh. Slowly, as though pulled by an invisible string, I made my way into the parlor to sit beside her portrait.

If ever a painting seemed to possess a life of its own, such was the case with Marthe's. And, although I had always been aware of its pull, with Marthe now gone, its power seemed even more formidable. When I walked into the parlor, I could feel her presence pulsing from the canvas.

I sat on the sofa, where I knew that Charles had positioned himself when he gazed at the portrait with Grandmother's hand laced through his own, and looked up at its massive frame. Marthe was as she hoped to be, eternal in her beauty. As her spirit flowed through the room, the painting remained the heartbeat of the apartment.

Even if she had not asked, I could never have taken the painting down from the mantel or sold the apartment to new owners. It would have felt not only like a betrayal for all that she had done for Alex and me; it would have felt like a crime.

At night, I stayed tucked inside my tiny room that was cluttered with my essential belongings: my clothes, my notebooks, and my novels. Even the old Mickey Mouse doll from my father, I brought closer to my bed. I felt that if I were to live in the apartment any longer, it would be best to essentially barricade myself in this little room. That way I wouldn't feel as though I was trespassing amongst all of Marthe's things. While I no longer felt that I was Marthe's guest, I was still not the mistress of the apartment, even if Marthe wished me to own it in part after her death and my father was nowhere to be found.

I pulled the edge of the sheets closer to my chin, as outside the sound of airplane engines rattled through the sky.

51.

May 1940

In the days that followed Marthe's funeral, I continued to worry that I had yet to receive any response from my father. The radio, which Marthe had never touched while she was alive, I now used more than ever. I carried it with me in and out of every room, to receive the latest news.

I kept the apartment dark, rarely pulling back the heavy curtains in the rooms that Marthe had always ensured were filled with sunlight. I stayed in my nightgown and robe, believing it wasn't necessary to get dressed.

Alex, concerned that he hadn't heard from me, surprised me with a visit. "Where is Giselle?" he asked. "You shouldn't be living here all alone."

"I told her to take the week off so we could both grieve," I muttered.

"You look terrible." He took his jacket off and draped it over a chair.

"I've been searching for news about my father. I never heard back from him after I telegrammed about Marthe."

"With all that's going on with the war, any communication would be difficult now . . ." He reached over to brush a strand of hair from my face.

"You look like you haven't slept."

I nodded. It was true. It had been impossible to sleep in the apartment all by myself. I felt Marthe's ghost everywhere. Wherever I looked, I felt her presence, whether it was in her collections, her painting, or even in the empty vases that in better days were always filled with colorful blooms.

My tiny room was the only place that didn't have her fingerprints all over it. But the radio reception was poor in that part of the apartment, so as much as I wanted to cocoon myself in that room with my notebooks and novels, my thirst to hear the news broadcasts took me into the rest of the apartment.

"I think you should come live with Papa and me . . . I'm worried." Alex's concern was written all over his face. "And this is really not your home."

A memory flickered through my head of my childhood apartment. The wooden kitchen table, my mother's bookcases. My bedroom with its flower coverlet.

"I could go back home, to our old apartment. Papa wanted me to live here because he thought I shouldn't be alone . . ."

"Exactly. And that's why you shouldn't return home either, but should instead come with me, to a place where people can watch over you." He touched my wrist. "Please," he said. "Please, come."

And so I packed my suitcase yet again. I folded the dresses, placed my journals on top, and wrapped the photograph of my parents in a wool scarf.

"I suppose I should bring the Haggadah and *Zemirot* book, too?" I said, seeking Alex's guidance. "It wouldn't be safe to leave them here unattended."

"No, you should take them with you."

"If you can carry my valise, I'll carry the books," I offered. I had not looked at them since I showed them to Marthe before our dinner with the Armels. At their suggestion, I had kept them out of sunlight, always wrapped in several layers of brown paper, in a box underneath my bed.

"It would be my honor," said Alex as he snapped my suitcase closed.

I followed him out of the apartment, guarding my mother's precious books close to my chest.

When we arrived at the Armels' apartment, Solomon was there with Alex's father. The dining room table had become a makeshift workshop now that the store had been shuttered.

The two men were hunched over the table examining what looked like a centuries-old book.

"I'm sorry for the mess," Monsieur Armel apologized when he saw me come through the door. "We're deciding the best way to repair this binding."

I smiled. I loved the sight of them examining a book that looked as old as the Haggadah I now carried in my arms.

"I didn't want Solange to be in that apartment all by herself," Alex said as he approached his father and Solomon. "I thought she could sleep in the spare room."

Monsieur Armel looked up from the book. "You're absolutely right," he agreed without any hesitation. "A young woman shouldn't be alone during such dangerous times."

I felt my cheeks flush. I did not like to think of myself as vulnerable, yet it was a great comfort to know that Alex and his father were looking out for me.

"Our home is always open to you, Solange," Monsieur Armel added.

Solomon wiped his brow with his handkerchief. "Perhaps we can revisit this tomorrow, Bernard. I have to think about the best way to do it. Whether we sew the binding or use glue."

"Yes, yes, of course," Monsieur Armel agreed. He stood up and stretched his back. "But let's not take too much time. I promised this to the Freys before they leave Sunday."

Less than a week later, we all sat in front of the Armels' radio and heard the terrible news. The German army had routed the Allied forces in the low countries. Within a matter of days, they had already conquered Belgium, Luxembourg, and the Netherlands. They were now well on their way to crossing into France. The speed and relentlessness of their victories took every French citizen by surprise. It made the Germans now seem invincible.

"If they enter France . . . my father . . ." I could barely get the words out. Alex reached over to me and pulled me to his side.

"He is at a military hospital, not the front," he attempted to reassure me.

But all I could imagine was the rain of bombs and gunfire. My father, who hated chaos, trying to maintain order amid all the bloodshed.

Monsieur Armel looked pale. He reached over and lowered the volume, but he must have also accidentally adjusted the tuning dial because now all that emerged from the radio was static.

I looked down at the floor, and part of me wished I could have been like Marthe, capable of shutting myself off from what was happening in the outside world.

When I was younger, I remember catching my mother in the kitchen happily tapping her heels to the sounds of Charles Trenet. But now the radio was no longer a source of pleasure or entertainment, only despair. The buzzing from the static was ominous. Though we were in a living room, it sounded like we were in the middle of a beehive.

As we had dreaded, the next day, the German army entered France.

But instead of a huge, thunderous outcry, Paris fell strangely silent.

It was the second week in May, a time when the city was normally aflutter with spring. Parisian women were typically excited to stroll through the streets wearing lighter fabrics that matched the romantic feelings of the new season. But now Paris seemed to be holding its breath in nervous anticipation, instead of savoring the opportunity to exhale from its long winter.

"Everyone's afraid," Alex said as he stepped toward one of the floor-to-ceiling windows that overlooked the street. "Did you notice last night they crowned the streetlamps in blue paper? They're blocking out the light to make it as difficult as possible for the Luftwaffe to bomb the city."

"They've already sent instruction manuals to most of the apartment buildings. 'Dim your lights. Close your window shades.'" Solomon shook his head and began to collect his things. "The next thing they'll tell us to do is to close our eyes . . . They will make the city dark, because if the Germans come, they won't want us to see."

Since learning the news of the Germans' entering French soil, we all continued to be on edge. I could sense how much stress Monsieur Armel seemed to be under, and I wanted to minimize my presence and ease his burden as best I could. I rose earlier than everyone else so I could use the washroom in private, and I dressed before either Alex or Monsieur Armel awakened from their dreams.

I found the tin where they stored their coffee, and brewed it so it would be ready for them when they awoke. I washed whatever remained in the sink or was left on the table from the night before. Monsieur Armel had spent every evening since I arrived working late into the night, and it was not uncommon to see a cup or small plate on his desk.

That morning, however, when I went into the kitchen, I found Monsieur Armel and Solomon together at the small table drinking coffee in the midst of what appeared to be a deep conversation.

"I'm sorry . . . I didn't realize anyone was awake in the apartment just yet."

"No need to apologize, Solange," Monsieur Armel said, lifting his hand from the table slightly in a gesture to assure me. "Solomon and I have just been talking, that's all."

Solomon looked up and managed a small smile in my direction. Since the Seder at the Armels', we no longer looked at each other as awkward strangers, but as members of the extended Armel family. He had even written a condolence card to me, expressing his regrets when Marthe died.

Between his fingers, Solomon clasped an envelope containing a few francs. I suspected Monsieur Armel was still trying to help support his one and only employee, who had a wife and children to feed. He quickly slipped it into his breast pocket as if ashamed.

"I should be going, Bernard." Solomon stood up and began collecting his things.

"Give Rachel and the children a kiss for me," Monsieur Armel said, patting him on the back. "And don't worry. I'm not going anywhere without the world's best book restorer. We will all leave here together, I promise you."

After Solomon left, Monsieur Armel returned to his seat and placed his head in his hands.

52.

May 1940

I have a proposition for you," Monsieur Armel said. "I have not told Alex about it yet, as he would never have permitted me to ask you."

"Yes, you can ask me anything," I told him. "I'm forever indebted to your kindness to me."

"Let us speak no longer of any debt, Solange. Your grandmother saved my son, so I am the one who will always be indebted to you. But now we have more immediate matters to address, and time is of the essence. Every day that passes, the Germans get that much closer to Paris. I don't want to be caught in a situation where it's too late."

I folded my hands in my lap and waited to hear what Monsieur Armel had to say. "You may ask me anything. With my father away, I feel as though you and Alex are the closest thing to family I have now."

"I have written to every contact I have, in the hope that I can sell my remaining inventory. But everyone seems to share the same problem as me. All the best Jewish book dealers are trying to liquidate their libraries to get out of Europe."

I was puzzled. "But how can I help?"

Monsieur Armel clasped his hands together, and I saw his knuckles turn white. He was clearly uncomfortable with what he was about to say.

"Do you remember meeting a gentleman by the name of Frédéric Clavel the other day, when you were having coffee with Alex?"

I nodded.

"Well, he came by yesterday. He told me he knows about a particular dealer that is interested in purchasing your Barcelona Haggadah."

I sat quietly for a moment, soaking in his words.

"He does?"

"Yes. Evidently, he had seen it years ago, just as I had, when it was still in your grandfather's possession. He knows how rare and valuable it is, even if he didn't let on when Alex mentioned it at the café."

I hesitated for a moment. "Well, in fact, he did ask me there and then if I was interested in selling it."

"And if my information is correct, you told him you weren't."

"Yes, that's right. Luckily, Alex spoke on my behalf."

Monsieur Armel smiled. "I'm sure he did. And I'm sure he conveyed to Monsieur Clavel that if you weren't willing to sell to us, why would you sell to him?"

"Exactly."

"But what if your book could get us all out of France?"

I raised an eyebrow. "I'm not sure I understand."

"The amount of money Clavel says the dealer is willing to pay would be, shall we say, considérable."

He paused after emphasizing that last word, and then looked down at the table briefly before lifting his eyes toward me.

"By all, do you mean your family and Solomon's?" I wasn't sure whom he was including in this statement.

"And you, Solange. Of course, you, too."

I felt a sense of relief wash over me.

The Haggadah and the less valuable *Zemirot* book were precious to me because they represented a lasting connection to my mother. But I believed those books also had a destiny all their own. They were what had initially brought me to the Armels, and I was willing to sell them if it could save those I loved.

"Of course, I'll sell the book if it can ensure us all safe passage."

"I know this is not an easy choice for you to make, Solange. Especially not knowing what has happened to your father."

I looked down at the floor. It had now been months since I heard from my father. And the radio broadcasts all reported that the area where his military hospital had been located had been heavily bombed.

"I know I wouldn't want my daughter to be alone in Paris. I'd want her to go where she'd be safe."

"Yes, that's why he wanted me to move in with my grandmother . . ." I nodded my head. "My safety was his only concern before he had to go."

"And that is why Alex asked you to come stay with us. It is human nature to want to protect those we love."

Monsieur Armel's words affected me, and I struggled to fight back my tears. "I'm so happy my mother left me such an important gift. Who knew one book could save so many lives?"

Monsieur Armel's color had returned to him. He stood up and embraced me, and I could feel the warm pulse of his heartbeat pressing into mine.

That afternoon, I went into the guest bedroom where I had been staying and unwrapped the Haggadah. I held it in my hands. Its weight had always felt substantial to me, but now it seemed even heavier, infused with a deeper meaning.

I looked over the illustrations once again, lifting the dry, yellowed pages one by one. I remembered how Alex had explained many of them when we were alone. The stylized depictions of the matzo and the plate of the bitter herbs; the drawings of the plague of locusts, darkness, and the death of the firstborn. The colors of red, blue, and gold on the figures were still surprisingly vibrant even after so many centuries.

As I continued to turn the pages, the story of the Israelites' journey from Egypt was not lost on me. If Monsieur Armel managed to negotiate the sale of the Haggadah, I knew the money would be used toward our own exodus. My suitcase remained underneath the bed where I now slept. I was ready to leave whenever Monsieur said the word.

Every day that passed, the tension escalated. It was the last week in May and the shops were nearly empty, the grocers having nothing to offer. As the cherry blossoms fell to the ground, we looked at the sky and prayed the Germans would hold off their bombing. But our prayers were not answered.

Just as we were finishing lunch on June 3, the air-raid sirens began to sound. The noise was blaring. We could hear an ominous rattle in the sky, and we knew we had only minutes to get to the bomb shelter across the street.

All I remember was Monsieur Armel, shouting: "Now!" Alex and I, unable to speak, locked eyes for a split second before we all jumped up from our seats. We left everything where it was: the bread on the table, the radio still broadcasting the news. Everyone realized there was nothing more important than getting out of the apartment building alive. No one mentioned a single rare book or my priceless Haggadah. We just rushed out of the apartment, and as the sky went from blue to dark gray, all we could do was hope we got inside the hatch before the city was engulfed in a blaze of red.

Once inside the dark, damp chamber, we saw the flickering of flashlights and families crouched together. I kept close to Alex, grateful to have a warm and comforting body next to me.

In the corner, I saw a mother trying to soothe her small children, while not far from them two older boys, around nine or ten, were debating whether it was better to die by bombing or by poison gas.

"Gas," one of them finally decided. "There wouldn't be any blood," he said pragmatically. The other one nodded, as if impressed with his friend's practical reasoning.

Inside, I had a pit in my stomach. What had the world become that children were now discussing their own death, as though it were a menu option? As I looked around and saw the blank faces clustered amongst us, I realized that our emotions might be the first thing we are forced to abandon in war. That the numbness that engulfed our senses was the only way we could sustain ourselves against all the chaos.

Hours later, when we were told it was safe to return to our apartments, we stepped out of the open hatch and into the light. Our eyes had become so used to the darkness, that now the sunlight threatened to blind us.

The roads were paved with broken glass and debris. Store windows were shattered and streetlights were pulled out from the pavement like rootless trees.

As Monsieur Armel steadied himself on Alex's arm, we all looked in the direction of their apartment building, breathing a sigh of relief that it still stood intact. We began to make our way back, the shards of broken glass crushing under the soles of our shoes.

Although the apartment had not been damaged in the bombings, we all remained quite shaken. Many buildings were not as lucky, and smoke could be seen rising from the neighboring destruction. Torn curtains floated out of broken windows, like apparitions. A broken desk, cleaved in half, managed to find its way into the street, perhaps thrown from a building during impact. Around us, debris floated like a flock of dying birds.

We would later learn that the epicenter of the bombing was in the Auteuil quarter, dangerously close to us. The Germans had sought to bomb the Renault and Citroën factories that bordered the city, but the nearby areas had also suffered extensive damage from the one thousand bombs that had been dropped.

If we needed a wake-up call, we now had one. The radio blared the reports of the French causalities: hundreds feared dead, dozens of fires, and fifteen factories destroyed. We all knew that the warfare would only escalate and that the danger to Paris would increase.

I could see the anxiety on Monsieur Armel's face and knew that he had been finalizing the negotiation with Clavel's contact.

"Monsieur Clavel has a dealer meeting us in Marseille that will be the liaison for the collector that is purchasing the book," he informed us.

"We leave in four days for the south," Monsieur Armel announced later that afternoon. "We can take only our essentials. Solomon and his family will be coming with us, too."

He looked exhausted. "Solange, you will need to take care of both your father's apartment and your grandmother's.

"I've already paid a deposit to an organization that is helping to arrange the transportation of Jewish travelers out of France. They'll be securing our transit visas and boat tickets. But we must not waste any time. The visas will have an expiration date, and the boat from Lisbon won't wait for us."

. . .

As Monsieur Armel and Alex prepared to leave, I had two apartments that I needed to close. My childhood home was now devoid of most of my sentimental attachments. I had already moved most of my journals, clothes, and even the old Mickey Mouse doll from my father's to my grandmother's. My father had taken care of what paperwork there was before he left, and there was little of value that remained except for my mother's beautiful bookshelf, which I knew I could not possibly take with me. But if I was going to sell the Barcelona Haggadah, I needed to replace it with another book that could keep me connected to my mother, something of sentimental value. So I returned to the apartment to take one last piece of her before I left Paris.

"Do you want me to come with you?" Alex asked as he stood knee-deep in his family's living room trying to figure out if there were any books they had overlooked that they still might be able to sell.

"No, that's kind of you." I shook my head. "But I think I need to do it myself."

Less than an hour later, I arrived at my childhood apartment, quietly opening the door to the entrance and walking up the narrow stairs as I had done so many times in my life.

When I entered, the apartment already looked sparse. Although it was early spring, the rooms were cold, and if emptiness had a smell, this was it. It struck me then and there that the smells and sounds of life are what created a sense of warmth within a home. The same could be said about Marthe's apartment. Without the fragrance of her fresh flowers, the trail of her perfume, or the sound of her heels against the wooden floorboards, the apartment seemed more like a mausoleum than a home.

The only bit of color remaining in our old apartment was my

mother's bookshelf. I walked over and scanned the shelves, which were lined with scores of novels and slender volumes of poetry. If I could take only one book that encapsulated my memory of her, it had to be one that I remembered her holding between her hands. I reached for the book of fairy tales that she had read to me so many times when I was a child, and placed it in my bag. The cover was worn around the edges; the paper had yellowed. But when I opened the book and smelled its pages, it reminded me of my mother. I was bringing with me the fragrance of my childhood when I slipped that tattered old book into my bag.

As I walked toward my bedroom, I had the strange sensation that I was moving through the rooms of a dollhouse. Everything looked smaller than I remembered it. My bed with the floral coverlet now looked childish to me. My chair, with its pale yellow cushion, also didn't look like it befitted a grown woman. Even my wooden desk contained traces of me from another time. I lifted one of my old notepads and saw that some of the sentences I had written over the years had transferred through the sheet paper. Like an old palimpsest, the words were etched into the wood.

But I would take nothing from this room on my journey with the Armels. I had already removed what I needed. And now I had in my possession one more book from my mother. I felt at peace with the notion that I might never return to this apartment. Unlike Marthe with her apartment, Father did not own his. How many months in advance father paid the rent, I did not know. And it was likely that the landlord would take possession of our apartment once the rent ceased to be paid and neither my father nor I reappeared.

So I silently said good-bye to the rooms where I had spent my childhood, and the furniture on which I had shared meals with my parents or read my books.

I shut the door and walked toward the living room one last time. I took a piece of paper from my father's desk and sat down to write.

Dear Papa,

I have written you more times than I can now count, but my letters have remained unanswered. I don't know if you're alive or dead. I pray that you are safe and unwounded, and that it is only the channels of communication that have prevented you from telling me how you're faring . . .

I placed my note in an envelope and wrote on the front, *For Papa.* Then I quietly walked out the door.

When I arrived at my grandmother's apartment, I was surprised to discover Giselle's bag in the vestibule.

Perched on a stepstool, she was dusting with a feather brush the ornaments on the shelves flanking Marthe's portrait, her gray hair pinned behind her ears.

"I wasn't expecting to see you here," I said as I placed my bag down and walked closer to her. "Please tell me you and your family are safe and no damage happened to your home from the other day."

"No, Solange, we were lucky, thank God."

I placed my hand on her back and helped her down from the stool.

"And still after all the chaos, you come here . . . I had hoped you'd be able to spend more time with your family now that Marthe is gone."

Giselle placed down her feather duster on the lower shelf. "I have spent nearly all my adult life here, Solange. It's hard now to know what to do with all the extra time I have."

My eyes softened as I looked at her. She was still strong. And with her silver hair and blue-gray eyes, she appeared attractive despite her age.

"I have kept this house sparkling and the household running for fiftysomething years. During the rare times when your grandmother's coffers were low, I went weeks without being paid. But your grandmother never went back on her word. She always managed to come through for me." Giselle's voice began to waver slightly. "Do you know I received a letter from her lawyer? She left me a small pension for my retirement."

"Yes, it's so well deserved," I answered. In my conversation with Marthe's lawyer, I was surprised how much thought Marthe had put into the planning of her estate. In addition to creating a fund for Giselle, she had also put a considerable amount of money aside to pay for the annual maintenance of the apartment.

"You are now nearly the same age as your grandmother was when I began working for her," she said, her gaze firmly focused on me.

"You have the same dancing eyes, and soulful intelligence. I cannot properly express how happy it made me to see you come into your grandmother's life."

I could feel the emotion thick between us.

"And knowing your loyalty toward my grandmother all these years has been a great comfort to me," I added.

Giselle lowered her gaze. "I know you no longer need me. But it was important for me to come back to the apartment for one last good-bye."

I smiled, and could feel the emotion welling inside me. Tears began to form at the corners of my eyes.

"I, too, am going away now, Giselle. I'm not sure when I'll return, but you needn't worry, the apartment will be well cared for. Marthe will still rule over the apartment." I lifted my chin in the direction of her portrait. "Just as she wanted, and just as she should."

"We must assume that I won't be coming back for some time," I told her. "So we should remove anything that is perishable and clear the cupboards and icebox. Take whatever is left home for your family," I told her.

So she packed up the flour and sugar, the jars of fruit preserves, and even the tins of dried herbs. I then went into the little room where I had slept since December, and made sure nothing had been overlooked. I left the Mickey Mouse doll from Father and a few of my old notepads. Taking only the journals of Marthe's story that I had filled over the past two years.

It was only after I had embraced Giselle and we said our good-byes that I allowed myself to amble through the apartment one last time. I pushed open the French doors to Grandmother's bedroom, which had remained untouched since her death.

Giselle had made up the bed. The pillows were crisp, the silk shams puffed up like clouds. And in dazzling colors woven above, butterflies danced within the upholstered headboard. I could almost hear the beating of their wings.

I walked down the hallway and stood gazing at the portrait of Marthe rising over the fireplace, ruling over the room. I heard her voice in my ear, as if she were still there beside me, telling me another story, and sharing with me her wisdom from a well-experienced life.

"Go," she said, urging me onward. "I am as I should be, safely ensconced in my home. And I'm still young and beautiful."

I felt the warmth flowing from her pearls around my neck. I gave one last farewell to all her beautiful ceramics, the two matched rhinoceros horns, the velvet bergères, and cushioned settee. All those things that Marthe had handpicked and kept so dear. And in those final glances, I pressed them each into my mind as though they were pieces of her that would remain forever beautiful and untouched, like a secret treasure chest sealed from prying eyes.

Only then did I reach into my pocket for the key to the apartment. I stepped out and quietly locked the door.

53.

June 1940

In the days before our own departure, we could hear cars being packed, the men and women shouting at each other as they tried to tie their suitcases atop their cars and cram as many people inside.

"Can't they leave more quietly?" Monsieur Armel complained. He lifted his fingers from the typewriter and pressed them to his temples.

From the Armels' tall living room windows, I could see several cars loaded with trunks and suitcases. Carpets tied to the roofs. Dogs ran alongside the cars.

"Where will they all go?" I asked Alex, who now stood beside me.

"To the countryside. Burgundy, perhaps. Some to the south. No one wants to be here if there is another bombing."

I was surprised that I didn't feel panic. Instead, a numbness had overtaken my body as if I couldn't allow myself to think further than a few hours ahead.

"It will take them all day to get out of Paris and probably several more to get any further."

I touched the sleeve of his shirt. We had all been counting the days until our own departure, and the frustration and impatience with the situation was thick.

I peered down at the streets, my eyes again falling upon the abandoned dogs.

"Those dogs were once beloved pets, but now their owners are just leaving them . . ."

His hand slid down to squeeze my fingers.

"We're not leaving anyone behind." He came closer and whispered into my ear. "You know that, Solange. Not you, not Solomon, not his family."

"I know," I said. "But I wish we could take one with us . . ."

He shook his head. "I do, too, but the car will be too tight as it is with Solomon's family.

"Someone will care for them. I promise you."

I couldn't help but wonder if what he said would prove true. If the Germans came into the city, would they be kinder to the dogs than they would to the men and women whose lives fell into their hands? I knew there wouldn't be enough kindness to go around for both.

We left at the crack of dawn, moving as silently as mimes, gesturing what to bring and what to leave behind. Outside, black birds flew overhead, and the sky was cloudy as quartz.

We packed only the essentials. The car would be taking seven people, so the children would have to sit on Rachel's and my laps. The suitcases were loaded and secured atop with rope.

I stood just outside the car waiting for Monsieur Armel's signal that I should sit inside. I felt Alex slide up against me. "I want to give you something before we set out."

He reached into his pocket. "Consider it a promise," he whispered as he pulled out a gold ring and slipped it on my finger.

I stared at the slender gold band, hardly able to believe my eyes. "It was my mother's," he whispered. "Papa gave it to me last night." He leaned over and kissed me. "We're leaving everything behind, Solange. So this is my first step to putting down roots, wherever we end up."

I felt my heart in my throat. My hands reached for his. I wanted Marthe's watch. I wanted to believe it was possible to make time stand still.

But Monsieur Armel had a schedule to maintain. Both Alex and I heard him barking orders for everyone to get into the car.

As Rachel slid in with the children, Monsieur Armel came over to Alex and me and patted him affectionately on the back. "Congratulations to the two of you . . . We'll celebrate once we get to Marseille, but for now, there is no time to spare."

Solomon sat on the passenger side, with Alex, Rachel, and me squeezed in the back with the children.

We were already packed tightly against each other, with one in the middle. Leo, the more restless of the two children, was on Rachel's lap, and the young boy was fidgeting to get comfortable.

"Let me take Eva," Alex whispered to me.

Eva had just turned six, but she was finely boned and felt nearly weightless on my lap.

"It's no bother," I told him. "I find her a comfort." The warm smell of the little girl's skin close to mine was soothing.

"We have a long ride ahead of us." He squeezed my hand. "You must tell me if your legs get tired from the extra weight."

I tightened my fingers around his, marveling with the new sight that my ring finger was no longer bare. The gold band shimmered in the light.

"I will, I promise," I told him. And my heart fluttered. I nearly wondered if the precious butterfly clasp, which I now had hidden beneath my hair, beat its wings against my neck.

Monsieur Armel took one final look to make sure the suitcases were tightly secured. The night before, Monsieur Armel and Solomon had carefully examined the Haggadah one last time before packing it in several layers of protective paper.

"We must try to make sure the car doesn't get too hot or too cold. Changes in temperature or humidity can cause the pigment to lift off the page. We've told the dealer the illustrations are intact, and we'll need to ensure we deliver it that way."

"Yes," Monsieur Armel agreed. "We wouldn't want any of the illustrations to detach."

They had prepared the Haggadah as though it were a priceless jewel. Not only was it wrapped in protective paper, but also in a cushion of white sheeting. Then, it was placed in a separate box along with two other books Monsieur Armel hoped to sell. Everyone in the car knew the books were our currency. Since we had not been successful in getting sponsorship to the United States, we would go to South America, where no sponsorship was necessary, and try to make a new life there within the expatriate community.

"It is not ideal," Alex had confided to me, "but perhaps eventually we can then make our way to North America. Papa just doesn't want to wait here until it's too late."

I understood. Time was of the essence. With the oceans already filled with battleships, no one knew how much longer passenger boats would be able to cross the Atlantic. Once we got to Marseille, there was still much we had to do before we got to Portugal and began our voyage. We needed to pick up our transit visas at the Spanish embassy, as well as a certificate of health and good conduct for each of us. And our entry visas to South America. It was no wonder that Monsieur Armel didn't want to squander a single minute. The organization HICEM, which was assisting us, would also need to be paid in full so we could receive our boat tickets.

"Are we all set back here?" Alex's father opened the back door of the car and leaned in.

Rachel pulled Leo close to her chest, and the little boy gave off a little whine.

"Shhhhhh," she whispered into his ear. "Bernard, I think it will be best for everyone if we start to drive."

"Agreed," he said as he shut the back door and made his way to the driver's side.

Monsieur Armel turned on the ignition, the rumble of the engine sending waves beneath our seat. From the front of the car, Solomon quietly uttered: "May God be with us."

54.

June 1940

We were packed like sardines. Even with the windows rolled down, we were hot and uncomfortable. Our thighs pushed against each other, and our arms touched. We could smell each other's breath.

I had not expected to see the roads as crowded as they were. Both in front and in back of us, large sedans packed to the brim with valises and trunks surrounded us. We saw carts loaded with families, too. Some carried with them furniture, or cages with brightly colored chickens. On a flatbed truck, we saw an old piano secured with several yards of rope, with mattresses and suitcases buttressing it from all sides.

After nearly three hours of driving, Rachel suggested we pull off the main road and try to find an inn so the children could use the bathroom and have something to eat.

It was a good thought. None of us had eaten breakfast, and the children had grown increasingly restless under the cramped quarters.

Leo had been whimpering for the past hour in Rachel's lap, and she had tried to no avail to soothe him.

"I'll try to pull over soon," Monsieur Armel agreed. In the rear-view window, I could see the fatigue in his eyes. None of us had slept well for the past few nights. Solomon also looked exhausted. His olive skin was sallow, his hair was unruly, and his clothes were creased. It was hard to imagine the quiet and elegant Rachel being drawn to such a rumpled character.

"*Maman, Maman,*" Leo was crying in his sleep.

Solomon turned around and spoke to Rachel in Yiddish. She caressed the little boy's hair with her hand as she answered him.

"We're sorry he is complaining so much. I hope it's not disturbing everyone."

"He's such a pest!" Eva chimed. "Papa told us we had to be on our best behavior!"

"Shhhhh!" Rachel admonished the little girl. "He isn't feeling well. Let him be." She shook her head to show her dissatisfaction with Eva's behavior. "We all just need to get out and stretch our legs."

A few hours later, we found an inn and piled out of the car, our legs wobbly as if we had been at sea. Rachel still had Leo in her arms as she stepped out. Eva ran ahead of us, and I hovered behind to try to have a few moments of privacy with Alex.

"I feel sorry for the children," I said softly. "We're all so cramped from the drive."

Alex shook his head. "We'll let them run around here a little bit. They probably haven't experienced the French countryside before." He stood there looking a bit pale, his white shirt and pants now as creased as Solomon's. The house before us, with its thatched roof and the tractor stacked with bales of hay, looked like a painting. Even the sunlight appeared preternaturally golden.

I stepped closer to him, hoping to feel the graze of his hand against mine. The air smelled of spring, a perfume of freshly cut grass and blooming honeysuckle. For a brief moment, I wondered what it would be like if we traveled no further. If we managed to find a farmhouse somewhere and raise a family quietly under the canopy of trees and scampering animals.

"It's so peaceful here," Alex said as if reading my mind. "It's a shame we can't stay longer, but I think Papa is hoping we can make it to Orléans by tonight. We will see how crowded the roads are," Alex said, breaking the silence.

I took a deep breath of the air. I did not want to imagine reentering the car and squeezing against the others again.

"Then, hopefully we can make it to Dijon." Alex leaned over and kissed me. His eyes remained closed as our lips parted. "I never had the chance to thank you for agreeing to sell your mother's Haggadah."

I felt his breath warm against me, and saw the dark rounds of his eyes.

"I would like to believe it was destiny," I whispered. "Without that book, we would never have met each other."

Alex's fingers tightened around mine. "I wonder if Rabbi Avram and his wife are smiling down on us. All these years later, the book has been passed down through countless hands, creating a story with each of its owners."

I smiled. This book, which had been created to teach the ancient traditions of the Jewish faith, had now inspired love and also helped ensure our survival. I was not thinking of Rabbi Avram or his artistic wife, however. I was imagining the woman who owned the Haggadah before me. My thoughts were solely of my mother.

That evening, a farmer outside of Bourges agreed to let us use his loft in exchange for some francs Monsieur Armel offered for us staying the night. When we all climbed the wooden ladder, we discovered that the accommodations were sparse. We would be sleeping on mattresses that smelled of straw.

Leo seemed unlike his playful self. He hovered close to his mother. His pallor was chalk white.

I undressed behind the stacks of hay, pulling my nightgown over me like a tarp. Beneath the white cotton, my skin flushed. I kept Marthe's pearls around my neck, believing they were safest there.

It was cruel to be so close to Alex and not be able to touch him. The slender gold band on my finger felt like a promise, and now, beneath my nightgown, I could feel the pull of my body yearning to be close to his. Alex had brought the box with my Haggadah and the other valuables into the loft so they wouldn't be left in the car overnight.

He placed them between our two mattresses. And as I lay down on the bed, I closed my eyes and imagined the books forming a bridge, hoping he, too, felt my desire flowing through the space between us.

In the morning, I found Monsieur Armel crouched on an old wooden crate speaking with Solomon. He held a long twig in his hand and he was drawing a map on the dusty floor.

"If we don't encounter any problems, we can get to Lyon from here by the evening."

Solomon's eyes were focused on the ground. He looked haggard, as if he hadn't slept all night.

"That will keep us on track for meeting Clavel's dealer Thursday morning."

Solomon nodded.

"Our own exodus." Monsieur Armel nodded in agreement with Solomon. "Let's hope the waters also part for us in Marseille just as they do in the pictures in the Haggadah."

· · ·

Leo had slept curled at his mother's side all night, his cheek pressed to her chest, his arm draped over the width of her body.

"*Lieblinge*," Solomon whispered as he knelt down closer to them. "Darlings."

Rachel's arms instinctively stroked her sleeping child as she was roused from sleep. The sight of such pure, maternal affection warmed me as I slipped away to get dressed behind the bales of hay. When I emerged, Alex had already put his pants on and was buttoning his shirt.

"Seems like we'll be off as soon as the children and Rachel are ready."

I nodded. I was nearly ready. All I needed to do was put on my shoes.

Alex and I glanced over at Rachel, who seemed to be whispering to Solomon. Her face looked pained. Leo was still in his pajamas and she cradled him in one arm, his legs dangling over her lap.

We both sensed something was amiss.

"I think she just told Solomon the child has a fever."

We watched silently as Solomon placed a hand on Leo's forehead. The little boy shivered slightly at his father's touch.

Solomon's face was also now pale. He said something again in Yiddish that neither Alex nor I understood. But Monsieur Armel, who had a working understanding of the language, seemed to understand perfectly well.

For several minutes, we stood silently, unsure of what would happen next. Rachel was now rocking little Leo in her arms in an effort to soothe him. Eva, who had awakened and dressed herself, now walked over to Alex and me.

"He's sick." Her voice sounded very much like an annoyed older sister. "*Maman* is saying we should let him rest here before we go any further."

My heart sank. I knew this was an impossible request. There was no way we could make it to Marseille in time to meet the dealer if we delayed ourselves by even a day here. Time was of the essence if we were going to get out of France.

"I'm very sorry, but we all must leave today. We need to bring him with us; we can't leave you here alone." Monsieur Armel's voice was firm.

"He just has a cold, Rachel," Solomon insisted. "Look, even his eyes are red and his nose is runny. Let him sleep in the car. I'm sure it will pass by tomorrow or the next day."

I could see the look of anguish on Rachel's face. Clearly, the child was in terrible discomfort.

Again she muttered something underneath her breath as she placed Leo down and reached for her clothes beside the bed. He clenched his eyes shut and he looked like a newborn rabbit, his eyes swollen and rimmed with pink.

No one but Rachel seemed to think he was suffering from anything more than a cold.

In less than fifteen minutes' time, we were all headed toward the car.

We arrived just outside Lyon by sundown, and Solomon carried Leo up the stairs of another farmhouse that was renting two rooms for the night.

"I'm sorry you're stuck in here with us, Solange, but they don't have any other options for us," Monsieur Armel apologized. "A young lady should have her own room, or at least sleep with a mother and her children. But no one wants to risk you also getting sick. We're already in too-tight quarters with the car."

"I don't mind," I said, and it was true. I was happy just to be able to stretch out on a bed at night after sitting in such a twisted position in the car for so many hours. Secretly, however, I wished I could be alone with Alex in the room.

Monsieur Armel looked at his watch. "The farmer and his wife have invited us to join them for dinner tonight." He stood up and walked toward the window. Outside there was nothing but fields and orchard trees. The urban splendor of Paris was far behind us now. It seemed completely possible that the owners of the farmhouse had never laid eyes on Notre Dame or the Eiffel Tower. I closed my eyes for a moment and tried to imagine I was not cramped in a small room in the French countryside, but back sitting in my grandmother's elegant parlor. That instead of the damp smell of wood and straw, I was inhaling the delicate bouquet of violets.

We settled down for dinner around a large wooden table and several mismatched chairs. A basket of thick bread was passed to us by the matron of the farm, and we all tore large slices and filled our hungry stomachs with the warm and yeasty loaf.

Solomon had remained upstairs with Rachel and little Leo, but Eva was enjoying the opportunity to be the only child at the table.

"Have a little more chicken," the old woman urged Eva. "It seems like you have quite a journey ahead of you." She looked kindly onto the little girl. "And such a pretty dress you have!"

The woman's vision must have been cloudy or else she was just being kind. Eva's dress was now almost in tatters. Smudges of dirt created unattractive shadows across the front placket. The hem had come partly undone on the skirt so that it hung unevenly. But Rachel had tied the girl's braids neatly, and her blue eyes and fair hair gave her an angelic quality that was apparent even to those with the poorest eyesight.

"We were not lucky enough to have our own," the old woman lamented. "So it's nice to be able to put up two families for the night." She turned to me. "I suppose you'll be a mother soon."

I blushed, turning the ring that Alex had given me before we left. Alex didn't answer her. He simply placed his hand on mine and smiled.

But our affectionate moment would be short-lived. Later that evening, as the radio was brought out, we heard the terrible news that Italy had declared war on Great Britain and France.

We all felt under a black cloud. Leo's fever had not abated, and Rachel was now even more insistent that they not travel any further.

"His nose is still running and he's lethargic," Solomon informed us later that evening. "I told her there will be good doctors in Marseille. I know we have to maintain our schedule."

Monsieur Armel appeared visibly torn. Our schedule would not allow a single missed day. Everything had been planned. The meeting with the dealer could not be rearranged. The ship leaving Lisbon would not wait. The transit visas had already been ordered and had an expiration date. Our schedule had to be maintained with clocklike precision.

"Rachel." He said her name quietly. "You know we cannot stay . . ."

Her eyes fell to the floor, then shut closed. "I wouldn't be a mother," she whispered as a single tear fell down her cheek, "unless I at least asked . . ."

By now we were all sick of being in the car together. The evening before, Rachel had scrubbed Eva with a bar of laundry soap and towels soaked in boiling hot water in hope of preventing the spread of Leo's germs. I could smell the fresh scent on the girl's skin. I tried to channel my grandmother and still make myself look presentable. I had not bathed since we left Paris, but I took out a little vial of rose oil and pressed it behind my ears and at my pulse points. My hair, which was now limp and without curl, I pinned back in an artful chignon.

We were like bedouins at this point, with all our worldly possessions packed into the car, traveling on roads that brimmed with other people like us, all trying to get as far away from the capital to places where they thought they'd be safer. I thought of the Haggadah safely wrapped in brown paper and crated in the trunk, and the story of the Israelites' exodus now resonated deeply within me. I felt a connection to my mother, with her family, as I grasped Alex's fingers through my hand.

Leo was now wrapped in a blanket. He complained the light hurt his eyes, and Rachel tried to create a cocoon for him where his face was pressed against her breast.

It was still nearly one hundred kilometers until Marseille, and Monsieur Armel was determined to get there before sundown. My Haggadah was safely in the back, and I closed my eyes imagining the rabbi and his wife who had initially created the beautiful book all those years ago. Soon it would be passed into new hands, with a new life ahead of it.

For the next several hours, we rode in the crowded car. We spoke little, hoping to let Leo sleep as much as possible. Outside we passed stretches of farmland. Small villages made of fieldstone, and a single church steeple that pierced the sky. Occasionally, Monsieur Armel would be forced to stop for petrol, and all of us, except for Rachel and Leo, would pile out of the car and stretch our legs and breathe in the fresh air.

The bread and cheese we had packed at the beginning of our journey had been finished, and our stomachs rumbled with hunger. At the petrol station, Monsieur Armel bought us sandwiches and we sat outside with our faces tilted toward the sun.

"We probably have four more hours or so until we reach the city," he told Alex and me.

Alex nodded, chewing on the last bites of his sandwich, and I sighed. The constant traveling had depleted me. I was exhausted. Leaning against his shoulder, I looked at the packed car, which seemed to sag from the journey. The black doors were covered in dust; the wheels were caked in mud. All I hoped was that we would get to Marseille safely.

I fell asleep for the rest of the journey, only to be awakened by the noise of a bustling port city as we entered Marseille. Our journey suddenly felt terribly real, far more so than even when we had first loaded our suitcases or closed down the apartments. In contrast to the countryside of the past few days, I now saw the familiar terrain of an urban setting. Though there was something far more exotic to Marseille. Unlike Paris, with its elegant stone buildings and imperial grandeur, here the city had a uniquely Mediterranean feeling. Many of the buildings were as white as the seagulls that circled overhead. As we drove closer to the port, I could hardly believe my eyes. The water was the most extraordinary color I had ever seen. Blue and veined like marble. Boats in the harbor sounded their horns, dockmen hollered, and seagulls sqauwked. Outside a tobacco shop, at least ten men in military uniforms stood smoking cigarettes, their eyes tracing the girls who floated by, their cotton skirts lifting like sails.

It took us at least another hour of driving through the city to find a vacancy in one of the hotels that could accommodate all of us.

Finally, Monsieur Armel found three vacant rooms, not far from the port in a hotel that looked like it was something out of one of my mother's old novels. The building, once majestic, was now in disrepair. The facade was crumbling, the stucco was cracked, and behind the wrought-iron balconies, the hotel's tall windows were kept open, their dingy curtains fluttering like old dresses in the sea air.

As we began untying the cord that secured our suitcases to the roof, Monsieur Armel took charge.

"Solomon, get Leo inside and we'll tell the concierge to call him a doctor. There's a pharmacy down the block." He reached into his pocket to offer some money for Alex. "Why don't you try to get some fever powder for him to make him more comfortable?"

I remembered my father mixing those sachets of powder in a glass of water when I had a temperature. I felt a longing for his calm and his wisdom now. I knew he would have been able to speak with the pharmacist about what would make Leo feel better. I loathed the war, the vacuum that had swallowed up the normal channels of communication. My mind began to rush as I wondered how he'd be able to locate me once we left France. I imagined him returning to our apartment to find my note, and knew that it was essential that I write him again before we left Marseille, just in case there was the slightest chance he had returned safely.

Alex stood watch over the car as we brought our valises into the hotel. Just before Monsieur Armel returned to park the car, the trunk was opened to remove the box with the books.

"Oh my God!" Alex's voice scorched through the air. I turned and peered into the trunk. Unbeknownst to us, the well-intentioned farmer had placed a bottle of wine in the trunk as a parting gift to us. The bottle had broken and flooded the bottom of the car. The crate that contained the Haggadah was partially stained the most terrifying color of Bordeaux.

I grew pale and my stomach felt as though it had just been sliced through by a sharp blade. I reached to touch the box, and the corner was soaked through in red wine. "It can't be!" I cried out. It seemed like we were both having the same nightmare.

In perfect synchronicity, Alex and I stretched our hands to pull the box closer to us.

I had no idea if the wine had soaked through the crate, but it was clear the wooden box was affected by the spill. As I touched the saturated corner, I felt as though we were touching a painful wound.

"Don't panic," Alex said in a vain attempt to appear that he had the situation under control. But I could hear the fear in his voice; the terror was palpable. The Haggadah was our ticket out of France, and if it was destroyed, we were going nowhere.

"We need to unwrap them now," he said. He lifted the books from the crate. The box and the bottom layer of packing material were clearly affected by the wine, but the brown wrapping paper seemed pristine. Still, we needed to check.

Quickly I began to pull the paper off of the Haggadah, while Alex removed it from his father's books.

As I lifted the Haggadah out of its layers of protective paper, I was relieved to discover that it had not been affected by the wine spill. But the book had not come through our journey unscathed.

"Look," I said, showing him one of the red-and-blue-colored decorative birds. The rich blue color was flaking and cracking. It looked as though some of the pigment was lifting off from the page.

Alex turned white. "The wine spill must have caused a change in moisture." He took the book from me and began to inspect the other leaves.

"Luckily, it only seems to be on that page."

"But how will we be able to repair it?" I was so upset, I could hardly breathe.

Alex's face still looked grave. "It will depend on Solomon," he said softly. "He'll be the only one who can restore it. If it can be done at all."

Poor Solomon was already beside himself worrying about Leo. The doctor was called as Rachel waited by the sick child's bed. Monsieur Armel brought Solomon into our room, where the book was laid out on our bed.

"Solomon, we have an issue with the Haggadah . . ." His skin was pale and the strain on his face was evident. "Without the money from these books, we're not going anywhere."

Solomon leaned over and appraised the damage.

"It's as I feared. Consolidation has occurred."

Monsieur Armel let out an agonizing sound, a grunt that sounded almost like a dying animal. "I needn't tell you that our passage out of France depends on this book. You realize that more than anyone here."

"Is there any way we can repair it?"

Solomon was quiet. "It's not going to be easy, Bernard . . . I'll need to seed a gelatin between the pigment and the parchment." He shook his head. "It will be difficult and time intensive . . ."

"But do you have the supplies and instruments to even do that?"

Solomon nodded. "I can make an adhesive with gelatin and some wheat starch . . . Still, it will not be easy. We'll have to keep our fingers crossed that I can reattach it to the parchment."

As Rachel tended to Leo's fever, Solomon immediately set himself in motion. He took the small black satchel he had brought with him and removed his instruments. Half of them looked like they belonged to a surgeon, and the other half to a painter: two flat sable brushes, three with rounded tips; several scalpels; cotton swabs; a tweezer, and something else that I didn't recognize. Later, I would learn it was a spun-glass burnisher for removing threads from illuminated manuscripts.

He took the book and laid it on the towel, and used the tip of his scalpel to start lifting the **corners of** the pages to make sure there was no other damage. He no longer looked at it as a casual observer would, but as an expert restorer analyzing the damage with razor-sharp eyes.

We watched transfixed, all of us holding our breath as he began to prepare the necessary adhesive.

"Seeding the gelatin beneath each little flake will take hours and require my full attention," Solomon informed us. "It is best you leave me so I can concentrate on the work . . ."

We all understood and were about to leave him to his work when there was a knock on the door. It was the doctor, who had finished examining Leo.

Solomon got up and walked over to speak with him.

But the doctor did not lower his voice when he told Solomon his diagnosis. We all heard it as clear as a bell.

"I'm afraid, Monsieur Weckstein, your son has come down with the measles."

Just when we thought we had experienced the worst-possible blow, we received Leo's diagnosis. All of the adults knew what this meant. Leo would have to be quarantined, as would Eva, who unlike the rest of us, had not yet had the disease.

"I will speak to the hotel director about making sure all the necessary precautions are taken. But keep him in his room. He has spots in his mouth. I suspect the rash will appear on his chest by tomorrow."

Words escaped us. As Leo's fever escalated, Rachel kept vigil. She applied cool compresses to his forehead and spoon-fed him broth that the hotel owner's wife brought up to his room.

· · ·

Alex went out to the pharmacy and bought fever powder. In his satchel, he carried some provisions for a modest dinner. Some bread, cheese, a jar of cornichons, and a few sprigs of parsley, which he said was the only bit of fresh greens he could find.

"You've done well," Monsieur Armel murmured softly. "Better than I expected, and we'll make do." He looked exhausted. He had spent the past hour shuttling between negotiating with the hotel owner, who was not as compassionate as his wife, to let the sick child remain quarantined in his room, and keeping Solomon focused on trying to save the Haggadah despite being distracted by the news of his ailing son.

As I was lucky enough to have my own room, Alex suggested we have dinner in my quarters.

The idea was a welcome distraction, and I began to prepare the space. I opened up the windows, allowing the briny sea air to fill the room. It felt good to inhale a fragrance that was both foreign and invigorating. Outside, I could hear the bustling sounds of the city, which felt reassuring. Taxis honked, men shouted to each other on the streets, and I could hear foghorns blaring from the port. It was unfortunate that we could not leave directly from Marseille, but at this point, only a few transatlantic ships would risk taking civilians through the dangerous waters for fear of being torpedoed. And we were informed we had no other choice but to leave on a boat from Lisbon. I looked around the dingy hotel room. The walls, once painted white, now looked like the color of newsprint. The only adornment in the room was a single framed portrait of a woman in a field holding a basket. It amazed me that in only a few weeks' time, my living arrangements had gone from one extreme to another. I heard Marthe's throaty laugh in my ear, as if she were there in the room with me, gazing at the completely artless painting on the wall.

Somehow, however, I had to create a space for everyone to eat. I looked around the room and tried to find some inspiration. The bed was made up in white sheets and a simple cotton coverlet. Improvising, I removed the coverlet and placed it on the ground. I took the writing tray the hotel had provided down the hallway and washed it with soap and water.

When Alex entered the room . . . "It's not much, but it's more than I expected to find so late in the day." I smiled and took the bag from him, kissing him sweetly on the cheek.

"Do you have a pocket knife so I can cut the bread and cheese? I'll put it over there," I said, pointing to the freshly washed writing tray. "We can pretend it's our little feast."

"Did anyone ever tell you that you're perfect?" he said as his arm pulled me onto my feet. He brought me into his arms and kissed me. His mouth tasted of parsley. Of spring and possibility. I kissed him back, my entire body melting into his.

That evening, as Leo slept in the room next door, his rash flaming over his little body, we managed to get Rachel to come in and sit with us for a few minutes before returning to her son.

With little extra space to spare, we all sat on the floor with our legs slightly draped beneath us. "It almost feels like a Seder," Alex said to all of us. "We've left nearly everything behind, and a long journey is still ahead of us."

I looked around the room and felt that I had been absorbed into the most extraordinary family. My heart was full. For the pages of the Haggadah were no longer just ink and vellum to me. They had sprung to life, a narrative continuing before my very eyes.

Solange

There is part of me, the writer, that would like to end my story here. Our makeshift dinner on the floor of our hotel room. My new life beginning with a journey from a port in the South of France, where seagulls circled in the salt-laced air.

I would like to pretend that from there, everything worked out as it should have. That we all escaped France safely, and then managed to build a new life first in Rio de Janeiro and then in New York. That Monsieur Armel rebuilt his rare book business with the help of his handsome and hardworking son.

But as I learned from my grandmother, every story, every life, has its own light and darkness. That beneath the veil of white powder are secrets we all wish to hide.

Years later, when I became a wife and a mother and eventually a novelist, my children would plead with me to tell them the details of my own life story. Their favorite episode was the chapter in which I arrived in South America with their father and grandfather, with nothing more than a suitcase filled with three dresses and a photograph of my parents, clutching the hand of their father, whom I believed to be my most prized possession of all.

They loved for me to tell them how the Haggadah was saved, and how despite the odds being so stacked against us, we managed to escape the Nazis. That we boarded a steamer ship and built a new life in a city where the tango parlors played long into the night and where women tucked camellia flowers into their hair.

I treasured these moments with my children, their eyes wide, their imagination open. It was one thing to finally see my stories published, but my greatest pleasure was when I sat in the big cushioned chair in our Manhattan living room and entertained my children with my stable of tales. I was still young, barely in my thirties, but how I relished capturing their attention! It was hard in those moments not to think of Marthe, all those years ago, when I sat across from her in her parlor, clinging to her every word.

So the story of the Haggadah became a legend in our household. I went into great detail about how Solomon had labored for hours. How with the thinnest tip of his brush, he applied the gelatin, seed by seed, so the colorful pigment that created the red and blue feathers of the decorative bird was reattached to the ancient parchment. The children always breathed the sweetest sigh of relief when I described how the dealer took the Haggadah from Monsieur Armel and handed him enough money to pay the agency that was assisting with our tickets on the SS *Angola*, thus ensuring our passage across the ocean to safer shores. I peppered into the story how on the same ship we met the creators of the children's book series Curious George, Monsieur and Madame Rey, who, like us, would eventually find their way to New York and became lifelong friends.

. . .

But there was a part of the story that I could never share with my children.

You see, shortly after our arrival in Marseille, and just before the Germans marched into Paris, Eva also came down with the measles, and her case was far worse than Leo's. We waited for days in that dingy hotel hoping that she would recover quickly. But the child's fever would not abate. Her face flushed scarlet. Her chest was covered with a terrible rash, tiny red circles that looked as though she had been stung by a thousand angry bees.

The appointment with the doctor who issued the health certificates, the last bit of paperwork necessary for our exit visas, could not be postponed. And we could not exchange our tickets on the ship for new ones. If we waited any longer, we'd never have enough time to get ourselves to Lisbon. Monsieur Armel tried to explain our situation with the organization that was arranging our travel and paperwork, and he was told nothing could be changed. There were too few boats, and our visas would have an expiration date.

"Aren't there any other ships?" Rachel begged. And even if we had the time to find another ship, we wouldn't have been able to afford the passage, as our current tickets could not be refunded.

"Eva will not pass the health examination," Solomon said in a voice steeped in resignation. "And if we were to try to sneak her on board, we would risk infecting those on the ship. I could not live with myself if that happened."

Rachel looked exhausted. She could barely manage her words through her fatigue.

"What are we going to do?"

Solomon spoke carefully. "You and Leo will go now with the Armels. If we're lucky, Leo will pass his medical exam now that the fever has dissipated. I will stay behind with Eva until she gets better."

"I'm not going without you," Rachel said, pushing through her tears. "And I'm not leaving without Eva, either."

"Yes, you will," Solomon insisted. "I'll find a way to eventually join you. You know how resourceful I am . . ."

She shook her head. "I will not risk separating our family." Her voice had suddenly become stronger. Almost defiant. She stood up and looked at him with fierce eyes. "No, Solomon. No."

The following afternoon we departed for our medical exams, leaving Rachel as she tried to cool Eva's fever with an ice bath and cold compresses, with Leo still fast asleep.

The waiting room outside the doctor's office was filled with immigrants. Some dressed in dirty pinafores, others in their Sunday best. The doctor examined me first, his stethoscope cold on my chest, his mallet striking my knee. He listened to my breathing and then felt my abdomen with a quick, brisk touch. With the same mechanical movements, he stamped my paperwork and the Armels', clearing the way for the three of us to leave France. But none of us felt joy or the slightest pang of relief. We felt something far more terrible. When we returned later that afternoon and looked at Rachel with her tired eyes, her daughter resting on her lap and her fingers laced through Leo's hands, we were flooded with a sense of guilt.

And so this chapter of my life story I hid away deep within the channels of my heart. I held my own children close, smelling the fragrance of their hair and the sweet scent of milk from their warm cheeks, and I created my own version of the story when we all arrived in South America and then, years later, made our way to New York. When my daughter asked about my pearl necklace, gently tugging on the emerald green clasp, I placed my hand over hers and told her how I inherited my affection for butterflies from my grandmother. That true love felt like the beating of wings.

It is a painful truth that every life has its own regret. With Marthe, I believe it was the fact that she never fully made peace with my father. That she died before receiving absolution from him, even though she had gifted all of her worldly possessions to both of us in the end.

But for me, it was the reality of having to leave Solomon and his family behind. That was the shadow not only I, but also Alex and his father, would take with us to our grave.

The day we left the Weckstein family in Marseille, we all felt that our hearts were ripped from our chests.

Monsieur Armel and the rest of us did not want to leave them. At the last minute, we all agreed we could try to find a way to book a later passage on a ship out of Lisbon. But Solomon knew more than anyone that the tickets could not be refunded, and that this was our only chance to leave.

"I have some money from my grandmother," I insisted. But Solomon would not hear of it. "We have our children," Solomon said, shaking his head no. "My family is together." He looked at Monsieur Armel, who had taken him under his wing since he arrived in Paris five years before. "And you must now go with yours."

To this day, I can still hear his words in my head like a requiem. At that point, we had no idea of places like Auschwitz or Treblinka. We left Marseille convincing ourselves that somehow Solomon and his family would find a way to get their visas before our ship departed from Lisbon. And should that not happen, they'd find a way to keep safe.

And so we loaded the car to make our way through the Pyrénées, a three-day journey to Lisbon with hardly a word uttered among us. Before leaving, we had peered into the room of the two children. Leo was still recovering; he appeared as thin as paper. But Eva was still in the throes of fever, and her face was flushed a painful red.

But it was the image of Solomon in his black suit, stained with salt rings, his delicate white hands clasped in front of him, that was almost too painful for words. For we all knew that it was he who had restored the damaged Haggadah. It was he who, in the end, had really saved us. His sacrifice, made so quietly and without drama, was lost on no one.

The novels that line my bookshelves now are the same ones that my mother once loved. The French classics, the fairy tales. We also have an extensive library with rare Jewish books, ones that Alex doesn't like to keep in his shop on Madison Avenue. In the corner, there is a special section for my own novels that I've had published over the past decade, in twenty different languages, that Alex always chirps proudly about to our friends.

But this is the book I never published. The one that reveals the story of my father, my grandmother, and ultimately my guilt about Solomon and his family. The secret that I left behind an apartment in Paris, with its rightful owner forever presiding above the marble mantel. The key to its front door sits in the side of my desk drawer, where my children and grandchildren will someday find it when I'm no longer here.

Shortly after Alex and I arrived in South America, I discovered that my father had perished after being forced by the Germans to march to the Northwestern part of France. So for years I instructed Marthe's attorney, then later his successor, to pay the annual fees on her apartment from the money Marthe had left me. I know that one day my granddaughter will marvel at the Boldini portrait, that my grandson will finger my old Mickey Mouse doll, and my daughter will sit on the dove gray sofa and stare at her great-grandmother, with whom she shares the same russet hair and dancing eyes.

Like everyone who looks back on their life, my hope is that my children will see me clearly and without judgment. As a woman not so unlike her grandmother. A woman partly of reinvention, a woman of shadow and of light.

An apartment in the ninth arrondissement of Paris was opened today, revealing an opulent, art-laden home that appeared to be untouched for nearly seventy years.

Dominique Debos, an estate assessor, said, "It was like stumbling into the castle of Sleeping Beauty."

Most interesting was a portrait discovered above the mantel of the original owner, Marthe de Florian, by the nineteenth century portrait painter Giovanni Boldini. All that is known is that Madame de Florian's granddaughter inherited the apartment in 1940 and appears to have paid from abroad the maintenance until her death this year. Her heirs had no idea that the apartment existed until notified by their grandmother's attorney in Paris.

"It is a snapshot of a lost way of life," Debos said. "On the shelves, we discovered rare Chinese porcelains covered in a veil of dust and an original Mickey Mouse doll. In one of Madame de Florian's desk drawers, love letters—tied in satin ribbon—were found."

A neighbor, forty-eight-year-old Alain Hommeriche, said, "I wondered why it was so quiet next door."

The painting of Madame de Florian by Giovanni Boldini is expected to go up for auction later this year.

Author's Note

In 2014, my dear friend Kara Mendelsohn sent me an article that would become the inspiration for this novel. It described the recent discovery of a mysterious apartment in Paris that had been shut for nearly seventy years, ever since the start of World War II. The heirs to the apartment had no idea it even existed until it was first mentioned in the last will and testament of their recently deceased grandmother. When the apartment was finally opened after all that time, it served as a time capsule, as its sumptuous Belle Époque—era furniture, Chinese porcelains, and other fine works from the nineteenth century filled the rooms. But the most intriguing item was a painting of a beautiful woman set in a magnificent gilded frame. It was of the heirs' great-grandmother, the original owner of the apartment, who was a courtesan by the name of Marthe de Florian.

The painting of a young Madame de Florian in her silk gown, its billowing, gauzy sleeves slipping off her bare shoulders, displayed a woman of obvious sensual charms. The auctioneer who was eventually called in to appraise the apartment's antiques and valuable works of art, a Monsieur Choppin-Janvry, suggested the portrait was done by the nineteenth-century artist Giovanni Boldini, who was renowned for his portraits of famous socialites like Consuelo Vanderbilt and

Marchesa Luisa Casati. The auctioneer later confirmed his suspicion that Boldini had painted the portrait after he found love letters from Boldini, tied in satin ribbon, in Marthe's bedroom vanity. The painting of Marthe de Florian would later be sold at auction for 2.1 million euros, a record price for a Boldini painting.

As many of my readers already know, all my novels are inspired by questions to which I do not know the answers. Reading about this mysterious apartment, my mind was filled with them. Who was Marthe de Florian, and how did she come to be painted by the acclaimed painter Giovanni Boldini? How did a woman born Mathilde Beaugiron, the daughter of an impoverished laundress, become a "kept woman" of cultivated luxury and pleasure, living in such a wondrous apartment in the bustling ninth arrondissement? And most important, why did her granddaughter, Solange Beaugiron, who some historians believe was the writer Solange Beaugiron-Beldo, close up her grandmother's apartment just as the Germans were approaching Paris, and never return to it again?

There were few published facts to go on at the time I began writing the novel. Little was known about Marthe de Florian except her original birth name, Mathilde Beaugiron. In 1888, a census listed "seamstress" as Mathilde Beaugiron's occupation. Records also indicate that Mathilde gave birth to two boys, both of whom were named Henri. One died shortly after birth and the second, Henri Beaugiron, was said to have grown up to become a pharmacist. Henri's paternity was not revealed on his birth certificate.

The exact date that Boldini painted the portrait of Marthe de Florian is also surrounded by conflicting reports. A 2010 newspaper article in the *Independent*, a UK newspaper, stated it was painted in 1898, but other sources suggest it was painted in 1888 when Marthe would have been around twenty-four. After studying Boldini's paintings, I believe the portrait to have been painted closer to 1898, when Marthe was thirty-four years of age, not twenty-four. I don't believe the image depicted of the woman in the portrait is one of an ingénue, but rather, of a mature woman who was in full command of her beauty and charms. And so I have written the novel using that date. Neither I, nor my reseach associates in Europe, were able to locate an official death certificate in France for Madame de Florian. In recent months a letter has surfaced written in Henri Beaugiron's hand, which states her death to be August 30, 1939. For the purposes of the novel, I have made her death eight months later in order to coincide with Solange's departure from Paris just prior to the German Occupation.

Solange Beaugiron remains as equally mysterious as her grand-mother. I was lucky enough to have my dear friend and art historian, Costanza Bertolotti, discover a 1938 article from the French news-paper *L'Humanité* that references a Solange Beaugiron. According to the article, Solange was the daughter of a pharmacist and by the age of seventeen had already become an aspiring playwright. Her first fully written play was entitled *Miss Mary*, and Solange sent it to the theater Danou in the hope it would be performed. The article further states that, unfortunately, the theater put on a play eerily similar to hers that was attributed to another writer, André Birabeau. Solange publicly accused the director of the theater of first sending her play to Birabeau. I have used this morsel of information by making Sol-ange a budding writer in the novel.

But that is all I could determine about the true facts of Marthe's and Solange's life, and so I have had to largely imagine the rest. In the end, we will never know the exact reason that this beautiful apartment was sealed for seventy years, nor why Marthe's grand-daughter continued to pay the maintenance on it until her death but never actually returned there. Just like Marthe and Solange, the apartment maintains its secrets and seduces us to enter into a world that defies time and exalts art and beauty.

Acknowledgments

Many people helped me with the research for this novel. Costanza Bertolotti, who assisted with locating and translating the resource material and also provided a wonderful sounding board as I fleshed out what details and facts we could discover. Kathy Abbot, an amazing costume historian, who assisted me on the research for all of the underpinnings and other details of the clothes worn in the late nineteenth and early twentieth centuries. I was fortunate enough to visit her at Towson College and look at the costume archives there, to see up close the capes, gowns, and corsets worn during the nineteenth century, so I could accurately bring Marthe's wardrobe to life.

To Lisa Leff, an author and professor at American University, I send a special thank-you for assisting me with the historical research of the novel and going over the manuscript with me. Your wealth of knowledge in French Jewish history proved invaluable. Thank you also to Gail Shirazi at the Library of Congress for sharing your wonderful contacts with me, and to Anne Brener for introducing me to the beautiful *Zemirot Yisrael*. And to Diane Afoumado of the United States Holocaust Memorial Museum, who also helped as a sounding board early on as I tried to draft a workable plot for the novel. I am also indebted to Doris Hamburg for sharing her incredible knowledge of manuscript conservation work with me. Author and dear friend, M. J. Rose, has cheered me on with this book since its conception and has kept me anchored through the process.

Martin Fletcher, journalist and author extraordinaire, who generously agreed to write the newspaper "article" that appears at the end of the novel. Pieralvise Zorzi, who chivalrously escorted me to Caffè Florian in Venice as well as beautiful Ferrara, Italy. Charlotte Gordon, who showed me the images of the sumptuous Peacock Room at the Freer Gallery in Washington, DC, that became the seeds for Marthe's love of Asian ceramics. And of course, my cherished early readers, Nikki Koklanaris, Kathy Johnson, Victoria Leventhal, Robbin Siegel, Tina Spitz, and, my mother, Ellen Richman. A special thank-you for Gus Kasper for being a wonderful intern, Shauna D. Jones for helping verify my French inheritance laws, and Jardine Libare, my dear kimono sister, I'm lucky you're only a phone call away.

To my wonderful and supportive agent, Sally Wofford-Girand, who has nurtured each of my six novels with great care and always keeps me reaching higher and higher with each book. To my editor, Kate Seaver, and publisher, Leslie Gelbman, at Berkley Books, thank you for providing my novels with a wonderful home and support as they are ushered into the world.

Lastly, the biggest thank-you of all to my husband, Stephen Gordon, who is always on hand to both solve a pesky plot issue or to provide legal expertise. You will forever be the dark-haired green-eyed boy in all of my novels.

Readers Guide

THE

*Velvet
Hours*

by Alyson Richman

1. The author references shadow and light in the novel. Discuss the aspects of shadow and light in Marthe de Florian's life, as well as in Solange's. Do you think both women come to terms with their pasts at the end of their lives? Or is there an element of regret?

2. Charles gives Marthe the gift of the pearls partly as a gift of beauty, but also as a gift of financial security. Do you think Marthe does the right thing when she sells the necklace?

3. Marthe is not educated, yet she is immensely curious. How would you describe her self-education? Do you think her material possessions reflect her pursuit of knowledge?

4. Marthe belongs to the demimonde, the world of secret pleasure. What do you think of Marthe being a kept woman? Do you think it enabled her to be more liberated than married women in French society, or was her life more restricted?

5. Discuss the essential role the Barcelona Haggadah played in the novel. For example, it enables Solange to learn more about her ancestry, it brings her into the Armels' bookstore and also, in the end, enables Solange and the Armels to gain safe passage. What else did the Haggadah bring to the overall story?

6. Above all, Marthe loves art and beauty. The author describes the sumptuous furnishings in the apartment, the butterfly- and bird-painted china, the fresh flowers, the rose-scented baths, and the gold-embossed stationery. Do we have these rituals of beauty in the twenty-first century? Are there any of these lost rituals that you'd like to bring back into your daily life?

7. Solange and Marthe forge an unlikely friendship. What do you think they each teach each other through their friendship?

8. Solange says: "What I realized at that moment was that my grand-mother believed that as long as the apartment remained the way she had created it—her portrait above the mantel, her collection of porcelains, and the other pieces of art she had hand selected—she was convinced her memory would also not be extinguished." Do you think that heirlooms help us maintain a memory of our loved ones, or are our shared stories what help connect us to the past? Are the two linked? How? Is one more important than the other? Do you own something that is linked with a story, and does it connect you with the past?